Her Broken Beasts

SHADOW WORLD
BOOK ONE

AMBER ELLA MONROE

Her Broken Beasts (Shadow World 1)
Copyright © August 2022 by Amber Ella Monroe

All rights reserved.

No part of this publication may be reproduced, stored in a retrieval system, or transmitted in any form or by any means, electronic, mechanical, recording or otherwise, without the prior written permission of the author.

This is a work of fiction. The characters, places, incidents, and dialogues in this book are of the author's imagination and are not to be construed as real. Any resemblance to actual events or person, living or dead, is completely coincidental.

Book Summary
HER BROKEN BEASTS (SHADOW WORLD 1)

A witch whose magic is stolen by her family. Three ruthless, possessive, hot-as-sin demons who seek to overthrow their king and claim their mate. They need each other to raise hell.

While trying to find a loophole to a spell, I accidentally summon a monster—a powerful, dangerous, dark entity from the shadow world. No worries, I'll just send him back.

That was the plan... But one night of chaos and seduction left me powerless and kidnapped by the beast who'll use me to do anything he commands. Especially once he discovers the power I possess.

To fuel my magic, I'll need massive otherworldly power. Power which can only come from a trio of beasts at my side.

Altair. Morpheus. And Dominik. My three beastly saviors promise protection and pleasure. Each stroke of lust fills me with enough power to raise hell on shadow world.

I crave their savage touch just as much as I seek vengeance against the evil that stripped me of my magic.

As the stakes rise, the madness unfolds, but my devils will destroy anything that stands in their way. The agreement I forge with them will cost me. Either my life or my soul. Or maybe both.

Trigger Warnings and Inclusions:
Descriptive violence/language
Why choose reverse harem
No cheating
No MM
Knotting
Attempted SA (not between romance interests - this book is romance with an HEA)
Smexy times with supernaturals & double peen-ed supernaturals
Double P
Double PP

CHAPTER 1

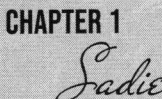

HAVING shadow magic in the blood makes one a target. And guess what? I've become a target.

I could've been born anything but this. Anything but a prisoner of magic.

Being chained to a wall and poisoned by relatives whose only aim was to prevent me from casting spells had me wishing I was born a mundane human in a not-so-normal, mundane-ish world.

I could do epic shit even without magic. I could make a difference in society without drawing from my blood lineage.

But no...

I'm Sadie—freaking—Carrier.

"Tell me, Sadie! Tell me where she is!" My half-brother, Finn, barked so hard that his spittle flew in my face.

I jerked away, shielding myself from his violent aggression.

Finn had a way of fueling his magic with anger. I'd seen what he could do. Saw the way he tortured his enemies in fits of rage.

"I told you already. I don't know where she is," I panted as I pulled hard against the chains. My bindings were heavy—strong enough to hold ten grown men.

Finn exhaled, rolling his eyes as if he didn't believe me.

"You had me snatched while I was on my way to work. People are going to be looking for me when I don't show up, wondering where I am," I told him.

He smirked and huffed with skepticism. "You actually think those people give a damn if you show up or not?"

"You're such an asshole."

"I'd be much nicer to you if you actually cooperated, you know," he replied.

"Do you think I'm stupid enough to believe that?" I countered.

"You're the one who's lying. You don't know where your sister is? You two have a connection. Why is the blood spell not working? What did you do?"

He opened up the cut on my wrist even more with his sharp, perfectly manicured fingernail. I had already bled enough after his failed attempt at a locator spell.

"Stop!" I screamed. "My connection to Sydney is broken!"

Finn gripped me by the neck, wrapping his fingers around my throat. "You lie!"

"Finn! Enough," Finn's evil mother, Magda, chided from the entrance of the vault. "Don't mark her. She's promised to another. That vow was written in blood. Bruise her anymore and she's useless."

Magda was just as evil. She had raised a monster. She stood by and watched her son chastise me for hours. The only thing she cared about was getting rid of me.

Finn grunted. "Don't worry, mother. I'm sure that bastard will see some use for her, whether she's dead or alive, as long as she's delivered in the flesh. Her uterus is all he wants, no?"

I shivered.

Magda pointed a finger in my face. "Your sister—she doesn't know what she's done. She doesn't know the trouble she's caused. She doesn't know the danger we all face."

I believed my sister knew exactly what she'd done, but I kept my lips sealed shut.

"When I find that busy little slut, she will hang upside down until she passes out for her treachery," Finn said.

"She did nothing wrong," I countered.

"Bullshit," he replied with a wave of his hand. "She stole the moon orb. She—"

"You don't know that!" I interjected.

"Like hell I do. The orb belongs with the coven. With its leader."

"And that would be you?" He didn't miss my sarcastic tone.

Finn frowned. "I should've known the two of you would pull something like this. You probably had it all planned out. Scheming with your underhanded ways behind my back. I should've had you two thrown into hellfire. The two of you should be dead, just like your mother."

I crumbled under his insistent verbal abuse.

"You can't even look at me!" he bellowed out. "You're guilty. You two schemed and carried out plans behind my back. I can see it all over your face."

He was wrong. But only partly.

My sister Sydney and I never planned anything behind his back. Our plans never got to the execution stage. Or so I thought.

The moon orb was gone and my sister was missing. There was a strong possibility the two events were connected. The coven thought so, throwing those two coincidences together and concluding that she stole the damn thing to get back at Finn.

Or she could've just gone on one of those expeditions with her research team. She was into anthropology and she was absolutely obsessed with ancient history. This could've all just been a misunderstanding and bad timing. Maybe someone else stole that moon orb. Maybe Finn was accusing the wrong person.

Now that Sydney had abandoned us, she'd have no chance in hell to beat Finn. Our parents' swift and suspicious deaths left two open seats on the council—one of them being a High Priest or Priestess and the other being a

Guardian. And, not to mention, the most important position of all—Regent.

My sister and I had talked about it, knowing fully well that my father intended for one or both of us to join the council.

Finn was a mess. He was spiteful and often let his judgment overrule the most rational solution.

My sister was older by only a few years, and she was always seen as the outspoken and most plausible leader. She was like my mother.

I, on the other hand, got more of my father's traits. They said I was too unpredictable and my magic, too unstable. And there was something about my nature that made me incompatible with most. Plus, I was already betrothed to another.

That's why it had to be my sister. She was my better half. And now she was gone, and so was the one thing my coven depended on—the moon orb. The mystical object that contained all of my coven's secrets, knowledge, and history. Apparently, without it, we were lost.

But we all knew the real reason the moon orb held the highest value over all of our magical objects. It was the most powerful and had fueled many spells to date. Every rising leader knew that. And we needed every ounce of power if we were going to continue extending our services to humans and protect them from evil.

The orb had a way of predicting terrible events. We had used the warnings in the past to shield ourselves and mundane humans from threats.

Finn, who had a prized collection of material possessions, claimed he had every right to the orb as our next High Priest, which he had prematurely installed himself as. He believed the induction ceremony couldn't go on without it. He figured my sister stole the orb's powers to keep him from rising, so he was prepared to do anything to get it back.

"I never should've trusted you sluts," Finn continued his verbal onslaught. "Of course, you're just like your mother, who only pretended modesty. She was only half the woman my mother is." He pointed at Magda who only gave a half-crooked smirk.

I was just about sick of this shit. Him insulting me. My sister. Now, my late mother. And then, demanding things from me like he owned me. Well, he didn't own me.

It was time I fought back like my sister did. I was a dead witch one way or the other. Finn and his mother hated that my older sister and I survived the tragedy that took our parents. If they planned to punish me, I preferred they get it over with sooner rather than later. I would never tell them how to find my sister, even if I knew where she was.

"Do you have anything to say, Sadie?" Finn reached out and squeezed my cheeks with his thumb and forefinger. He squeezed so hard that my gums hurt. "Where is your damn sister?"

I looked him straight in the eye. "For the last time, I know nothing, you fucking bastard!"

His eyes widened, and the color red sparked in them. It was almost as if he was possessed by an evil he couldn't control. He'd been that way ever since I could remember. Even though he didn't like being called a bastard, it was the truth. My mom was always convinced that Magda stole my father. And Finn...well, he thought it went the other way around when my father re-married my mother. Because of how badly Finn treated me, I was ashamed to share blood with him or even call him my brother at all.

It made little sense. I still grappled with the truth and lies, trying to understand things as they were.

"You call me a fucking bastard?" Finn huffed.

Filled with rage, Finn shoved me hard and my body flew more than a foot back and slammed against the stone wall. Pain seized my spine and the metallic taste of blood in my mouth brought about confusing and conflicting images and memories.

"You have until tonight to tell me where your sister is." Finn leaned down where I lay on the ground. "If you don't, I will bleed you dry right in this place, and then I'll hand you off to your betrothed in a bloody box. See if I care what happens to you in hell where you belong."

"But I can't!" I blurted before I could stop myself.

"What do you mean, you can't?"

"I...I...I told you, the connection is broken. She must've done something to unlink us."

He rushed for me, pointing his forefinger in my face. "You're going to fix the connection. As I said, you have until tonight to get yourself together. I'll have someone come in and remove the magic-blocking chains, and you'll remain in this cave until we know where that little rubbish-hunting bitch has gone."

"You can't keep me here forever," I said.

"Oh, I can. And I will. I can't draw power from the moon orb right now, but I certainly can draw from you. And you can bet if your sister did something to jeopardize the orb's powers, I'll keep both of you locked away, where your only use to the coven will be to fuel our spells."

I looked away, swallowing down my sorrow and regrets. I wanted to find my sister, too. I was worried about her. She always had a knack for disappearing, but her sudden unexplained absence seemed strange. Finn's reasons for finding my sister were sinister and self-serving. I didn't want to see him win.

"Well?" Finn shifted in front of me, hands on his hips. "You're going to find your sister, Sadie, or else."

"Or else what?"

"I'll just have to make a call to the police precinct where you work and put in a little anonymous tip about who...and what you really are. If they found out you were actually a witch with ties to the dangerous supernatural roaming their city, what do you think they would do, huh?"

I jerked at the chains. "You wouldn't."

How dare he threaten my job? My one and only real job. The one I worked so hard to get. All I ever wanted was to make my mark on this world, outside of my coven duties. There had to be more to my existence than banishing evil spirits from this realm and exorcising demons for the mundane. I actually enjoyed working alongside homicide detectives down at the local precinct, even if it was for a shithead boss. Even if it was only entry-level and on a junior salary.

Finn's eyes narrowed. The unibrow on his forehead lifted. "Oh, I would. The truth is, I don't care what they think about us, sister. Outing our family sooner rather than later would be a fine power move now that my mother is on the city's council and has the senator wrapped around her little finger."

Behind him, Magda smirked.

"Fine," I said, resolved that he wouldn't leave me alone unless I agreed.

"Good, because I wasn't going to give you a choice either way. It's time you stopped pretending to be a fake detective for these mundane humans and use your real powers to do some real work."

"Just give me until tonight," I replied.

He grinned. "Make sure that your magical battery is supercharged, sister."

I cringed when he called me sister.

"Tonight will be spectacular!" he added.

I exhaled out a ragged breath, nervous because I knew I was just biding time.

Finn was going to be disappointed. Very, very disappointed.

I had vowed never to do spells again. I hadn't used my gifts in so long, I was thinking my magic had abandoned me.

How could I track my sister when my magical abilities hung in the balance?

And what would my evil half-brother do when he found out?

CHAPTER 2
Sadie

MY MONSTER CAME to me again in my dreams. Or maybe I was on the verge of death, still clinging on to hope and never-ending fairytales. They weren't real. They were never real. But these dreams seemed real...

Ten feet tall. Of beastly proportions. The monster's presence could command the attention of Kings and Queens. His alabaster skin was decorated with cords of muscles and thick veins that resembled a maze. From his head, horns that resembled black ice were erected. Black and blue hair swept past his collarbone. His teeth were a stark white. His incisors, sharp. And his canines, long enough to inflict a deadly bite.

He looked like a god. But how could that be? I knew my otherworldly creatures, and I knew them well. He wasn't a god. He was a creature of the night. Demon. I couldn't bring myself to utter the words of his true form, knowing it was true. And knowing that it didn't matter one way or the other.

"How did you get in here?" I squinted against the bright light blinding me, trying to get a better view of him.

"You let me in." His deep, raspy voice drew me in like a moth to a flame.

I caved to my knees and the chains around my wrists and ankles clanked against the floor. I looked around. I was still in the vault. Still a prisoner. But something felt different.

I was alone. With the monster.

At this moment, it felt as if only he and I existed. Nothing else.

"How?" I croaked.

"In your dreams. I slipped through."

The creature was beautiful. Like a work of art. Structured from only the finest elements. His long raven-colored hair swept across his face and shoulders, blending in with his wings.

I shook my head. "But..."

"You invited me in. You need me." A pained expression marked his face.

I yanked on my chains and frustration set in. Even in my dreams, I was still Finn's prisoner.

"Is this a game?" I asked.

"You know it's not. I am real. So is this." He moved closer, leaned down, and slipped his long claws under my chin.

His touch ignited something inside me. Something carnal. Something deep within. "You know how to make this very real, Sadie. Yet you only summon me in your dreams."

It felt real. And this didn't feel like a dream. The weight of the chains felt real. His touch felt real. These emotions felt real.

He rose, still caressing my face, and I rose with him. Unable to fight the urge to touch him, I laid my palm on his chest. He was hot to the touch, and I reared back a moment before placing my fingers on his flesh once more.

He was real.

"I have always been real," he whispered, leaning down and slipping a finger between the seam of my lips.

I parted my mouth, and he replaced his finger with his lips, kissing me with hunger.

"Only you can drop the veil..." He muttered between kisses. "It doesn't have to be this way. Only in your dreams. Only when things get so bad you can't stand the pain. Let me take it away. Let me take you away from it all."

The creature in my dreams wasn't lying. This wasn't the first time he came to me. I always thought of him in my times of need. And he came every time. Sometimes, he came even when I least expected it.

We all dealt with stress differently. I dealt with it by imagining things. Bad things. Unreal things. Naughty things.

"Not real..." I whispered, chanting it over and over again to make myself believe it.

This only angered the monster before me, and he snarled, pressing me back into the hard stone walls. "Let me demonstrate how real..."

Groping me by the thighs, he pressed his core into mine until I was spread wide to accommodate his massive size. Passion zipped up my spine and flames of desire swelled between us.

His huge hands cupped my ass and the look of determination on his face was the only sign I needed to understand that he meant to have me. Right here and now.

He guided his thick dick between the drenched folds of my sex and drove just short of thirteen inches deep. Red-hot searing pleasure took me by force. Penetration alone took me over the edge and I came apart in his arms, screaming out in climax.

I wrapped my legs around him just as he started to pound himself in and out of me while holding my body fixed to the wall. His thrusts were carefully guided, plunging back and forth into my sex with his monstrous size.

"Soon, Sadie..." he rasped, canines distended and gliding against my throat. "Soon, this will all be real. Call to me. Release me. You know how. I've been waiting."

"But I—"

He covered my mouth with a kiss. "No buts. Just say it. Tell me what you want."

"This. I want this," I panted.

"You want more than this. I can feel it. You're stronger than you think. You deserve more than you know."

"I..." I shuddered and then screamed when a climax took me. I felt a smile spreading across my lips in the aftermath. It's what I loved about sex with him. I could never predict my orgasms. He liked to control when they happened.

"There you are," he growled. "Fuck. Do you know what you do to me?"

Pheromones heightened between us, and his arousal stimulated me even more. My slick coated his thick shaft, and I clenched around him as he throbbed uncontrollably.

His knot swelled inside me and another climax took me. His wings were gone. I dug my fingernails into his flesh, raking them down his back.

This was pleasure. His engorged knot plunged deep inside me. His seed flooded my insides. He came, marking me with his essence.

This wasn't real. He'd be gone in the morning.

He kissed my lips. "You know how. Release me. It's time."

My beautiful monster faded away.

"Wait!"

I reached out, but my monster was gone. Standing in his place was ex-Headmaster Tymon, who wasn't even one-fourth the monster's size. The little man couldn't have stood over four and a half feet tall.

"My goodness. You're burning up! Come now before it's too late," Tymon said.

"Tymon, what are you doing here?" I asked as he slipped the key into the locks holding me in the vault.

I looked behind him, expecting to see that controlling bastard, Finn, and his evil mother.

"No matter. We have to get you out of here. I made this magical artifice to get you out. *Hurry now.*"

He jostled the metal, jerking aggravatingly at the chains and pushing the key artifice into each lock.

I hadn't seen Tymon since way before my sister vanished. I had believed he left with some members of the outer court after the council members bickered about several issues, including who should rise as the next Priest.

Tymon used to be a devout coven member while my father was still High Priest. Decades ago, he acted as headmaster at the day school for children with magical abilities. My sister and I had attended there for almost fourteen years before we transitioned into a private, homeschooled setting. Most recently, his peers deemed him an accomplished artificer and historian, but they put him on duties that didn't involve the use of his magic—which was lost to him…or so I thought.

Tymon bowed his head as he worked. His long white hair shaded his face and pointed elf ears. He shaved his sharp horns off years ago before he attempted to fit into human society, but it was apparent that he was back with the coven.

Most supernaturals who looked too…well, supernatural often found out that blending into human society was difficult, especially when they were judged because of their differences. The mundanes considered us cursed. Not all of them were judgmental, though. In fact, a small percentage of them envied and even sought our talents.

"Why are you helping me?" I asked Tymon.

He glanced up, apprehensively. "Why would I not do this? You don't deserve this. Go before it's too late."

Dirt clung to my clammy skin. Sweat coated my chest and my hand went to my neck where the monster scraped me with his fangs. "Did you see a monster? A beast. With horns and wings. His skin was black. His hair was...blue. Very dark blue." As the description left my mouth, I realized how ridiculous I must have sounded.

"A monster? Where?" He choked out a short laugh and threw me a bag. Even for an earthly supernatural, some things were just too absurd to believe. "Put this robe on to cover yourself."

Heated embarrassment stretched across my limbs when I remembered Finn stripped me down to my sports bra and undies. I tossed the robe over my shoulder, tensing up when I sensed the telltale signs of tingling between my legs, reminiscent of my intimate time with a sex beast.

"Tymon, I'm serious. The monster was right in here. Right before you came in. Did you see a monster in here with me?" I pressed the issue.

"You want to know who the real monster is? Finn, that's who. *That* monster?"

"No, not Finn." I felt like I was going to puke.

Tymon ran to the entrance, looked both ways, and then ran back over to me. "Then who? What monster are you talking about?"

"I...Never mind."

"Get up! Go. I can't hold the invisibility spell up much longer."

I shook my head. "I can't. You don't understand. He's going to find me."

"You have to try. Leave now before it's too late."

"Where will I go?"

Tymon pursed his lips together. "Just leave now. You're not safe. Finn will come back. They have a most gruesome punishment planned for you. Go now!"

I grabbed up the bag. "And what about you?"

"Don't worry about me. I'll see you again."

He marched me out of the vault and into the night. Two of Finn's guards sat by the door with their heads leaned down in what looked like the most uncomfortable position. They were both asleep, snoring like babies.

"You did that. You put them to sleep. You have your magic back, Tymon. How—?" I whispered.

"I always had it. Using magic comes at a price, so I only do so for important reasons," he said while rushing along a trail. Rows of tall bamboo trees hid us well. "If I were you, I'd get as far away from here as possible. Just like your sister did."

I frowned. "Do you know where my sister is?"

He shook his head. "No one knows where your sister is. And that scares me..."

"Me too, Tymon."

"That's why you have to go now," he said, rushing me. "Get away from here. Go find your sister. Both of you should stay away from Finn and his new coven."

"That's easier said than done."

Before I could utter another word, a trail of light started making a beeline from the main mansion to the bricked-in hole where they had me chained.

I gasped. "They're coming."

"If you don't run, they'll find you."

As he issued the stark warning, footsteps approached us on the narrow path.

Tymon was right. Even if I had nowhere to go, I had to go, anyway.

We both took off.

CHAPTER 3
Sadie

I RAN until it felt like I couldn't run anymore. Dodging across busy streets and stopping in dark alleys to catch my breath and make sure Finn's henchmen weren't after me put a toll on my body. I didn't know how long I could keep it up.

Aside from the occasional looter, drunk, or late-night party animals and socialites, no other mundanes were on the street. It was almost two in the morning. Normal people were sleeping. Normal people...not people like me. People like me were haunted by their demons. Demons here on earth. Like Finn. Or was it just me and this recent string of bad luck?

I fumbled with the mood pendant hanging from my neck as I reflected on my dilemma. If I fidgeted long enough, I could talk myself out of the evil plans of retaliation that fueled my thoughts.

I couldn't go back to my apartment. At least not tonight, so I stumbled into a twenty-four hour library near a community college.

After chugging down as much H2o as I could from a water fountain, I snuck into one of the quiet study rooms. I'd done this so many times before when I needed time alone, time to think. This time was no different.

Except I was too tired to think or do anything else besides slump against the beanbag chair on the floor. My feet were sore from running across gravel roads and littered sidewalks. My lips were parched, and my lungs were overworked. Exhaustion set in. I curled up into a ball and welcomed the darkness...

But all I saw was light...

...at the other end of my dream.

This time, another monster appeared in the place of my alabaster-skinned monster. This beast was different. His complexion wasn't like any human's. He was ashen-complexioned. He bore a striking resemblance to the monster who often riddled my dreams. Although this one favored his human side, the aura surrounding him told me he was not a creature of this realm.

The monster who visited my dream while I was stuck in chains was a frequent guest in my head. He'd been coming to me since my magic manifested. Way before I became a woman. I had dreamt of monsters before as a child, but those were only innocent dreams. They weren't like this. The dreams I'd been having lately were purely carnal in nature. The purpose—to replace my pain with pleasure.

My monsters never disappointed. They knew exactly when I needed them. Once, they were absent from my life for a long period. A time when I put my energy into my studies instead of my magic. My mother had insisted on it—telling me my foolish fantasies about make-believe monsters would get me nowhere. So I had shut them out...for a long time.

I almost forgot they were a part of my life at one point, but after my parents died, my monsters visits grew more frequent.

As if nothing else mattered, my attention shifted to the present monster.

His hair was astonishingly silver—almost white—and tail-bone length. He was large and strong, just like the alabaster monster.

It was so strange that I often felt like the names of these monsters were on the tip of my tongue, but I never called them out loud. Not in my dreams. And certainly not while I was awake. My instincts told me there was a reason for that.

I lifted my upper body and glanced around, taking in my surroundings. I was still in the private study room, but something had changed. It felt like I was floating, but when I swung my legs over the edge of the chair, I cringed when the sole of my feet hit the floor.

"You're in pain," the monster spoke. His thick baritone echoed the small space.

"Yes. Make it go away," I whispered. It felt odd to request this from a total stranger, but I had already assured myself that this was something the monster could do for me.

The monster knelt beside the chair and cupped my feet in his big hands. "The pain? Or the man who did this to you? Which one would you like me to make go away?"

The monster lifted his gaze to mine.

I swallowed, understanding completely what he implied. "Do you know what happened to me?"

"I'm in your head. Yes."

"So, you're not real, either?" I asked.

"It depends." *He stroked my feet, massaging them until the tenseness faded away from my soles.*

The silver-haired monster massaged the discomfort away. Instantly calmed and feeling safe in the presence of him, I tried not to think about anything else other than what was happening in this moment. But that was hard when someone wanted me dead.

"And the other one like you? Where is he?" I asked.

He frowned. "Other one?"

"Why do I dream of monsters?" I whispered aloud.

"You need us. And we need you," he simply stated.

"You? Need me?" I repeated, in disbelief that someone as majestic as these monsters would need little old me. I barely had my magic, and even when I did, I never flaunted my gifts or used my powers much at all. As Tymon said, the use of magic came at a price. And I was the frugal type.

Massive hands crept up my legs. The monster smoothed his hands against my ankle and up the insides of my thighs. Wearing nothing but a pair of flimsy panties under the robe, I felt exposed to him.

A flash of arousal provoked the fire already blazing in my core, and I wrapped the robe tightly around me.

"No," he grunted, taking my hands and placing them on the bean chair on either side of me. "I want to see you just as you are."

"But..."

"You keep too much bottled up inside. Your potential. Your magic. Your cravings. You bury these things deep and they become a burden for you. You summon me because you need my help. You need release." *As he spoke, he pulled the robe away from my body.*

As he stood, his tight leather pants disappeared in an instant.

When my gaze landed on his groin area, I froze at the sight. He had two dicks, one directly above the other, both standing at full attention. His huge sac, which looked as if it was full of semen, hung low and heavy against his thighs.

I licked my lips as flames of hunger danced through my core.

Both dicks were the same size. Massive and intricately veined. He was perfection. His hand stroked the top dick in an upward motion until he reached the shaft. Pre-cum oozed from the gaping slit. Then, he switched to the lower dick, stroking it in a slow downward motion, until his fisted hand brushed against his swollen balls.

"Oh..." It was all I could muster.

"Does the sight please you, Sadie?"

"It does."

"And the others? Do they please you too?"

I swallowed, feeling awkward that he would ask me such an intimate question about the other monsters from my dreams.

"Your pleasure is of utmost importance, so you can tell me the truth," he urged.

I nodded. "He does. They do."

He slid a finger under my chin and made me look at him. "They do what?"

"They please me."

The monster grinned. "Hmmm. But it's my turn now."

With a clawed paw, he raked my soaked panties down my legs and then parted my thighs to get a view of my glistening pussy. My sex clenched and leaked when he raked his gaze over me. He picked me up, switching places with me so that he was outstretched on his back on the bean chair. Then he yanked me over him and positioned my thighs on either side of his face so that I was straddling him in a sixty-nine position.

"Sit on my face," he commanded.

I lowered my pussy slowly, moaning when his tongue intercepted my clit. His tongue was strong and large, lapping me with hunger. I looked down, catching the sight of his forked tongue flickering in and out of me.

He used two hands to stroke his two dicks simultaneously as he devoured my pussy. Shocked beyond limits and aroused beyond measure, my mind drew a blank as I drooled over this monster's well-endowed throbbing dicks.

I rocked my hips and moved up and down his stiff tongue, using it like a cock until I reached my peak. I bit my lips hard, but a shallow scream still escaped me.

Suddenly, he stiffened and came. Both cocks released an alarming amount of cum, shooting out like a geyser. Some of it sprayed my face and mouth. I licked it up and opened my mouth for more.

Even though I was more than satisfied and elated from the first orgasm, my monster continued to lap up my juices with his tongue, holding me fixed onto his mouth with his big hands now that he had stroked himself to completion.

"You are delicious, Sadie. The energy you feed me is off the charts. Your power is without limits when it comes to this. When we finally have you all to ourselves...when you finally come to us...just imagine how much sweeter this would be..." *he moaned, groping my ass, licking my forbidden hole and making me quiver.*

"How do I come to you?"

I was extra curious. My monsters had always come to me. I had never gone to them...wherever they were.

"And where?" *I added.*

His lips parted but the answer didn't come out.

"Why do you not come...outside of my dreams?" *I demanded.*

"We are stuck..."

I gasped. "How can I help?"

"The more you feed us..."

. . .

"The more you feed us....what?" I blurted out into the open air. *"M—"* The monster's name was on the tip of my tongue. Something starting with an *M*. Yet, I couldn't get the entire word past my lips.

I sprang up with a gasp, sweaty, and with my core aching as my breath left me in gasps. Still wrapped in a robe with my panties still intact, I looked around the room.

I was still here. The monster was gone.

It was as if none of it ever happened.

What the fuck?

These sex dreams were making me crazy.

No wonder people thought I was the unstable and unpredictable one.

Not only did I dream of things that most people believed were fairytales, but I also dreamed of three of them.

Three demons. The same three demons had infiltrated my thoughts and dreams for years.

It all started with an innocent spell I cast as a child, asking the spirits to send me a triad of guardians. I had fully intended to have one for me, one for my sister, and the other for a close childhood friend of mine. But when I learned I was the only one who could summon and see the demons, I knew they were mine and mine alone.

In the beginning, I would only sense them whenever I was lonely or scared—basically when I thought I needed them the most. And they came every time, even if it wasn't in the flesh but only in my mind.

As I grew older, my guardians fulfilled more than basic needs. And when I lost my innocence—became a woman—my relationship with my demons deepened.

Each demon was different. They had distinct personalities, which made each reunion unpredictable.

One was dominant and often told me when something wasn't good for me. Another was secretive but attentive. And the last...he was both untrusting of me and arrogant.

But there were those who would still argue that my triad of men was only a figment of my imagination.

Someone yanked the door open. The woman's eyes widened when she spotted me on the bean chair.

"Oh, sorry. I thought this study room was vacant."

She slammed the door shut.

I exhaled and slumped back on the bean chair. I heard signs of the library coming alive all around me. I had to get out of here. I had to keep going.

My sex demons were a distraction from the real problem I faced. If I didn't find my sister and warn her about Finn, things could get a whole lot worse.

CHAPTER 4
Sadie

THIS WASN'T A GOOD IDEA. I shouldn't have stepped foot in my aunt's fortune-telling shop, but I didn't have any other choice.

My aunt, who many knew as Mistress Naima, didn't seem surprised to see me. She blinked once and put the glossy-covered feng shui manual she was reading down on the counter.

She glanced at me over the rim of her eyeglasses and flashed me a bright smile. She took off the spectacles, allowing them to rest on her chest from a ruby-chained neck strap. Her wheat-complected skin was flawless, and she reminded me of a beauty pageant queen with the way her makeup was so perfectly done. She kept her hair neat—tightly wrapped into a high bun with loosely curled tendrils flowing against her temples. Back in the day, she was always the center of attention at any family gathering.

Aunt Naima tapped the counter with her long red coffin-shaped nails. "Why am I not surprised to see you?"

I sighed in relief. I honestly thought she would tell me to turn around and leave. I had no idea if Finn had poisoned her against me or not. If so, I was prepared to run as fast as I could again.

"Well, come on in." She waved me in. "What is it?"

"I need your help."

"My help?" She pushed her hand against her hip. "Why would a being as powerful as you need my help?"

"Keep it down, Naima. No one knows I'm here." I bit my lower lip and looked around.

I had to be careful about what I said in public, and her shop wasn't empty. Some local teenagers were perusing the aisle, admiring all the artifacts, herbs, potions, and other trinkets lining the shelves.

I was having second thoughts about coming here now, but it was too late.

After realizing that going back to my apartment right after I narrowly escaped Finn's evil plans for me was a bad idea, I secured a bus ticket using a computer at the library and left the city. Now I was in a small town I thought I'd never visit again. Too many *familiars*. Just being here, I risked someone recognizing me. I hadn't been here in three years. I liked to think that I looked different.

"You're probably right, but I'd keep a low profile around here. No one could ever forget those innocent green eyes and gentle smile," Naima said.

"Just in case you haven't noticed, I'm not smiling. I'm serious. I need help."

"Don't we all, child? Mika left minutes before you walked through the door. Didn't you see her out in the parking lot?"

I shook my head. "I don't think so. I came through the back and slipped around the side."

Mika was Naima's adopted daughter. She took the girl from the orphanage when she was just eleven years old and had been raising her for the past six years. Mika had a troubled past and her bad behavior was always blamed on her prior traumas. The only support system she had in her life was Naima, who tried to show Mika that she could turn her life around and break the cycle of anguish.

"Well, you couldn't have missed her. She has a brand new shiny motorcycle she borrowed from her guy friend who I tried to warn her about," she said.

Now that I thought about it, I did see someone revving off on a motorcycle as I raced into the shop. They had on a helmet and I figured it might have been one of Naima's regular customers. If the leather pants, steel toe boot-wearing person was Mika, she had obviously taken a drastic personality change. The Mika I knew used to dress in preppy designer outfits, not skin-tight leather.

Naima continued on about Mika. "That boyfriend of hers is nothing but trouble. He provides for her, you know. Gives her things that aren't good for her. But alas, she's old enough to do whatever. I've done what I could for her. I'm tired and I don't have much longer on this earth." Naima's tone held a hint of sadness, and I felt sorry for her.

"I could maybe talk to her if you'd like. They have some openings down at the precinct in the records department. When all this crap blows over, I can put in a good word for her."

Naima's eyes brightened. "That would be great. She needs her independence..." And with a curt smile, she added, "And a job. Now tell me, what's bothering you?"

"I have to do something before it's too late. I just can't wrap my head around what exactly to do."

"Hmmm, well, I might be able to do a reading for you," she said.

"I don't want my future told. Not exactly. I just need direction...*guidance*." I looked toward the door when the bell rang as the teens exited the shop. Rushing toward the entry, I clamped down the locks so no one else could enter.

"You would be surprised to know what your future held, Sadie," Naima exclaimed, coming out from behind the counter and walking over to an aisle of snow globes.

"Sure I would. It's just too bad that futures change. All it takes is a shift in one's fate, whether it's by a natural or unnatural occurrence."

"Smart," Naima confided. "Is this about your betrothal, by any chance?"

"Betrothal?" I cringed. "Of course not. That's not for another few months. My twenty-first birthday, remember?"

"Hmmm, you're right? Well, that's soon."

"Yeah, but I don't even want to think about it." Honestly, I was hoping for some freaking miracle to happen. But miracles didn't exist obviously.

"Your betrothed...what's his name? Samuel? Samson? I'm sure he's getting sick of Finn's shit, too. If you're lucky, maybe your betrothed will come to take you earlier."

I rolled my eyes and grumbled. "I've been wishing and praying that Samson finds some hot nice woman in France while he's there on business and calls off the betrothal altogether."

"We all know that's not happening. There's too much to gain from a union between a Carrier and a Wulfric."

I folded my arms. "Like what? World domination? My parents promised me to Samson and neither one of them are here to actually give me to him, so shouldn't this agreement become null and void?"

Naima clucked her tongue and shook her head. "Not a chance. Not with Finn as overseer of the Carrier estate and coven leader."

"Why did I have to get betrothed to someone? Sydney didn't, so why me?"

"You are the carrier, that's why," she said nonchalantly.

I rolled my eyes. "Both of us are of Carrier bloodline, ma'am. I'm sold away, but she's just free to do....whatever." I waved my hand in the air.

"No. I meant, you are *the* carrier. As in you carry the trait of your mother. The trait of an omega witch, which means you are more than likely to bear multiples, which keeps our link to the ancestral realm alive. Your father was a twin, you know?"

I sighed roughly. "I know. But Sydney—"

"Sydney has already proven she's not a true carrier. Even your mother knew that. She did a reading on both of you when you were babies."

A sour memory tore through me and I fought to keep that image hidden. My sister, however, suffered the greatest loss, losing a soul that never had a chance to place his or her mark on this world. It all happened so fast. My sister fell in love, and like a hopeless romantic, she thought she could run away with her mundane boyfriend, but cruel fate had other evil plans. The baby in her womb never stood a chance.

I didn't blame her for distancing herself from the coven when it happened, leaving the state, and often times, even the country to chase after ancient artifacts and...broken dreams.

"And why do you think Samson chose you to marry?" my aunt asked.

"Because my sister is strong. She would've fought my father's decision," I said, solemnly.

"Never underestimate yourself again. You're strong too. Fighting isn't always the answer." She grabbed my arm. "You, my child, have the gift of a leader. You chose to delay, even forgo, your happiness for the greater good. Our link to the spirit world will never be severed because of it."

I hoped she was right. I was willing to sacrifice a lot for my family. My true family.

"And the men of Samson's family always bear strong, powerful offspring," Naima added. "Samson's mother was a lower witch, but she has magic nonetheless. Samson's father is the Alpha of their pack, and soon Samson will take his place. Our coven—*your* future coven—will then possess the earthbound guardians it needs to thrive."

"But maybe the prophesy is a lie. Maybe the gene skipped my sister and me. Maybe I'm not who they say I am. *Maybe* it ends with us," I said.

"No, darling. Do not wish that on yourself," Naima replied, her tone filled with anguish.

"But so much has happened..."

"I know, I know. Let's just give things time to work out. As for your inquiry about world domination, yes. Domination is what I see in your future. Maybe not of this world, but of something, darling. Maybe even of this coven. You can take it back from Finn one day."

"Anyway, that's not why I came today. I don't want to talk about that stupid betrothal or Samson. My sister is missing," I told her.

"We got the message, darling. Finn has a bounty out on her head."

I bit my lip and then nibbled on my fingernails, wondering if there wasn't a bounty on my head by now for escaping him. His wrath must have grown exponentially since finding my chains broken and me gone.

"He thinks Sydney took that damned moon orb," I spat out.

Naima pointed at me, shaking her head. "Language, missy."

"And he wants to be Regent. I just know it."

Finn had not come outright to say this, but it was obvious. He was on his way to formally declaring himself High Priest of our coven. The next apparent path would be Regent of Covens—a position my father also held before he died. And the Regent controlled all thirteen covens. Since my sister was oldest, I always thought she would receive the title after my father, not Finn.

I sighed. "I have to find Sydney."

Naima tossed me a doubtful glance. "Are you sure that's what you want?"

"I—"

"Or rather...are you sure that's what she wants? I mean, she disappeared for a reason."

I ran my hands up and down my arms as a brief chill raced up my body. "I just think she's in trouble. She'd never leave without saying anything to me. It all seems so strange."

"What was the last thing she told you before she left?"

"That she wanted to kill Finn."

Naima burst out in laughter, holding her belly as she doubled over with amusement.

I propped my hand on my hip. "Aunt Naima, certainly you don't find this funny. I want to kill Finn too, but that doesn't mean I want to *actually* kill him."

Naima shook her head. "You're not making sense, darling."

"I hate him," I said, clenching my fist. "But I'm not going to kill him."

Naima pursed her lips, casting me a perplexed look. "Well, someone else will. I can almost guarantee that," she said, as if her prediction was a fact.

"Killing him won't solve the issue. One of his cronies will just pick up where he left off."

"And gods forbid that insipid selfish bitch mother who birthed him claims the honor." Naima rolled her eyes.

"And then the coven would really fall hard. She's as corrupt as they come, and the coven is rotten to the core."

"Well then, you know what you have to do."

"And what's that?" I asked, folding my arms across my chest.

She laughed. "What did we just talk about, like five minutes ago? A living legitimate heir. Carrier. Gene. A union with the Wulfrics leading to more resources to overthrow Finn. Duh! Isn't it obvious?"

"Yeah, no," I exclaimed sarcastically. "What I will do is find my sister so we can get the hell away from here. Together.

You can come too, Aunt Naima. I know you never liked it here."

Naima exhaled deeply with her lips pressed tightly together. "I'm going to die here, darling. This is something you have to do on your own. And probably without your sister."

My heart dropped. "What do you mean?"

"I can't help you find your sister, Sadie. I don't have what it takes, but you do."

"I honestly think my magic has abandoned me, Naima."

Naima leaned over and picked up my mood pendant and glanced at it. "The stone says you're scared, darling. Don't be. Magic is never really gone. It's like faith. You just have to believe."

"When I turned my back on the coven, I turned my back on my magic. It hasn't returned the same since. I've tried. All I've managed to pull off are beginner spells that don't require the use of my powers. I can do magic just not the powerful ones my father taught me."

"Well, what about all that work you're doing down at the precinct. You interned there, and they finally found a position for you, right?"

"Right." I shrugged. "They did."

"So, you mean to tell me you didn't use one bit of your magic to solve all those cases they put you on?"

"Nope. Not one ounce of magic," I replied. "That was all me. I've got smarts too. You're not the only genius in the family."

"I wish that were true. I just read the cards. Unfortunately for me, casting magic spells is in my past. That's the thing about our coven's curse. As we grow older our magic fades away making way for the next generation of witches."

"But you and mom found a way to stop that from happening, right?"

"She followed through with it. I didn't. We didn't know the dangers back then. Plus, trying to stop the inevitable requires a lot of sacrifices. One I'm not willing to make."

"I understand."

Just then, the rain started pounding the top of the roof and thunder rumbled in the distance.

"Oh, great," Naima grumbled.

I walked around her shop, admiring all the pieces up for sale and on display. Naima wasn't just a mere fortune teller. She and my mom used to be two of the most powerful witches in the coven before Finn and his kin took over. My half-brother, Finn, believed his side of the family was more worthy of leading. But, they were just corrupt.

I came across a tall oval standing mirror sitting in the corner of the wall. The shiny gold framing caught my eye. The piece was elegant and beautiful. I glanced at myself standing there, wondering what my future held. Naima's gifts and cards often painted a vivid picture, but I had been taught enough to know that fate could change. One's fate often changed a dozen times over in their lifetime. What she reads today might not be what she read tomorrow.

"Do you have somewhere to stay tonight, Sadie?" Naima asked.

"I think so..." My voice trailed off as I analyzed my frame in the mirror. Washed-out skin-tight black jeans and a cropped top were my choice of attire for today. Black boots from my work uniform completed the look. It was all I had in the duffle bag in the car when I escaped Finn.

"I have a small bunk bed upstairs. You can stay here for the night, if you like. That hail storm is likely to cause some major distractions on the interstate. You don't want to be traveling back in that." Naima's voice drifted off.

"I took a bus," I replied.

"Even worse," she quipped.

Still in front of the mirror, I turned to the side, taking in my silhouette.

How strange. While I was looking at myself, it appeared as if nothing else was in the background. I only saw my image within a cloud of mist. And yet, when I turned around, numerous urns lined a shelf behind me. I took a look at my reflection in the mirror again and smiled.

Even though I was a mess and my long, dark wavy hair was pulled up into a crooked, unkempt ponytail, I had to find joy from something. I stayed inside most of these days, forgoing vitamin D, so my olive skin with natural reddish brown undertones was looking a bit under the weather.

"What is this piece, Naima?" I asked her as she flipped the door sign from "Open" to "Closed".

"It's been in the family for a very long time. It's not for sale. Loki likes to look at himself."

"*Loki?*"

She giggled. "My cat."

I blinked. "You named your cat after a Norse god?"

"He was already named. I found him on the street in the cold, wet rain. Collar said Loki. He answered to it, so it stuck." She shrugged.

"Oh."

Naima was always taking in some poor, unfortunate soul. She was kind that way.

I looked around the shop some more, carefully watching my step for fear of stumbling over a trickster cat named Loki.

"No need to tiptoe around. Loki's probably upstairs napping." Naima peered over my shoulder. "Are you losing weight, darling? Those pants are sitting a little low on your hips."

"I don't think so. But this mirror is strange," I said, going back to the mirror after nothing else held my attention.

I frowned. Although I knew Naima was standing right behind me, I couldn't see her reflection with mine in the mirror.

"It's probably over three hundred years old. Of course, it looks strange to some."

"Can you see your reflection?"

Naima laughed. "Of course I can. And all the rest of the stuff behind us. Can't you?"

I squeezed my eyes shut and then focused again, but it was still the same. All I saw was my reflection among a cloud of mist. I didn't want to press the issue, but sooner or later I'd have to tell someone about these weird dreams and premonitions I'd been having. The thing was, who was I going to tell that I'd been having dreams about three sexy demons fucking me on a nightly basis?

Heat and arousal rose up my core. I turned away from Naima, desperately trying to get my shit together.

"I hate to see you so sad. So, tell me, if you won't allow me to read your cards, and I don't have the means to help you find your sister, and I can't legally break off your betrothal to Samson, how can I help you?"

Feeling a smile tugging at my lips, I spun around. I parted my mouth to speak, but before I could get my thoughts out, a lightning bolt pierced through the glass window.

We both jumped at the same time, turning toward the source of the strike.

A strong wind rattled the door on the frames and suddenly the whole door was ripped from the threshold.

I gasped, hands to my chest, trying to find my breath.

I couldn't believe a storm was strong enough to yank the door off the hinges. It turned out, I was correct.

After the dust settled, Finn's mother, Magda, stood in the doorway.

Crap.

CHAPTER 5
Sadie

"WHAT THE—" In disbelief, I backed up a couple of paces.

That selfish bitch was here in the flesh. They'd found me, but how?

I should've never come here. This should've been the last place to go with a whole coven after me.

"Magda," Naima gasped.

"Mm-hmm," Magda smirked, then her gaze fixed on me. "There you are, you sneaky girl. Time to come home and do what you promised."

"Over my dead body." Naima placed her body in front of mine.

"Naima, no!" I cried out just as Magda raised her hands and unleashed all of her powers at Naima.

"As you wish," Magda hissed. "I'm tired of you placing hexes on me anyway, you old hag! Time to die."

Two lower male witches entered the establishment as Magda fought Naima with the force of an entire coven. I grabbed the nearest weapon, punching my fist through a glass cage and wrapping my fingers around the blade of a dagger.

The male witches had their powers, but I didn't have enough of mine. I used what little strength I had, holding them off until I couldn't hold on any longer.

"Don't come any closer!" I held up the dagger.

"Or what?" One lifted his hands, collecting the negative energy around him. "I don't think you know how to use that, little girl."

"Try me," I screamed, gripping the handle so tight it hurt.

A flash of something filled his eyes as he glanced from me and the blade, and then to something behind me. The mirror.

I held the blade straight out, closing my eyes just as a magnetic force surged inside me. And as if by some magnetic force, one of the lower witches jolted forward, and the dagger impaled his heart.

Gasping, I released the blade's handle just as he dropped to the floor in shock.

What the hell just happened? Did I just stab someone? No. It was as if the witch just threw himself on my dagger.

"You'll pay for that." The second witch hurled a deadly force at my head.

I ducked, and the force hit the mirror, breaking the glass on impact.

The surge I experienced only seconds earlier faded away and I felt lightheaded. When the second witch came for me, there was nothing I could do to stop him.

Then I saw the most horrible sight in front of me. Aunt Naima gasping for breath, dying as Magda took all of her life force with powers I had no idea she possessed.

"Naima," I screamed just as she collapsed on the floor.

Her eyes were dull as they locked with mine. She whispered one last word. "Believe."

As her body lay lifeless, my emotions slammed into me like a missile.

This time, when the second male witch directed his deadly fireball at me, I seized up. Jolts of electric shock nailed me hard. My jaw snapped shut, and I accidentally bit my tongue. The scream I felt ringing in my ear never reached past my lips as everything went numb and I flopped on the ground, twitching hard. My eyes were the only thing I could move. The interior of the store was already on fire.

Hands grabbed me, hauled me up, and dragged me out of the shop. The bell rang on the way out, but moments later, the shop was engulfed in flames. Tears welled up in my eyes and spilled down my face.

Out of my peripheral, I spotted someone speeding across the parking lot on a motorcycle. It was the same bike I spotted when I entered the shop earlier.

Mika!

Mika jumped from the bike and it skidded across the asphalt. "No!" she cried out, and then turned, racing toward Magda. "You said you wouldn't harm her. I told you everything you wanted to know. I told you where to find Sadie. Why did you do this?"

My heart felt as if it had shattered into a million pieces the moment I learned that Mika had told them where I was. How could she do this? Now Naima was gone, and the shop was up in flames.

"What do you care?" Magda said, thrusting Mika aside and then turning her back on the girl. Over her shoulder, she yelled, "Deal with it. At least you got what you wanted. Your debt is paid in full."

Oh no. No, no.

The cronies took me away while Magda ordered them around. As I glanced back at Mika, I watched her sulk, with her long braided hair hanging down her back. Did she regret what she did? Because I regretted coming out here and putting Aunt Naima in danger.

Mika covered her mouth and burst into tears as she collapsed to her knees on the pavement. She was powerless. Born a mundane. There was nothing she could do. She'd already done the worst.

The distant shrill of the fire trucks grew closer. Of course, there was nothing I could do either. It seemed that Magda and her cronies had paralyzed me.

I could barely move. Barely breath. It felt like I was gagging as I tried to scream and holler for help.

Magda ordered two men waiting by a dark van to tie me up and gag my mouth.

I ground my teeth together and tried my hardest to fight back. I was surprised when I kicked one of my kidnappers in the chin.

"The magic is wearing off," one crony informed Magda.

She came to the back of the van, shot me a death stare, and hissed. "Must I do everything myself."

With the wave of her hand, I was out like a light—hurled into darkness.

CHAPTER 6
Sadie

I WOKE IN THE COLD—DARKNESS all around me.

I couldn't muster a word because I was gagged. I twitched and turned as a man carried me over his shoulder, only to realize that my arms were bound.

I tasted bile in my mouth. The vile memory of my aunt being murdered was engrained in my head like a rotten sore. I was sick with rage; my heart ravaged by fear.

I should have known. There was no escaping Finn and his ugly mother. They'd get what they wanted one way or another—only because they were wicked enough to do anything to get it. They would do the devil's bidding to achieve their aims—whatever it was.

I often wondered what it was. They had the family's ancestral home and land. They had the coven. They had the backing of influential political and religious figures. What more could they want?

Besides the whereabouts of my sister and the magical moon orb, what else *did* they want? It always seemed that with every ounce of power they gained, they always sought more and more. Always unsatisfied. Never fully satiated.

I could either give them what they wanted and hope for some miracle in the end or fight. Either way, I knew I had to be strong.

I forced myself to calm down and focus on my surroundings. It was so dark. I tried to use my powers to filter through the darkness, but those were lost to me now. How could I believe my magic would come back full force when one of the worst things had just happened to me?

I was no stranger to death. My parents had protected us from the most gruesome dealings of coven business, and yet, there was death all around me. Having worked for some time as an intern in the homicide unit of the local precinct and then having the fortune of being hired once my internship was up, I'd seen it all.

I wasn't afraid of death. I wasn't afraid of the end.

The footsteps of the man who carried me crunched on the gravel. The familiar smell of sulfur and dirt filled my nostrils. I was right back where I started. In this musty cave. Only this time, they brought me deeper inside. Tymon had risked blowing his cover for nothing. Naima had lost her life because of me.

Other footsteps echoed behind and in front of the first man, indicating that there was a line of people heading somewhere. Unintelligible grunts told me that they were some of Finn's loyalist henchmen—various supernatural entities—pledged to do his bidding for life. They were supernatural, but had no magic. Yet, no one would underestimate them because they were prepared to die for Finn and his cause.

A sudden turn by the man carrying me and a swift change in the air suggested that we were in another area of the underground cave. The air was drier and there was less oxygen to take in. Or maybe it was just me, being gagged and all.

I once recalled a story my father told me about there being a lower level of the cave on our ancestral lands where they took those coven members who were sentenced to be punished. No one ever came out unharmed. Some never came out alive. In fact, they were never spoken of again. Almost as if they were wiped off the face of this earth.

What had I done to deserve such fate? If they were going to kill me all along, they should've done it earlier. It was obvious I didn't know anything about where my sister or the moon orb was. We'd been busy over the past few months, and it didn't really help that we had a small disagreement before she disappeared. Well, not a small one. A rather big one about where to keep our parent's urn.

We were both frustrated, but we were wrong about taking that anger out on each other. Now there was a big possibility that I'd never see her again.

My stomach turned and perspiration melted from my pores. I couldn't stand the scent of the odd smells lingering in the room.

A door creaked open and locks were either dismantled or applied. More footsteps could be heard as the men marched on the gravel.

Suddenly, someone ripped my blindfold off. I gasped at the sudden beam of light shining in my face from a series of red-flamed torches. Those torches and the candles lit along the walls in the room seemed to increase the temperature tenfold. The room was constructed from stone and, in the center, was a blood-stained round table.

I inhaled sharply, but my scream of terror only came out as a sharp gulp. After almost choking on a lump of bile, I swallowed it down. It slammed like a hammer in the pit of my gut. Bones were scattered everywhere. A few skulls had been tossed in the corner. Books and other odd artifacts decorated the wall as if this were a museum. A death museum. A place of horrors.

Finn shifted into the room and pointed to the center stone table. "Chain her to the altar."

I fought every second as the men chained me, as instructed by Finn. They were strong and my attempts to break free were futile as they forced me onto the stone while they grabbed up the chains.

"Make her keep still," Finn demanded, as he fumbled with some concoction in a bowl off to the side.

With his command, one of his henchmen, craned my arm behind my back in the most unnatural painful position, causing me to cry out.

"Be careful!" Finn shouted. "You'll spoil the meat."

The meat? What the hell? What did he plan to do? Pan-sear me on this altar?

Grimy hands manhandled me to the point of even more pain. With the sharp edge of the knife, one of the henchmen cut all of my clothes away until I was stark-naked.

Anger and embarrassment flooded my veins. I couldn't even look away from Finn as he stared at my body as they readied me for whatever evil ceremony he had planned.

What an animal!

I couldn't stand to stare at him anymore, so I squeezed my eyes shut. They had to cut away my bindings, but at this point, I had lost hope and my arms slumped to the table once my wrists were free.

The next thing they cut away were the ropes around my ankles and then proceeded to pull my legs apart. Cold chains struck my lower leg and sheer terror awakened in me. It was all the adrenaline I needed to act. I erupted, kicked one of the henchmen in the throat, and jumped off the table. I shoved past the other henchmen and bolted for the exit.

"You stupid fucks. Get her!" Finn commanded.

His henchmen scrambled into action, immediately lurching behind me.

My heart hammered as I stumbled out into the hallway, my eyes wide, looking for the door to this smelly cave. I wanted out of here. Even if I had to run out naked to gain freedom.

The gravel was slippery beneath my bare feet and I skidded around the corner, pushing my body off a corner wall to propel myself away from those henchmen. The sharp edge of rocks cut into the soles of my feet, but I knew the pain was small in comparison to what Finn would do to me if I was caught.

I slammed into someone's hard chest, stumbled backward, and hit my ass hard on the ground.

"You're not going anywhere, you little rat!" One henchman grabbed at me.

I ducked out of his grasp and then slid away from another, but the third time, I failed to cheat my cruel fate.

They caught me, and less than a couple of minutes after I raced away, I found myself back in the dry chamber.

I'd used all my strength the first time trying to fight them off, so when the chains clamped tight around my wrists and ankles this time, I gave in.

Finn ripped the gag off my mouth.

He looked down at me as if I was some pawn in a little game of cat and mouse. The mood pendant hanging from my necklace caught his attention and he reached down for it and snatched it from my neck.

"Bastard," I blurted, as he held up the moon pendant and inspected it.

Not only had he violated me, but he also took from me the only physical thing that brought me solace when I needed it. The necklace was a gift from my dad. Every time I wore it, he said it would remind me of how incredibly talented I was. My different moods at any given time represented my many talents.

"Give it back," I bit out, jerking upward.

"Not a chance in hell." He dropped the necklace into a bowl. "I told you what would happen if you tried to disobey me," he said.

"You gave me no time. You—"

"Be real. You ran. Used the magic you said you didn't possess to free yourself. You never had plans to find your sister for me. You know where she is."

"I-I don't," I stuttered, jerking against the chains.

"Doesn't matter. Because I had a plan for this. Just in case either of you ever got separated from the coven, I came up with a backup plan."

"Backup plan." Hell, I didn't even know what his initial plans were, let alone a backup plan.

"The moon orb is missing, which means we can't use it to do the coven's work. But we can draw from a Carrier."

"If you're trying to do what I think you're trying to do, that only works when two Carriers are present. Siblings. There must be multiples to fuel that kind of spell."

Finn grinned. "Never forget that I have Carrier blood too. My brother died in my mother's womb, but I have a sibling, nonetheless. We kept his ashes outside the family tomb for a reason. Our bastard daddy was good for something after all, wasn't he?"

He stroked my face. "The spell calls for the blood of siblings. Never said it had to be from the same set of parents. Yet, we are still from the same bloodline."

I cringed, rearing back and pressing my spine hard against the stone table.

"What are you up to?" I croaked.

"You'll see." He turned and fumbled with something on a table.

"It won't work," I shot at him.

He spun around. "It will."

Fire danced in his eyes. My gaze locked with his in a magnetic tug I couldn't pull away from.

"Nothing you wish for will ever come to fruition. It never has." I should've been wary of taunting Finn like this. He never liked being teased or told he couldn't do something.

Anger flared around him. "That's because of brats like you and your sister who don't like to share. Sydney ran off with my moon orb and you've thrown away your magic. Just like that." He snapped his fingers. "You two have plotted against me for a long time."

"How could that be true? You're the one with the coven, the ancestral lands, and even the church behind you."

Finn grimaced and looked away. He was trying to hide something. Did I hit a nerve?

"Oh," I breathed. "The church? Have the other priests abandoned you, Finn?" I taunted.

He said nothing to me, but demanded one of his henchmen to go fetch a few tools.

"I understand now. The moon orb gave you the power to anticipate threats and predict attacks on the church and our coven. Now you can't do that. Not without the orb."

When Finn wrapped his fingers around my throat, I didn't anticipate he'd squeeze hard and long enough to cause me to see white. I grabbed at his hands, clawing for breath.

"I didn't ask for your assessment," he hissed, loosening his grip.

Realizing that I was doomed one way or the other, I continued. "Your magic is superficial, Finn. It's always been. Coming from a source you never had...and you'll never have it."

He slapped me across the face and I tasted blood.

"Say nothing else or I'll call upon shadow world demons after I'm done with you and have them rip you to shreds this very night," he warned.

The picture he portrayed scared me, but I needed him to know that I knew the game he was playing.

I swallowed in an attempt to wet my dry throat. "You needed us together. Sydney and I. To fuel your spells. We've been close enough this whole time. Until...we weren't . And the moon orb right at your fingertips was just the icing on the cake. It allowed you to see deeper into the future, but at a price. A crystal ball may be able to predict attacks, Finn, but it doesn't stop them."

Finn huffed. "Fuck that moon orb! I don't need it anymore. You think you're so smart? Wait until you see what I've got in store for you."

"Just the other day, you and your mother were trying to push me off on Samson. Now, it looks like you want to kill me." I tugged against my restraints with a grunt.

He shot her a twisted smile. "I'll deal with that dirty dog, Samson, too. After I get through with you."

I clenched my teeth as icy anger shocked my core. "Soon, everyone will see you for who you truly are. Someone who claims to protect his realm but all he does is form alliances with crooked goons and delays the inevitable. My sister saw you for what you were. A fake and a fraud. No wonder she ran away."

Finn gave a short laugh. "Of course she did. You're the stupid one. You're still here."

Finn always had a way of making someone feel less-than. And in that moment, I felt like the weakest link in the coven.

"Doesn't matter now. Just as you've always been, you're going to be the sacrifice and I will get back what I lost," he stated. "Maybe your sister will come running then. Then again, maybe she won't. She's probably too busy trying to find a new coven home. Without you."

His last two words cut like glass. I couldn't deny the truth or falseness of his claims. I could only speculate as to why Sydney up and left without telling me or confiding in me.

"And remember that magic you suppressed deep down inside so no one could use it against you?" he asked, and then just like I thought, he didn't wait for me to reply. "It's time to drive it out so we can play."

Finn picked up a knife and began chanting a spell from an old grimoire. He dipped the sharp end of the blade into a bowl of cleansing brew, washing it clean, and then held the knife up in the air where the shiny blade glinted against the moon light beaming down through the cracks.

"You don't know what you're doing, Finn. Stop. You don't know what you're welcoming into this realm," I warned him.

"Yes, I do."

He plunged the knife into my side. White hot pain seared through me and I bit my tongue hard. Liquid warmth pooled beneath me on the table and I lay in it, unable to move because of the scorching hot pain.

Finn took the same knife and slashed it down his open palm. He held his hand over a bowl where my blood had already pooled and squeezed. "You'll see..." he sneered.

He grinned a gory, menacing smile as he picked up the bowl and held it to his lips. After uttering a spell I didn't recognize, he drank from the bowl. Blood dripped from his mouth and onto the floor as he consumed the entire contents.

I wanted to vomit, and it felt like I was going to die. His wound seemed to magically heal but I lay there, bleeding out and fearing that this might actually be the end.

"Immortality is the only option in this world, don't you agree?" He laughed pridefully.

So, that's what he wanted. He wanted more than power over the majority. He wanted to live forever. Well, there was no such thing. And even if he had found a loophole spell granting him this power, it would come at a price. As I lay there dying, it was obvious what that was.

"Isn't this what you wanted, Sadie? Just say the words. Relinquish your full powers to me for eternity, and I will grant your wish. To be free of your coven duties. To be mundane. To be left alone to live a life of apparent squalor. Go on...say the words."

It was true. I wanted no part in Finn's dealings or the coven if they were behind his evil plans. Living life mundanely would be better. As for squalor, that was rubbish. I knew how to take care of myself.

I parted my lips. Finn leaned down, cupping his hand against his left ear. "Go on...say it. Let me help. *Infiius Expesis Asime*," he babbled.

Twelve other witches from our coven gathered around and they began chanting the spell. One by one, they slashed their palms and drained the blood into the bowl.

This was low. Somehow, Finn had convinced them all to relinquish their powers to him. When they were done, Finn grew stronger and directed all of his newfound energy to me.

An invisible force constricted my throat, restricting my breathing. I clasped my chest, trying to draw in air.

Infiius Expesis Asime. Sadie, say it! He was in my head. *You have two options, sweet Sadie. Die or relinquish.*

My lungs burned so badly it hurt to the point where I would say anything to get him to allow me to breathe. And then I did. I said the words, but not the ones he wanted me to say.

"Partum Le fantôme Asime!" I blurted.

At my command, a cyclone burst through the room and blasted the whole entire right side of the wall away.

When the dust settled, a large entity—an eight-foot-tall red-eyed alabaster demon—appeared in the center of it all.

Finn was livid and looked batshit scared, fearful of the apparition that just occupied the room. "You fucking bitch! You executed the wrong spell."

Holy crap, what had I just done? Who or what had I summoned?

CHAPTER 7
Sadie

THE EIGHT-FOOT-TALL demonic monster from my dreams was real. He was here. And in the flesh.

Something told me this wasn't a dream. How did I know that? Because I usually woke up when dreams turned into nightmares.

Moonlight beamed down on the monster's alabaster skin. Huge horns erected from his head and blue-black hair swept across his back as the cyclone whirled around us. It was the most majestic thing I'd ever seen.

The storm never ceased. It was as if the demon brought the darkness and chaos with him.

Several witches were tossed against the stone walls by some invisible force where they landed unconscious, never getting up again. The remaining witches led Finn in a chant, but nothing they did banished the monster from the vault. When they realized what they were up against, the rest of the witches fled the vault, leaving Finn alone to fight the darkness.

I tugged at my bounds, but I was still strapped to the table in a puddle of my own blood which lay cold beneath me.

"Be gone, demon. You're not wanted here," Finn shouted out.

The demon monster pushed forward, slamming into Finn with a muted thud. Finn slid across the floor on both feet, but managed to keep himself upright. He threw up the knife and slashed a wide arc just as the monster came for him again. Finn was trained in martial arts, and he used all of his skills to keep the monster at bay, but to no avail.

Finn raised his arms, gathering up a massive amount of energy from the cyclone. When he hurled the force at the monster, the ball stopped a few inches in front of it. With one effortless lift of his clawed hands, the monster reversed the force, and it knocked Finn several feet back where he crashed into the stand where they kept all the blood. The liquid spilled over, splashing onto Finn's head, coating his face.

The monster pointed at Finn. "Touch her again and I'll snap you in two."

"Demon, you're not of this earth. Where did you come from?" Finn demanded.

"Hell. And that's where you'll be going soon."

Finn spat blood on the ground. "Why are you here?"

The monster turned, pointing a finger at me. Of all the things I could've thought of in that moment, I only thought of the times when I dreamt of the monster and me tangled among silken sheets, with me crying out his name in the throes of passion. Yet, every time I woke up, I couldn't remember the monster's name.

"I'm here for my queen. She's mine," the monster stated.

Finn laughed. "She's no queen. No queen at all. Besides, you're too late, demon. I've taken everything from her and more."

I never said the words. Not the words Finn wanted me to say, anyway. So what was he talking about?

The monster frowned as he assessed me on the table and then he lifted his hand and my chains broke, granting me freedom.

"She is useless, demon. She used all the power she had left to summon you and now she is useless."

I folded upward but found myself swaying from the blood loss and I collapsed right back onto the stone table. I was on the verge of passing out again. I could feel it. It usually only happened when I overexerted myself during a spell. And besides a spell, summoning a demon from hell would do that to just about anyone.

While the monster ran to my aid, Finn lurched for the mood pendant and scooped it up from the floor.

"No!" I yelled as he fled the vault with my necklace and the vitality he stole from me.

A thunderous movement erupted all around me and the ground shifted.

When I witnessed large pieces of rock and concrete breaking off from the sides of the wall, I knew my life would be over in a matter of seconds.

All around me, I could hear the echoes of a spell that only Finn would have executed.

He was trying to kill me. Or it—the demon. He was trying to trap us in here.

I held up my fist, trying to call whatever powers were left within me to stop it, but it was too late.

I scrunched my eyes close and used my last breath to call out to my spirit sisters to let me join them quickly in the afterlife. I didn't want to feel the pain that I knew would come from having tons of rocks crush me to death.

The monster swept me up and hauled us across the room as everything came crashing down. It all sounded like a massive earthquake as dirt and dust came pouring into the mouth of the cave.

If it wasn't for the massive monster covering my body with his, I'd be dead.

Other than dust and debris lessening the visibility around me, nothing touched me or fell on me.

When it was all over, there was silence—and the unbelievable ragged breaths of the monster as he took most of the rocks coming for us to his back and side.

If I could've surrounded us with a protection spell, I would've. But Finn had taken something away from me—something I feared I could never get back.

Suddenly, the demon folded upright again. "Argh!" A handful of rocks rolled off his back.

I turned around slowly, glancing up into his face. I still couldn't believe he was here in the flesh. The demon who had visited my dreams since I was a girl.

He was angry. His flesh was *black alabaster*—like the stone, which was said to be rare and unique. As dark as he was, he seemed to glow like sunlight. His skin looked hot to touch.

"Hold tight, my queen. I'll get us out of here," he said, holding his right arm up in the air.

White-hot vibrations surrounded the demon and then puttered out quickly.

"Dammit," the demon bit out. "I exhausted all my strength to get here."

Fully aware that I was still naked, I wrapped my arms around myself and stayed huddled against the wall.

The demon was half-naked himself, only covered in a wool loin-cloth and black vest. Intricately knotted copper amulets dressed both of his forearms.

"How did you get here?" I breathed.

He turned swiftly. "You summoned me, queen. Demanded my actual presence. I broke exile to save you."

"Why do you keep calling me that?"

His forehead creased and his eyebrows came together in the center. "You are Sadie. You are our queen."

A vivid image flashed in my mind. The image of three immortal guardians with massive horns and gigantic wings flanking me. It was like déjà vu, as if I'd lived in that moment before.

"*Our* queen?" I mouthed.

Before he could explain, water began flooding into the cave from between the rocks. Within seconds, the water was already shin level.

"Oh my God." I hopped up to a standing position. Modesty, at this point, was only second to survival. Yet I still attempted to conceal my nakedness from the demon. The same demon who had presumably already seen me naked. The same exact demon who brought me to orgasm numerous times over and over again...in my dreams.

As the demon frantically searched for a way out, I began to panic. The water was now waist-deep on me, but only about thigh-level on the demon.

When the demon reached for me, I caved, moving toward him in a split second. His name...was on the tip of my tongue, but I couldn't bring myself to say it.

He wrapped his arms around me, and although the water levels were still rising, the rhythm of my heartbeats began to slow down.

"We can get out of here alive. But it will require massive energy on both of our parts."

His rock-hard body pressed against mine as he kept me as close as possible around the rushing waters. My legs weren't even touching the floor anymore. The demon was holding me suspended against him.

"I can't access my magic right now," I panted.

"I can help you. And you can help me. My source of power grows through energy."

"What kind of energy? How?"

"Sex."

Sex.

I should've known it. All demons required some form of energy to exist, whether it was through reaping souls, drinking blood, feeding off energies, or whatever else kept them alive.

After the mention of sex, the demon's manhood came alive between us.

"I'm sorry, Sadie. I can't let you die in here."

"Why are you apologizing?" I asked.

Without answering, he bent low and took my mouth firmly in a soul-sealing kiss. My body came alive. Even in my dreams, I hadn't recalled a moment this magical.

Heat washed over me. I didn't even notice the threatening ripples of the water rising up my body as he held me close. I wrapped my legs around the demon.

Fire flared in his eyes and I saw my reflection in his irises. I gasped, leaving my mouth open to his wanton kisses.

"Don't be afraid, Sadie. I'm going to fuck you. I'm going to fuck you now to save you."

He backed us up against the rocks until my spine was pressing against the cold, hard, jagged stones.

The instant connection I felt with this demon fueled this moment. And even though I could not use my powers, I felt the remnants of my magic stirring around in my veins.

The water began circling around us, creating a vortex of energy.

I leaned into him and enjoyed the kiss. He angled his mouth until he was kissing me hard, fast, and deep.

He cupped my breast and rolled my nipple between his thumb and forefinger. I bit out a gasp and arched myself against him. When his hot lips connected with my throat, leaving a hot trail of desire, I felt my sex clench, hungry for what I knew would come next.

"I promise you, Sadie, when we get out of here, it's going to be different. I'll have more time to explore every fucking inch of your lovely body."

"The water..." I rasped. "I need you."

Even if I died in here. In this cave. By drowning. I would have left this earth as a happy woman in the arms of this demon. Maybe, he'd even be the one to take my soul to its final resting place when it was all over with.

The bulbous tip of his hard shaft probed at my opening. With the first two inches inside, I leaned my head back until it rested on the cave. He was looking right at me, staring into my eyes, captivating me.

"You know me, Sadie. Say my name," the demon commanded.

My lips parted in a gasp as he pushed in another couple of inches.

His eyes were the color of coal. And within the irises, glimmers of gold danced.

"Please—*Ah!*"

He drove home, catching me off guard. My insides knotted and pleasure grew rapidly as my sex adjusted to his thick width. His manhood had to have been a good twelve inches deep inside me and almost as thick as my wrist, stretching me wide. I widened my legs even more just to accommodate him and dropped my face to his collarbone.

I thought he was already seated fully, but then he drew back almost all the way out and sunk himself deep to the hilt. I screamed, and rocks fell from the top of the cave.

I wasn't afraid anymore.

I could barely take the hot sensations running through my veins. The pleasure was out of this world. The first orgasms funneled through me like a whirlwind. I was dizzy with emotions. Hot with need.

He thrust savagely. Hard, deep, and deliberate plunges that took me over the edge over and over again.

From somewhere deep inside, new magic surged. Against the demon's skin, the vibrations from his own powers entered me.

Release was so close for him. I could almost taste it.

Something changed within me. It felt exquisite. Like lightning heat bolting through my core.

"Say it, Sadie. My name. *Say it.*" His deep, masculine voice echoed throughout. It was all I heard. Nothing else mattered.

He plunged hard within me.

"*Altair!*" I screamed his name. My demon savior's name was Altair.

Altair roared out in pleasure.

Relief came. For both of us. Hot, electric, blinding release.

Pressure spread out to all corners of my body and then dissipated, leaving only spine-tingling gratification.

Water spun around us. Droplets showered us as if we were in the middle of a torrential downpour. I was drowning in it.

I opened my eyes and lifted my face to the blinding light above us. Energy radiated outward and upward until there was an earth-shattering blast.

Sex with Altair was absolutely mind-blowing...but was this death?

CHAPTER 8
Sadie

I WAS in Altair's arm in what seemed like another dimension. The air felt different somehow, denser, more polluted, and I struggled to breathe. Mere seconds passed, and the monster landed on an enormous boulder overlooking the beach.

Rough waves crashed into the shoreline and toppled over the tall cliffs. Moonlight rippled over the surface of the sea. The world—or wherever we were—was bathed in twilight.

"Where am I?" I panted, glancing around, my hands still squeezing Altair tight, hoping this was real and that he didn't let go.

"No worries, Sadie. We're still in the earth realm."

"You...saved us," I whispered. My eyelids were heavy as a deep slumber set in. I was so weak. It was as if something vital was stolen from me.

No...not if. Something *was* stolen from me.

"We can't stay here. Too many lurkers," Altair said, looking down below at the beach. Even after midnight, people still visited the beach. "Where does my queen wish to rest?"

"Home. Take me home."

"It is not safe..." His voice trailed off.

"No. Not that home. I have another place. I'll show you."

I touched his right temple, putting a vision in his mind of a ranch house my father used to take us to for private family vacations. In fact, it was where my sister was gifted the grimoire on her thirteenth birthday and where I manifested the idea of summoning three protectors.

"That's enough. You'll drain yourself. I'll take you there," he whispered.

Ice-cold numbness shocked my body and I couldn't remain conscious enough to see that the monster took me where I felt the most comfortable. I knew Finn wouldn't look there. He knew nothing about the place. No one knew anything about it. Only my father. My mother. Myself. And my big sister.

I thought about the ranch house overlooking a tranquil lake. I thought about how secluded it was in the forest. It's where I should've gone in the first place.

I should've decided a long time ago.

I should've gone AWOL just like my sister.

The monster looked down at me in confusion. It was right then that I knew he was in my head, just like the other red-headed and silver-haired beasts of my dreams.

It was over now. Finn had what he wanted. He'd leave me alone.

I wanted to believe that...but I couldn't.

I woke up with super tight, sore muscles and with no sense of time. As I propped myself up on the soft cushions, I wiped my eyes and blinked a few times into the shadows until I spotted Altair's massive form near the window.

It was still dark outside. Or had I missed more hours than I realized?

Altair turned around. "Yes. You've been sleeping peacefully since dawn yesterday."

He was in my head again. How was he doing that? I hadn't let him in.

"It's my gift. And it's how I stay connected to you. I can't turn it off. Not unless you ask, of course." He grinned, flashing sharp incisors.

I smiled shyly, pulling the blanket across my shoulders and hiding my bare skin. "You can turn it off, for now."

"Very well."

He sat down on the ottoman next to the bed. A bowl of water and a washcloth sat on the end table.

I glanced down at my side to examine the deep cut. To my surprise, my flesh had already healed.

"I healed you in the cave," he said.

"Are you still in my head?"

"No. I am not."

"Do the others have the same gift?"

"My kindred, you mean?" he asked.

I pulled myself up until my back was against the headboard. "*Kindred?* Is that what you call the other demons who frequent my dreams?"

"Yes. The three of us...we come from the same bloodline—spawned from a king of demon blood. We have many gifts. Some, the same. Others...different. As do you." He reached out and picked up a lock of my sleek black hair, admiring the way the tresses curled around his fingers. "I imagined our first physical meeting, but never like this. You are perfect."

"Not so perfect if I continue to fail."

"But you haven't failed. You haven't failed me. I broke away from the Nebulae plane because of you."

"Is that another realm?"

He nodded. "Nebulae was the only land on which my kindred and I could roam until you pulled me out."

"Why?"

"We were exiled. By decree and by magic. You broke the magic holding us there. The decree still stands."

I couldn't imagine being exiled from my home. "Decree by...?"

"My father. We were caught conspiring to overthrow him, which is true. It's not something we hide."

I frowned. "Overthrow him?"

"A very long time ago, we made a blood pact to take Shadow World back from my father."

"The others are free too, then?"

"They are. We all felt the curse lifted from us when we heard your cries for help. We can jump realms now apparently. But we had to make a decision. Your spell was only strong enough to allow one of us through to this realm without detection. In a split second decision, we agreed I would go. It won't be long before one of my father's messengers realizes that I have broken the rules of exile, and he'll come for me."

"And what will happen to you if he does?"

"I'm not worried about myself. Only you. I can't have anyone know what you can do."

I chuckled under my breath. "What are you going to do? Keep me hidden and locked away?"

I was only joking, but the serious look that swept across Altair's face told me he'd been considering this.

I scooted to the far edge of the bed and swung my legs over the side. "I don't have time to be locked away like I'm a slave. I've already escaped one lunatic—"

"I assure you, my queen. You will not be treated like a slave."

Somehow, I believed Altair. At no point when they came to me in my dreams had I felt like a slave. If anything, I felt peaceful, guarded, and...sexually liberated.

"In any case, I have to find my sister. My half-brother, Finn —he's responsible for a lot more than just threatening to kill me on that sacrificial altar. Before they found me, I was with my aunt. They killed her. And Mika helped them because they poisoned her against us. I have to avenge my aunt."

I squeezed my fingers together and balled my hands into fists.

"It wouldn't be wise to run after your sister so blindly. We don't know where she is, and for all we know, she might not want to be found. She has escaped this evil half-brother you speak of and we shouldn't interfere with that."

Altair was right.

"We are fated to protect you. Don't you remember summoning us when you were only a child—only having just lived a decade?"

I tipped my chin and caught his eyes. They were bright gold now, reminding me of the harvest moon. The darkness had completely disappeared.

"I was so little. I didn't know what I was doing."

I remembered the day like it was yesterday. My sister and I, having been born in the same month but in different years, always celebrated our birthday during the same moon time, in May, when the grounds were most fertile for planting.

On my sister's thirteenth birthday, my parents gifted her with a grimoire. While I, who was only ten, received another doll to add to my growing collection. I had outgrown dolls by that time. Sydney wasn't supposed to receive her grimoire until her sixteenth birthday, but she got it early. At the time, our coven was dealing with difficult foes and many were dying bloody violent deaths trying to defeat them.

Rabid werewolves. A savage vampire or two. And several restless spirits.

In my father's words, me and my sister had to learn to protect ourselves just in case the unthinkable were to happen.

At the time, I knew it wouldn't help one bit to become jealous of my sister's present, but I couldn't help my feelings. Rather than showing animosity to her, I constructed my own spell without the use of any grimoire, asking the spirits to help me summon three guardians.

If the unthinkable happened, my sister, our childhood friend Millicent, and I would always be protected. And the unthinkable did happen.

My spell was successful, but things didn't quite turn out the way I thought they would.

My sister couldn't see the three demons. Only I could see them.

My sister couldn't summon them either. Only I could.

And our friend, Millicent...well, her family left our group for another rival coven, joining them because they thought my father was cursed.

Over the years, I realized the demons I summoned were mine and mine alone. But they weren't just in my imagination. My demons were real. And now I had proof.

The eight-foot-tall alabaster beast standing in front of me couldn't have been a hallucination. Unless, of course, I was dreaming. But I wasn't. I had pinched myself a dozen times already.

"If my summons was all you needed to free yourselves from this exile, why didn't you ask me when..." I swallowed and heat crept up my chest.

He gently tipped my chin with his fingers. "When I was inside of you in the dream world, you mean?"

I nodded. "Yes."

"Because it is still too soon, Sadie. You're only months away from your twenty-first birthday, but your most greatest powers have still not surged. A spell of that magnitude could've killed you, if you weren't ready."

I bit my lip. "I see. Finn started the spell and—"

"You finished it," Altair said. "But not to his benefit."

I cringed. "He took what he could from me and now I'm left empty. Without my powers, I doubt I could perform a simple fire spell at this point."

"You could, but I wouldn't advise it. You can harness powers from an alternate source until you find out how to reverse what that dimwit has done."

"How? I mean, where do I get that kind of power?"

Altair grinned. "Me. And the others. We are at your disposal. You can channel us. You've been doing that all along."

I crossed my arms over my chest. "Why do I feel that channelling you comes at a price?"

"If you want to stop your half-brother, you need to channel a powerful source. And yes, it comes at a price, if that's what you want to call it."

"What's the price then?"

CHAPTER 9
Sadie

BEFORE ALTAIR SPOKE, I knew the price would be high. I already owed him for saving me. My debts with this demon were racking up.

He prowled over to the window again. The curtains were shoved back and moonlight gleamed inside. I couldn't get over how flawless his skin was. He remained in his demonic form—alabaster skin and exquisitely toned body on full display. His horns were almost the same color as the night, only darker with a strong, majestic glint of silver. On his massive back, two mounds swelled from where his wings would unfold when needed.

I blushed, remembering the way he took me in the cave and pleasured me like my life had depended on it.

"The price, you ask? We need to feed."

I pursed my lips, contemplating Altair's answer. "Well, good thing there's not a shortage of food around here. You can hunt and fish anytime you'd like."

"From you, Sadie. We must feed from you."

"Oh." I swallowed. "Oh, I see."

"Humans. Or mundanes, as you call them, do not sustain demons for long. They are an energy source for us, but not the only source. I can go through one hundred humans, but they will never appease me the way you do. You taste exquisite, Sadie, especially when I'm giving you pleasure."

I blushed as a warm sensation unfolded between my legs. I was wet instantly just thinking about how his massive shaft felt when he was inside me, stroking me to completion.

I wiped the perspiration from my forehead. "You've been feeding from me through my dreams?"

He nodded. "And likewise, you've been channeling us for your spells. Sadie, you were strong before you summoned us when you were a child. But when you called to us when we lived in the Shadow World and began to channel our powers from there, that gave you untethered access to magic that others didn't have. My brothers and I...we allowed it."

I figured this much. It made sense now how I was able to execute some of the most complicated spells during our moon rituals, while others could not.

"I was just a child," I whispered.

"My kindred and I...we knew that. But for us, it was fate. The moment you summoned us demanding our immediate protection, we knew you were our queen."

"The queen of what? I have nothing."

He smiled. "You have us."

I sighed and got up to join him at the window, wrapping the sheet around my body. "I was always taught that all magic comes at a price either way, whether or not it's being channeled from something."

"You are correct. Wielding change requires a sacrifice more often than not. That sacrifice or price may not be known at the time. So, there needs to be a balance of give and take at any given time. I think you understand that more than your peers."

My spine tensed as he spoke. He knew so much about magic—as if he was used to wielding it quite often. "What do you mean?"

"Your halfbrother, for example, seems to think there should be no limits to his powers. He was so willing to strip you of yours that he ignored the potential consequences for himself and others."

I frowned. "Finn is a complex individual. Although I hate him for what he's done and the destruction and division he's caused within our coven, I understand no one lives without having flaws. My father tried with him. Tried to show him the way, but apparently, his efforts didn't work."

He slid his palm across my cheek. I closed my eyes, reveling in the peaceful feeling his touch brought.

"You are not like Finn," he said.

"No."

"Then let's not talk of him again."

My eyes flew open.

"I promise you, Sadie. Finn will reap what he's sown. Now that you're with me, he won't be able to touch you."

I swallowed. "I can't run forever. Maybe my sister can, but I can't."

"You won't have to. That's why you have us."

"But where will I go? Even if he's taken my magic, I'm still traceable."

"I'm taking you with me. To Nebulae."

I gasped. "How will that be possible?"

"With you, anything is possible. But I can't stay here. I can feel the cloaking spell we put up already dissipating as we speak. My father's reach includes most of the earth's territory. If he knows I'm here, he will hunt me down. If that happens, he'll know how I got here."

"I...I can do another cloaking spell for you. Luckily, it doesn't require deep magic," I muttered.

"No, and even if it did, you can always channel me for that."

"But I haven't yet agreed to your proposal." I blinked, looking up at his perplexed expression. "What if I free you from me? I summoned you. You and the others are tied to me in some way. What if I release you and send you back?"

"That's not something I desire. And you know very well that you don't want that either."

My breath hitched when he slipped his hands between the blanket and caressed my bare thigh.

He leaned in and brushed his lips against my ear. "Now that we have you, we will never leave you to walk this earth alone. You were meant to be with us."

A shiver crept up my spine. "So, you've decided..."

"Yes. Once my father is dethroned, everything will fall into place. But I need you to do it, just as you need me."

"And what about Fi—"

"Shhh." He placed a finger on my lips. "Don't utter his name again. I am already so angry that if I wasn't here, I'd be somewhere with my fingers wrapped around that dimwit's throat, squeezing the life straight out of him."

Negative energy surged around us. Some of it even slipped its way inside me. Like a sponge, I took it all in.

I had only just realized that getting a demon angry to fuel violence wouldn't bode well for my plans or intentions. I could very well use Altair to exact revenge in the most brutal way possible, but that would almost certainly result in the loss of lives.

"I would if you asked me to. And...it would," Altair whispered.

He was in my thoughts. *Again.*

"I thought I told you not to do that," I chided him, but the more he touched my heated flesh with his strong hands, the more I pressed myself against him.

Altair hoisted me up. It took milliseconds for my feet to leave the floor and wrap around his waist. The sheet fell on the rug about his feet and I looped my fingers around his neck.

His manhood was already hard and pressed solidly against my belly. My pussy clenched in anticipation. I was so greedy and ready for him to take me into the clouds again.

His incisors pushed gently at the veins on my neck.

"I...I have to tell you something before you decide...you know, about me."

"I've already decided. I decided the moment I knew you existed. But tell me now, anyway. What is it?"

"I...I'm still betrothed. Set to marry Samson Wulfric on my twenty-first birthday."

Altair pulled back and searched my face. His eyes were glowing red. And for a moment, I thought his possessive nature would spiral into something much worse.

"You never belonged to him. You belong to me." He thrust his cock inside me, plunging deep until he was buried to the hilt.

I cried out.

My body convulsed into an instant orgasm, and I forgot everything. Everything except Altair.

He placed me on a table nearby and pummeled me until I couldn't form words. Only screams escaped my lips.

So much energy flooded the room. There was a river of magic around. The air was so thick with it, the pressure of it expanded outward and the walls and other unstable furniture pieces in the room shook with so much force.

I wanted more. *More.*

My need for him was paralyzing. Every plunge took me higher into the clouds.

Something blossomed around his cock, stretching my pussy. Something was forming at the base. It almost felt like a knot, twisting and growing deep in my wet cunt.

"Do you feel that, Sadie? Do you feel your slick coating me?" he asked.

"Yes!" I gasped.

"Your body was made to take me. To take my demon seed. You're an omega witch—rare and sacred—perfect for taking my knot and breeding."

At the mention of breeding, I squeezed my sex tightly around his thick shaft.

His wings shot outward and a long tendril shot up from behind him. *His tail.* It wrapped around my waist, taking the place of his hands.

He slid his hands upward above me, pressed his palms into the wall, and fucked me hard.

I was slick. Juices spilled from my cunt down his thick thighs. He slid in and out of me with ease, stroking back and forth without missing a beat until my clitoral orgasms synced up with deeper g-spot convulsions.

He knotted, locking himself inside me.

Long streams of hot cum splashed into my womb and he held me hard against the wall, filling me with seed.

I was beyond elated. On cloud nine, and not ready to come down yet.

I rested my head on his shoulders and panted, trying to get my breathing back to normal.

My cunt wouldn't stop clenching around his shaft and he was still leaking seed into my already overflowing pussy.

My only regret was not demanding Altair's physical presence way before my life desperately depended on it.

Sex in dreams was bliss.

But this was...out of this world.

Suddenly, a bright-colored rift opened up to the left of us.

We were both so shocked to see it happening. It jolted both of us out of our euphoric moment.

"Fuck," Altair growled, without parting from me. He couldn't either way. His knot was still lodged and locked deep inside me.

"What is it?"

"It's a Grugger demon from Shadow World trying to come through. It must have sensed all the energy we created and came to steal from it. *Hold still.* I'm going to banish this thing back to where it came from."

His wings and tail disappeared and he captured me with his arms so I could carefully unseat his cock. My feet settled on the floor.

"Fucking vulture," Altair spat out and then held up his hand. With a flick of his wrist, he sealed the rift and it dissipated. "If something from the Shadow World tracks our energy like that again, my father will hear of your existence and my escape in no time. We have to get to Nebulae *soon.* "

CHAPTER 10
Sadie

I HAD NEVER CHANNELED power intentionally from a demon, but I guess there was a first time for everything.

I had pulled energy from Altair and his kindred before, but not knowingly.

So I had to wonder, was I really all that powerful to begin with? Questioning myself brought up the conversation I had with Naima. Maybe I was a fluke witch. Maybe my coven's existence actually ended with my sister and me.

There was no way in the world that the spirits would allow Finn access to old magic, knowing he was a lost cause. But I had been wrong before about everything.

Even now, I wondered if my parents were in the spirit world. Their deaths were so sudden that the living elders often said their souls would never rest in peace, and so they would never find the spirit world.

Yet, I couldn't believe that. I wouldn't believe it.

Buried in the building's rubble, which blew up after a bomb ignited with my parents inside, crime scene investigators eventually found bones that the coven reburied on consecrated grounds. Other than an act of terrorism, police detectives never discovered why the terrorist chose that chapel to carry out his attack on the innocents.

My parents had only been trying to help the church, whose clergymen believed an evil spirit was haunting the grounds and a few of its members. Exorcising demons was one of the many ways my parents earned their living.

Finding out the reason this calamity happened to my parents was perhaps the number one reason I worked at the police station, but even after years of digging, nothing new ever came about.

Even my sister warned that I should just let it go. Our parents were gone and they couldn't be brought back or contacted in the afterlife. It was just an unfortunate tragedy resulting from them being in the wrong place at the wrong time. For my sanity, I tried to believe that—some days, anyway.

I sighed and brought myself back to reality.

Altair was seated across the narrow table from me, watching me as I fumbled with the elements used to fuel my spell. We had searched for and found everything on the same lot where the cabin sat. Altair had even helped me collect everything.

Aside from exorcising demons, my mother was also a devout supporter of natural medicine, so it was no surprise that we could forage various herbs and exotic plants right in the backyard.

I picked up the wooden bowl with all the elements inside and began muddling the leaves together into fine dust. If I had my magic, I wouldn't have needed to do anything the old-fashioned way, as my father would describe it. Yet, thanks to him, I could create just about any spell the *old-fashioned way*.

"I still don't understand how this is possible. How you're here," I said, as I worked. "Finn was stealing my magic when I summoned you."

"It was a life or death situation. Your conscious mind must have known that. You must've used whatever energy you could to get me here," he replied, leaning forward and glancing into the bowl.

"What did it feel like...being summoned?" I asked.

"I can't really describe. Hmmm, it's like a pull toward something. It's like a call that I have to answer to...or else."

I paused. "Or else?"

"Or else I lose everything, including you. And that can't happen."

I looked down at the table. My mind went languid, devoid of hope. "It will happen eventually. It seems I keep getting caught up in things that threaten my life."

Altair took my hands in his, directing my attention away from my work and to him. "Listen, I won't let anything happen to you."

I swallowed. "And if something were to happen to you?"

His lips twisted and then he drew them in thoughtfully. "That's why there's three of us. We are your protectors."

Imagining life without my three protectors pained me. Before, I had them only in my dreams...and that had been enough. I didn't want to think about what I'd do if I couldn't call on them when I needed them most.

"I don't want to think about that. Tell me more about the summoning."

He got up, slipped behind me, and began kneading the tension from my shoulders. "When you summoned me, I traveled through a funnel cloaked. It's why my father's demon force wasn't able to detect me. If you can manage the cloaking spell, for both of us, that would be best."

I closed my eyes for a moment while he worked his magic with his hands.

Altair knew exactly what I needed when I needed it.

I relied on my demons more than I knew.

I smiled. "I can do it...the spell. I won't stop until I get it done."

"I know you can. We could travel uncloaked, but the less detection we have, the more time that would buy us to execute our attack on Shadow World."

"You've been planning this a long time, then."

He nodded. "And it's time to execute. I think that's something me and the others can all agree on."

"I know we can't control much of fate, but why now? Why did it have to be a life or death situation?"

Altair sighed. "My kindred and I agreed to wait until you were a woman to come to earth to get you, but then my father exiled us. The only connection we had outside of Nebulae was you. You linked yourself to us in both mind and soul. Your power allows you to reach us despite the odds. We knew you were our only chance...but if we waited just a little while longer you might already be at your full potential and not at risk—weakened like this."

"You mean on my twenty-first birthday?"

He nodded. "But we never predicted the sudden upheaval in your life."

I frowned. "Unfortunately, the coven mess started way before my parents perished. They shielded my sister and I from most of it, so I didn't know until it was too late and they were already gone." A lump rose in my throat as I recalled receiving the bad news. My entire life changed that day. And then, I learned that Finn and his mother had assumed guardianship of my sister and I, as well as the coven.

"You didn't reach out to us for many moons after that."

"I was broken. I even questioned whether I wanted to use magic anymore." I shifted in the chair. "The three of you always came to me separately. Never together. Except at the beginning, when I first summoned you all." I couldn't stop myself from pondering.

I caught his gaze, eager to get through to the blankness in his eyes that stared back at me.

"We're like brothers, as you'll soon discover. We aren't happy when we lose. And when we lose together, it's never a good time."

"That's understandable. My sister and I fight too."

"Probably not like us."

"Why do you want your father removed?" I asked.

"He *should be* removed. Our father exiled us because we always questioned him and did the opposite of whatever he wanted."

"Children sometimes do the opposite of what their parents ask and then they get punished for it. I'm no different."

He grinned. "Well, your exile was probably to a time-out corner or something like that. Ours was to another realm."

I giggled. "Not really. My father was strict. Whenever we did something wrong, we were grounded for weeks at a time and forced to read literature that would bore the dead. I mean, besides my sister, who wants to read about rock formation?"

Altair chuckled right along with me.

"Our forced exile isn't the only reason why we're going to remove him. He killed our mothers. When we found out that he cast them into hellfire, we tried to kill him." He looked sheepishly off to the side. "We failed. Demons as old as he is are incredibly hard to kill."

That statement alone sent alarm bells ringing. This coup Altair was now trying to take on would be dangerous. "He must be powerful, then."

"He reigns over Shadow World. Draws his powers right from it. Of course, he is."

"And if he is your father, that makes you a...crown prince."

He nodded. "One of the crown princes of the Shadow World."

"Right," I said, thinking of the others. His kindred.

I wondered how this would work out once I was reunited with the others. Altair had already proven himself to be possessive, declaring that I never belonged to Samson.

I had feelings for all three demons. I had developed feelings for them even before I knew they were real.

"I am a possessive soul, but I am not jealous of my brothers." He raised his voice when he stated this. "It is already prophesied that we will share what is sacred to us. *You.*"

My heart skipped a beat. "I was only wondering. And I told you...if you go into my head again without my permission, I'll send you right back where you came from—*without me.*" I cast him a teasing grin.

He returned the grin. "And that will be another punishment I cannot accept."

Turning back to my work, I poured the contents of my brew into a glass bowl and then set the bowl upon an altar of some old books.

I reached out for his hand and he gave it without hesitation.

"Shall we begin?"

"Let's proceed."

I clasped my hand with his. "I'm warning you. Finn left me empty. I'm going to need a lot of your energy to pull this off."

"Take what you need, my queen."

I began.

"Nebulae. Asente. Zoist. Asime."

Altair gasped and his fingers tensed while entwined with mine as I funneled power from him into the spell.

Nebulae. Asente. Zoist. Asime.

The room exploded into a cloud of mist. Black and gold specks floating up around us.

"Asente. Vasdio. Asime!"

We landed with a plop on floors made of marbles and in a mansion so grand, I thought I was on the set of a movie.

Altair reached upward, pulling me up from the floor.

Our arrival in this place hadn't gone unnoticed.

Two figures I recognized slowly rose from their chairs.

My demons.

At long last, I was with my demons. *Finally.* We were all together. In the flesh.

My attention drifted to the silver-haired rake with the Amazon-god-like physique who stood slightly behind the other. He was the taller of the three. His skin was an ashen gray and amulets adorned both his wrists and ankles.

The red-headed brooding rogue presented himself partially in his human form—with olive-toned skin riddled with tribal tattoos and massive horns on his head. He parted his lips, revealing his forked tongue.

"It's about time you got back." The silver-haired rake was the first to speak.

"We were beginning to think she might have murdered you for your powers, brother," the rogue exclaimed, undressing me with his eyes. A suspicious gleam marked his playboy-like features.

"You never should've doubted my plan. We are here," Altair replied. "Sadie, meet the others in the flesh this time. This is—."

"I know who they are. Morpheus…and Dominik." My eyes shifted between the two demons as I named them.

Morpheus grinned. A lock of silver hair fell over his eyes as he continued to assess me.

Dominik's eyebrow rose a fraction, and he licked his lips as he glanced from me to Altair. "You don't plan on keeping her for yourself now, do you, big brother?"

CHAPTER 11
Sadie

EXECUTING SPELLS WAS EXHAUSTING, even with the help of a powerful demon. After the brief reunion —in the flesh, this time—my body gave in and it felt like my knees would buckle.

If my demons hadn't been there to catch my fall, I might have cracked my skull open.

That wasn't the first time I had performed a spell so powerful, and with the way things were going, it likely would not be the last.

I sat up in the bed, which had to have been California-king sized, maybe bigger. All around me were mounds of pillows and soft, silken sheets that caressed my skin as I shifted through my nap.

Nap? Well, I had no idea how long I'd been sleeping and there were no windows that I could see, so I had no sense of time.

The room was vast, exuding feng shui vibes. I felt at ease and at peace. Protected. And safe.

For once in my life, I thought about nothing else but this moment. Myself. My demons.

It's not selfish to take care of oneself, my mother would say...

But how come I was feeling guilty?

Even if I only had a moment like this to take off my big girl panties before the hard work began, I would be...happy.

Speaking of big girl panties...

I peeled the sheets back away from me, realizing that I was utterly naked.

Someone, one of my demons maybe, must have thought it was okay to deprive me of clothes.

There wasn't a closet, a dresser, or a strap of clothing in sight.

But there was an additional adjoining room. The reflection in the mirror on the door revealed a porcelain bath sink. So, at least there was a bathroom.

Everything was just surreal. And different.

I could tell I was on a different elevation in this realm. I was light-headed and it felt like I was floating.

That would be something I'd have to get used to—if I was going to stay here.

As I slipped out from under the sheets, I noted how quiet it was. It was just as if I was alone in this big place. I recalled the enormous room that Altair and I teleported to when we first arrived. If the great hall was that big and this bedroom was this size, I could only imagine what the rest of the rooms would look like. It all reminded me of something out of a magazine spotlighting the rich and famous.

Although my sister and I had everything we ever needed, my father still chose for us to live way below our means. Money was no motivator for either my sister or me. And to this day, millions of dollars left behind by my parents for our future endeavors still sat untouched in investment accounts. One day we'd get around to sorting stuff out or send it off as a donation to one of our favorite charities.

As if the marble floors would crack under my feet, I tiptoed into the bathroom, which gave off the same vibes as the bedroom. Someone had polished everything from floor to ceiling.

Fresh towels were stacked on a rack against the wall. And all the hygiene products I could think of were tucked into a basket on a bench.

Still, there were no clothes.

Evidently, my demons walked around shirtless since I met them all that way. Hopefully, they didn't expect me to walk around in the same manner.

Before I literally passed out from sheer fatigue, I recalled Dominik and Morpheus eyeing me like I was their favorite dessert or something.

It pleased me to know that they were just as attracted to me as I was attracted to them. I had always worried about that. After all, they had come to me in dreams.

I turned on the shower, and the water steamed up instantly before the first drops hit the tile. I climbed in, taking a washcloth, soap, and shampoo with me, and emerged myself under the gentle stream.

The shower pelting down felt like instant acupuncture to my body. I hadn't realized it over the last couple of days, but my muscles ached from having to run nearly a mile to get away from Finn.

I closed my eyes and let the water slide over my face while rubbing my skin to wash away the suds.

A vision flashed before my eyes. My demons and I were together in the shower. They were tending to me, washing all the aches and pains away from my body. I gasped as my fingers passed over my clit, already swollen with need.

Apparently, I could also conjure up demons in my mind. There was no stopping my imagination. I wasn't sure that I wanted to.

Before my carnal thoughts got out of hand, I switched off the water and stepped out of the shower.

After applying skin oil to myself and drying my hair a bit with the towel, I wrapped it around myself and secured it tight.

Just before venturing back out into the bedroom, I got the urge to test a theory.

Nebulae was a magical realm, so that meant there was lots of magic here—right in the atmosphere.

I plugged the sink drain and filled it with water. Stepping back, I held my hand above the porcelain and uttered a chant, trying to replicate the energy of the moon orb.

There was only one way to know for certain if my sister had something to do with the disappearance. And more importantly, replicating its energy would pull me closer to it.

My attempts didn't work, and instead of replicating the energy of the moon orb and its location, I saw something else in the water. Shown to me in the basin was a vision I would've given anything to unsee.

My demons were in hell. Attached to pyres. And lit on fire. All three demons screamed in agony as the flames licked up their bodies, devouring them whole.

My scream caught in my throat and I lunged back, panting in distress.

Terrified over what I just saw, I pushed myself out of the bathroom into the bedroom, oblivious to what awaited me there.

Somebody with considerable strength caught me by the waist and crashed against me, holding me fixed to the wall.

It was Dominik. Even without looking behind me, I knew it was him.

I could smell him. He smelled the same way he did in my dreams. Like licorice and cotton candy.

"Witch," he hissed. "You would light us on fire?"

To my horror, I realized what he was talking about.

"No...I..." With my cheek smashed up against the wall, it was hard to form words.

"I was in your mind, Sadie. I saw what you saw."

Aggravated that my demons had no respect for my fucking privacy, I lashed out. "Who told you to go in my head?"

"What game are you playing, witch? Are you trying to trick us into thinking you are our queen?"

I should've known Dominik would be the most difficult to convince. Ever since I conjured him and the others, he had proven to be the most stand-offish. Although I loved him just the same.

He didn't come to me as often as the others. Only when I demanded punishment for what I had done.

Only Dominik knew about my wicked side—or so I thought.

Only he knew what evils I was capable of, despite the good deeds I had always been favored and praised for.

No one knew about the time I lured a serial killer vampire down a dark alley, only to use my magic to drain him dry and then leave him out in the daylight for the sun to burn. Needless to say, the supernatural's most-wanted list got shorter because of it, but I always felt guilty even though I had taken a dangerous paranormal creature off the street the hard way. My coven didn't deal with threats that way.

We weren't bloody or violent, but apparently, I had that type of evil in me. And no one knew. Just my demons.

Dominik came to me in my dreams afterward, convincing me that this was who I was. Keeping my true nature bottled up inside would do me no good.

"*Answer me.* You have no words now, Sadie?" He reached up under my towel and stroked my thigh. "What say you now...*queen?*"

I moaned. His hands felt so good on my skin. And just like with Altair, the thought of being with Dominik in the flesh and without restraints was out-of-this-world enticing.

I parted my legs, rocking back into his hands as he stroked my sex.

Pressing his lips to the back of my neck, he groaned. "Your cunt is always wet and ready, Sadie. Would you like to be punished?"

"Yes, please..." I croaked out.

"You've been a bad girl, Sadie. Allowing my brother to take your cunt so you can get into his head, trying to convince him of how innocent you are."

He drove a finger inside of me and worked it back and forth into my sex. Fireworks exploded when he tipped something deep within me. My juices drained down from his fingers and down my thighs.

"Pretending that you were weak when you came to our domain." He shook his head and clucked his tongue softly. "*Bad girl.* What else are you hiding, Sadie?"

"Nothing else. I promise." Dominik removed his fingers, and I pouted, grunting sharply in protest. "Please," I begged.

"So, you're not my bad girl?"

"I am, Dominik. I've been bad," I moaned.

He groaned against me, sliding the forked end of his tongue along my neck. "Mmmm."

He gave me his fingers again, this time, two of them. With his hand wrapped around the back of my neck, he held me pressed to the wall and finger-fucked me until I was shaking uncontrollably in climax.

My cries echoed throughout the room and high into the dome ceiling where the vibrations made the chandeliers dance.

He spun me around and yanked my towel from my body, throwing it aside.

As if I were his and his alone, his eyes swept the entirety of my body from toes to the crown of my head. All the while, a massive erection grew between us. My attention dropped to it. All along his thick shaft, veins pulsed furiously with life. He was just as big as Altair was. There was no doubt I found every inch of him pleasing.

This time, he wrapped his fingers around my throat and captured my lips against his. He kissed me passionately and hungrily.

He pulled back. "Why did it take you so long to summon us to come to get you?"

He looked angry and enamored at the same time.

"I didn't know I could. It was...it was a dangerous time in my life."

He grunted. "Not too dangerous for me. Mark my words. Whoever that bastard was that tried to punish you upon an altar before my brother came down to get you, I'm going to butcher him."

Arousal quaked through me. I felt shameful for feeling such erotic feelings toward Dominik's vow of violence toward my enemy.

"But for now, queen, I need your pretty little mouth on my fucking cock."

He pushed me down to the floor. The moment I leaned forward, his bulbous head pushed past my lips.

At first taste, I moaned as tremors rode up my spine.

He wrapped his hand around the head of his cock, holding it up while I licked the underside of his cock.

"Just like that, Sadie," he moaned. "*Fuck*. You're doing this so well."

With his fingers threaded through my hair, he shoved his cock deep into my mouth. My knees felt unsteady on the marble floor as I rocked my lips back and forth over Dominik's monster cock.

He slammed to the back of my throat, impaling my head against the wall. Filled to the max with his manhood, my only option was to breathe through my nose. Over and over again, he fucked himself into my mouth, driving more and more of himself inside, inch by inch, until he finally reached the back of my throat.

"*Yes*. Suck me like a slut," he rasped.

I gagged once or twice before I found his gigantic size somewhat accommodating. Even then, the light became darkness as I faded in and out, suffocating because of his lustful assault.

My arousal leaked from me as a rapturous climax fluttered throughout my core.

Fully intent on bringing Dominik pleasure, I pleasured him with my tongue for what seemed like an eternity. Until finally, his seed burst from him, spraying against my palate, down my throat, and leaking from my lips.

He pulled back. Streams of cum still shot from the slit. I licked at his cockhead as he moaned in pleasure and squirted the remaining bits of his seed all over my breasts.

I panted as he helped me up from the floor. With his thumb, he wiped a smudge of cum from the corner of my lips.

With his eyes flashing a deep red, he asked, "Will you betray us?"

I swallowed. "No."

He blinked once, spun around, and exited the room without another word.

Holy fuck. What the shit had just happened?

But even when we were only together in dreams, he fucked me like a phantom. The whole thing would appear to be over in seconds, but I knew that was impossible because Dominik always thoroughly satisfied me.

Just like Altair's gift was mind-reading, Dominik's expertise must have been mind-fucks.

I was at a loss for words.

Why would he ever think I planned on betraying them?

CHAPTER 12
Sadie

THE LAST THING I wanted to be was a prisoner—*again.*

Grown men had trapped me so many times before. First, my father arranged my marriage because he truly believed it would be good for me and the coven. Then, Finn took advantage of a terrible time in our history to strip me and my sister of our powers. And my demons... although I knew they meant well by keeping me in the Nebulae realm, I hoped they weren't as overbearing as I predicted they would be.

I assembled a tunic out of a cashmere throw, twisting it around my body until I could walk comfortably. Then I walked out of the room to investigate my new home away from home. There was marble, glass, and crystal everywhere. Each time I took a step forward toward the grand spiral staircase, I felt like I would break something.

The mansion seemed empty, and my demons were nowhere in sight. But I sensed one of them nearby.

Dominik maybe?

Well, probably not.

I doubt he'd approach me again after accusing me of becoming a potential traitor. Yet, I had seen even the most innocent souls become devils.

The first room I entered appeared to be a library. Many books lined the shelves. Small trinkets made from some granite-like material I couldn't identify were tucked between the books and decorated various end tables around the room.

I spotted a small chest sitting on a table. It was no bigger than a miniature jewelry box. After hesitating, I lifted the lid and rose-scented mist floated up into the air.

I snapped it shut and walked to the next art piece—a vase filled with fresh black-colored roses. I touched a petal, and the flower seemed to come alive, bending backward and then spreading its petals until the flower was completely opened to me.

Every nook and cranny of this place seemed to be filled with magic.

Someone came into the room. I turned around swiftly.

"Morpheus." My breath caught in my throat after I uttered his name.

Out of all three demons, he was the most difficult to figure out. I'd never seen his emotions left out of control and unchecked.

He had long silver hair that only the angels were said to possess. His ashen gray skin was flawless, and he was devoid of any tattoos or unnatural marks.

The instant I took a step back and shifted to the left, the stem of the rose curved again. Its actions reminded me of a sunflower, bending toward the light at sunrise.

"The flower is drawn to your magic. It feeds off of it," Morpheus stated, walking inside the room.

"But...Finn stole my magic," I said.

"Most of it," he corrected.

I blinked, following him around the room with my eyes, wondering what new things I'd learn next. I knew I had nothing to worry about concerning Morpheus. He'd always been attentive to my needs and had never once confused the shit out of me.

"Do you know where I might find some clothes?" I asked.

"You don't have to find anything. Dominik went out on a run. There's a human-ish market on Nebulae. He'll find you some stuff from there."

"A human-ish market? You mean like a shopping center?"

Morpheus nodded. "We have humans in this realm, yes."

"They're here...willingly?"

Morpheus laughed. "Yes. Once it's safe for you to go out, we'll show you. The beings here like earthly things, as you can see. The house is modeled after something a human might live in. Prior occupants made it that way. Although

Nebulae is still a supernatural realm, there are humans—both willingly and unwillingly. Some have even sought sanctuary here."

"But you and your brothers are stuck here. You don't want to be here. That's what you've always told me in the dreams," I stated.

Morpheus frowned. "Our father exiled us to a place much worse than Nebulae."

"Then how did you end up here?"

"During the spell, our mage, Torstein, risked his life to alter our final destination. Instead of landing in a hellish realm, my brothers and I were cast away here. My father's original decree still stands. We are stuck—which is here in Nebulae, but Torstein made it so that our father can't touch us in this realm. You'd think we'd want to remain here with the death threats over our heads, but we are men of our word—our father will pay. So, we can't just stay here forever."

"What about Earth? Can he harm you there?"

"He most certainly can. Dominik says that you nearly encountered a Grugger as the two of you were trying to figure stuff out. Gruggers are beings of the Shadow World. As long as my father is in power, he reigns over both Shadow World and the human world. That means beings from both places can transport and travel without issues between both worlds—and they often do."

Morpheus had already reached the side of the room and had closed the gap between us. The closer he got to me, the more in tune I became with my feelings. He fueled something deep inside me, luring it to the surface.

He wrapped his arms around my waist. He didn't have to bring me close to him. I stepped toward him voluntarily, needing to feel his heat against my skin.

"How exactly are you going to break your father's spell?"

"That's where you come in. You're more powerful than you know."

I shook my head. "Not without all of my magic."

Morpheus grinned. "You don't need all of your magic. You just need us."

I gasped the moment he leaned down to kiss me. It was short and sweet but delivered a mind-boggling sensation. His kiss was a taste of what would transpire between the two of us.

Morpheus parted from me and held out his hand. "Come."

"Where?"

"I relied on Dominik earlier to bring you to the kitchen so you could eat what I've prepared. That never happened."

I lowered my gaze to the floor, wondering if he knew what had actually transpired between Dominik and me. After our tryst, I showered again, but I still smelled the sweet scent of his cum all over me. The scent was engrained in my memory, maybe.

I blushed. "I might have made him mad."

"Don't worry about Dominik. When he loves someone, he tries to push them away."

I swallowed. "Why?"

"Isn't it obvious?"

I thought about it for a minute, and when I didn't speak, Morpheus exclaimed, "Ah, he's not going to tell you this freely, but those he trusts have betrayed him before. Our father. His mother..."

"*His mother?* But I thought—"

"We are complicated, Sadie. Let's talk more after I feed you." He linked his fingers with mine and took me out of the library and down the narrow corridor leading out into the main hall.

It didn't take us long to reach the kitchen. The piping hot smells of food from the platter in the center of the kitchen island reminded me it had been a while since I had eaten anything worthwhile.

"I get no pleasure from denying you what you need, Sadie," Morpheus said, lifting the lid and revealing an assortment of food.

"Did you cook all of this?"

He nodded. "We rarely eat human food, so I hope I did this right."

"It looks amazing. And it's a lot. Are you going to join me?"

He raised an eyebrow. "Oh, I will. Very soon, I will. I'm trying to be a patient person. Only when you are fully fed and nourished, will I help myself to what you offer." He licked his lips, and I blushed at the thought of what he could do with that tongue of his.

"Yes, that too," he added.

I swallowed as warmth sprouted along my core, tingling out through my fingertips and toes. "You mean sex?" I whispered bashfully. "That's how you feed from me."

"We prefer that way." He picked up a hot buttered roll and held it up to my mouth. "But there are other ways."

I couldn't contain my hunger anymore and took the bait. The first bite of the delicious roll was satisfying. My belly silently cried out for more.

Morpheus's forked tongue slipped past his lips momentarily before disappearing again as he watched me chew with avid concentration.

I finally understood it.

Sex wasn't the only way my demons could feed.

They fed off every emotion I expressed—even gratification from something as simple as eating.

We were in the kitchen for a good while talking over the platter as we took small bites. My bites weren't so small, of course. I probably ate enough food for both myself and Morpheus.

We were so consumed in the meal, we didn't notice Altair come in with two baskets filled with clothes.

I blushed.

"Don't stop on my account. You have to eat." He pulled out a chair and joined us. "How are you feeling?"

I smiled. "Good. I got a good nap in."

"That was more than a nap, Sadie." He chuckled.

"Well, how long was I sleeping for?"

"Probably a whole day in terms of human time. But time moves slower here in Nebulae, and night comes and goes whenever it pleases."

"That's weird," I exclaimed, popping a cherry in my mouth.

"I can see that you have both fed well," Altair noted, while this time directing his comment toward Morpheus.

Morpheus grinned. "She is delicious, brother, but I am still famished. Although you said she would test my patience."

"Well, you're the one who said you would wait until after her peak. Abstinence will be hell for you," Altair challenged.

My face reddened as my demons talked about me right there in my face.

Altair leaned back in his chair, crossing his arms over his chest. "Where has Dominik gone off to?"

The others had finally noticed. I secretly wished I could have all three of them here. I was having such a good time and had learned so much from them.

I only hoped that Dominik had come to grips with whatever was bothering him. I knew the anger he displayed towards me earlier would disappear eventually. I couldn't just come here and expect them to trust me right off the bat.

I looked up and my eyes locked with Altair's. It took me only a second to realize that he had funneled through my thoughts as I was having them.

Altair stood. "What did he do to you? Did he hurt you?"

"No, I...he thought I...he was just..." I mumbled, trying to paint a clear enough picture for Altair, but all I could think about was Dominik's cock down my throat and his fingers wrapped around my neck while I gagged on his semen.

As I fumbled around with an explanation for what had transpired between Dominik and me, Altair barged from the kitchen. The moment he shouted out Dominik's name, I knew things would get worse.

Morpheus and I followed him into the great room. Dominik seemed to have just gotten back into the house. He set down a tote full of leather-bound books just as Altair came for him.

"What the fuck?" Dominik blurted out.

Altair said nothing as both men collided in the center of the room. Dominik, who'd been thrown some ten feet into the opposite wall, lunged back up. Waves of anger poured over him just as he morphed into his full demon form. With both men in that form, and if it wasn't for Dominik's fiery red hair, it would've been hard to tell them apart through the madness.

"What did you do to her?" Altair shouted.

"What? Is this what this is about?" Dominik barked out.

"You can't treat her like a dog, Dom! I mean it."

"I've not treated her like a dog, brother. I only did what you did. I fuck her because we need her. I fuck her because she is ours to keep. And most importantly, I fuck her to heal her."

Somehow, Dominik's statement only angered Altair. Dominik charged again and the men ended up rolling all over the floor.

Morpheus tried to jump between the two. A forceful blast threw him back. "Fresh Hell," he exclaimed, getting up off the floor.

"Stop it, you two," I shouted, as magic tingled from the tips of my fingers. Even as I forced as much of my powers to the forefront as possible, I still didn't feel confident in myself. I took from the turbulent energy in the room to make up for what was lacking inside me.

I let go anyway, executing a spell I never once had to use.

When it was all over with, both men were shackled to the floor with magical chains they couldn't break. For added protection, I erected an individual jail cell around both of them.

My actions shocked all three demons. My actions also weakened me. Morpheus, who was only two feet away from me, reached out to me, grabbing me just in time. If he hadn't, my feet would've left the floor.

"Are you okay?" Morpheus asked.

I nodded, leaning against him.

"See! She traps us," Dominik bit out and then tried with all of his might to snap the chains. Jolts of electricity blasted from his body as he tried to get himself loose.

"Shut up, Dom. You caused this," Altair challenged.

Dominik breathed heavily. No amount of force he exerted against his bonds would release him. "You mind-read her all the time. Why do that if you trust her, brother?"

Altair's bold stare lifted to meet mine, and he stared blankly. "I trust her with all of our lives. Enough to bring her here."

Dominik inhaled sharply. "You haven't seen what I've seen—"

"That's enough, Dom," Morpheus snapped.

What did Dominik mean? What had he seen? Was he talking about my vision from earlier with them on the pyre?

My mind spun with the possibilities. It became too much for me to handle.

Altair pressed himself against the front of the cell as I let my head fall to Morpheus's shoulder. "She needs to rest. Or she'll pass out."

Dominik rattled his cell. "She'll let us out of here first."

I lifted my head off Morpheus' shoulder and then raised my hand. Before I could exert my magic to release them from the cells, Morpheus gently covered my fingers and guided my hand downward.

He shook his head. "*No*. They'll remain in the cells until they've settled down. I will not allow you to overexert yourself any further like this."

I didn't argue or challenge him, but neither did the others.

Dominik slumped down in the cell and sat on the floor. Altair leaned back against the bars.

Morpheus lifted me from the floor, cradling me into his arms. As we were walking away, Dominik yelled, "You will leave us here like animals, Sadie? Brother?"

Morpheus ignored him, and I was too exhausted to feel guilty about anything. Just as long as Altair and Dominik couldn't tear each other's heads off, everything would be fine. For now.

I was back in the grand bedroom. Morpheus laid me on the bed and then climbed in after me, pulling sheets over us. I cradled myself to him.

"Thank you, Morpheus," I whispered against his chest.

"I should thank you."

"For what?"

"Because we need you here more than you know. All of us. Me. Altair. Dom. I know you'll be the light that saves us from the darkness."

I wanted to believe him.

But what use could I be, and how could I have faith in myself if the execution of a simple magic spell left me defeated?

CHAPTER 13
Sadie

MY DEMON PROTECTORS brought me gifts.

Apparently, they knew how to win my heart even when things were up in the air.

I unraveled the spell that kept Altair and Dominik latched away in a cell for hours. The moment I did that, both men bolted from the mansion in need of energy and claiming they wouldn't feed on me while I was weak.

They needed sustenance after fighting with each other, and lots of it.

When I inquired from Morpheus about where they went, he explained how there were thousands of rifts all over Nebulae that allowed massive amounts of energy to pass from the different realms at any given time.

According to Morpheus, the only bad thing about feeding off the unknown was that you were never guaranteed to feel satisfied afterward.

But back to my presents...

I was so happy about them, I found myself grinning like a fool. When was the last time someone got me a gift? I couldn't even remember.

It took me almost half an hour to unwrap everything.

Altair bought me clothes. Among the garments were extravagant form-fitting gowns that I never would've worn on the earth realm. I would probably feel like Cinderella or some other Disney princess wearing the extravagant dresses. Most of the relaxed wear left nothing to the imagination, but I had peaked out of the windows already and glimpsed what some of the other inhabitants of this realm were wearing. Especially by the women inhabitants who were mostly scantily clad.

Morpheus gifted me with more personal but necessary items, like bottles of bath oils filled with flower petals, sweet perfumes, hair ties, and even a box with an assortment of combs and brushes. When I saw his offering, I knew he was the one who had stocked the bathroom for me.

Dominik was the only one who did not leave me anything. But I didn't blame him. He wasn't like his brothers. He didn't wear his heart on his sleeve like Morpheus. And he definitely wasn't as attentive as Altair.

My protectors also had important duties on Nebulae. Just as they had taken on leadership roles in the Shadow World, they became devout leaders in this realm as well.

Altair had territorial disputes to deal with. Morpheus had patrolling duties. And Dominik...well, he does whatever he does.

They were by no means followers, and I knew without a doubt they were meant to be commanders in every way.

I met Minerva, their housemaid, shortly after they left. The woman didn't talk at all. She was deaf and mute. But she cleaned up the mess the men had made after fighting. She did it with little fanfare as if she was used to it. She even brought me breakfast tea and biscuits to enjoy as I sat on the window seat people-watching.

Just as I was told, humans lived in Nebulae. They walked about, conversing with supernaturals as if it was the most natural thing to do.

This morning, I only saw a handful of species.

Humans, but just a handful.

Demons and demonesses, like my protectors and Minerva.

A couple of gargoyles walked around with their wings hanging out.

Two green, leathery-skinned leprechauns kept hopping out of bushes scaring the unsuspected.

And one peculiar-looking being who had to have been a mix between a fairy and a demon chased after a miniature pet poodle.

From my position on the window bench, I heard the doors of the mansion open and the sound of enormous feet clomping against the marble.

I stiffened, knowing that it was one of my demon protectors coming home.

Exceptionally anxious, I readjusted all the pillows comfortably on the bench around me and waited.

Without knocking or announcing himself, Dominik opened the door and crossed over the threshold. He still had his wings spread and had to lower them a bit to get inside.

"Dom," I gasped.

The sight of my demons always left me breathless.

A rush of erotic thoughts flooded my mind and there was nothing I could do to get rid of them once they started.

"Sadie." He placed a box wrapped in black shiny wrapping paper on the table next to me. "I've come to apologize."

I swallowed, looking up into his eyes. I knew he was sincere about his apology. "You were just being yourself. You are who you are. I would question me too if I were you."

"And yet, I am sorry if I scared you."

"You don't have to be sorry."

He tilted his head. "You didn't like the way I treated you, no?"

I blushed, biting my lips, but the truth slipped right from my mouth, anyway. "I liked the way you made me feel, but..." I looked down at my fingers.

He stepped forward, lifting my chin upward so that I could meet his red-hot stare. "But what, Sadie?"

"I don't want you to think I'm a traitor."

His lips thinned and the red glare diminished until his true eye color—an icy blue—took its place. "You are not loyal to your coven anymore. You had no choice but to abandon them, but abandon them, you did. Is that not an act of traitorism?"

My breath caught in my throat as anger nearly overcast my emotions. I wanted to slap Dominik and kiss him at the same time. But why?

He grinned, showing lovely pearly whites and a pair of the sharpest incisors I had ever seen. "It's alright, Sadie. They don't appreciate you, you see. I would've done the same thing."

"Why do you taunt me like this?" I demanded. "Do you want to break me?"

Dom leaned down and rasped in my ear, "In order to transform, sometimes you must first break."

"I don't understand," I whispered.

"You are like the lotus tree that quivers during a storm. Roughened by the wind, all the petals fall off. You doubt your worth. But the tree is still a glorious sight. When a branch breaks, you doubt your strength, forgetting that the tree is deeply rooted and built to withstand the test of time. Lose faith in yourself and give up, and the tree will die. Persevere, and the tree will hold steadfast in its current state or transform."

I thought about his words and what Morpheus said about Dom. I was beginning to understand. Dom had been broken before.

"You're talking about yourself," I stated in a low voice.

His eyes widened in surprise, but his usual guarded expression quickly shaded that demeanor out.

"I hope you enjoy the gift. I selected it for you yesterday," he said.

I reached for the box and untied the bow, which was also pitch black. I was never the type to rip into my holiday presents. Not like my sister, anyway, who joyfully ripped every wrapping sheet to shreds. I figured he would comment on how slowly I exposed the contents of the package, but he waited patiently, studying my every move.

Inside was a stack of leather-bound journals wrapped carefully with twine. I took them out, tracing the intricately threaded covers with my fingers. I'd never had custom journals before.

When I opened the journals, they were lined and blank, just waiting for me to add my notes and sketches to them.

I smiled.

I wasn't sure how he knew, but I wrote all the time. If I wasn't working on spells, I often wrote my thoughts just to get them out of my head.

In fact, as a child, I used a journal just like this to write the spell that brought my demons to me.

"How did you know?" I breathed.

"How could I not know?" he returned.

"Thank you."

"I'm glad you like my gift." Dom turned swiftly and headed toward the door.

As he was preparing to leave the room, I called after him. "Stop."

He halted with his hand on the doorknob.

"Can we talk more?"

I didn't want him to leave. I wanted him to stay. Maybe I needed breaking so I could become stronger.

He turned and eyed me. His heated stare equaled the unmatched hunger growing in my body.

"You want to do more than talk, don't you?"

I blushed.

Dom's nostrils flared. "You are in heat, Sadie. Have been since you arrived here."

"I can't help it."

"I know. My brothers and I all serve a purpose, as you witnessed when we came to you in your dreams. But this time, you need someone who will be gentle. I cannot guarantee you *I* will be gentle."

"I just...I want..."

Dom closed the distance between us and captured my lips with his mouth. He was right. He was none too gentle. The kiss was feverish.

His touches on my body were, in and of itself, transforming. The dark energy that flowed from him to me proved to be overpowering, but I opened my mind and soul up to Dom and bathed in the power emanating from us.

"Sadie, once I start...I won't be able to hold back."

His voice was low, with an animalistic tremor I had never heard before. My body trembled at the sound of it, causing me to take a step back, away from him.

I looked up into his eyes to make sure Dom was still there and that his demon had not emerged. Even if it had—even if he had shifted into full demon form, I would've still craved what he offered.

"How could a feeling so pure..." He stepped toward me as he spoke, bridging the distance I'd only just created between us.

He reached for me, his right index finger eagerly moving toward my left arm. One touch sent a wave of pleasure coursing down my spine. My legs instantly felt weak at the knees. I hastily grabbed the edges of the window sill and crushed my ass into the hard surface, just so I could remain on my feet while my insides raged on with passion. His eyes were all over my body, undressing me even without touching me.

I wore one of the white silk dresses Altair gifted me with nothing underneath it. But when he stared at me the way he did, it felt like the fabric was falling away, baring my naked body to his amorous eyes.

Slowly and slyly, his fingers traced a pattern down my arm, leaving a trail of goosebumps in its wake. I didn't realize I was holding my breath the whole time. Not until my throat ached.

He looked back up into my eyes, his head cocked to the side as he completed his question. "How could this be wrong?"

"...well..." I started, but the rest of the words died on my lips. It wasn't wrong. This felt right.

Yet, I was supposed to be mad at him for the chaos he led last night. But how could I get through my heats without him? Without his brothers? How could I pretend not to notice the wetness between my thighs, at the crux of my legs, just beneath this gown?

Just how?

My lips remained parted as I tried to speak. When I attempted to say another word, he flattened his right index finger against my lips, instantly shushing me.

"Shhh. Your thoughts are loud," he whispered with a slight shake of his head.

He leaned in toward me. His cock molded against me through his pants. It was so hard it intensified my arousal right away. His finger slowly slipped away, only to be replaced by his lips on mine.

He kissed me softly, his lips barely even touching mine. He could've kissed me harder, but he refrained, just so he could gauge my response.

I could resist.

Heck, I should.

But the feel of his lips on mine, his hot scalding breath all over my face, and his hard meaty cock pressing hard against me were all too much for me to resist.

"Is that better?" he rasped.

My lips seemed to have a mind of their own. "I want you to be you."

I slowly parted my mouth, letting him in.

My eyes closed, but I could tell he was smiling. I felt his lips stretch against mine, evidencing a soft smile. I wrapped my arms around him, pulling him close as I deepened the kiss.

At this point, I didn't know what I was doing anymore. I didn't even care what was right or wrong. Quelling this flaming heat between my legs was the only thing that felt right at the moment.

He gingerly swept me off my feet and into his brawny arms. I tightened my arms around him, clinging tightly to him.

I wasn't afraid of falling. No, I was aching to be close to him.

My legs wrapped around his body just before he placed me on the window sill. When he kissed me again, he wrapped his fingers around the thin straps of my see-thru gown, and then he pulled, baring my firm nipples which were just as erect as his cock.

He fondled my breasts with both hands while his tongue thrashed its way inside my mouth to engage mine in a tango. When I pulled away for a breather, my head tipped backward, bearing my neck to him.

His lips left mine and proceeded down my neck. His fingers crawled beneath the gown, roaming overT my naked pussy as he kissed his way down my torso.

A hungry gasp escaped my lips. I reached for his pants and hastily unbuckled his belt. Barely a moment later, our garments lay forgotten on the floor.

He lifted me into his arms yet again. My legs were swift to encircle his body.

And then I felt his thick, hard cock bumping against my clean-shaved pussy. He roamed the dripping wet entrance for a painfully long time. It was only a few moments, but to me, it was forever.

"Please..." I said, my head thrusting back as I tried to control my craving for his hard cock.

"Say the words," he whispered. "I'll fuck you, alright? I'll give you what you need. What you want."

He nibbled my left earlobe, and then he exhaled, his steamy breath streaking into my ear.

"I just need to hear you say it..." he added.

"Fuck me already..." I said.

My voice was a little too loud. But I didn't care.

"Please..."

I trembled with need as I spoke.

His cock molded against me again, this time finding its way inside of me. He was inching his way inside of me. I didn't want that.

Slow and steady would not work for a woman in heat. I needed something harder. Faster. More intense.

Definitely not this. Not from Dominik. Just as he said, he and his brothers all served different purposes.

So, I reached down to meet him, my pussy gliding all the way toward his balls. That single action forced his full length inside of me and parted his lips with a gasp.

I covered his lips with mine, silencing him with a kiss while I slid up and down his cock. He guided me along his shaft, but his pace didn't work for me.

I bounced faster, harder, each move of my body causing my breasts to jiggle and bounce. I could tell he was holding back, allowing me to maintain control. His demon side rippled just under his skin, dying to come out.

"I'll be good for you, Sadie. I'll try. Only for you," he groaned, squeezing my ass and going deep.

"'kay. Please, Dom—" The knot—Dom's knot—blossomed, cutting off my words.

I threaded my fingers through his hair, knotting his strands tightly just like he was knotting me.

It felt so good. I screamed out in pleasure.

He buried his face in the space between my neck and shoulder. Sharp teeth gently scraped the skin on my neck.

"I'm going to mark you, Sadie, and let everyone know who you belong to. That way there will be no mistake that my kindred and I will crush anyone who tries to hurt you."

My sex clenched around his cock in answer. I slipped my fingers around his neck and brought his lips closer to me.

"Do it, Dom," I urged.

He wasted no time breaking the skin and sinking his canines into my flesh.

I cried out as pain and pleasure exploded through my veins. Only a moment of comfort paralyzed me, and then it was over. Only pleasure remained, and the world revolved around us.

Not even the deepest of kisses could silence either of us. We moaned and gasped, our bodies equally throbbing.

When I felt his cock throb and jerk inside of me, I knew he was only a few strokes away from climaxing. I didn't stop coming until he shot his thick, hot cum inside of me, and even after that, the remnants of my orgasm still fluttered through me.

Our passion blended into one continuous storm.

"I was trying to be gentle for you," he rasped.

"I know. That was good, Dom. That was perfect." I kissed him and then added, "But in the future, I want Dom without filters."

He grinned. "As you wish."

With his knot locked inside of me, we remained connected. The evidence of our union slowly slid out of me, but what we had done would never leave me.

Dominik had marked my soul for eternity.

As for what came next for me and my three demon protectors...I could only imagine...

CHAPTER 14
Sadie

AFTER WHAT SEEMED like a few days of walking through the halls of the mansion, a formal tour of the entire place was in order. My demon protectors had promised, and I was going to hold them to that promise.

There was a whole underground level that I had yet to see. That level had been vacant ever since the last owners moved out and my protectors took up residence.

The last occupants were the vampire king and queen of Nebulae, but they jumped realms at the first opportunity. They used to sleep in the dungeon levels, and Morpheus had even claimed they left behind a coffin or two. It all seemed so morbid. And I was certainly glad that my demons didn't sleep in coffins.

But I wasn't as interested in the underground dungeon as I was in Nebulae as a whole. After looking through the glass at everyone who passed by the mansion, I was curious about this realm. It was risky, but I want to get out and see things.

I felt better now. My strength was back. My powers were growing. My magic was still a bit shaky, but I was working on that.

Soon, my protectors would be strong enough to cloak me entirely. When we ventured out eventually, I wouldn't have to worry about someone spotting me and taking word back to Finn's minions, or worse, my demons' father. They weren't ready for that yet. Hell, I wasn't ready for it. I knew it would happen someday, but I could agree with one thing concerning my protectors—we wanted to be ready for it.

At tonight's meeting, Altair, Morpheus, and Dominik would decide the best way to launch their attack.

All three of my protectors were seated at the head of the table with me directly across from them. They were all so dominant; I often wondered how they shared leadership over so many things without butting heads. Well, since my arrival, I'd only seen Altair and Dominik bicker and physically fight about one thing. It also seemed they had put that behind them. Altair wasn't in a bad mood and Dominik had apologized.

"So..." Altair started, clasping his hands together. "Let's start with the most pressing matter...growing Sadie's powers back to where it was before Finn intervened."

Dominik sat back in his chair. "He is lucky we don't have access to earth right now. If that were the case, we wouldn't even be talking of him. He'd be a dead man. Powers go back to Sadie. Problem solved. But since you took so long to cross over from Nebulae to earth, he nearly succeeded."

Altair growled. "I teleported as fast as I could, and you know that. That cloaking spell the Cave witches did for us took some time."

My posture stiffened at the mention of witches. "Wait? Cave witches? There are witches here?"

"Yes, Nebulae has a prominent coven. They live in the mountains. In huts. And in caves. Thus, why we call them cave witches. They're not as powerful as you though. It took seven of them to get me cloaked so I could transport from Nebulae to Earth. You performed a cloaking spell by yourself with limited access to magic," Altair noted.

He was right, but with limited magic, the spell had taken a toll on me.

"The only thing is, we now owe the Cave witches a favor or they'll start threatening to out us to our father's minions," Morpheus exclaimed.

"They'll get access to Shadow World magic when we get it. And I doubt they'll go spilling the news to my father anytime soon. The Cave witches are outcasts from Shadow World too," Altar replied.

"Then what do you propose, regarding Sadie's powers?" Morpheus inquired. "Our original plan was to feed from each other, but that was before Finn stole most of her magic. Now, there's no way we can feed from her to fight our father while leaving her vulnerable."

"You're right. She can't do magic *and* feed us at the same time right now," Altair said.

"Well, why not?" I asked, biting my lips.

"As much as we want to feed from you multiple times a day, you wouldn't be able to handle it in your present state," Dominik replied.

"And if Finn had never stolen my powers, you would...feed... multiple times a day?" I had to admit, the idea appealed. Sex with demons who give pleasure? Count me in anytime.

Dominik grinned. "Your appetite is just as great as ours, Sadie. Why do you think we haven't teamed up on you yet?"

"Dom!" Morpheus's warning growl made Dominik back off.

Dominik held up his hands. "Alright, alright, but I'm just telling her the truth."

"So, I have an idea," I started. "I can do magic, there's no doubt about that, but since I get exhausted earlier than I should as a result, then it means I need an alternate source of power."

Altair frowned. "Alternate source?" He looked back and forth between Dominik and Morpheus. "Who?"

I giggled. He thought I meant someone else. "That's not what I meant. You three are the only men I'll ever need. I promise. What I meant was a thing...not a person."

"Thing?" Morpheus inquired.

"In our coven, we funneled magic through an object. The moon orb. As much as I enjoy...our feedings..." I cleared my throat just as a blush fanned across my face. "There's another way I can harvest powers that doesn't require depleting the three of you of your energy."

Altair leaned forward. "Do tell."

"I attempted to generate a replica of the moon orb the other day." My gaze met Dominik shyly, thinking back to how he caught me while I was doing my spell. "It didn't work but it's only because I didn't give it much time. I can do it. I just need a few elements. Maybe you have them here in your realm. Maybe those cave witches might even help."

"You mean you can construct another moon orb like the original?" Dominik asked.

"Probably not as good as the original, but I have high hopes that I can."

Morpheus smiled. "We have high hopes that you can too."

"And you might even be able to draw from it too," I added.

"Let's focus on your needs for now. You construct the moon orbs for your needs. Our father's execution can wait. It's not like he's going anywhere," Altair stated.

Morpheus leaned back in his seat, crossing his arms over his chest. "Nice. So, that will allow us time to use our resources to raise whatever army we can against our father. We'll breach shadow world in no time, and then you won't even need a moon orb, queen. You'll have access to shadow magic and us, as you see fit. Stopping Finn will be easy then. I, for one, would love the honor to go down to earth and rip out his spleen."

"I'm just worried about my sister," I said.

"I promised her we would help her with her sister who's missing," Altair started.

"Finn thinks she took the moon orb," I offered.

"Well, how could that be? The moon orb is highly traceable. And wouldn't your coven be able to detect her magic if she used the orb?" Dominik challenged.

I sighed. "That's the thing. My link to my sister is broken, and no one has been able to trace the moon orb. It's like it's off the grid or...out of service."

"You mean *destroyed?*" Dominik offered.

"Yes, my sister might have destroyed it, jeopardizing Finn's access to the spirit world and to shadow magic. That sounds like something she would do to spite everyone."

"And you just want to know what she did and where she went, right?" Morpheus inquired.

"Right. If she's even alive..."

Meetings between Altair, Morpheus, and Dominik could go on for hours, even a whole day with the number of issues that were virtually laid out on the table. Most of the remaining issues dealt with Nebulae and how they wished to maintain some presence here even after their takeover of the Shadow World.

When moonlight crept through the windows, fatigue set in. I guessed I was so used to falling asleep at nighttime that my body and mind couldn't give each issue the prolonged attention it needed.

Things would get better. If I planned to stay here or follow my demons anywhere else where the atmosphere was similar to that of Nebulae, I had to adapt.

I promised my protectors I'd regroup with them later on after taking a quick nap, but when I got back to the room, all I could think about was how I fit into the equation concerning their plans.

I propped up some pillows, tucking them around me, and then sat up in bed with one of the journals Dominik gifted me and began working on the spell for the moon orb.

The list of elements I needed took up almost half the page. Most of the exotic plants were hard to find on earth, so I couldn't help but wonder if I'd be able to collect the elements in Nebulae.

My first outing was scheduled in three days from today and I could hardly wait.

Cloaking spells and a new moon orb—these two things were high on my priority list at the moment. And then, I knew I would have to delve into the darker magic—the magic I would use to allow my protectors to breach the shadow realm. That's what I was preparing for. And whether or not I liked it, my demon protectors were right. I had to play it safe or the entire plan would go to hell.

As I was scribbling a drawing of the orb, glass shattered from downstairs. Mayhem ensued.

My back stiffened like a board as I sat up and listened.

My demons were fighting. Again.

I threw the covers off me and raced down the spiral staircase. The meeting had been moved to the library for some reason.

This time, all three demons were going at it. Fangs distended. Wings unfolded and bumped into everything.

"What are you three fighting about now?" I demanded.

"Morpheus here wants to call a truce with the Stone clan. They've been fighting us for years, trying to guard a rift that doesn't belong to them," Dominik blurted.

Somehow I should have known Dominik would be right in the middle of an argument.

"Don't be so quick to claim the right of use brother," Morpheus shot back. "We've been here under a decade. The Stone clan has been here for centuries."

"For centuries, my ass." This came from Altair. He jerked at a chair that had been tossed over, turning it right side up again. "They fled to Nebulae after being defeated by another gargoyle clan in their mother realm. Don't you think it is quite arrogant of them to claim exclusive access to a rift that has direct access to shadow energy? We need that rift. If I have to rip apart that gargoyle prince to get to it, I will."

"That is not what we decided years ago. No! There has to be another way. A way that doesn't involve making another enemy," Morpheus shot back.

"Brother!" Dominik pounded his fist on the table. "We have enemies lined up from here all the way to hell. You'll have to go tell that Stone clan prince to get in line. If he is afraid his rival and successor will somehow break through the rift, he'd better be battle ready. Running and hiding out in Nebulae won't ever solve a thing."

As the demons argued, my attention whipped back and forth between them. My heart raced with anger and my mind spun. Power tingled in my fingertips but I tried my hardest not to use any magic.

Putting all three demons in chains for their unacceptable behavior at the same time would be a death sentence for me. If this was going to be the norm, maybe I somehow needed to realize this was the way my protectors hashed stuff out with each other.

The crazy thing was that I saw the rationale behind all of their arguments, but I hated to see them fight like this. As if they weren't brothers. As if they wouldn't have to team up in the near future to defeat their father and whatever other enemies they had lined up from here all the way to hell.

I needed a breather.

When I backed out of the library to retreat to a quiet place, none of them noticed. They were too busy trying to convince each other that their particular plan was the most feasible.

I raced out into the great hall, grabbed an overcoat from the side table, and threw open the front doors to the mansion.

Nightfall greeted me, but the moon was bright enough to light the path before me.

There was hardly anyone roaming around, so I stepped out into the night.

As I walked in awe of the beautiful scenery, the magic in the air sunk into my pores. I parted the overcoat a bit, and a warm breeze coated my skin like a blanket.

Looking behind me, I couldn't see the mansion anymore. Just the tops of trees and high hills.

A firefly danced in front of my face. Upon closer inspection, it resembled more of a hummingbird. Or maybe it was both. Or perhaps it was some hybrid creature only native to Nebulae.

I giggled when it circled my head and then followed it a few feet until it disappeared high above.

The sound of water trickling down a hill caught my attention. I walked toward the noise, but I never made it far.

Something—someone—some creature grabbed me from behind and yanked me behind some thick, black-colored hedges.

CHAPTER 15
Sadie

MY SCREAMS WERE CUT off by cold, meaty hands.

I knew without a doubt and even before this kidnapper pulled me behind these thorny bushes that he wasn't one of my demon protectors.

Something was wrong.

It's that gut feeling of anxious anticipation you get whenever you're awaiting something. You don't know what it is yet, but you know it's terrible. Then, it claws at you, making you observe and analyze everything hoping to figure out what it is until it's too late.

Yeah, it's that, but so much worse.

My kidnapper cackled behind me. "We've got you now, little pet."

We?

Oh my God. I saw their shadows stretching on the ground and there was definitely more than one kidnapper.

"Let me go," I hissed through his clammy fingers and then used my nails, hoping to claw my way out of his grip.

"Really, what does that demon jerk even see in her?" one snorted, and for a moment, my whole body went rigid. I blinked a few times, dazed and disoriented as one of the goonish-looking creatures looked at the other before back at me. "She's a frail little human if you ask me."

I had no idea what these things were. They reminded me of lizards. Their skin resembled a snake and they seemed to camouflage with whatever they stood by.

They resembled...lizards.

The ring leader—the one with my hands pulled painfully behind my back—licked my ear with his long wet tongue.

I shuddered. "Stop it."

"She tastes like an earth girl," the ring leader chortled.

"I haven't fucked an earth girl in half a decade," another said. "Perhaps we should sample what's so good before sending those demon jerks her cunt filled with our seed, huh?"

I almost vomited.

The ring leader pushed me a couple of feet away from him and stripped me up and down with his beady eyes. They surrounded me, leaving no space between them to allow for a successful escape.

I could always try. Or I could blast them to hell with fire magic. I wanted to so badly. No one was coming to my aid.

It was almost pitch black outside and I could barely see. These lizards—their irises shined like iridescent lights in the dark.

"Let's do it, Jask. Let's show those demon jerks how it used to be here in this realm. *What we catch, we keep*," the other tittered.

"But the High Priest Finn said she's gotta marry a prick. He says—" one of them started to say.

"—I don't care what he said. We can have our fun first."

My attention shifted back and forth between them. "Wh-what did you just say?" Had they mentioned Finn's name? Or was I hearing things? Imagining things again?

The ring leader laughed. "Don't look so frightened, girl. You'd be better off with your folk, no? Not with these impetuous demons who call themselves princes."

If I was understanding correctly, these lizard men knew Finn. Had connections with him. That could only mean...

Finn had found me. *He knew where I was.*

Holy Fuck.

When was this going to end? When would he stop chasing me?

I looked around for any sort of weapon, something that I could use to ward them off while getting help. But it was too late.

As soon as I opened my mouth, one slammed his palm right over my piercing scream as tears welled at the corner of my eyes. Another wrapped his lizard tail around my legs so tightly I thought I'd trip.

"Take her to the den," one instructed.

I kicked and screamed, desperately clawing at them.

I grabbed hold of a tree limb and clung to it as the ring leader tried to carry me off. Pretty soon, the branch would break.

I couldn't fight my way out of this. These lizard men were strong. Almost as strong as my protectors.

I began to whisper and realized I was chanting a spell. A spell that would turn the lizard men to stone.

A taloned claw grabbed my throat, cutting off my incantations. "Oh no, you don't, you little witch."

All breath seemed to leave me as I mouthed Altair's name.

Suddenly, the hold that had been latched onto me loosened, and I stumbled to the ground, grasping at my throat.

My breath came in pants. I could barely register what was happening as the lizardmen that had their hands on me were screaming, their yells piercing the night.

I watched, horrified as one of the lizard's heads exploded like a sledgehammer to watermelon as a shadow blacker than the night shifted back and forth like a phantom.

Another death-chilling scream rent the air. Something cold, wet, and thick splashed on my right cheek. I wiped at it, thinking it was my blood, but it wasn't. The secretions smelled foreign. Not like blood.

Everything felt like slow motion as I watched in horror. Right in front of me, blood spewed out of the lizard men's bodies in rapid succession as the sound of their dead bodies hit the hard ground.

I glanced down in shock. Soulless mutant eyes met mine. Their insides spilled outward, still pulsating. I could even make out their spines, pulled out of their bodies. My stomach churned just as the blood drained from my face.

A shadowy mist slowly rose from the carnage and materialized into a—

Altair.

In two seconds flat, he shifted partially out of his demon form. His red eyes remained. His chest heaved up and down as sheer fury rolled down his body in massive vibrations.

"Altair," I whispered as he slowly strode towards me. His body was so rigid and tight that I knew he was on the very edge of snapping for what I had done. I had known my protectors had enemies, but I never would have thought they would come for me this soon.

"W-what the hell were they?" I panted, pointing at the clumps of reptilian flesh and bones.

"We call them *Licanis* here. *Lizardfolk*."

I thought so. "I...I didn't see them."

His lips twisted into a frown. "I figured."

"They mentioned Finn. They mentioned my betrothal. I think Finn has tracked me here."

Altair blew out in frustration. "That figures too. But how?"

I bit my lip. "With no moon orb, Finn has to draw powers from something else. Something powerful."

"The coven," Altair offered. "He did that in the cave, remember?"

"No. The coven couldn't have recovered that quickly. I think...I think he's channeling the spirit world."

"Spirit world?"

"It's where my ancestors' souls go to rest once they find peace. The magic there is virtually limitless. As incoming High Priest, he has access to it on demand." I exhaled. "Here I was thinking losing me, my sister, and the moon orb would set him back, but he'll find a way to get back at us. And he has."

He shook his head. "He's going to be relentless, isn't he?"

I nodded.

"So, do you see why this was a bad idea, Sadie? Going out without us?"

I swallowed, wringing my hands together. Unspent magic tingled at my fingertips. I wanted to do something drastic to end it all. *End everything.* "Yes...I guess."

"You guess?"

His voice was so menacing and low that it came off as nothing more than a snarl of sorts. It made me flinch, especially as he hauled me up off my feet and glared at me.

"You need punishing," he stated.

I licked my lips and his attention fell to my mouth. His expression softened and he drew his bottom lip in momentarily. For a moment, I thought he was going to kiss me. I wanted him to. The way he made quick work of those sneaky lizardfolk was impressive.

I knew I shouldn't have been turned on, especially since he had slaughtered two beings with no remorse.

But why should I care? Those lizard men were planning to... fill me with seed just to get at Altair and his brothers.

Finally finding my voice, I swallowed. "W-what will you do?"

"Do?"

"To me. What will you do to me?"

He moved quickly and pressed his heated chest against me. I fought a whimper when he trailed his tongue up to my neck, nipping at it with his sharp fang.

"Have you learned your lesson? Almost getting kidnapped once again because you underestimate the need for our protection? Every time I kill, do you understand what that does to me?"

I swallowed while my body tensed up, unable to process the rapturous heat racing through my body.

His large, rough hand made its way into my hair before he tugged on my strands. He cupped my scalp with his palm, causing me to look up at him as he towered over my body.

"Tell me..." I whispered.

"Violence feeds me negative energy. Negative energy breeds more violence."

I gasped.

"But not for you, my queen. Never for you."

"I know you won't hurt me."

He kissed my forehead. "No."

I pressed my palm into his cheek and raise his head. "Be it negative energy or positive energy, you need both."

"Yes, but I never wanted you to witness..." He paused and then waved his hand over the pile of limbs. "...bloody carnage."

"Then if you are who you say you are and I am your queen, this won't be the last time I see such things, now, will it?"

"Let's get you away from here."

In a blink of an eye, Altair unfolded his wings and wrapped my entire body with them. I felt as if we were falling and spinning at the same time.

A balloon of black energy expanded around us. Rather than pulling from me, Altair drew from the essence of the fallen lizard men. This created a powerful source of energy from which he teleported us from the streets back to my room in the mansion.

I thought for sure I would hit the marble floor hard when we landed, but he lowered me with grace and ease. I felt my dress being pulled from me and my back hit the mattress. I thought he would waste no time, giving me what I most obviously needed. His touch. His love. Him, inside me.

When he left me on the bed to go stand by the window, I pouted. "What is it?"

He didn't even look away, and I felt my body freeze up in disappointment. His expression was stoic, giving nothing away. For the first time since I summoned Altair, I had drawn a blank about what was wrong with him.

But, there could only be one thing...

"This betrothal...Finn and others will try to use it to trap you," he said.

I lowered my head. "I told Samson a long time ago that I didn't want to marry him. He knows it, but he doesn't care. Our families made an agreement. It's like a contract to him. Some kind of business transactions. He can have whoever he wants but he wants to trap me in a loveless union instead."

"Don't worry, Sadie. He won't win. They won't win. Unless you want him to, of course." I didn't miss the pinch of jealousy mixed in his dismissive tone.

I cringed. "Of course not." I couldn't help but tilt my head to the side; my mouth pulled into a straight line. "You can't be...jealous of him. Are you, Altair?"

I crossed the line when I asked him this, but I honestly hoped he didn't think Samson would be a threat. Even if this mess with Finn hadn't developed, I would've done anything to put off my marriage with Samson until he realized that following through with a betrothal wouldn't benefit him in the way he thought it would.

Altair remained in the shadows, but his jaw flinched.

Without a doubt in my mind, he was still angry about me running off and almost getting kidnapped by lizardfolk, but I didn't think this Samson situation would upset him even more.

"Jealous?" he repeated with a snarl. "Why the fuck would I be jealous of him? A weakling who cannot protect you but wants to marry you? You know he only wants one thing, Sadie. One thing from you."

I swallowed as displeasure welled up in my throat. "What you want? My magic."

Altair growled and turned around. "Do you think that is all I want? Just your magic?"

My gaze dropped to the floor in embarrassment. "I have to wonder."

His body went even tighter for a moment, and I knew I had hit the mark. He was in my head. I didn't care. I wanted him to be. That's how he found me. That's how my demons protected me. I had invited them into my head long ago before I knew what I was doing.

Altair grabbed a handful of dried rose buds from a bowl I'd been using earlier and crushed them until they were almost dust. His eyes grew colder and the air in the room dropped a few degrees. He was right. Feeding on violence like he had done tonight only brought intense emotions for him.

He crossed the room and closed the distance between us. Bringing a lock of my wavy, black hair to his nostrils, he breathed in roughly.

"I have loved you since you summoned me, Sadie. You sealed our fate when you sought my eternal protection. Whatever you choose, my devotion to you will never waiver."

He was so compelling. His magnetic pull was so inviting.

"I choose you, Altair. I'll always choose you and your brothers."

In one forward motion, I was in his arms. His lips claimed mine. When it felt like I was floating on a cloud, he pulled us over to the bed and sat down.

"Enough talk of earthly men. I've had enough of that. Now, sit on my lap, my queen," he demanded with a stern look.

I was already wet between the legs and I knew it would leak if I moved, but my body sought to obey Altair's every single command.

Pressing the lips of my sex together, I was already becoming rather slick with the need for him. There were no panties to drench because I didn't wear any.

I'd never seen him like this before. Hot and bothered, equally with anger and hunger. His emotions further fueled my need for him as I propped myself down onto his lap with a gasp upon realizing how hard he was for me.

He reached under my long dress, pinching my sensitive clit. "No one will ever fulfill you the same way. Not like us."

"No," I gasped out. "Not like the three of you."

"Look at you. You're practically gagging for it. See how your pussy creams for me. Look at how much slick you produce, my queen." He slid a finger through my juicy and wet slit, proving his point.

"I...Altair," I breathlessly whimpered before looking into his eyes. I'd never seen him so angry with me before that I wanted to appease him. I wanted to apologize and thank him for saving me, but I also needed to remind him I only wanted to be with them. My trio of shadow world demons.

"Do you want to know why it's always me who races to you when it comes to these situations you keep getting yourself into?" he asked, kissing me on the shoulder.

He had my attention. I nodded and waited for his reply.

"The energy gained from wreaking havoc and instilling violence is addictive. Very addictive. Just like the energy you feed us with when we fuck you whether it be in your dreams or in reality. We prefer to fuck you, my queen. Violence is a last resort but is sometimes needed."

"Do the others feel that way?"

"Morpheus and Dominik gain the most strength when they feed off of violence. Negative energy. Just one kill and they will more than likely go on feeding rampages which leave bloody trails in their wake."

"I kind of knew this about Dominik," I said. "But Morpheus...he seems calm."

"Because he's good at abstaining. It is true what they say. The quiet, nice-looking people are the ones you have to watch out for." Altair grinned.

"So, I've been told."

"I'm telling you this to say this...there will come a time when there will be violence. Morpheus won't be able to abstain and Dominik will indulge as he always does. We'll have to choose violence to succeed. To protect you."

"I know. Now that I'm here with you all in the flesh, I've learned more than you think."

"So, from now on, you'll obey when we ask you to stay in a certain place." He raised an eyebrow.

"Hmmm, let's see." I bit my bottom lip and pretended to think.

"I guess you need another lesson, don't you?" he growled softly before leading me onto my knees on the floor. My mouth watered when his cock tented his pants. I wasn't like this before, but he had trained my body to want more.

I stared up at him, making him groan. "Fuck, Sadie, you're fucking beautiful on your knees for me."

"Yes," I breathed out. "I'm sorry for not listening."

"Show me how sorry you are," he snarled. "Show me before I take you across my knees and spank you so hard you won't be able to sit for days, much less get out of this bed unless it's to spread your pretty thighs for me."

"Altair," I whimpered out, my body feeling as if it caught on fire because of his words.

I slowly undid the buttons of my lace gown as I softly nuzzled his manhood through the tight cloth barrier. I felt like a cat in heat, wanting nothing more than his cock in my mouth, which caused him to chuckle. "Needy, aren't you?"

He lifted my chin just as I was about to apply my mouth to him.

I licked my lips. "Please..."

With that, he lowered his pants, and his cock sprung free. Thick pre-cum was already gathered at the bulbous head as he led me to settle just at the edge of the bed. "Do you like this sort of play, Sadie? Does it make you feel better when you lie to yourself and me, denying how much you're enjoying getting fucked senseless by me? If you like this game, my queen, you can just tell me. I enjoy breaking and taming you so that no earthly man will ever satisfy you."

Jealousy.

It was jealousy that I could see swimming in his eyes.

"Altair," I mewled softly. "There's no need to be jealous."

"I'm not," he snapped as he guided my head forward towards the tip of his cock with his large, rough hands. "Now hurry up and suck my fucking cock, Sadie. You think you're allowed to summon me without feeding me?"

Once more, my heart fluttered in excitement to know that he completely owned me as my eyes pierced his. He needed this, and I needed to show him how serious I was.

"You don't have to be," I whispered.

"Then you know what to do."

"Yes, Altair."

Licking my lips, I bent forward and lapped at his fat cockhead, cleaning off the thick pre-cum that coated his length. White pre-cum gathered at the end, translucent and shimmering, reminding me he wasn't human at all.

My core throbbed rather painfully, needing to be plugged up once more by his cock all over again despite doing it almost daily. Altair didn't even bother to suppress the groan that spilled out of his mouth as my soft lips wrapped around his shaft, and he chuckled.

"Fuck, my queen. Suck that big cock that you love so much," he crooned at me, tipping his head as I opened my eyes to look at him. His monster cock was a snug fit. I closed my lips around the tip, bobbing my head slowly. He grunted, rocking his hips in and out of my hot, wet cavern. "Such a filthy slut, aren't you? Yeah, just like that. Now use your tongue as well. Ah, yes, Sadie, you know what to do. You got to work hard if you want to please me and prove you've learned your lesson, or I'm going to spank your ass so hard that you'll be feeling it for days."

He gripped harder onto my hair, tilting my head back so I would have no choice but to take more of his length down my tiny throat. I shifted uncomfortably on the floor as my hands went to dig into his thigh. Wetness collected between my legs and dripped down my thighs.

In fact, I couldn't believe my body's reaction to this rough treatment from him.

He smiled wickedly at me, his eyes glowing red.

"Are you enjoying this?" he taunted me, immediately rewarded with my flushed face. Finally, he let go of his grip on my hair, pulling my mouth away from his cock. I let go with an audible pop, my tongue still lolling out as he bent forward and pushed the straps of my dress down to collect at my waist.

His eyes traveled to my breasts, and he licked his lips.

"Say it, Sadie. Say you'll never disobey me again."

"I'll never disobey—"

He forced his thick, rigid cock inch by inch down my throat, cutting me off. He throat-fucked me until saliva leaked down my neck and through my cleavage and then pulled away.

"Now stand up and take off your dress, Sadie," he instructed me.

When I was done, he eyed my naked body with appreciation and then led me back to the floor, continuing to use my mouth as a cock sleeve.

"Good...my queen. So good," he cooed, petting my hair condescendingly as he used my hot mouth for his pleasure.

"Now, touch yourself for me. Get yourself nice and wet for your punishment."

He was so big and swollen every time he pushed between my lips. I thought of how deliciously sore I'd be tomorrow if he rammed so roughly in my dripping, wet cunt the way he plunged himself down my throat. I noisily hollowed out my cheeks, bobbing my head earnestly.

I knew he was growing closer to climaxing as I shoved two fingers into my wet pussy while I used my thumb to rub it in circular motions around my swollen, throbbing clit. His balls clenched while copious amounts of pre-cum leaked out of his cock as I greedily slurped it up.

I gagged and choked as I continued to suck his enormous cock to the best of my abilities. The thought of having him enter me and splitting me open caused me to start fingerfucking myself as I tried to bring myself to orgasm.

"I guess you really do need discipline, don't you?" he chuckled darkly. I shuddered violently at the way he stared at my body as if I was nothing more than a plaything for him. It was the way his majestic alabaster-toned skin along with his curved horns contrasted with his red eyes. His red, devilish eyes and massively muscled arms told me he could kill in a flash if he really wanted to. Yet, in reality, I seemed to have power over him. The energy we created was also mine to take.

I gagged against his length as he only groaned and forced me to swallow around his steel rod. "Are you finally going to be a good girl, Sadie? Or maybe I should lock you up here instead. Me nor my brothers will come to please you."

No. I didn't want that. *I needed them.*

I bobbed my head in compliance.

I gagged, and my throat tightened even further as if I was trying to milk him for all he was worth, for the inevitable. I couldn't even think straight anymore as my fingers flew across my throbbing clit. My hips were bucking in my hand as I lost myself in the crashing waves that overtook me.

However, right before I could jump over the edge, Altair ordered me to stand up, and I obeyed without missing a beat.

Then, in a whirl, he pushed me onto the bed, bending me over. Finally, he went to nudge my legs apart and pushed my fingers away. One hand cupped my pussy while the other tightly held onto my hips.

I gasped, digging my fingers into the plush sheets when he probed my wet entrance with his thick fingers. I have no idea how long he held me down, teasing me for almost half an hour or so, much like I did before with his cock. I was a blubbering mess, pleading and crying for him to fuck me for being so bad.

Losing count after my first four orgasms, I was oversensitive to his every touch that I wanted nothing more than to stop. Yet, my cunt wanted to be stretched by the monstrous cock. I shivered when he laughed and outright moaned when he replaced them with his fat cockhead.

"Oh, God," I whimpered, thrusting and bucking my hips in an effort for relief. Heated sensations gathered in my core. I wanted nothing more than to be used by him. And then... cherished by him.

He was Altair. Oldest of his three brothers. Demanding, and controlling, and knew what he wanted and had a plan for getting it. But, instead of pursuing his completion, he kept dragging his thick cock, slick with my arousal, over my pussy. This was bordering torturous to have him tease me this way.

"Please," I panted, desperate to feel him penetrating and spearing my inside was making my head spin.

"Keep begging for it," he demanded, rubbing his cock along my pussy, between my legs. It only allowed him to nudge my clit in a way that made my body jump underneath his touch. I felt as if my body was on fire. "Come and tell me how much you want this."

"Yes," I repeated, shaking from need. My head was spinning, and my stomach was clenching with need. "Please, inside. I...I want you inside of me. Please, rip me apart, so everyone will know that I belong to you. Mark me up. Use me..."

He brought his hand down hard onto my ass. It echoed around his bedroom, along with my crying. He continued to spank me hard, my body lunging forward each time as I drooled all over his sheets. "Answer me, Sadie."

"Oh, yes, yes, please," I babbled, trying to rock my ass back onto him. "Please, Altair."

"Bring your ass up more."

I pushed my peach-shaped ass back where he could reach me, spreading my legs wide.

"Good girl."

With a throaty grunt that made my nipples pebble, he shoved the entire length of his cock inside of my tight cunt in one perfect, single motion. Thanks to how wet I was already, my cunt didn't even put up much of a fight as my back hollowed out. I had no choice but to bite down hard on my forearm to keep myself from crying out when he sheathed himself inside of me.

He wasted no time in setting a ruthless, savage pacing and long strokes into my tight channel. I could feel my wet heat gripping his cock as my walls fluttered around him, trying to adjust to his size. And judging from the way he used me so thoroughly, I knew he wasn't trying to savor every second like it was going to be his last.

No, because it wasn't his last. He fucked me like he owned me.

"You're loving this, aren't you?" he questioned, and I could hear him maniacally laughing. He squeezed my ass and smacks it hard again. My flesh wobbled before he leaned down to hold himself over me while nipping hard on my earlobes. "Such a sweet cum-hungry little slut, aren't you?"

"Yes," I choke out. I couldn't believe he was still hungover from the violence he inflicted.

"That is what violence does, my queen."

So good.

So fucking good.

I should've been ashamed for wanting it like this. If this was what violence brought out, I wanted more of it. Needed more of it. And I would have more of it.

"Naughty, dirty girl. But you are perfect," he moaned.

I gripped the pillow until my knuckles locked while little moans tumbled out of my mouth. I openly moaned when he slammed into my cervix.

"Ah!" I cried out, my whole body lifting momentarily off the bed as I screamed.

"Now, now," he tsked, still thrusting so hard into me that his thighs slapped against my ass. "I know how much you want me, but you still need to be quiet, Sadie. Or Morpheus and Dominik will want to punish you too and I don't think you can handle that right now."

Oh, my God. Why did the idea appeal to me? I licked my lips.

I tried slapping one of my hands over my mouth, but nothing seemed to work. It felt so good. My back-to-back orgasms rendered me helpless.

"No need to hold in all this energy, love. I owe you this," he whimpered into my ear.

After a series of deep plunges, he pulled me up by sliding his broad arms around my stomach. He dragged me away from the bed as he sat back down onto the bed seat with me on my lap and fully seated onto his cock with my back on his chest, facing away from him. He shoved three fingers into my mouth while the other went to fondle and pinch my nipples, and I couldn't even think.

"Bounce on my fucking cock," he commanded. "If you want my cum filling you up, work for it. So come on, work on my cock, my queen."

"Mn," I nodded, sucking hard on his fingers in my mouth. I rose a few inches and then dropped onto his cock. Every time I sank onto him, a shudder wrecked down my spine, and I dug my nails into his forearms.

"I'm going to cum deep inside of you, Sadie," he snarled, and it almost sounded like a promise. 'I'm going to fill you to the very brim with all my thick, hot seed. And since you like being fucked hard like this, you're going to get off on it, yes?"

"I will," I finally confirmed. "I want you, Altair. I want you so bad."

I didn't know how long I continued to bounce on his cock, but the lightheadedness and the bliss came hand-in-hand until my thighs gave up. Then, as I slumped onto him, he murmured some praises as he took his fingers out of my mouth and swirled them over my clit as his mouth clamped down on my shoulder, biting into me, marking me.

It was enough to trigger my orgasm through utter ecstasy. I put my hands over my mouth to keep myself from crying too loudly as my pussy clamped hard onto his cock. I threw my head back, blinded by my orgasm. Yet, he was relentless. He kept pinching my nipple, circling my clit, biting and sucking at my neck.

He then grabbed the back of my neck, crashing his lips hard onto mine as we swallowed one another's moan. I cried out as I felt his cum erupting from his cock as it pulsated, shooting right into my womb and coating my insides with his potent demon seed. I kept grinding onto him, riding him in an attempt to draw out every last remnant of his cum as our tongues battled.

He pulled away from our heated kiss, and I thought he was finished. But he wasn't as he buried his face into my shoulder and bit down hard again and then licked the droplets of blood off my flesh. The sharp pain mixed with the pleasure made me gasp at the sensation of my pussy flooding with the sticky white mess as I closed my eyes, trying to catch my breath.

Finally, he released his tension with a sigh. His climax filled me with the type of magic supernatural beings killed for. And I took it all in.

"Truly, you have the power to instantly stop my heart if you wanted," he muttered lightly, kissing me on the lips. I couldn't help but notice how soft his voice had gone, and I realized just how much he was worried about me. "You will always be pursued."

I turned around on his lap to fully face him. I still straddled his thighs because I still needed him with me.

"But I'm not afraid, Altair. Never forget that."

He exhaled. "What would it take to convince you to stay away from danger?"

"I want you and your brothers to stop bickering, for once. Or none of this will ever work."

He nodded. "We will try. For you."

"And I enjoyed the meeting from earlier. I want us to do more things...together."

He rose an eyebrow.

I giggled and gave him a quick peck on the lips. "I wasn't just talking about sex, but other things."

"Like?"

"When was the last time you and your brothers sat around a table and ate together? Like a family meal?"

His eyes shifted to the left as he thought about it. "Never."

"I thought so," I replied. "When we were little, my parents always made us sit down to dinner together once in a while. My sister and I always hated the idea of doing that, but once we were there, my parents couldn't shut us up. We talked about everything under the sun, and it brought us closer together as a family."

"Then, what are you proposing?"

"Let's have dinner. Just the four of us. And I'm going to do all the cooking this time. I just need you to acquire the ingredients."

"Minus the ingredients for hexes, I would assume." His lips spread in a slow grin.

I locked my arms around his neck, and kissed him, longer this time. "I don't need ingredients to hex you, my king."

He returned the kiss passionately. "I'm sure my brothers would agree to it, so let's do it. No fighting, I promise."

"I'll hold you to that. Or else, there will be consequences."

CHAPTER 16
Sadie

COOKING for myself and no one else was easy.

Cooking for three demons who preferred feeding on emotions rather than copious amounts of death-by-chocolate-cake...now that was hard.

I had overestimated myself. Not only did my demons agree to me cooking a big dinner for them, but they wanted to watch.

*Er...um...*I didn't see that one coming.

But, I guess.

In any case, I was getting distracted six ways to Sunday and had already literally burnt up a few rolls, but was able to discard them in the trash quickly before anyone commented.

The kitchen was hot. I was a hot mess in my flour-covered apron. And the demons were in a heated conversation over a game of chess that I had somehow convinced them to play to keep them from distracting me.

Cooking on earth was far easier than cooking in Nebulae. The next time I suggested a family-type dinner like this, I was going to order takeout.

But I was going to pull through. After all, I was the one who suggested this. I expected them to hold up their end of the bargain by not fighting, and we were all going to sit down and have a nice meal while talking about...things.

Yeah, things. Tonight was one of those nights that I didn't want to talk about the chaotic state of things or the fact that Finn knew I was in this realm and that my demons had enemies who held lifelong grudges.

Suddenly, over the butter sizzling in the pan, things became deathly quiet.

I glanced over my shoulder to see why they were so quiet. Despite being hundreds of years older, they obviously knew how to have a good time and not take things so seriously. This was the side of them I wanted to see.

"Stop shaking your fucking knees," Dominik snarled at Altair as he studied the chess pieces.

I cleared my throat to remind them not to get too rowdy and willed myself to turn around before getting caught overseeing them.

"Why?" Altair snapped in retaliation.

"It's fucking annoying," he retorted, his fist meeting the table. "You're trying to break my concentration and you know it."

"Hey, let's not start this now," Morpheus interjected. "Especially if you all want to eat," he added.

Altair grinned. "We're going to eat, alright."

"I get first servings." Dominik licked his lips. "You still abstaining, Morpheus? You know you wanna."

Morpheus's face heated over in a blush as he shifted his gaze to me. He bit his lips, deep in thought.

"I think you've suppressed your appetite long enough, little brother," Dominik teased.

"Shut up," Morpheus warned.

I pressed my lips together to stop the throbbing sensation that was on my head rather than between my legs usually. I had hoped that a "family" dinner might have helped them solve some of their quarrels.

"That's right. Dinner is almost ready," I called out, hoping a simple distraction would stop a fight from breaking out.

Luckily, it worked as Altair tilted his head to the side when I went to pour them all a glass of wine.

"What are we having?" he asked curiously.

"Those juicy T-Bone steaks with a seafood mac and cheese," I beamed proudly. "I've also got—"

"Not interested," Dominik cut in and immediately saw Altair and Morpheus kicking him from under the table, but he didn't even wince. Instead, his nose flared as he narrowed his eyes at them. "What? You know it as well. You don't want human food for the night."

"O-oh," I murmured. I should have been used to Dominik's rude and outlandish behavior, yet it still stung slightly. It only stung more because I presumed Altair and Morpheus might have thought differently as my shoulders sagged. "Okay...do you have something else in mind?"

"Yeah, something much sweeter," Dominik answered with a wicked grin.

"I'm making some chocolate cake," I offered.

Morpheus sighed.

I crossed my arms over my chest. I was prepared to tell them to make their own damn food the second they opened their mouth, but they exchanged knowing looks with each other. That was when I knew something was up and they were already planning something.

"Sadie, we can get anyone to come here and make human food for you all you like, but when Altair came and said you wanted us to have dinner together, I got a taste for something else," Dominik said, eyeing me up and down. He then got up from the table.

My stomach heated in disappointment. "W-what then did you have a taste for?"

Dominik chuckled. "You."

"W-what are you doing?" I whispered breathlessly as I watched with bated breath the way Dominik unbuttoned his pants, letting them pool down his legs in one swift motion alongside his undergarments. No matter how many times I'd seen their cocks, it made my heart skip a beat, especially how it sprung up and hit his naval.

"Um..." I licked my lips.

"Sadie, I think you know exactly what he wants for dinner," Morpheus huffed out a laugh, and from the way he nor Altair moved, it was as if they knew from the start. Their eyes were practically glowing with unkempt lust now that Dominik had broken the façade they were all playing along with.

"And that's not something we're going to sit here and fight about," Altair added.

"Look at you," Dominik laughed, grabbing my wrists roughly and causing me to yelp when my body crashed hard onto his. His other hand snaked around my tiny frame, his eyes penetrating my very soul of the pain-pleasure. "You don't even know what you're drooling for."

Was I drooling? I couldn't tell.

It looked as if they really were trying to make a meal out of me with their insatiable appetite.

"Not so rough," Morpheus chided from the sideline, leaning back in his chair.

"She likes it rough," Dominik spoke with cool authority.

My core throbbed.

Why was I turned on with getting treated like some sort of fuck doll for these three demons...at the same time? I had them all separate, but never together.

"I'm getting impatient, brother," Altair rumbled.

In an instant, the chessboard was shoved off the table and clattered to the floor. With lightning speed, I was plopped on the table and then flipped over. My face was planted on the placemat as Dominik pushed my legs apart and bowed me into a doggy-style position.

"There you go. Present that pretty pussy to us, my queen," Altair moaned.

Morpheus peeked over Dominik's shoulder. "Pretty indeed. I want to devour her whole, brothers."

Shame pricked at my cheeks, and yet, something was freeing in giving into them.

Slick, thick honey leaked from my slit onto the table and down my thighs. Given the deep growls and trouser unzippings that echoed around the kitchen room, I knew what they were thinking.

"Fuck, such a naughty slut. I bet you were expecting this. Boring us with your human food when all we wanted was your body," Altair groaned hoarsely before one rough finger came in contact with my juicy slit. He massaged me in circles. I whimpered, my body filling up with pleasure as I lay there, held down and felt over by demon brothers.

"P-Please...I've never had so many...at once." I pleaded through my quivering lips. I wanted to tell them I had never had sex of this magnitude, but they knew.

They knew...

But would they cater to me or fuck me with savagery?

"Don't be afraid. Your body was made for us. You're an omega. You're unique. Your body will conform the way it needs to to accommodate our size," Dominik said.

A finger wrapped around the waistband of my skirt before the sound of something ripping went out, echoing loud in the air.

I gasped when a hand slapped my bare pussy harder, and I was more than sure it was Dominik. Or maybe Altair, whose patience I had tested repeatedly. Not knowing made the experience all the wilder.

The next thing I knew, Dominik flipped me over onto my back. His nose pressed right against my folds, sniffing me like a wild animal in heat before groaning.

"Fuck, you're dripping, and we barely even touched you. Maybe you were already praying for you being the main course, huh?" he growled, running his tongue against my folds as I cried harder in utter ecstasy. "You want us to eat together and fuck together. Is that what you want? Let's go prep you up then, yes?"

He didn't wait for my reply before cramming two big and thick fingers into me. My toes curled, and if it weren't for Altair and Morpheus, I would have inched away from just how rough he was while stretching me out to no end.

"Ah..." I trailed off, carnal need racing through me

"Time to breed you up, Sadie, for who can wait until your twenty-first birthday besides Morpheus? *Not me*," Dominik groaned.

"Play nice," Morpheus scowled at his older brother. "We can all wait to breed her. She is our queen."

"We mean it," Altair added.

Dominik pushed forward, lifted my legs high into the air, and rubbed his member at the entrance of my puckered ass as the others looked on. Surely, if he entered me there, he would rip me apart with his massive size.

Altair and Morpheus took advantage and ripped whatever was left of my dress and apron, leaving me completely naked and vulnerable. They began to play with my nipples, touching them and pinching them harder, making me cry from the pleasure ricocheting through every inch of my body.

"So soft," Morpheus growled against my ears. "Do you like it when I touch you? Tell me you like it."

His thumb circled my taut nipples, playing with them. I threw my head back with a moan, both pain and pleasure ripping through me and sending jolts down my body. I rocked against Dominik's fingers. Each of them tugged at my puffy nipples right in the kitchen until I purred like a kitten in the heat.

"Y-Yes, I like it..." I whispered, followed by a gasp when I felt Altair harshly pinching my other nipple.

My whole body was already flushed with need, juices running down my ass. "I love it so much."

Busy drowning in the ecstasy of being pleasured by two demons, I didn't understand when Dominik aligned his cock along my entrance. Without warning, he slammed forward and pushed all his thick length into me.

I cried out and my eyes closed shut. The abundance of slick coating my sheath prepared me for his sudden onslaught, thank the gods. When he started moving inside me, I felt nothing but pleasure.

Altair and Morpheus continued to play with my nipples using their fingers and tongue, trying to ease the pain of having Dominik's well-endowed turgid shaft stuffed inside me. Ever the impatient and sometimes heartless demon that he was, he did not give me any time to adjust fully and started pounding into me like a madman.

Using me brutally for his pleasure only.

His cock slammed into me again and again, and the sound of loud our wet skin slapping echoed in the air. He made sudden and rapid movements, making pain and pleasure both blast through the region between my thighs as he dug his nails into my hips.

I was screaming, whimpering, begging—for more and for less.

My whole body trembled under the heavy weight of the one who played with my body as he pleased.

"Tightest little cunt ever," he groaned, pistoning deep and harshly inside of me. "Fuck, this is heaven. Cry for me, Sadie. Say my name. I want to fucking break my slut in. You're swallowing and tightening up so much like a good breeding whore and choking my fucking cock...while my brothers watch. You like that, don't you?"

"*Dom*...oh fuck," I wailed.

"Brother, go a little slower. She is precious to me. I don't want her fucked to death on the table," Altair snarled, capturing the bottom of my chin and turning my head to look up at him. I stared at him, my mouth falling into silent screams as Dominik pushed in harder and harder. He brought a thumb closer to my face and wiped away beads of sweat, pressing a soft kiss on my head.

"It's okay, Sadie," he whispered. "I'm here." He kissed my lips passionately.

My heart fluttered because, despite his dominating nature, he still tried to comfort and cater to me.

"Join me if you want to, but don't ask me to slow down," Dominik seethed with a low voice. "Just look at her face. She fucking wants this." He fisted his hands in my hair and pulled my head back, tearing me away from Altair so they could all see my lust-filled face and the way my voluminous breasts jiggled.

"Please..." I trailed off, not sure what I was even begging for.

Dominik started to speed up as Morpheus stood up, his nose flaring. My eyes drifted to his tented cock, eyes widening at the thickness of his two cocks, growing in length and girth. My mouth watered at the sight of two purple bulbous heads dripping with pre-cum.

"Now, it's my turn, Dom." Altair nudged his brother. "I'm the oldest. Don't be greedy."

Looking down between my legs, I watched in hunger as they switched sides.

Dominik pulled out of me in a swift motion, leaving me empty. I groaned in dissatisfaction. I wanted to be filled again.

Dominik moved aside and Morpheus moved to the head of the table as Altair worked his fingers in and out of my sex.

I leaned over and took one of Morpheus's two cocks in my mouth while wrapping my fingers around the other.

Snarling, Altair stroked himself while waiting between my legs with his seed beading on the tip. With an anguished roar, I watched in horror as the demon within him broke free. His fingers quickly elongated until they were claws and tightened around my hips, digging into my soft flesh.

I stilled eyes widening because, in his demon form, he was much more aggressive.

Animalistic.

Demonic.

He pressed the head of his monster-sized shaft against my puckered back opening. With a snarl, he thrust forward, burying himself entirely inside my puckered opening. I gasped at how he pushed the head of his thick cock past the ring of muscles at my anus.

I couldn't speak, let alone break out into a scream. My mouth was full of Morpheus.

I could feel my tightness clenching around him, feeling him compressing deep inside me and knocking the breath out of me. He was rough, and seeing Dominik watching me being used only made me wetter.

"Oh fuck, she's tight," he praised and made smooth and slow movements, allowing me to take small breaths before he started increasing his speed more and more.

He tried to be gentle with me but could not restrain himself and began to be more abrupt, thrusting into me with a force that made my insides burn.

Dominik, being the impatient one, stood over us and grabbed his cock, stroking it as he watched. He reached across and spread my thighs more, allowing him to get a close-up look as Altair fucked my ass. Morpheus slid his hand down my belly and played my clit like a guitar.

I cried, thrashing and gasping, feeling as if they were breaking me from the inside. Their sudden and rapid movements made me feel as if I was going to pass out at any moment. I couldn't hold back anymore.

I moaned.

"P-Please..." I cried, my voice faint against their harsh animalistic groans.

What did I expect from three powerful demons?

While my legs shook and my whole body thrashed in ecstasy, I heard a murmur coming from Morpheus, who was still fucking my mouth harder and faster. I couldn't hear it well, but then I felt a hot liquid suddenly pouring over my tongue.

I came in unison with him as he stroked my clit at just the right tempo and angle.

Dominik, who was stroking himself through his climax, showered my chest and belly with his warm seed.

And Altair, who was locked deep within my ass, came so hard his cum spilled from me when he came.

When it was all over, I collapsed back on the table, spent.

My breaths were short and ragged. My visions turned into little dots no matter how many times I blinked.

Taking turns, my demons leaned down, each one kissing me passionately. I accepted each kiss, wrapping my fingers around their necks and plunging my tongue against theirs.

"You see, Sadie. One thing we don't fight about is how best to please you," Altair said, scooping me up.

"Indeed," I whispered.

I knew before he took the next step where he was taking me.

"Can we do that again? Together?"

"Indeed." He winked. "No dinner required."

I was asleep in his arms before he reached the stairs.

CHAPTER 17
Sadie

I ENJOYED a little fun just as much as the next person, but time didn't seem to be on my side.

I had to get to the bottom of how Finn was able to trick my ancestors into tapping into powers from the spirit world now that the moon orb was gone.

With my spell to construct a new moon orb almost complete, I had yet another project on my to-do list.

If Finn could just continue his destructive behavior some other way, then that could stall the interim plans my demons and I had to infiltrate Shadow World.

I had to stop Finn in the meantime.

Just as Altair had said, Finn would be relentless no matter what. Now, I almost wished I had killed him when I had the chance while I was on earth. None of this would have happened.

Yet, I wanted some of it to happen.

I glanced at Morpheus as he sat across from me on the window seat. The demons alternated every day, choosing which one of them I would pull magic from to fuel my spells.

It was Morpheus' turn today.

I enjoyed his company on days like this because he was always the calmest. My father always told me I would never perfect a spell during the height of chaos. Morpheus was the opposite of chaos. He was serenity.

As I worked a piece of twine around a bundle of herbs, I called him away from the window seat.

He got up, smiling. "Are you ready for me again?"

"No. I won't pull from you until I know it's going to work. Spell is not quite ready, but I wanted to ask you something."

"And what is that?" He pulled a stool over to my work table and sat near me.

I blushed. "Why do you abstain?"

"It's something I vowed to do the moment you summoned us for protection. I had a vision that I would wait until you peaked and that just stuck. I haven't been with anyone else since that vow."

It pleased me that he was waiting for me. "Peak, as in my twenty-first birthday?" I asked.

He nodded, and then reached out and twined some of my hair around his finger. "And remember...time progresses differently here. On earth, your twenty-first birthday is only weeks away. I can wait that long, I think. Can you?"

I grinned. "I can. You please me in other ways, Morpheus. You always have."

"I'm glad. Also, I'm sure you'll find it to be more advantageous if you wait."

I put my work down on the table, giving him my undivided attention. "How so?"

"If I told you now, it wouldn't be a surprise, would it?"

"Tease," I giggled, swatting at him under the table with my foot.

He just caught my foot in his big hands, placing it on his lap next to his maximum-sized packages. I licked my lips, remembering the way I sucked one of his cocks while fist-pumping the other.

"You'll drive me insane waiting, Sadie. I think you know that." He kneaded my foot, massaging the arch and between my toes.

I moaned and my pussy creamed. "I think you deserve it. After all, what woman wouldn't want a man with two cocks instead of just one?"

Morpheus's nostril flared outward and his majestic eyes gleamed. "Be careful now, little witch. You know I'll set you right here on this altar, spread your legs wide, and lick you raw until you can't take it anymore."

My clit pulsed as soon as this hot and explicit imagery formed in my mind.

He leaned forward. "So, what will it be? A pussy-licking or a spell-casting?"

"*Um...*" I swallowed.

He chuckled, deeply. "My dicks will be worth the wait. *I promise.*"

I sighed as he continued with his massage and then requested the other foot.

"How did I get so lucky?" I asked.

"I could ask you the same. I knew we were fated to have a queen, but I never imagined one as perfect as you."

"Then, what did you imagine?" I turned the tables on him.

"Hmmm. A fire-breathing sorceress bitch with two heads, medusa braids, and eight soul-sucking tentacles—like an octopus."

"What!" I gasped, appalled at his depiction, jerked my feet away, and tossed some pebbles at him.

He laughed, swatting the fallen pebbles from his lap. "I'm only kidding. But my brothers and I have fought a monster like that before. *She was hell.* Turns out she's unkillable."

I gave him a wry smile. "Nothing's unkillable. If it draws breath, it can be killed."

"Easy for you to say. You're a powerful witch. When we fought that octo-bitch, we would chop off a head or cut off a tentacle only to see it grow back before our eyes. Although we didn't kill her, we did trap her on a desolate realm where she can waste away for all eternity for her crimes."

"Crimes?"

"Much like Finn, she steals from the innocent to maintain her vitality. Cutting off her access to innocents will stop her indefinitely."

Suddenly, something dawned on me.

I jumped up from my seat and raced over to the bookcase where I kept my journals of notes. "I think I know how to stop Finn."

Morpheus came to join me, observing my actions as I flipped through the pages. "How?"

"I'll cut off his access to the spirit world. It will stop him from accessing magic he needs for a majority of his spells. He'll be livid. And powerless." I bit at my fingernails, contemplating this thing.

"Hmmm, that sounds easy, but why does it seem like there's something more to it?" Morpheus asked, slowly.

I slapped a journal closed and a hollow thud echoed in the air. "Because there is more to it. I need a coven of witches. I need to convince the cave witches to help me do this."

CHAPTER 18
Sadie

THE BARRIER DENYING Finn access to the spirit world was active. I should've felt triumphant in my success, but I didn't. It was bittersweet—no, the execution of the spell didn't feel life-changing at all.

I knew I was only delaying Finn's next dastardly effort to destroy something good, just like he tried to destroy me.

All of this was probably like a game to him. He would always come back tenfold. We shared blood, for goodness sake. We had the same father. And although my father got little time with Finn in his earlier years to steer him in the right direction, he still inherited my father's persistence. But so did I.

The cave witches were helpful but they were now gone. And now, I owed them a favor. Our circle of eleven was just right to execute the spell. Without them, I probably couldn't have done it. Plus, we had three powerful demons from which to harvest magic. Each demon shared the load equally, but luckily there were plenty of rifts open tonight for them to refill their energy wells. That's where they were now—scouting for magical rifts in the realm, drinking up all that they could.

I had to wonder, how much energy loss did a demon have to endure for it to be detrimental...or deadly? The last thing I wanted was for them to become so weak that they couldn't protect themselves against a greater threat, like their father, who they believed would kill them on sight with no questions asked.

I sunk under the steamy waters in the jacuzzi until I was chin deep. The heat from the overhead sauna above coated my body, clouding the bathroom with mist. I had only just discovered the moon door up above, but I kept it closed tonight.

The scenery was nice; I had to admit. But just as my demon protectors needed to refill, I needed to decompress after such a powerful spell.

I lowered myself further, taking a deep breath before dipping my head beneath the surface of the water. I closed my eyes as I collapsed to the bottom of the jacuzzi.

As the water rushed through my ears and pushed against my eardrums, a vision came to my mind.

My sister was near at ocean, surrounded by a cliff and a maze of connecting tunnels. It felt as if I was there with her, looking over her shoulder.

Directly in front of her was a blue hole—a marine cavern. From my position, I could see that the sinkhole was deep. If she took one step, she would fall inside.

"Stop," I warned, holding out my arms while trying to reach her.

"No. I have to." She looked back at me and raised the moon orb over her head. "I'm sorry, Sadie. I have to."

A funnel came out of nowhere, taking her down under into the deep blue hole.

"Nooooo."

"Sydney!"

I came up for a breath, hard and fast. Water sloshed over the sides of the tub as I gained my bearings.

My lungs burned and I coughed up some of the bath water.

I grabbed a towel and wiped my face.

What the hell had I just seen?

After lifting myself out of the jacuzzi, I unplugged the drain and sat on the side of the tub until all the water drained out.

Was my vision true? My mind loved playing tricks on me, even when I was a child.

Foresight was never one of my gifts. I could never master the techniques. So, where was I coming up with these strange and scary images?

I didn't want my vision to be true. I couldn't bear it if my sister was gone.

A tear ran down my face and dripped onto my thigh with the other water droplets.

"Where are you, Sydney? Where in the world are you?"

I came to many hours later with a start and in a rather interesting situation. I was tangled up in a maze of arms and legs. I wiped the haziness from my eyes.

Altair, Morpheus, and Dominik had joined me sometime in the night and I hadn't even noticed. Each demon was fast asleep. One of them was snoring a little but I could figure out who.

I knew the bed was monster-sized for a reason, and apparently, this was it.

I grinned.

This was literally the first time all three of my demons slept by my side. Before, depending on who came to keep me company at the time, they would sleep or nap with me separately.

How odd. I didn't even remember them joining me on the bed.

Had we...?

No. I would've remembered if I had sex with them last night.

Making sure not to wake any of them, I crept over their massive limbs. It wasn't easy. One of them grabbed the pillow I'd been sleeping on and pulled it close.

I covered my mouth to stop a giggle from escaping my lips and tiptoed quickly into the bathroom to get ready for the day.

By the time I finished and walked back out into the room, the men were just beginning to wake up.

Altair yawned. "Mmmm. Well, hello beautiful."

"Morning, sleepy heads. Or afternoon. Or night. I can't tell." I giggled, walking towards the windows and parting the curtains. It resembled daylight outside, but within hours it would probably be pitch black.

Dominik pulled himself up and leaned against the headboard. "The queen witch is awake. It's about time."

I stood in front of the bed in a long negligee that I knew was see-through. Folding my arms over my chest, I asked, "When did the three of you join me?"

Morpheus scooted himself all the way to the foot of the bed, seating himself in front of me. "Hmmm, I think it was right after your bath. At least, that's when I came in. Then these two knuckleheads followed." He hitched a finger behind him.

"We came to share some magic, but you were already asleep," Altair said.

"Well, I'm awake now," I teased, just as Morpheus slid his fingers up my thighs.

His cocks twitched under his loincloth, making a tent with the fabric as he massaged my thighs. My pussy practically creamed as I stood there in front of him. When he licked his lips, juices coated between my legs.

"She smells delicious, brother. Are you going to have at her? If not, I will," Dominik stated from his position resting against the headboard.

"We never agreed on who gets first dibs this time," Altair challenged, sitting next to Dominik, leaning back against the headboard as well.

I grinned. "Patience, you two. Morpheus has already claimed that honor today."

"And she's spoken," Altair said.

Morpheus wasted no time untying the straps of my frilly negligee and parting it to reveal my breasts. I straddled his lap, my legs on either side of his thighs. When he captured my nipple between his lips, I moaned. He sucked and lapped until my nipples were puffy and wet from his teasing.

Behind him, his brothers looked on, obviously becoming aroused from the show.

"Are you going to fuck her pussy this time, little brother?" Dominik asked.

"Maybe," Morpheus rasped.

His two cocks were swelling under my wet sex by the minute. If he wanted, all he had to do was lift me and thrust himself inside. I was slick with need. Only in my dreams had I felt Morpheus inside of me. I wanted him for real. He wanted to wait, but I wanted him now.

"Please, Morpheus..." I panted, pushing my nipple into his mouth.

"See, brother. She's begging you to fuck her cunt," Altair growled, pulling off his pants and stroking his thick erection. "If you won't, I most certainly will."

"You'll wait for it," Morpheus growled and flipped me over on my back.

He went straight for my pussy, pushing his tongue through my drenched slit and licking all around my clit. I cried out and shuddered. I grabbed his horns, guiding his mouth all over the lips of my pussy.

"How sweet is she, brother?" Dominik asked.

"She is fucking delicious."

"Don't you want your cocks inside her?" Altair urged.

Morpheus growled into my pussy and a climax fluttered through me.

"How do you abstain from fucking her? I don't understand it," Dominik pressed.

Morpheus stopped eating me out long enough to reply. "You will never understand. But I will fuck her. I'm the one that's going to be inside this sweet little cunt when she peaks."

I gasped when Morpheus descended face first on my pussy again, plunging his tongue into my hot sex. He looked up into my eyes and drove his forked tongue in and out, curving it upward until he activated my g-spot.

"You are fucking her tight cunt with your tongue. That's not abstaining. That's cheating," Dominik bit out.

Morpheus's long tongue slid out of my pussy again to reply. "Don't be jealous, Dom. There will be more than enough honey left for you to eat. I'm done talking about this. I won't talk to you when my mouth is full."

Morpheus dove again headfirst between my legs, eating me out like I was the last meal. I wasn't sure there would be anything left when Altair and Dominik finally got a turn. Orgasms kept rolling through me like an endless river. And Morpheus lapped up every last drop, plunging his tongue into my pussy until I was spent.

By the time he was done having his fill, I was already super sensitive. When Altair and Dominik touched me, preparing me for their oncoming onslaught I shivered beneath their caresses.

All three demons were ready and poised for what came next.

They looked delicious. Beads of sweat dripped off their bodies, making them look even hotter. Unable to resist, I reached out and trailed my fingers down the blocs of their abs, stroking their cocks and testing their readiness.

Their moans of pleasure sent electricity through my body. I wanted to feel that sensation over and over again.

Rising on my hands and knees in front of Morpheus who was now erected on his knees on the bed, I started to lick both of his identical cocks. Pre-cum already leaked from the tips, but his massive sac was still filled with seed.

Altair slid under me, lining his turgid shaft up with my pussy. And Dominik propped himself up behind me, leaning down to lap at both my wet slit and puckered hole.

Morpheus grabbed his top cock, twisting at the head, and rammed the bottom cock down my throat.

I parted my thighs, ready to satiate a need so great I was blinded by it.

After Dominik prepared my ass with his slippery wet fingers, he slapped my ass hard with his palm.

I gagged on Morpheus's cock as a scream ripped out my throat.

"Ready, brother?" Altair asked, pushing his cockhead past my swollen lips.

"Now," Dominik grunted.

Both monster dicks filled me up at the same time. I saw stars, stripes, and fireworks. The climax that followed the moment they entered me was explosive.

At first, two cocks thrust into my pussy and ass simultaneously. It almost became too much to bear, but the orgasm that took over my body rendered me too helpless to protest.

Eventually, they slowed their tempos and began to ram into me alternatively. And that feeling was bliss.

Each plunge sent me to a higher level of ecstasy from which I didn't want to come down.

Morpheus came first with both of his cocks. Copious amounts of seed shot down my throat and over my face as he reached his climax.

Altair and Dominik came one after the other, filling both of my holes with their potent seed.

The force of being filled to the max was so invigorating, that it sent me tumbling into my own rapturous orgasm.

The moment was so powerful that I screamed. The room itself shuddered, flower vases blew asunder, furniture smashed into the walls, and anything that wasn't fixed to a secure surface lost balance and shattered on the marble floors.

I gasped, gathering up all the energy in the room, and took it upon myself. My veins were on fire. The magic I'd just pulled inside threatened to break free from me even though there was no escaping my appeal.

When it was over, we collapsed on the bed. When I looked up at the ceiling mirror above us, we were an entanglement of sweaty, cum-drenched arms and legs.

For the first time in...forever maybe...my demons were speechless.

I looked back and forth from one to the next and said, "I think I'm ready now. I'm ready to fight."

CHAPTER 19
Sadie

"RENELLUS ANGIUUM ORBITUS."

I drew from the powers stored within me. I had stored up a lot over the past week or so in anticipation of this. Holding up the veil between the Shadow World and Nebulae so my demons could storm the gates was a monstrous task in and of itself.

"Orbitus Asime," I chanted. *"Renellus Angiuum...Orbitus."*

I held my fingers over the newly manufactured moon orb. This time, the orb was crafted from elements generated under the Nebulae moon, not an earth moon. Being so new and from a realm where magic wasn't as potent, the orb wouldn't be as powerful, but it would work for this occasion.

Sweat beaded across my forehead and the saltiness scorched my tongue, but I ignored it. I even quickly dismissed the droplets of blood draining down from my nose onto the altar, where I performed the spell.

I was going to hold up this veil, no matter what. I wouldn't let go until I knew all of my demons were safely back with me. Even if I had to die to do it.

The moon orb only revealed to me glimpses of what was going on with my demons in the shadow world. Because there were three of them, my attention was stretched all over the place.

They were being attacked at the gates. Blood was everywhere.

Their goal was to get in and get out. The wizard who orchestrated the spell that made their father's decree of exile finale was still alive. If they wanted to break the curse, the wizard could not be allowed to live.

With the way things were turning out, it didn't look like they would reach their father's throne in enough time. There wasn't enough time for that. The moon orb and the energy from which I drew could only last so long.

Even so, I could see that they tried.

Several times I wanted to look away as monstrous beasts fought with my demon protectors with no fear. It was worse than the fight Altair had with those measly lizardfolk.

Sharp pain speared my heart and I clutched my chest. I gasped as an image of Altair forked by a spear flashed in the moon orb.

Oh, God.

Had I sent my demons to a fight they couldn't win?

I closed my eyes and chanted another spell. Doubling my efforts had the potential to get me in trouble. If I overexerted myself, this wouldn't end well for either of us.

It was up to me to keep the veil up. If I didn't, my demons could get lost forever in the shadow world.

Suddenly, I heard one of my protectors calling out to me. It sounded like Morpheus.

I gathered the last elements and performed yet another spell.

It was now or never.

As I spoke the incantations, blood from my nose leaked onto the altar, but I wasn't going to give up.

Once Altair, Morpheus, and Dominik teleported back to Nebulae safely, I had to seal the veil and cut Shadow World's access off to Nebulae.

"Please let them be safe. Please let them be safe," I whispered under my breath.

Magnetic electricity from the moon orb scorched my fingertips. Pulling the energy from it, I called my demon protectors back to me, back through the veil.

Chaos rang through my head as if I was there. Angry growls from the rabid beasts that hunted after my demons tormented me. Ear-piercing screams from flying vultures as big as dinosaurs cut off my concentration. Thunderous marching from zombie foot soldiers running toward the rift I created sent panic straight through me.

"Oh, my God. Now. Where are you? Altair! Dom! Morpheus!" I screamed. They were supposed to have hopped the rift by now, but where were they?

I couldn't keep the shadow beasts out for long. It was only a matter of time before some of them jumped their way into Nebulae.

I struggled to breathe and the moon orb began to lose its light.

Suddenly, when I thought all was lost, my demon protectors hopped the rift, escaping through the veil.

I quickly chanted the incantation, zipping up the veil before anything else came back through.

On the white marble floors lay four breathing forms.

Altair. Morpheus. And Dominik.

The other white-haired old man in the black cape...I had no idea who the heck he was.

Morpheus and Dominik got up and dragged the old man in the black cape over to the altar.

"Drain him!" Dominik demanded.

"What!" I shrieked, frantically shifting my focus from the old man to Altair, who had not gotten up from the floor. "What's wrong with Altair?"

"He was hit. He's bled out," Morpheus said.

"No..." I mumbled. His once alabaster skin was now cloudy and dull gray. He looked almost—dead. His chest was moving...but barely.

Dominik grabbed me by the forearm and dragged me back to the altar. "This one has powers we need. Drain his cheesy ass. *Now*."

Sensing his impatience, I did as Dominik said, locking my gaze on the old man and blurting out the magic formula to steal one's powers.

The old man cracked and clutched his throat. "You will fail. You won't—" Frozen in time by my hypnosis, the man lost his ability to speak.

When the magic of this being was inside me, I halted the spell and threw myself upon Altair.

The old man struggled to right himself. "You bloody bastards. If you think you can win, think again. After all, your father knows best."

Dominik's stark-white fangs and pitch-black claws distended. He roared out in frustration and clawed the old man across the face, decapitating him. His head landed some ten feet across the room.

"We could've gotten that cheesy wizard to tell us more about father's plans? Why did you do that?" Morpheus bit out, pointing at the headless body.

"Because I felt like it," Dominik hissed between clenched teeth.

While they were fighting, I pumped Altair's chest over and over again, trying to get him to speak. His lips were cold. He wasn't breathing anymore.

Realizing that Altair was gravely injured, I screamed out in frustration, sending my magic haywire, destroying anything too weak to fend for itself and everything fragile inside the room—including my newly constructed moon orb, which shattered into dust.

Altair's cold hands came up to my face. "Told you that you could stop my heart."

His hand slumped down to the floor.

No. This couldn't be happening.

CHAPTER 20
Sadie

"YOU'VE OVEREXERTED YOURSELF, SADIE."

Morpheus placed a small cup of tea on a saucer on a dresser near the bed.

I left the cooling cloth on Altair's forehead to address Morpheus. "As long as he's getting better, that's all that matters."

Morpheus took my hand in his. "But that's not all that matters. If Altair knew you were going to do this to help him, he would've forbidden it."

"I only did what you all would do for me. I gave you all I had left. It's not like we can't get it back. I'm sure we can get it back," I said while trying to convince myself.

Morpheus sighed. "We brought that shadow magic back to you. You stole that wizard's magic so you could get what you wanted. To learn where your sister is. You used it all on Altair. He would've gotten better on his own. It would've taken much longer than we had, but he would've gotten better."

"Right. It would've taken much longer. Now that your father knows that you and your brothers can breach Shadow World anytime you want, they're going to be ready the next time. They know the decree has been reversed now that the wizard is dead. And possibly, they may even launch a counterattack. I don't want Altair compromised like that if that happens."

Morpheus shook his head. "It won't. You made sure of it. You sealed the veiled. None of the residents here have seen anyone from the Shadow world. We took a risk opening that veil, but because of your powers, we sealed it back up. The only way it will open again is if you open it."

I glanced over at Altair as he slept on the bed. "I don't know if I want to after all of this."

"Sadie, we're not on this quest to come out unscathed. Me and my brothers are very well aware that one or all of us may die bringing down my father."

My lips tightened in anger. "Now you know that wasn't part of the deal. You call me your future queen, but what am I to be the queen of if none of you are by my side?"

"Everything," he whispered.

Altair coughed in his sleep, disrupting our moment. His skin had healed over where the spear had pierced him right below the heart, but according to Dominik, he had internal injuries which would take longer to heal.

They could heal faster than any normal mundane, but they weren't invincible.

And the spears that were used to fight back weren't just regular spears. They were magically fortified for an army to lay waste to any supernatural force.

"In any case, we would never go into an all-out war, leaving you drained like this, vulnerable like this," Morpheus said.

"So, what will we do?"

"Dom and I will decide tonight whether one of us goes and one of us stays."

"But I don't want you to go back to the Shadow world alone. Your father will kill you, won't he?"

Morpheus nodded. "If we go back to Shadow world, he'll want to kill us, yes, but Shadow world wasn't what I was talking about."

"Then what are you talking about?" I asked, cautiously.

"Now that we're truly free to leave Nebulae, we have to search for loyal foot soldiers. We have to hunt down the horde we lost."

"Horde?" I whispered.

"Yes, Sadie. A demon horde to help us take down our father."

Suddenly, Dominik sauntered into the room. When he saw me tending to Altair still, he retracted his claws and folded his wings out of sight.

"How is he?" he asked.

"Better. Thanks to Sadie," Morpheus replied.

Dominik sat on the edge of the bed and held his palm out to me. "I fed from all the open rifts I could find. Take from me. You need your strength and Altair needs to wake up."

I swallowed. "Are you sure?"

"Yes. I can go out and try again later. Unfortunately, Nebulae isn't like the shadow world or earth, for that matter, where we can easily find a powerful source of energy."

"Okay..." I agreed, crossing my legs on the bed and taking his hand. I rose the other hand over Altair's heart.

As I was distributing the energy, something caught Morpheus's attention.

"Someone's on our doorstep," he said. "Continue. I'll go see who it is."

I completed the spell just as Morpheus drifted from the room to go see who had arrived.

"Are you okay?" Dominik asked, leaning over to kiss my forehead.

"Yes, I'm fine."

"Have you eaten today?"

"I have. Morpheus made me pancakes while you were gone." I smiled.

"Sorry. The last time I tried to bowl an egg in water, I made egg drop soupy-something with the cracked shells still inside it."

I burst out laughing. Leave it to my demons to lighten the mood. I needed that.

"Well, that makes two of us that needs to learn how to cook," I said.

Morpheus stuck his head back in the room. "Dom, come downstairs now."

"What is it?" I perked up.

"Sadie, you might want to stay up here. This will upset you."

Despite his warning, I slid from the bed at the same time as Dominik. "I don't care if it upsets me. What is it?"

Morpheus nodded toward the downstairs area. "Come."

I exited the room first, and Dominik followed closely behind me. Before I made it halfway down the stairs, Dominik took it upon himself to scoop me up, carrying me the rest of the way until we reached the first level. He did quite often. Maybe I was a little slow. Or maybe his strides were just too long. He took two to three steps at a time.

Both Dominik and Morpheus stood in front of me when we made our way outside to the courtyard, where there was a visitor. A male.

Apparently, Morpheus found it necessary to magically chain him to the water feature he stood next to so he couldn't leave.

I gasped when I recognize someone from Finn's inner circle. A lower male witch, who they called Reuben.

"Tell them what you told me," Morpheus demanded of Reuben.

Reuben's gaze drifted to me. He looked me up and down, and then at Dominik and Morpheus, who had morphed into their true demon forms, horns and all.

The look of discontentment on Reuben's face was rather telling. "You conspire with monsters now, Sadie?"

"No one gave you permission to question her." Dominik's bark thundered throughout the courtyard.

Reuben flinched before saying, "It's about what you did."

I met his accusing eyes. "What did I do?"

"You cut off access to the spirit world," he said.

I folded my arms across my chest. "Tell me something I don't already know."

"You didn't hear me, Sadie Carrier. You cut off access to the spirit world to everyone. *Everyone.*"

I gasped. "What?"

"That spell you did was powerful beyond measure. We felt the magnitude of it even on the earth realm. We know you did it to get back at Finn, but you have cut off a source of power from all the covens who have ever accessed it."

"That wasn't my intention."

Reuben jerked at the chains, causing my demon protectors to flinch, ready to attack if needed.

"In either case, Samson Wulfric, your betrothed, has also been notified of what you did. Finn demands that you stick to your side of the bargain. Or else."

Dominik growled. "You don't get to threaten her."

"I'm just the messenger," Reuben stuttered.

"Then why didn't Finn or this Samson come to say so himself?" Morpheus challenged.

Reuben lifted his chin.

"He's expendable," I answered for Reuben. "Finn wouldn't dare."

Reuben frowned. "The covens are mad, Sadie. And your betrothed feels rather humiliated and insulted that you would renege on your agreement. You'd better fix this. You'd better keep up your end of the bargain."

CHAPTER 21
Sadie

"SO, what will we do with that messenger boy?" Altair sat up in the bed.

I was happy to see him alive and alert. He was gaining his strength back by the minute. Even now, his essence dominated the room, almost overclouding the auras of his brothers. But that was Altair in a nutshell. He was older, and without a doubt, he was the most rational of the bunch.

Dominik was unpredictable, like me, so perhaps that was why I understood all of his faults.

Morpheus was level-headed and always calm under pressure. He would keep everyone from going batshit crazy. He would keep everyone from inflicting unprovoked violence just because we wanted to. But there was a side of Morpheus I hadn't seen. The side Altair warned me about weeks ago. I hoped we never saw that side because it would probably mean that all was lost and that we had lost.

"I say go out there and kill him. He's probably just a fucking distraction," Dominik said, waving his hand out at the courtyard.

"Leaving him chained up in the courtyard under the blistering sun with no food or water will kill him," Morpheus said.

"Well, leave him then," Dominik replied.

I sat back on the black velvet couch in the library while crossing my legs. "He's a messenger, so I say we send a message back."

Dominik shook his head. "You mean to send him back to earth. No way."

"I never said send him back to earth. I said send a message. There's a difference," I retorted. I snapped my fingers and produced a tiny slip of paper from thin air. I drew an ancient rune on the paper using magic and sent the paper over to Dominik using teleportation.

Dominik grinned as he caught the slip in mid-air. "I like how you think, love."

"That would only rile him up more," Morpheus offered.

"And the angrier he gets, the sloppier he becomes," Altair added.

"Then what about all these covens who claim they don't have access to the spirit world?" Morpheus inquired.

Dominik waved his hand again, dismissing the issue. "Fuck 'em. They'll get access when Sadie gives it to them. Finn is no rightful leader of any coven, and only Regents dictate access to the spirit world. Am I right or am I wrong, Sadie?"

Dominik surprised me with his knowledge of our chain of command. From this point up, I'd been schooling them about how the network of covens worked.

"You're right, Dom. There were twelve covens in our network, and my coven is the thirteenth and most powerful. In our world—mainly earth—witchcraft is a legitimate religion. The status entitles us to the same treatment as most churches, including the churches we protect. One Regent rules over a network of smaller and sometimes larger covens the very same way a king might rule over his country."

"Like your father was High Priest and Regent before he died," Morpheus added.

"Yes. My father was regarded as the prime power figure in our network. He was respected." No one missed the sadness in my tone. "So, yes, you're absolutely right. Access to the spirit world must be granted by the Regent. There is no standing Regent, for he is dead," I said, blinking away my tears.

"So, you were within your right to cut him off," Altair concluded.

I shook my head. "I don't lead my coven. I am no High Priest nor Regent."

"Neither is Finn," Altair countered.

"*Yet*," I added. "He wants to be both, not just Priest. I can see that now."

"It is custom for the offspring of such a figure to takeout after he or she dies," Morpheus said.

"That's not how it works. We have rules and customs. Finn has already grabbed the title of High Priest of our coven, and he's clearly on his way to declaring himself the Regent of Covens."

I frowned, swallowing down the bitter taste in my mouth.

"Is that not a title you would appreciate?" Morpheus asked.

"That's just not me. My sister maybe."

"But your sister is gone, and you are a Carrier. Your father was Regent," Morpheus replied.

"Of course I am, but that doesn't mean leading a coven is my fate," I argued.

"Your fate is to be our queen," Dominik stated loudly.

I hoped that was true. Why I favored being queen to demon protectors rather than a Regent of Covens was a mystery to me. But I felt strongly about it. My decision was made a long time ago.

"Then why should she listen to anything Finn has to say?" Morpheus asked. "If he's so big and bad and believes he should be Regent, he would be able to reverse the spell himself. He wouldn't have to send a messenger to beg our Sadie to do it for him. He is nothing. A non-issue. I agree with Dom. I say we stuff his messenger down a live volcano and wait for it to blow. That's the message we should send. A messenger bag of bloody, charred body parts."

I bit my bottom lip, contemplating the plan. "I know Finn. I've known him almost all of my life and yet he's become very sporadic. But if I'm guessing right, Finn makes the most mistakes when he feels that he's being ignored. Take, for example, those lizardfolk he sent to terrorize me. And now he sends Reuben here to threaten me into returning. It's obvious he's up to something big. Something bigger than stealing the Regent title. If we do nothing, he will make another mistake. I'll leave the barrier up over the spirit world for now. As a Carrier and my father's daughter, that is my right."

Altair propped his right ankle up onto his left knee and stroked his chin. "And what about this Samson dude?" His eyes met mine disparagingly. "Do we need to go fillet him?"

I exhaled sharply. "Other than demand that I marry him, he's done nothing wrong. I can't kill my blood. It's the worst thing I could ever do."

Dominik rose swiftly. "Then there's no more to discuss concerning either of these cowards. Send that messenger back down to earth. Tell them you belong to us. Tell them you will become our bride. *Bride of monsters.*"

CHAPTER 22
Sadie

I LAID in bed most of the next day with my journals and a pile of pillows around me. I was nervous as heck, thinking about how and when Finn might retaliate. Maybe this was why I wasn't fit to be Regent either. I was always questioning my decisions, hoping I made the right one.

It wasn't like I had my parents to talk it over with. Or my sister to argue with about this thing and that thing.

But I did have my demon protectors. And even though they saved me from myself and sacrificed their goals to keep me safe here in Nebulae, I'd protect them, too. I was prepared to do anything to keep our squad intact.

Even now, Altair slipped inside the room, bringing a sandwich with him.

"I brought you a snack." He set the tray on the nightstand.

I put my pen and journal down on the pillow next to me as Altair crawled onto the bed. "Thank you. But, I'm not very hungry."

"You need to eat. You haven't eaten all day."

"Well, neither have you."

His large weight made the bed sink as he propped himself up on his side on top of the sheets. "I'm good. I was out rift hunting all last night. It's Morpheus's turn."

The men were taking turns scouring Nebulae and feeding. They made it a point that one of them would always be here in case someone from Finn's group managed to teleport back here. Who knew what that idiot had up his sleeve? Yet, I wasn't afraid of him anymore. I wasn't afraid of anything. But my father always told me that people who feared nothing made stupid decisions. Had I made a stupid one in letting Reuben go back to Finn? Should I have had him killed?

"You are free to go outside of Nebulae. Why haven't you?" I asked.

He rolled over on his back and folded his arms behind his head. "I will. Dom has gone to the earthly realm already, but there was no sign of our horde there. We'll look again tomorrow. I think I'll go this time."

A knot rose in my throat. "I want you to be careful. Should I do a cloaking spell for you?"

"No. We can't hide anymore." He picked up one of my journals and flipped through the pages.

I smiled when I saw Altair looking through my notes. The skin on his forehead creased and wrinkled in confusion as he scanned my diagrams.

"I don't understand this," he said. "It's not English."

"No. It's an ancient underworld language. I was taught to use it to develop my spells. I sometimes translate them into English." I giggled.

"Hmmm. I will teach you shadow language one day. You will need it; most of my horde only understands that one language. And I want them to understand you."

I grinned and climbed on top of him. "Do you want to know what I need you to understand?" I licked my lips teasingly as he looked up at my body.

"Fuck, Sadie," Altair growled as I ground my hips down on his lap. I leaned down and kissed him while his cock stirred underneath me.

Likely unable to contain his dominance, Altair reached up and grabbed me by the back of my neck, his fingers curling into the hair at my nape. They tightened there, gripping me firmly and holding me in place.

"I want you to fuck me now and always, Altair," I whispered against his lips. "That's what I need you to understand."

"Then have all of me. Take what you need," Altair crooned into my ear as he moved his hand from my nape to run his thumb over my nervously bitten lips, parting them with his thumb, which he pushed into my mouth.

I sucked his digit, closing my eyes and imagining him coming on my tongue.

He let his hand drift down to my neck, clasping it tightly. I licked my lips and swallowed hard, my throat moving under his palm.

Suddenly, out of the corner of her eye, Dominik entered the room.

"Don't stop on my account," he said, inviting himself all the way inside and taking a seat on a bench in front of the bed. "I want to watch."

Cream spilled from my pussy onto Altair's groin as my arousal increased. Dominik opened up his pants, slipped his hand inside, and pulled out his meaty cock.

Letting out a moan, I massaged my pussy across Altair's hard shaft. Letting out a low growl, he flipped me onto the bed on my back, pinning me down into the mattress.

I wasn't wearing any panties underneath my long lace gown and as his swollen manhood brushed against my clit, I gasped with need.

As Altair laved at my neck, nipping at the tender skin there to leave a trail of light bruises right down to my spine, I kept my eyes fixed on Dominik, who was stroking his hard length slowly up and down.

My stomach clenched with desire at the sight and the knowledge that Altair and I were being watched by Dom and that he was taking voyeuristic pleasure in seeing us fuck.

Just like that, I couldn't wait any longer to feel Altair inside. Arching my back, I pressed my wet cunt against his cock.

In response, he grabbed a fistful of my hair and twisted until his fist was fixed against my scalp.

Altair entered me roughly, burying himself in as deep as he could all at once instead of easing himself in like he usually did.

I let out a high whine of pleasure. "Fuck me," I moaned as my blood rushed south, making my pussy heat and flush. A glance at Dominik experiencing equal pleasure made my whole body shudder with delight.

I held Dominik's gaze as Altair worked his massive cock within my hot sheath, bucking against me to send his cock deep. He built up a hard and punishing rhythm, fucking me roughly into the mattress. My whole body and the bed rocked in time with his thrusts.

Dominik squeezed himself harder, stroking his meaty flesh in time with Altair's plunges. The dual pleasure of being watched as I was fucked roughly made me delirious as I felt arousal rush through me like I had never felt before.

"Are you enjoying this, Sadie? Are you enjoying the way my brother watches as I fuck your cunt like this?" Altair moaned into my ear.

"Look at her face. Her fucking nipples are hard. She's going to come, brother. Fuck her harder," Dominik urged his brother from his seat.

I lowered my face into the sheets and bit into a pillow as Altair drove into me long and hard. My screams were muffled. My pussy clenched around Altair's monster cock, increasing the friction and pleasure.

Dominik was right on the edge of his orgasm, just like I was. And Altair's knot stirred deep in my sex.

I bucked up onto his cock eagerly, and as his tip pummeled the spot deep within me, I let out a scream that rocked the foundation.

As my orgasm hit me, the flesh between my legs pulsed uncontrollably. Altair tensed and his knot locked inside of me. He grunted out into the room, fucking me in shallower strokes as he flooded me with hot streams of cum.

Dominik moaned and neared his completion. Cum shot out of his tip into the air with the force of a volcanic eruption.

Altair was so spent he fell on the bed, taking me in his arms with his knot still buried deep inside me. And Dominik was so spent, that he never got up from the chair. He sat there panting.

Morpheus barged into the room right then. His shoulders slumped. "Looks like I just missed the show. *Fuck*."

CHAPTER 23
Sadie

MY DEMONS and I were in the courtyard enjoying the sun and fresh breeze. I had somehow convinced them all to stay with me today to rest together. For the past week, they had been traveling to different realms, trying to find out where their father had stashed the horde.

How could a person hide a horde of hundreds? That was the million-dollar question.

But when it came to supernaturals, anything was possible.

And my protectors believed with all their hearts that the horde still existed.

I propped myself up on the lounge chair, taking in each of my monsters. All three brought me happiness, but all together, the joy they instilled in me seemed immeasurable.

Dominik sat on the edge of the water feature, twirling his fingers around in the water. Altair lay on his back on a bench, reading from a book. And Morpheus was walking toward me with the most beautifully arranged bouquet I had ever seen. He must have picked them from the garden near the courtyard.

He handed me the bouquet and then sat on the ground next to my lounge chair.

"Thank you," I said, drawing in the light aroma from the buds.

"I've seen flowers like this on earth, but we don't have them in Shadow World," Morpheus said.

"I'm sure there are other beautiful flowers native to that realm," I said.

"When we take you there, you'll be the most beautiful flower of all," he replied.

I enjoyed this. Spending time with my monsters. It was nice to know that our relationship didn't have to always revolve around them, always having to protect me.

By now, I liked to think I was strong enough to protect myself.

I had magic now. And even if I lost magic, I knew how to get it back. Not to mention the fact that my demons were an endless source of power.

Something I would always be grateful for was how they renewed my confidence in myself.

I would never let them down.

No. I would fight for my demon protectors the same way they fought for me.

Dominik got up from the water feature and brought over a glass vase filled with water and I slipped the flowers inside and then placed it on the table next to me. Then he spread out on the ground right next to Morpheus and folded his arms under his head while he glanced up at the sky.

"We're going to take you to all the realms known to us," Dominik said.

"All of them?" I grinned. "I'd love that."

"Well, not all of them," Altair stated after putting down the book he read from. "I don't think she'd like what she will see beyond the Dark Gates, for example."

"What are the Dark Gates?" Something cautioned me not to ask, but I did it, anyway.

"The Dark Gates is another realm. It's a division of Hell, really. The King of Shadow World runs it and it's an eternal prison," Dominik replied.

"So, you have a prison for bad supernaturals. And here I thought both good and bad were allowed to run amok without consequences for their crimes," I said.

"Not at all."

"Well, ironically, the spirit world can be the resting place of both bad and good spirits. It's why the Regent dictates what comes from it...and sometimes what goes to it," I told them.

"Must be a hard decision," Altair replied. "Everything isn't all black and white these days."

A tall beacon of light broke through the atmosphere, hovering high above the courtyard.

My protectors sprung up instantly and were surrounding me before the light burst apart and revealed Reuben, yet again.

"You again!" Altair charged, blasting negative energy at Reuben, putting the messenger in chains, locking them around both his wrists and ankles until Reuben was kneeling on all fours like a dog in the courtyard.

"Once again," Reuben panted. "You have attacked the messenger."

"Because we're sick of you dropping in, asshole," Morpheus bit out.

Reuben shrank back. "Do you want to hear what I've got to say or not?"

"You'd better have a good reason," Dominik said as his eyes glowed a smoldering red.

"Look, do you think I want to be here? I am a messenger. That is all," Reuben stated.

"For Finn," I added.

"I am loyal to the High Priest. Have been ever since I pledged." Reuben looked much too smug, given the circumstances.

His implications concerning where his loyalties lie did not go unnoticed. Anyone other than Finn could act as High Priest and Reuben still would have complied.

"I've brought a message back from Finn," Reuben started.

"Then speak," Dominik commanded.

"He s-says you can have the whore. She's—"

Reuben didn't get to finish. Altair snapped him up and held him high in the air by the throat. All the color left Reuben's face as he clawed at Altair's massive hand, begging for breath.

Altair set him down on the ground, but still left his hand wrapped around the messenger's throat.

Reuben squealed out the rest. "In his words...he s-said...she can be a fucktoy for monsters."

Dominik retrieved his dagger from his waistband.

"Wait." I held up my hand, halting him from making quick work of Reuben. "What else did he say?"

"Samson is away on a trip. When he gets back and when your twenty-first comes, Finn says he'll want to collect," Reuben said.

"What does Finn know?" I grunted out.

Reuben coughed, still trying to get a little more air, while Altair clenched him around the neck. "In any case, Finn commands you, yet again, to drop the barrier into the spirit world."

"Sadie is not his to command." Bitterness sharpened Altair's voice. His fury rippled across the courtyard.

"T-then what would you have me tell him?" Reuben stuttered.

"That is exactly what you shall tell him," Altair affirmed.

My mind whirled and mixed emotions surrounded me.

"There's one more thing," Reuben quipped.

My head jerked up. My interest was piqued. "What?"

"He says your sister, Sydney, might be trapped in the spirit world."

"He's a lie," I whispered harshly.

"He's had visions of her succumbing to an awful fate. The covens have confirmed that she is not dead. But she is not safe either."

I gasped and my heart twisted. Air turned rancid and burned in my lungs. I doubled over. Morpheus came to my aid.

"I'm not lying about that, Sadie. Your sister is in trouble. When you cut off access to the spirit world, Finn stopped seeing things. You know he can see things. Things that have already happened. Even though he can't make sense of most of it, that's his power."

There was truth to what Reuben was saying. Finn always had the gift of hindsight, even if his abilities were undeveloped.

And I couldn't stop thinking about the vision I had where Sadie stood over a blue hole and fell into it. Even then, I knew what I saw had been a warning. Now, I couldn't help but think if it was maybe a cry for help from my sister.

I walked off to think and decompress, and all three demons followed me.

"You don't have to do anything suddenly or at that bastard's command," Morpheus consoled me.

"I know. But if my sister is stuck in the spirit world, this barrier will hinder any chance of her getting out. But if I drop the barrier, Finn will use the magic against me. I just know it."

"You don't have to succumb to Finn's tricks," Altair stated. "You don't need to work with him for anything. There's another way to gain access to the spirit world to find out if your sister is there."

I swallowed, looking on hopefully. "There is?"

After exchanging knowing looks with his brothers, Altair said, "Yes. And we'll have to take the Shadow throne to do it. We'll have to do it now. We cannot wait for my father to strengthen himself because I guarantee that is what he is doing while we search high and low for what he has concealed. We may have to do it without our horde."

My mind fluttered with anxiety. "But..."

Morpheus wrapped his arm around me. "The risk is great, Sadie, but the reward will be even greater."

"Okay..." I breathed and marched back over to Rueben, who still rubbed at the bruises on his neck.

"Tell me, Reuben...why does Finn want access so badly, huh?" I asked.

Reuben squeezed his lips together and he looked away. Altair caught him about the neck again, just like a snake would latch onto its prey's throat.

"Okay!" Reuben croaked out. "I'll tell you."

"Speak now." Dominik pushed the dagger about a half inch into Reuben's skin.

Reuben squealed out. "He's trying to reach someone there."

"Who?" I demanded.

Reuben shook his head. "*I don't know.* Not your sister. Someone else."

I shook my head, quickly going over in my head who Finn might be looking for. "Someone evil, probably."

Reuben's expression shifted. His duplicitous nature revealed itself, and his eyes were filled with reserve. There was something he wasn't telling us.

I huffed. "The last thing I'll do is open up the spirits to him to abuse just so he can unleash evil on earth for his gains."

His eyes pleaded in exasperation. "But what about the other covens? They need the magic housed there too."

"Where were all the covens when I needed their help? Where were they when I called for the formal investigation into my parent's death? They didn't care. So, why should I give them access to the spirit world—a magical abyss that my father kept open for their benefit?" I retorted, black ice chilling my veins.

Reuben blinked. "So, what should I tell Finn now?"

I looked behind me at my trio of protectors, who nodded. They were leaving the decision up to me.

I turned my attention back to Reuben.

Who did Finn think he was? *A god?* He was a back-stabbing clown and a fool. Plotted to take what doesn't belong to him. Conspired behind me and my sister's back. Sent his mother to kill my innocent aunt.

My anger was building up inside and I couldn't hold it in any longer.

"So, what is your decision?" Reuben pressed, shrinking back from Altair's murderous stare.

"Tell him to go take a jagged tree branch and shove it up his ass!"

With that, I used my magic to blast Reuben back to the earth, wiping my hands of any hold Finn ever held over me.

Who's the bad witch now?

CHAPTER 24
Altair

AS SOON AS my boots touched the molten hot ground just outside the gates of Shadow World, I re-formed from the mist into my true form—my demon form.

Morphing into the beast revved up my adrenaline and gave me the stamina I needed to slay monsters who were just like me. Well, not exactly like me. The blood of an ancient ran through my veins and these devils clawing at me, trying to keep me away from the throne, were less than vermin.

My brothers, Dominik and Morpheus, fought alongside me. Their need for vengeance was just as great as mine. I felt their energy almost quadruple as we made our way across the land.

Thanks to Sadie, we had all the time we needed to find my father's ass and give him what he deserved—a merciless death fit for a back-stabbing king.

Sadie no longer had to stand by to close the veil, because when my brothers and I breached Shadow World, we knew there was no going back. We didn't tell Sadie, but we either planned to conquer or die.

The latter, dying, would not suffice. We had to protect Sadie. That meant one of us had to stay alive—if it came to that.

We were warriors. Bred to fight battles. So, even if it didn't happen tonight, it would happen one day.

Otherwise, why would fate bring three protectors to Sadie?

She was special. Her gifts and powers knew no bounds—and if there were limits, we would overcome them.

Still, to this day, we hadn't even touched the surface of what Sadie could do with her magic.

I liked to think we had an eternity for that.

My claws distended. I backhanded a demon mutt so hard across the face, that the thing toppled and flipped numerous times across the rocky ground before plowing into a pack of his fellow mutts. After its sudden death, I reaped its soul, shredded it into pieces, and consumed the energy it generated. And when his mutt pack came for me all at once, I blasted them with a fireball. Their body parts and chunks of flesh rained down from the air and landed on the ground.

I looked to the left of me, where Morpheus took his axe and chopped a Grugger in half. Green goo pooled out from its torso and slid from his sword after the kill.

The further we advanced toward the castle where the throne sat, Sadie's power seemed to wane. But she got us up to this point. The barrier she held up around us so that no more than a dozen foot soldiers at a time could breach had gotten us this far. We knew we would be outnumbered, so we had to be strategic about this and Sadie came through with her ideas.

"Brother, behind you!" Dominik yelled. He tossed me a dagger and I spun around, catching the weapon and burying it into the slimy vulture that tried to attack me from overhead.

"We're almost there," Morpheus called out, pointing at the castle where some of our father's guards stood unmolested and waiting. "Father will answer for his crimes."

We fought like that until we reached the steps and the demon guards who were protected by their swords and body armor.

Morpheus started to engage them in a battle. "Go!" He shouted. "I'll hold them off. Go inside. Find father."

"Come on, brother." Dominik rushed forward before I could warn him. As soon as he yanked the doors open, three demonic witches blasted him back with a spell.

Bloody Hell.

CHAPTER 25
Dominik

MY HEART STOPPED the moment those three bitch witches blasted me to the ground. I fought against their dominant magic, but something worked to hold me frozen in time.

My blood boiled inside me, but it wasn't my doing.

These witch bitches were trying to fry us from the inside out.

I doubled over in agony and tried to reach for the small dagger on my waistband to stab one of them.

They chanted old ancient magic in the shadow tongue. They were trying to kill us, right there, on the spot.

Probably on my father's orders.

He would never fight us. He wasn't that kind of king.

He used his treachery and callousness. He wasn't a warrior king like my brothers and I were prophesied to become.

Suddenly, I heard Sadie's voice in my head. Although she wasn't here during the battle, she was always at the forefront of my mind. I had once given up on chasing after my father just to say that I avenged my mother, who secretly hated me. My brothers couldn't even convince me to join their fight. But then there was Sadie. She was my reason. She would always be my reason to keep on fighting.

Renellus Tutema. Mourir Auxala.

Sadie's voice was in my head. She was reciting a spell.

Renellus Tutema Asime!

"Dominik, find your strength and grab your blade. Hurry. My hold in this place is waning."

I found the strength to do as she commanded, lifting my dagger. There was no way I could kill anyone. I was stripped of my own free will. So was Altair. He couldn't move an inch.

The blade shifted around in my hand. It sailed out of my fingers and into the heart of the first witch.

Hexe mourir Asime! Sadie continued her incantation.

Mourir meant death. Sadie had called for death to the witches. And drop dead, they all did.

My brothers and I were released from the spot and we pushed forward into the castle to find it almost devoid of any soul.

Only a few guards tried to stop us from getting into the throne room.

Once we breached the room, we expected our father to be sitting there waiting for us, as he always did, to remind us that his word was the final law, but he was gone.

On the throne was a blood-stained note. He had just left it. The ink was still wet.

It read: *My sons. I will never allow you to kill me. I could never allow it.*

Beside me, Altair roared out in frustration, snatched the note from me, and ripped it to shreds.

I understood his pain. I saw the same visions he did. Visions of our mothers with their throats slit and cast into hellfire.

"What does he mean by he could never allow it?" Altair screamed out. "*Bloody bastard.* I will find him. I will put my fist down his throat and pull out his heart and feed it to the vilest dogs!"

Altair threw a stone piece across the room. He trashed the room in reckless anger. A pool of liquid gathered in his eyes. He turned away from us to hide his pain.

"*Coward,*" Morpheus spat. "Where is he? Where is that coward?"

Suddenly, small foot patterings echoed on the stone floor behind us.

In shock, we all spun around.

It was Sadie. Standing there in the flesh, limping along, exhausted from overexerting herself.

"Sadie, what are you doing here?" Morpheus and I ran to her aid. "We told you not to follow."

"I had to," she whispered. "I wanted to go where you go."

The thought that she would put her actual self out into dangerous situations to be with us bothered me. Our Sadie wasn't afraid anymore. *That terrified me.*

Blood was smeared under her nose and remnants were on the back of her hand where she had wiped it off. That told me all I needed to know about the trouble she went through to get here with us.

"Sadie...we could've been killed...and you would have no protectors here...you..." I said.

I didn't get to finish my words. Sadie's knees gave out from under her and we had to catch her fall.

Just before passing out, she muttered, "No one will ever hurt you. I will not allow that either."

CHAPTER 26
Sadie

MAINTAINING two households had never been easy, but that was exactly what I and my demon squad decided to do. Well, sort of.

We couldn't leave the Shadow world vacant or else their father might try to come back to take over. Or worse, some other power figure might try to come in and steal the throne from them.

Altair and Dominik were with me in Nebulae settling matters here. They were still seen as leaders in this realm and the realm couldn't exactly run itself.

Morpheus was back in Shadow world. A group of hordesmen had already pledged their loyalty to the brothers, so Morpheus had backup if he needed it. Plus, we wouldn't stay in Nebulae for long. We planned to join him soon in the Shadow world, where I would be surrounded by all the magic I needed. It was almost too good to be true.

As Altair and Dominik spoke with all the leaders of each group on Nebulae, I poked through the refrigerator, looking for something to eat. Humans and human food were hard to come by in the Shadow world. Most of what I ate there, I had to manifest with magic. It looked like I'd be doing a lot of teleporting in the time being. I wasn't going to give up ice cream, that was for sure.

As I was licking the container, trying to get the last drop of chocolate from the bottom of the carton, the telltale familiar signs that something or someone was teleporting here sparked up in the kitchen.

I rolled my eyes and sighed.

Yet, I prepared myself to cast magic in case someone brought trouble with them.

I grumbled when no one other than Reuben the messenger folded out in front of me.

But he wasn't alone.

Hog-tied up like an animal and muzzled like a dog, Finn struggled on the ground at his feet.

Annoyance filled my body like petulant violence. I held my hand up, prepared to blast them straight back to earth without question, but he protested.

"Wait! Wait, wait. I came on my own."

"What fuckery are you trying to pull?" I dropped the ice cream carton and stepped back.

My squad must have sensed my panic because they sprinted into the kitchen.

"What! Don't kill me!" Reuben pleaded, getting down on his knees next to Finn, who thrashed from side to side on the marble floor, trying like hell to break free.

Suddenly, Altair picked Finn up from the floor and tossed him like a sack of the vilest shit at the wall. With a thud, Finn's body collided with the wall and slammed onto the floor.

Finn grunted and passed out cold immediately.

"You're next!" Altair barked out, causing Reuben to reel backward. "You keep coming here freely, bastard. You are a threat to our queen."

Reuben held up his hands in front of his face. "Look! I brought him to you. The covens don't want him."

"If you're trying to trick us..." Dominik warned.

"No, why would I? Why would I even come here with him if I were trying to do that?"

I placed a hand on my hip. "You keep showing up at inopportune times, Reuben. This is not a realm you want to fuck around in."

"I told you. I'm a messenger."

I frowned. "This isn't a message."

"No, it's not. It's a statement." His eyes drifted to where Finn remained hog-tied and unmoving.

"A statement and a fluke of a man tied up like a pig," Dominik added.

"Don't shoot the messenger," Reuben pleaded. "I realized I cannot win against you, Sadie. You may have abandoned us for your demons, but I cannot get behind him."

I smiled. "You know you'll probably be burned for this, right?"

Reuben visibly swallowed. "I don't plan on going back to the covens. I renounce my privileges, my vows...everything."

"Looks like he knows when to jump from a sinking ship," Altair noted.

Reuben said nothing. He only looked sheepishly at the floor.

"What do you want?" I asked. "There's always a motive."

He shivered. "I told you. I don't want to be on the losing side."

Altair grinned. "You've already lost." Then he grabbed Reuben by the arm and began dragging him out of the mansion.

"Wait! Where are you taking me?"

"Have you ever heard of the Dark Gates, my traitorous friend? That is where you're going. It will be your new home." Altair spoke as he pulled Reuben further out of the home.

"Noooooo! Sadie, save me from your demons!"

A series of slaps to the face by big demon hands woke Finn right up out of his sleep. As soon as he realized the state of affairs, he cried out for help and jerked against the chains binding him to the stone table.

"Hello there, sleepyhead," Morpheus greeted him.

"What are you doing to me? Where am I?" He cursed under his breath, and then his gaze caught mine. "You treacherous slut! How could you?"

"Call her a slut again and I promise you'll be nothing but shreds of flesh on this table when I get done with you," Dominik warned him, jamming his claws into Finn's side.

"This is no more than you deserve, Finn," I said. "You were going to kill me."

"Sadie, please...you don't understand. I'll do anything. I take it all back. Just let me go."

Finn was scared shitless of the demons. But of course, he had never seen a monster in the flesh. He only talked of them and banished them in spirit. My father and the Elders had done a perfectly good job of keeping the young people out of dangerous situations, so we never saw the dark side of things. But I wish I had. I might have been better prepared for everything.

"There is no escaping now, you murderous bastard. You're going to pay for what you did," Altair said. "Thanks to your two-timing messenger, you'll finally meet the end you deserve."

"Oh, my God. Fucking bitch. My mother is probably tracking me now. You'll never get away with this," Finn warned, tugging so hard against the chains that his wrists bled.

Dominik laughed out loud. "For real? You're calling mommie now. Well, mommie can't help you. You've gotta answer to your own sins. And she has to answer to hers."

Finn pointed a finger but couldn't lift his arm. "If you touch a hair on her head…"

Altair's lips thinned in fury. "You never seem to put your money where your mouth is, but allow us to show you how."

I walked around to the head of the stone table, making it a point to tug at the metal so it would tighten across his torso. "Hmmm, should I drain you dry?" I used magic to open up a six-inch gash down his side.

"Sadie, please..." Finn pleaded.

"Or maybe I'll just stone you to death?" My magic created an illusion of stones toppling down over him. He jerked on the table and screamed.

"Oh wait." I pretended to think. "I'll just drown you." As if his personal hell was reality, Finn began choking and spitting up water.

He heaved dramatically when I ceased tormenting him.

"It's no fun being on the receiving end of torture, is it?" I asked.

He shook his head violently.

"But too bad. Your torture is justified."

"What do you mean? I'm not the one who agrees to a betrothal and then sleeps with beasts," he spat.

"I never agreed to that betrothal. My father thought it was best, but if he were alive today, he would never make me go through with it. And you're the only one pressing the issue. Samson is nowhere to be found. And when he decides to show up, I'll tell him again—I'll never marry him. *Ever*."

"Doesn't matter one way or another to me," Finn shot back begrudgingly.

"And you lied. You said my sister was stuck in the spirit world."

"I-I-I thought she was," he stuttered.

"You thought?"

"It's complicated. You know better than me that magic complicates things. There was a touch of her essence in the spirit world. The coven Elders told me so."

I bit my tongue, hashing it over. The coven Elders would have no reason to lie about Sydney being in or having been in the spirit world. But if she wasn't there, where was she?

Altair jammed a knife against Finn's throat. "Tell her who you're hunting down in the spirit world."

Finn laughed. "Reuben told you that, didn't he? That untrustworthy dysfunctional prick. He switched sides like a twisted snake."

Altair broke Finn's skin with the knife and Finn gasped. "I'm not telling you anything."

"Kill 'em," Morpheus said sharply.

"No. No. No. Okay, okay." Finn's words came out in a rush. "Not a who. But a what."

"What then?"

"The moon orb, of course."

I rolled my eyes. "Here we go again with this shit. You said you didn't need the orb."

"Turns out I do. It's more important than you realize," he shot back.

"Not to me. Not anymore," I retorted back.

"But of course. You've sold your soul and your body to three devils like a common whore. Wouldn't your daddy be proud?"

This time, I was the one who slapped him across the face. His insults hurt like hell, but I wouldn't let his words get to me anymore.

My body still seethed with mounting rage. "You don't know what you're talking about, you sadistic freak."

"You're right. I know no more than you do. But I know who might be able to help you follow in your sister's footsteps." His lips spread in a grimy smile.

"I don't trust you."

"You shouldn't. I tried to kill you, remember?"

"What do you know?" I demanded.

"You have to promise not to kill me," he said, testing me with a frail stare.

I folded my arms across my chest. "Okay."

"And them?" Finn glared directly at my squad.

"They do too," I said quickly.

Dominik grunted. Altair huffed. And Morpheus sighed heavily. I guess I had just taken the fun away from them.

"On the day your sister disappeared, she met with a certain drug lord vampire on the other side of town," Finn said.

My soul sunk into my belly and the breath rushed right out of me. "A v-vampire?" This time, it was my turn to quake at the knees.

My demon squad sensed my anxiety and they crowded around me.

"What vampire?" I asked.

"Guess who knows more about the vampire drug lord than you or I?" Finn's eyes held a mischievous gleam. "She's an orphan. She's a traitor. And she got your auntie killed."

"Mika!" I gasped.

"Bingo." A callous grin stretched across Finn's face. Dominik, who was probably fed up with seeing the bastard grin like an evil freak, punched him in the face.

Several teeth fell into Finn's mouth and he nearly swallowed them. He spat out blood and bits of broken teeth.

"Come on," Altair said, wrapping his arm around my waist. "Enough of this. It's time to go."

"Wait, let me out of here," Finn demanded.

"Not a chance, you stupid fuck," Morpheus called out over his shoulder as we all left.

"But you said you'd release me..." The chains rattled as Finn fought against them.

"We said we wouldn't kill you. We never said we would let you go," Altair corrected.

"*Oh, no*...you fucking monsters. Demon-fucking bitch. Cunt whore. Scourge of the world. Vermin of Hell..." He called out every name in the book at us. *"Come back here..."*

Altair slid the door to the Shadow world dungeon shut, cutting out the noise.

Once outside, I pressed my back against the wall. "This is so draining. And Finn is the most aggravating of all," I said.

"Don't worry about him. He'll stay locked up in there until he rots, if you will it," Altair said, leaning in and kissing my forehead.

On the other side of me, Morpheus pushed my hair off my face and kissed the other side of my face.

I pulled them both close to me, returning their kisses. I could tell Dominik was feeling a little left out, so I pulled him between us and gave him a lengthy kiss.

"You three are my peace after the storm. My saving grace. I needed you."

"And we needed you," Altair added.

"There's one other thing we wanted to ask. Well, tell you and ask you." Morpheus said. "We might as well get it over with now because in a few short hours, it'll be another day."

I blushed. "Well, what is it?"

Dominik's mouth curved in an unconscious smile. "Happy twenty-first birthday, Sadie."

My lips broke off into a wide smile.

Morpheus reached in and slipped his arm around my waist. "And will you be our bride?"

CHAPTER 27
Morpheus

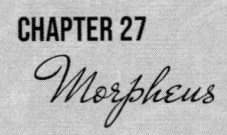

I WAITED for this moment for what seemed like an eternity.

Always knowing my queen would eventually be revealed to me, I held out hope as long as I could. Almost until I lost it. And then one day, a courageous girl summoned me to protect her...and the rest was history.

Sadie, our future queen and bride, came down the spiral staircase dressed in a long black see-through gown made of silk and lace. She was exquisite and wore the garment like the eloquent goddess she was.

Altair and Dominik flanked me as we waited at the bottom of the stairs for her. Something explosive was in order. This was a night I hoped she would remember forever.

When she reached us, I could tell she was nervous. All eyes were on her.

Despite her nerves, she went from one of us to the next, gifting us with a soul-stealing kiss on the lips.

"You look beautiful," I said, giving her more than a quick once over.

The cut of the dress left more than enough of her olive-toned, smooth skin for us to admire.

"Yes, she is exquisite," Dominik agreed.

"We have something for you." Altair handed me the ring box and I opened it in front of her.

Her eyes widened in surprise. "It's lovely."

I slide the ring on her index. "It's a mood ring. Almost like the necklace you wore. An engagement ring of sorts. Made from diamonds exported from the Shadow world. When the time comes and when you become our queen, we'll gift you with another."

"It's so pretty. There are three diamonds." She grinned.

"One from each of us," Dominik said.

She sighed and looked toward the window. Night had just fallen and she knew exactly what that meant.

When the moon reached its highest peak, she, too, would crest. That moment would be when her magic would be most potent.

I had abstained this whole time so I could be with her in that moment for the first time like I had always intended when she first summoned us for protection.

"Come." Dominik took her hand. "We have a bed waiting under the moon window."

As soon as we reached the library, which was fixed in the center of the mansion, she walked seductively over to the bed. We didn't need to instruct her and watched as she kicked off her stilettos and kicked them aside.

I was already aroused and ready to take her sweet pussy and I knew Altair and Dominik were, too.

She licked her lips. "Well, what are you three waiting for? The moon is cresting and I want to fuck."

She was wicked, and I loved it.

Without hesitating, we joined her, removing our clothes as we took turns kissing her soft lips. Her skin was even softer, and I took great care, caressing all the curves of her body.

She was just so perfect.

I was happy to share her with my brothers.

She deserved all three of us.

Altair leaned down between her legs and parted her thighs. Her sex glistened and he dove right in with his tongue, causing her to cry out in need. I sampled her honey too, and we traded off like that, eating her until she was drenched and raw.

Her thick slick was extra potent tonight. She smelled of honeysuckle flowers and English lavender. Among her people, it was prophesied that she would bear multiples for her mate. There was one thing they couldn't predict. They never predicted that she would be bred by multiple mates and bred multiple times. The time would come for her to become a mother. But right now, it was time for pleasure.

Sadie must have sensed my impatience. She lifted her legs over me and straddle my thighs until she was sitting on me. I folded up in the bed so that my chest touched her swollen breasts.

Altair and Dominik were at her back, kissing and nipping on her neck, lifting her hair so I could see the way they bruised her.

She was sopping wet and both of my cocks found her openings with ease. She grabbed the back of my neck, biting her lips. The hesitation on her face told me she was overthinking this.

I leaned in and kissed her. "Open your eyes, Sadie. Look at me."

She opened her eyes. Her emerald-colored gaze mesmerized me and I wanted to get lost in them forever. Just like her eyes, her body gleamed and shined majestically. Sweat peppered her skin as Altair and Dominik stroked her body until she was convulsing above me.

I grabbed her by the hips, placing my cockheads right where I wanted to fuck her. "Now, Sadie," I whispered in her ear.

Just as the moonbeam, her magic started to crest. She pressed her lips firmly against mine and sat down on both of my cocks until her pussy and ass were filled with me.

We all groaned as white-hot magic and powerful energy filled the room.

"Fuck him, Sadie," Altair groaned.

"That's right, Sadie. Fuck him just like that," Dominik urged, holding her ass and guiding her up and down my two thick cocks.

Everything intensified in a matter of minutes. Soon, Sadie was pumping up and down on my cocks with her breasts bouncing in my face.

"Fuck, fuck, fuck," I moaned. "Oh, fuck." I couldn't hold out any longer. I was going to explode inside her. The way her tight cunt squeezed me like a glove sent me reeling in ecstasy.

As my cocks knotted, she fucked her pussy deeper down my shaft. I locked inside of her and saw the moon and stars in her eyes. She came violently and the entire library shuttered. Nothing was safe from her erotic outburst of energy.

She threw her head back and called my name. In that instant, I came inside her—hot, hard, and heavy.

Dropping her head onto my shoulder, she bit down into my neck with her tiny human teeth. She marked me.

"*Ah*, God...Morpheus...that was so good," she panted.

"It was," I breathed.

Altair and Dominik helped her come down from her high and then they started kissing on her again, sending her back into a world of pleasure.

This went on all night. Altair, Dominik, and I took turns fucking her. We fucked her until we had nothing left inside to give her.

To me, it was all worth the wait.

Epilogue
SADIE

IT SEEMED I didn't know as much about Mika as I thought, and neither did Aunt Naima. Or maybe she did and was only trying to protect the girl from herself all along.

The only place I could think to look for Mika was at Naima's shop.

I knew it had been over a month since Naima's shop was set on fire with her still inside, but I didn't expect to see another shop sitting right in the parking.

It all seemed very strange. Surely, someone couldn't have set the shop back up this quickly. But the little mobile trailer was there, sitting in the same place. There were even burn marks in the parking lot and the trees were black from being scorched.

Instead of a sign that read Naima's Boutiq, the black and gold sign had been changed to Prism Apothecary.

What the hell? What the fuck was this all about?

Morpheus slipped his hand around my forearm. "I sense someone inside that trailer."

"Everything's changed. I wonder who opened another shop here. This was Naima's property. This couldn't have happened so fast," I said.

"We can check it out." Dominik looked around. He was always wary of his surroundings.

This wasn't the first time we had been to earth together since taking back the Shadow world. Most of the time we had come for other things like finding out what the coven was up to now that Finn was still in a Shadow world prison and hunting down the location of the powerful demon horde Altair and his brothers lost when they were exiled to Nebulae.

And the brothers were also tirelessly looking for their father, who had hurt them so much, they wanted to see him suffer the same way. I felt bad for them. Much like them, I was betrayed by a family member, but not by someone that close. I couldn't imagine what it would feel like to have been betrayed by a mother or father.

There wasn't a car or anything in sight in the parking lot, so I wondered if there was actually someone in the trailer, but Morpheus's instincts had never been wrong.

I broke off from the brothers, leading the way.

Before I could get within twenty feet of the steps, Altair stopped me. "Wait. I smell blood."

I frowned. "Blood?"

"You're not going in there," Altair stated.

I sighed. "Well, I'll just see what's inside." Before he could say another word, I blasted the door of the shop open with magic, fully prepared to deal with the consequences that it caused later.

But I didn't expect to see the horrific sight in front of me.

Mika, with her long braids hanging loosely, hovered over a body and appeared to be sucking blood from a person's neck. The person's body was still warm with life. They were alive, but barely.

"The fuck?" I mouthed.

My demon squad shifted in front of me as Mika looked up with blood all over her mouth and fangs as long as a vampire's.

Vampire...

Mika was a vampire.

She hissed and then popped up until she stood upright. After wiping her mouth with the back of her hand, she kicked the drained person aside, who was now dead.

Mika turned and raced further inside the trailer. I broke off from my demons and ran behind her. They followed.

"Mika! Stop!" I ordered.

She spun around, blood dripping from her mouth. "Leave me alone, Sadie."

"What happened to you?"

"What does it look like?" she hissed. "I'm transforming."

"T-transforming?" It meant she had died. To become a vampire, one had to die. "How did this happen?"

"Take a wild guess," she taunted hotly.

"Mika...I'm so sorry." She must've been so scared and alone after what had happened to Aunt Naima.

"Well, I'm not. And I see you're not either." She pointed. "How dare you bring those demons in here?" She hissed at them.

It was a known fact. Demons and vampires weren't on good terms. I couldn't even remember a time when they were.

"I..." I stuttered. I didn't know what to say. This caught me off guard. I came here for answers, but *this* was what I got.

"Well, what the fuck do you want, bitch?" Mika blurted out. "I've gotta go."

"Mika...are you just gonna leave that dead body here? Did you kill that girl?" I looked at the graying corpse she had so carelessly drained and kicked aside.

Mika frowned and started backing away. Her eyes were blood red, but not like my demons. She looked wild and savage.

Her lips trembled. "I was so hungry."

"She's rabid," Morpheus offered.

"No, I'm not," Mika snapped.

I took a step forward.

Mika picked up a book and threw it at me. "Stay away. Or I'll kill you."

Altair caught the book in mid-air and morphed out. One thing was sure, my demons didn't take threats likely and they certainly didn't take threats to my life very well, either.

"I just want to talk to you," I said.

"I didn't mean for her to die. I swear it. The fire...and..." Mika panted. "It was too late."

She was talking about Aunt Naima.

"Me neither, Mika. I shouldn't have been here. It was partly my fault, too."

She pointed at me. "You caused this."

"Mika, I'm trying to do everything to fix this."

"How can you fix this? My mom is dead!"

She was right. Death was final. There was no way we could bring Aunt Naima back, but there was a way for us to stop further tragedy from happening.

"I came to ask you about my sister. Did you see her meeting with a drug lord—a *vampire* drug lord—on the night she disappeared?"

That seemed to set Mika off, and that only made her angrier. Her fangs distended, and when I glanced over in the mirror, I saw that my demons had morphed out as well. Their fangs were distended, too.

Wait a minute! Mirror?

I glanced to my left, and to my surprise, the same mirror I saw in the shop when I came to ask for Naima's help was the same mirror that was standing there now.

Had it survived a fire? How could that be? And even so, had someone replaced the glass?

"Please don't make any sudden moves, okay?" I was afraid for her. The last thing I wanted my demons to do was hurt her.

She hissed.

I looked around the room. Sure enough, Naima's shop of trinkets, odds, and ends had turned into an apothecary. Medicinal bottles lined the walls. Much of the items from the old shop were still untouched by fire in this new shop.

"Mika, how did some of this stuff survive the fire?"

Mika looked around, just as confused as I was. It was as if she were out of it—high on some type of drug or hallucinogen that caused her to act strangely.

"I—I don't know. I just picked up what was left over in the ashes and brought it in here. I don't know anything about your sister. It's her fault if she's missing. She's the one who begged me to take her to see the drug lord. And now look at me! They told me the pills would make me better...make me forget what I saw when I saw my mom burned...but they lied. I took those pills like they said, and *I died.*"

I swallowed.

"I woke up in an alley and...I was so hungry." She clutched her belly.

"Why did you trade me to Finn and his mother?" I asked.

Her eyes started to water. "I had to pay some very bad people back. I didn't know they would do this. They said they just want to talk to you. That you stole something."

They had lied to Mika, just like they lied to me.

"I need you to take me to this drug lord," I told her.

"No!" Altair bit out.

"No," Mika said tersely at almost the exact moment as Altair.

Apparently, no one wanted me to win.

Mika shook her head. "No. I can't. They'll kill me."

Impatience seized my body. "You leave me no choice but to—"

Before I could call my magic, Mika dove behind a counter at the speed of light and grabbed a crystal ball. I had seen Naima use the crystal ball frequently to fuel her spells. Before I could stop her, Mika hurled the ball at my monsters as they tried to block her attempts to harm me.

The crystal ball shattered and broke. A large plume of smoke billowed up into the air and then floated toward the ancient mirror where the essence faded into the glass. The only two people left standing when the dust cleared were Mika and me.

And my demons...?

Altair. Morpheus. Dominik. *They were gone.*

"What have done?" My vision clouded over. All I saw was red as realization dawned on me that my men were nowhere in sight.

Mika's eyes widened and she started backing up and tripping over things.

She wasn't paying attention as she searched for an escape and fell backward over a black cat with green eyes, landing on her ass.

"Stupid fucking cat!" She got up and kicked the cat. The cat shrieked out in pain the moment it hit the opposite wall.

When I looked up again, Mika had already kicked open the backdoor. She used her vampire magic to shift out of sight.

A deadly silence filled the room when she was gone.

Everyone was gone.

I walked over to the mirror, but this time when I looked into the glass, there was no reflection staring back at me. "What—?"

Something soft brushed up against my ankles. I looked down to see the black cat stroking my leg with its body and purring. It looked up at me with its green eyes.

"Loki?" I whispered.

It purred.

I bent down to pick him up and hugged him tightly in my arms.

"Altair?" I called out. "Dominik. Morpheus. Come to me. Please."

No answer.

Just like that. *They were gone.*

***

Thank you for reading HER BROKEN BEASTS.

I hope you enjoyed Her Broken Beasts, the 1st book in the Shadow World Series. This is just the beginning for Sadie and her protectors. This is the first book in a planned trilogy.

The story continues in Bride of Monsters with answers to some of your questions, more character conflicts, some surprising revelations, and new adversaries. ;) And it's already out!

***

Message from Amber Ella Monroe

Thank you for reading HER BROKEN BEASTS.

If you enjoyed the story, don't forget to leave a review and tell others what you loved about it. Even a couple sentences about what you liked can say a lot.

·Visit Amber Ella Monroe on the web at <u>amberellabooks.com</u>.

SIGN UP FOR MY NEWSLETTER

If you enjoy romance with an edgier side, subscribe to Amber Ella's newsletter at http://smarturl.it/amberellas-list, and be one of the first to be notified of new releases, current contests, giveaways, and book-related news.

For paranormal romance novels, visit Amber Ella Monroe on the web at <u>http://amberellabooks.com</u>

About the Author

USA Today Bestselling Author Amber Ella Monroe pens seductive tales of paranormal romance. She also writes contemporary romance as Ambrielle Kirk. As a child, she never really dreamed of being an author. It was a destined path that chose her. Now she writes with her readers in mind, but the characters, of course, dictate the outcome.

Visit her website at http://amberellabooks.com if you enjoy romance with an edgier side or subscribe to her newsletter at http://smarturl.it/amberellas-list.

Sarah Wagner and

In August 2019, Sarah and Kate fou   ... *Today*, a community to share the lessons they have learned from their early career. Their aim is to encourage and support young ambitious women to unleash their full potential in the workplace by letting go of social conditioning and self-doubt. Determined to help the next generation of female professionals to rock their careers from day one, Kate and Sarah have written this self-help book as a graduation gift for you.

Over the course of the past year, *Unleash Today* developed into a global movement with an international team of twenty-nine members, spreading from Brazil to China, and ranging from marketing experts to editing specialists. Next to the book, the team offers motivational classes and webinars available on www.unleashtoday.com. In the course of 2021, the book will be followed by online courses to empower women from across the globe to discover their inner-confidence and unleash today!

UNLEASH TODAY

Sarah Wagner and Kate Surala

First published in 2021

Copyright © Sarah Wagner and Kate Surala

Sarah Wagner and Kate Surala have asserted their right as the authors of this Work in accordance to with the Copyright, Designs and Patent Act 1988

ISBN 979-8-6828-7064-6

This is from Sarah and Kate to you:
May you rock your first impression,
May you beam with confidence,
May you be freed from perfect standards,
May you network like a star,
May you love yourself,
May you smile at all conflicts you face,
May you step outside of your comfort zone; and
Unleash Today

Contents

How to Unleash Today.. 1
The Authors 3
How to Get the Most out of this Book 6
Embarking on Your Self-Discovery Journey 8
Your (W)Inner Compass 9
Your Bold, Authentic, Female Self 19
Unleash Today Challenge: Defining Your (W)Inner Compass. 24

Step One: Hello, Here I Am! 27
An Introduction 29
Your Appearance 31
Power Pose 34
Nonverbal Communication 37
Dress Code and Hair 43
Language and Tone 48
Mastering Your First Weeks 52
Other Tips to Unleash in Your Workplace 59
Unleash Today Challenge: How to Make a Grand Entrance ... 64

Step Two: Strengthening Your Confidence Muscle.. 69
An Introduction to Confidence 71
Hard Work and Resilience 74
Change Your Attitude: Raise Your Voice and Sit at the Table . 86
Unleash Today Challenge: Confidence 102

Step Three: I'm a Recovering Perfectionist 107
An Introduction to Perfectionism... 109
Choose Your 'Perfection' Wisely...111
Implement the New Excellent 128
Unleash Today Challenge: Perfectionism............................... 149

Step Four: Mastering the Art of Networking 153
An Introduction to Networking 155
Falling in Love with Networking... 158
The Art of Networking: You Can Learn It! 174
How to Get Comfortable with Promoting and Selling Yourself 186
Unleash Today Challenge: Networking 193

Step Five: Project 'Love' 197
An Introduction to Project Love 199
Turning Negativity into Your Superpower 201
Start Unleashing Your Inner Goddess 208
Develop Your Love Habits 217
Self Love at Work 229
Unleash Today Challenge: Project Love 235

Step Six: Dealing with Difficult Situations 239
An Introduction to Difficult Situations....................................... 241
Don't Run Just Yet, Lady!... 243
Speak Up, Don't Endure!... 250
Smart Ladies Manage Their Bosses 258
Keeping Your Emotions Under Control.................................... 270
Unleash Today Challenge: Dealing with Difficult Situations and People 275

Step Seven: Opportunities Don't Just Appear, You Create Them 279

An Introduction to Creating Opportunities 281
Learn How to Step Outside of Your Comfort Zone 283
Keep Learning and Never Stay Still 294
Unleash Your Growth with Others 308
Unleash Today Challenge: Learning and Growing 314

Your Unleash Today Journey 318
Notes 323
Acknowledgements 331

UNLEASH TODAY

How to Unleash Today…

In this section, we will be:

- Introducing ourselves
- Explaining the story behind *Unleash Today*
- Outlining how you can benefit from this book
- Guiding you on how to live your life in line with your values and purpose
- Showing you how to turn your female authenticity into your professional superpower

1
The Authors

> *Friends, partners in crime, and bold millennials changing the world.*
>
> **Sarah Wagner**

We met while studying in Maastricht, the Netherlands, in 2012. When we're together, our energy and motivation are limitless. Even being separated by over 8,000 kilometres during the COVID-19 pandemic, we found the joy and drive to write the book you are reading right now.

When we were growing up, everything seemed so straight forward. Good grades and diligent work would lead us to well paid jobs and successful and satisfying careers. Many years later, we discovered this wasn't the case. After we graduated, as junior professionals, we noticed we were facing visible and invisible barriers that held us back from becoming the women we believed we could be.

When looking for self-help books and mentoring, we had to accept that most advice was shared by successful women who were twenty years or more into their professional career. We could not find any books written by people who, like us, are in the earlier stages of their career. We were missing current perspectives on how ambitious women can thrive in their careers. That's how *Unleash Today* was created. Our mission is to share the lessons we learned so other young ambitious women do not have to go through the same experiences we did. This book aims to empower you, the next generation of young ambitious women.

By sharing the lessons we've learned and the most common pitfalls, we hope to help you avoid the mistakes we made. Our aim is to encourage and support young ambitious women to reach their full potential in the workplace. In this book, we show you how to excel in the workplace while being your authentic, powerful self. We openly share our experiences with imposter syndrome, how to handle difficult conversations with your boss, and how we have managed to build the incredible network of experts who have contributed to *Unleash Today*. We'll help women acquire the recognition they deserve by overcoming societal gender bias and redefining what it means to be confident and strong.

Research suggests that the largest gender difference in self-reported confidence exists below the age of twenty-five. The level of confidence of women in their mid-twenties is at a startling 32 per cent in comparison to men's confidence of 47 per cent. It is only by the age of forty that the self-declared confidence gap usually disappears, and the confidence level of women and men is on par at 53 per cent and 55 per cent respectively. By the age of sixty, women eventually rate themselves as more confident than men.[1]

We believe change is needed to ensure that women break the barriers society imposes on our self-confidence and unleash our full potential at an earlier stage in our lives and in the workplace. Our education system fails to teach girls to embrace risk, to leave our comfort zone. It fails to encourage us to be different and dare to behave outside the realm of societal expectations. We are on your side to build the resilience needed to rewrite the rules! It takes courage to stand out, but the fight is worth fighting for.

2
How to Get the Most out of this Book

In order for you to unleash today, we have developed seven steps that will prepare you to embark on your journey, or help you refocus on one that you have already started. To make the most of our time together, we encourage you to read this book in the order it is written, as each step builds on the previous one. This book is not only based on our personal experiences but accompanied by forty-nine stories from our experts sharing their unique perspectives. You can find out more about our established community of experts on our website (www.unleashtoday.com).

You'll gain the most from your *Unleash Today* journey by completing our exercises, taking notes, and highlighting as many sections as you like (go crazy with your colours!). We encourage you to read your copy with an open mind, as we raise some innovative ways of thinking and challenge some common preconceptions. We provide you with further career resources on our website, share fantastic tips in our newsletter, and an array of helpful insights discussed in our events.

Unleash Today is a handbook full of tips and lessons that will help you bring your whole self to your workplace. By the end of our journey, you'll know how to make the best first impression, train your confidence muscle, ditch perfectionism, master your networking skills, fall in love with yourself, learn how to deal with difficult situations, and continue growing in your career. It's time to set yourself free and unleash today!

3
Embarking on Your Self-Discovery Journey

> *Being your authentic self is a radically beautiful act of strength.*
>
> **Kate Surala**

When you enter your new workplace, you might feel a bit lost. You have reached your goal of graduating, spending a year abroad or interning at various companies. The question at the top of your mind is what next? What precise steps will you need to set in motion to start the career you have worked so hard for?

We're here to tell you that it's fine for you not to have a set career plan right from the start. However, we're also going to share a secret with you. If you want to make the most out of your twenties and thirties, you need to focus on finding your meaningful goals. Time is scarce, so it's essential that you start this crucial self-discovery journey sooner rather than later. Focus on finding yourself and identifying what is important to you.

4
Your (W)Inner Compass

> *Know thyself.*
> **Socrates**

Before starting your (new) career, you first need to identify your values and purpose, as these will help you to determine your professional goals. The next few pages will equip you with the tools to determine and pursue your (w)inner compass based on your values and purpose, which you can turn into more concrete and actionable steps. This should be a living vision that you'll adjust as you move forward. The important thing is to start putting your wishes, ideas, and goals on paper. You'll see that being organised and feeling in control of your thoughts will empower you. Let's get started!

Values

Your personal values are a central part of who you are and who you want to become. They are the lenses through which you see yourself and the world you live in. They form your personal truth and develop your self-confidence, self-esteem, happiness, and resilience. Your values will always remind you of who you are and what you believe in. When you're clear about your values, you'll be able to care less about other people's opinions and judgements.

How to Unleash Today...

Now it's your turn. Grab a pen and paper and get to know yourself by creating your own value system. Mark the most important values in your favourite colour in this non-exhaustive list of values:

- Achievement
- Adventure
- Authenticity
- Autonomy
- Balance
- Beauty
- Boldness
- Compassion
- Challenge
- Citizenship
- Community
- Competency
- Contribution
- Creativity
- Curiosity
- Determination
- Fairness
- Faith
- Fame
- Friendships
- Fun
- Growth
- Happiness
- Honesty
- Humour
- Influence
- Inner Harmony
- Justice
- Kindness
- Knowledge
- Leadership
- Learning
- Love
- Loyalty
- Meaningful Work
- Openness
- Optimism
- Peace
- Pleasure
- Poise
- Popularity
- Recognition
- Religion
- Reputation
- Respect
- Responsibility
- Security
- Self-Respect
- Service
- Spirituality
- Stability
- Success
- Status
- Trustworthiness
- Wealth
- Wisdom

Don't worry! It's natural for it to take time to identify your values. A good way to start is to look back on your life so far. Pick out moments when you felt spectacular and confident. Think about the key decisions you made and reasons that drove you to make them. Identify your values by writing down your three top successes and defining what key values helped you achieve those.

Successes / Spectacular Moments	Guiding Value
E.g. I won a marathon	*Discipline, energy, endurance*

EXPERT MEMORY

Sereena Abbassi, Independent Equity, Inclusion, and Diversity Expert in Bristol, UK

When you lose your values, you can lose your confidence. Your values are your anchor. They keep you grounded and centred—a reminder of who you are. My values and purpose are two sides of the same coin. I value self-reflectiveness, fairness, honesty, empathy, kindness, generosity, and full truths. My purpose is to help people connect with themselves so that they can better connect to each other. My values are my tools, the tools I use to carry out my work.

Growing up, I was a loner. I experienced being the new kid at eight different schools. Art and drawing were my only constant. My primary school years were spent with a sketchpad and pencil in hand. Spending so much time alone as a child allowed space for introspection, a connectedness, which is the same type of experience that we seek out in our adult lives through being in nature, meditation, and prayer.

Completely unbeknownst to me at the time, being a loner allowed me to discover myself without the bombardment of external influences. So, when I started to build relationships, I was able to see people in a way that they hadn't even seen themselves—their potential for greatness. Bruce Lee puts this beautifully in one of his essays, 'The Passionate State of Mind': 'We can see through others only when we see through ourselves. Lack of self-awareness renders us transparent; a soul that knows itself is opaque.'

Lesson learned
I found my values by looking within, and I found my purpose by looking outwards. Through my relationships and experiences, my engagement with the outside world. So, have experiences—have lots of them—though the most profound experience and relationship, you'll ever have, is the one that you have with yourself.

Purpose

Alongside your values, being clear about your purpose is equally important. A purpose provides reason for action, it is the objective or intention behind something. A sense of purpose is powerful, as it enables people to accomplish big things. A purpose gives people guidance and orientation in life. Your purpose can help you determine your goals, establish priorities, and make important decisions. It provides you with the necessary determination to succeed.

Studies show that people with a high sense of purpose, a sense of direction, remain healthier and physically stronger as they grow older. Other studies show that having a purpose in life can significantly increase your happiness, make you more productive and creative at work.

Then what are you waiting for? The issue is that, although many people seek to know their 'why', many just don't know why they are doing what they are doing.

What constitutes a purpose is deeply personal. Finding it is a process of self-discovery that may take years. However, once you have found it, it will help you create the professional life you desire. Don't just wait for random coincidences to determine your course.

> **EXPERT MEMORY**
>
> **Miisa Mink, Founder of the accountability platform DrivenWomen in Helsinki, Finland**
>
> I can still remember the 'aha!' moment when I discovered my purpose and how it made me feel. I was thrilled and scared at once. I was getting nowhere with some ideas I had and decided to take matters into my own hands. What would I produce if I created a brand and a business based on who I was and what I believed in? I had been building my clients' brands and it was always easy to hide behind that façade. Now it was time to create a brand that was stemming from my own heart and that felt scary.
>
> That early spring afternoon, sitting on a lush sofa in one of London's co-working spaces, I discovered my purpose by finally paying attention and taking the time to write things down. I listed everything I loved doing, my talents, and what I was good at. I wrote down my values and what I was like as a person. I dotted down anything and everything about the things and ideas that

I was passionate about. Then I started connecting the dots—and there it was, my purpose.

I discovered that I was passionate about equality and women's empowerment. But I was also a 'doer' and I wanted to see a real change in the world. I realised that one of my key talents was that I was able to give abstract things a form, so I took on a task of conceptualising the personal growth journey and making it accessible for all women. I knew I was onto something because I was both elated and extremely scared to start realising my vision. What if I failed? The hardest part is to look at yourself and to accept your brilliance. The 'doing' is not so tough.

Lesson learned
Building a career or a business is hard work, but unless you build it on the right foundation—your true self—it can feel frustrating. As soon as you start taking steps on your path the universe starts supporting you. You are safe in your purpose.

There are different ways to find your purpose. One way is just like Miisa, where you write down what you are passionate about, what you enjoy doing, and what your talents are:

What is your passion?	What do you love?	What is your natural talent?
E.g. Fitness	I enjoy exercising and trying new sports	Communicating with others

At the same time, it's often not the fun and easy stuff that leads you to your purpose, but the really difficult experiences that hurt you most. It may be the moment when you lost your job after working hard for years, the moment when you felt isolated and lonely after a family member passed away, or when you felt yet discriminated against in the workplace.

> **EXPERT MEMORY**
>
> **Sarah Wagner and Kate Surala, Authors of *Unleash Today***
>
> While writing this book, we realised that empowering other women to reach their full potential in the workplace is our life purpose. Speaking up about unfair treatment and reminding women of their rights and power comes very easily to us. It's also something we can't go without. Whenever the topic of empowerment comes up, we feel the urge to listen and engage—it's our passion. But we hadn't realised this until starting the writing process for *Unleash Today*.
>
> **Lesson learned**
> You're carrying your purpose within you; you just need to discover it. Actively seek out your purpose and look for it rather than waiting for it to emerge on its own.

Now write down a life purpose statement. Take a moment to write a description of how the world would look if everything was going perfectly for you. Our purpose statement is, 'Empowering young ambitious women and providing them with practical tools to be their authentic self in the workplace and unleash their full potential'.

ANSWER

Admittedly, it sounds easy. You just identify your values, think about what you are passionate about, and find your purpose. And... there's your inner compass that allows you to be your authentic self at all times, set your goals, and unleash today, right?!

We know this won't always be the case, so be patient with yourself. All we're saying is that you should start this journey now rather than later. For instance, you can begin with dedicating five minute blocks on a daily basis to develop your authentic action plan. Once you've found your purpose and values, you'll be equipped with an inner compass that will help you decide where you want to go. Once you have a clear vision, determine the path to your destination through concrete goal setting and start taking actions to move you in the right direction.

Make sure to align your professional goals with your life purpose rather than running from goal to goal without thinking about the 'why'. Ask yourself whether pursuing a particular goal is really what you want to achieve, whether it is relevant, meaningful and leading to your deeper fulfilment in the long run. Does it bring you closer to your purpose? Is it in line with your values?

Do you care about climate change and want to make an environmental difference? Would you like to care for your family and help them succeed? Do you want to travel the world and connect with other people?

Your inner compass will tell you when you are off course. But remember, you determine when your compass has to be readjusted, because your values or purposes may change over time.

Although this will require a substantial amount of self-reflection, it's time well spent. Attaining your goals will be much easier if your heart is in it as well. We revisit the topic of smart goal setting and determination of priorities in Step Three in more detail.

5

Your Bold, Authentic, Female Self

> *Trying to be a man is a waste of time.*
> **Sarah Jessica Parker**

Unfortunately, many women continue to feel the pressure to toughen up, lacking the space to be themselves. We may hide our female traits at work, afraid to let them shine and make them the new norm. We may be told to 'stop being too emotional', or to refrain from 'playing the mediator'. You shouldn't have to sacrifice your female traits at work. We encourage you to follow your heart and intuition and be your female self rather than conforming to the management, working or clothing style that was historically rewarded with success.

Gender stereotypes in society imply how we are expected to act, speak, or dress. They can be harmful as they don't allow people to fully express themselves. We're generally expected to be polite, nurturing, and accommodating, while men are encouraged to appear strong, outgoing, and bold. This makes it particularly difficult for women to take up the courage to be independent, smart, or assertive, attributes often valued and needed to succeed in the workplace. Be bold for change by being the best version of your true self. Throughout the book, we will share various tools to work on your confidence. We hope you perceive your boldness as your strength when you finish our book.

> **EXPERT MEMORY**
>
> **Louise Corbett, Founder of Exceptional Existence and Women Empowered Helping Women to Find their Voice in Hong Kong**
>
> The word 'woman' is truly one of my favourite words. Our strength, agility, softness, intuitive nature, and ability to love and nurture in a way that can make the world know that all is ok is our power.
>
> **We are here to be female:** After fifteen years in the corporate world, I often witnessed women sacrificing their femininity due to a deep seated belief that it is what is needed to progress in their career. For some reason, so many believe that if the majority of leadership roles are led by men then, in order to get to a C-Suite position, one must exhibit masculine qualities.
>
> **The Power of the Feminine:** When I hear a woman say she wishes she was a man, I die a little on the inside. I wholeheartedly believe that a woman can be a strong, professional, and extremely capable individual while standing strong in her feminine energy.
>
> My experience has taught me to identify some common feminine strengths that are recognised again and again. These include:

- A continual and primary focus on the wellbeing of the community and family (or the corporation).
- An ability to be nurturing and strong at the same time.
- A commitment to detail, preparation, and accountability.
- A sixth sense for risk and a sensible aversion to it (again perhaps with the first point in mind).

Lesson learned
Let the woman inside you shine in your workplace.

EXPERT MEMORY

Em Roblin, Canadian Coach and Consultant in Bali, Indonesia

I have a boldness about me. It's one of my greatest strengths. It often sounds like, 'I have a great idea!' followed by a grin and impromptu brainstorm over coffee. I can trace many key moments and turning points to times when I've been bold, instances such as:

- Stepping into the unknown by moving to a foreign country on my own without a solid plan in place,
- Putting up my hand to present a keynote speech at a high-profile conference in my non-native language without having full proficiency,
- Sharing a wild idea for a new programme without having a clue how people would receive it.

All of these examples make me feel alive. When I'm being bold, I feel full of abundance and possibility.

It's a beautiful feeling and I've been told that it's inspiring to be around.

But it hasn't always been so rosy. For many years, my boldness had a dark shadow, a powerful force that showed up as a deafeningly loud inner critic that would shout, 'What's wrong with you?!' It would break down everything I said and did and critique it.

I would end up feeling low. I started to question myself and question my ability to make decisions. I even began doubting my own intentions. It felt counter-intuitive to me that with more experience, I'd get less confident, but that's what happened. I found myself stumbling my way through things in real time.

I stopped being as bold as I previously was. I focussed on toning it down, challenging my anything-is-possible mindset, and learning to better control myself.

One day, I had just finished a meeting and was walking back to my office under the mid-afternoon sun. I found myself in curious conversation with my inner critic in a very different way than we had ever interacted before. I asked her where she came from and what her intention was. She told me she was there to look out for me, that she just wanted to help me have an easy life, and to help me fit in. It was an 'aha!' moment, I later discovered that talking to your inner critic as I had (and still do) is a trusted technique recommended by leading psychologists. Instead of avoiding it, get curious about it, and learn when it can be helpful to you and when it's pulling you away from who you are and what you want.

Don't get me wrong, I can still get stuck in a negative pattern of self-talk today. But it doesn't last long. When I notice it happening, I take action to shift my energy. My office neighbours laugh when they see me dancing in the hallway.

Lesson learned

The journey to truly shine our unique light is, well, a journey. I find great comfort in knowing that I'm not alone. May we each keep moving on our own paths to live out our potential.

6

Unleash Today Challenge: Defining Your (W)Inner Compass

Imagine you're jumping from one goal to the next, from one achievement to the other. You never pause to ask for the 'why' rather than the 'what'. Whenever you set your mind to a task, you complete it and succeed. You are a check-box queen. But what is the deeper meaning behind pursuing all these goals? You haven't found the real purpose in your life, the light in the dark that will guide you through the tunnel. You're unfulfilled, disoriented, and lost, longing for this ultimate fulfilment you had hoped to experience upon achieving your goals. You are looking for a fresh start. Where do you start?

ANSWER

How to Unleash Today...

EXPERT ADVICE

Marina Newington, Founder and Productivity Coach in London, UK

POWER is an acronym that is going to help you remember that you are the priority in your life. Finding your POWER requires you to dig deep, open yourself to new learning and new mentors, and visualise what success looks like and feels right for you.

- P stands for priority. First you need to make yourself a priority in your own life. As women, we are used to putting ourselves at the bottom of the list. We first think of our children, partners, work colleagues, friends, and pets—anyone but us! If you look after yourself first, you'll have the confidence, strength, and energy to be there for the people you care about.

- O is for Order. Do you ever feel like you spend the day running from meeting to activity, but not really getting anything done? If you are organised and in control of your schedule, you can rule your world instead of letting it rule you. You can then achieve your big goals with time to spare.
- W is about communicating with the World. It's so important to be able to connect with the people around you. If you work on your communication technique, build your support network, and learn to set boundaries, you will be able to share what's really important to you with the world around you, and feel supported in return.
- E stands for Energy. By focussing on eating healthy foods, fitting movement into your weekly routine, and getting enough sleep, you'll be able to unlock the energy you need to take on the world.
- R is for Roadmap. By taking these steps, you've fuelled your body and life for success, but where are you going? You have to figure out what's next. What's your why? What are your dreams and the actions you need to take in order to make them come true?

Lesson learned

Find your POWER by prioritising yourself, taking control of your schedule, connecting with the people around you, unlocking your energy and following a clear roadmap.

Step One:
Hello, Here I Am!

In this section, you learn how to:

- Make the best first impression
- Boost your confidence by power posing
- Master verbal and nonverbal communication
- Dress for success
- Master your first day in the office
- Ask the right questions

7
An Introduction

> **❝** *A good first impression can make wonders.* **❞**
> **Sarah Wagner**

Imagine it's your first day at work. You've just graduated from university or left your previous job. It's a new beginning and the world is waiting for you.

You'll probably be nervous when you first walk through the office or take part in your first meeting. You may have a million questions running through your head, fear that you won't grasp the 'in' jokes and worry that you'll struggle to adjust to the rhythm of the new environment. But you're not the only one! You might feel nervous attending the meeting, but don't forget you deserve to be there. After having passed hundreds of exams and written dozens of assignments, you've demonstrated that you're a capable young woman, able to embrace this new challenge.

Yet, other people won't just look at your CV and assume that you're qualified based on your grades and extracurricular activities. From the moment you set foot in the office, your behaviour will be examined closely. Your new colleagues will automatically evaluate whether or not you fit in. This will be based on your appearance, attitude and behaviour, working style, connections, commitment, and many more aspects. You need to be proactive and ensure you set the right tone from the start. It's important to create your own image before someone else does it for you.

8

Your Appearance

> *As a woman, dressing for success isn't superficial, it's being smart.*
>
> **Sarah Wagner**

Like it or not, you're always being judged by others. Research shows that people form an opinion of your personality, body language, and appearance in about a tenth of a second.[2] In our experience, women are often judged more quickly than men, particularly in male dominated environments where we tend to stand out from the crowd. This is why we recommend you think carefully about the impression you want to make and adjust your attitude, verbal, and nonverbal behaviour accordingly.

Let's start by reflecting on what impression you want to make. In order to control your image, you first have to create it. What personal and professional attributes do you want to convey? What do you want people to think about when you enter the room? Write your responses in the box below:

ANSWER

EXPERT MEMORY

Nina Pfuetz, Head of the Fintech Ratepay in Berlin, Germany

In my early twenties, people never perceived me as competent as my older colleagues. Therefore, I deliberately dressed in a conservative way. I would usually wear a blue suit and white blouse. Although I was used to wearing contact lenses, I would also put on my glasses and arrange my hair in a sleek ponytail. Dressing up like this helped me to enhance my 'perceived' competence.

When I met Hilary Clinton some years ago, she told me that, in her early career, she always came across as too female and caring. That's what led her to work on her perceived confidence. A few years later, her advisors told her she came across as super competent, but too harsh and not female enough. It's a very fine line to walk.

With this in mind, once I reached my late twenties, I took the decision to always be authentic rather than fitting someone else's expectations. I can still make deliberate decisions of what I wear or how to do my hair, but I play with it and adjust according to the environment, occasion, and what seems acceptable and natural to me, allowing me to be true to myself.

Lesson learned

Always be true to yourself, but be aware of how you come across. Be smart and take into consideration the environment you operate in. Adjust accordingly within the margins that still feel authentic to you.

9
Power Pose

> *Don't fake it till you make it.*
> *Fake it until you become it.*
>
> **Amy Cuddy**

Interestingly, we often think body language mirrors our feelings. However, psychologists have shown that the opposite is true as well.[3] When you change your body language, you change your attitude and how you feel.

If you're nervous or uncomfortable in a meeting, you tend to contract or collapse your body. It's easy to fall into a submissive position with crossed arms, slouched, and frowning. In these situations, make a conscious effort to stand or sit up straight, smile, and be engaged. You will begin to look and feel more confident very quickly. Don't let your body mirror your inner feelings, and vice versa.

To feel empowered, we recommend exercising the power pose, which we illustrate below. The power pose is the epitome of confidence. Push your chest out, stand with your hands on your hips and position your legs hip distance apart.

The power pose has been proven to increase testosterone and lower levels of stress hormones and cortisol.[4] Therefore, it increases your feelings of power and confidence.[5] Practising this pose will change your mindset. It will help you regain strength and believe in yourself in moments of doubt. Act the way you want to feel!

In order to benefit from the power pose, you should make time for yourself before meetings. Find a private place, like a bathroom, look at yourself in the mirror and power pose. Try to stand in this pose for two minutes. When you look at your mirror reflection, you will feel empowered and confident. Then close your eyes, breathe in deeply for a count of three, hold for one, and then breathe out for a count of five. Combining meditation and power posing provides relaxation and boosts confidence.

EXPERT MEMORY

Kate Surala, Co-Author of *Unleash Today*

We used to have a stand-up meeting every morning to discuss the day and individual action points for each team member. During the first meeting I attended, I looked around and noticed some people with crossed arms, others lingering in the back, and some tapping their feet or playing on their phones. People weren't paying attention and the environment didn't encourage people to ask questions. Instead of following the majority, I actively focussed on conveying a positive message by straightening my back, holding my head high, and uncrossing my arms.

Lesson learned

Be mindful of the power your body posture has on yourself and others. An engaging stance will captivate an audience, motivate others, and lead to more enjoyable and productive interactions.

10
Nonverbal Communication

> *Fie, fie upon her!*
> *There's language in her eye, her cheek, her lip,*
> *Nay, her foot speaks; her wanton spirits look out*
> *At every joint and motive of her body.*
>
> **William Shakespeare**

People subconsciously consider two questions when they meet you: 'Is she trustworthy?' and 'Can I respect her?'[6] This initial judgement is usually based on body language. Studies have shown that people who use positive nonverbal communication are perceived as more competent, persuasive, likeable, and emotionally intelligent.

Be conscious of your posture, as it impacts your success more than you might think! The power pose is just one example of nonverbal communication. Other examples include targeted gestures, body language, facial expressions, and style. Nonverbal communication is a silent language and mostly done unconsciously. Being aware of your body language at all times empowers you to control the first impression you want to make.

Your body language is very important. Here are some tips to support you adjusting your body language to make a confident impression.[7] The goal is to internalise them, so you perform them without thinking:

- **Take up space**, like standing or sitting with your legs apart, signals to others that you are confident and comfortable with yourself. Standing with your feet close together could imply insecurity.

- **Don't touch or scratch your face.** Fidgeting with your hands can be distracting to listeners and convey nervousness.

- **Use your hands confidently but in a controlled way.** Use them to reiterate what you are trying to communicate and the point you're trying to make. At the same time, make sure to control your hand gestures and don't use them excessively.

- **Refrain from holding something in front of your chest.** Holding something like a notebook in front of your chest can come across as closed and unfriendly. Instead, hold it below your chest or beside your leg.

- **Be conscious of your facial expression.** Smiling is a particularly powerful nonverbal communication tool, as people will remember your positive attitude.

- **Have a firm and steady handshake.**

- **Be present at online meetings.** When joining a call with multiple participants, we recommend switching on your camera and positioning your webcam to be at your eye-level by propping up the laptop with some work material, such as your copy of *Unleash Today* so it's right at your fingertips!

Facial Expressions

> *What does it cost to smile? Nothing. What does it cost not to smile? Everything, if not smiling prevents you from enchanting people.*

Guy Kawasaki

Research suggests that at least 80 per cent of communication is nonverbal, with facial expressions making up a big part of it.[8] We encourage you to make a conscious effort to use your smile to your advantage. You don't have to be superficially upbeat all the time, but having a positive facial expression makes you look engaged and professional.

Working in today's virtual environment exposes facial expressions more than ever before. If you are on a video call, make sure to control your facial expression at all times. You might easily forget how you look, and you don't know who might see your rolling eyes!

At the same time, we're aware that many women receive unsolicited comments on their facial expressions. In fact, a survey found that 98 per cent of women have been told to smile at least once in their life.[9] Of course, we don't want to contribute to those numbers, so never smile to please anyone. Only smile if you want to or if you see the value in it.

We also recognise that a woman's smile can have a deeper meaning and isn't only a sign of joy. It can also be a signal of submission or agreeableness at times, such as when choosing to refrain from reacting to (sexist) comments. In these situations, make sure that you send the right signal to your counterparty—is it really appropriate to smile if someone is making a sexist comment? You could stop smiling in that moment and say with a serious face, 'I don't feel comfortable with these comments.'

> **EXPERT MEMORY**
>
> **Kate Surala, Co-Author of *Unleash Today***
>
> After being told many times that I have a 'resting bitch face', I decided to remind myself to smile more often. In the beginning, I had to make a mental note to remember to smile rather than sticking to my default facial expression.
>
> **Lesson learned**
> Be aware of your natural facial expression and smile more in the right moments.

HELLO, HERE I AM!

Handshake

> ❝ *She had great eye contact, a firm handshake, and a focus in her manner that gave me confidence she took her work seriously.* ❞

Richard Pickard[*]

Who do we remember after a meeting? Not only those with a positive smile, but also those who welcome us with a firm handshake! Studies show that people are more likely to remember you and react more openly if you shake hands with them.[10] But it isn't just about shaking hands, it's about how you shake them as it reveals a lot about you.

To convey competence and confidence, you should make steady eye contact while holding a firm, but not too hard, grip for about one or two seconds. A firm handshake allows you to make a lasting impression, particularly as strong handshakes are often not anticipated from the opposite.

EXPERT MEMORY

Sarah Wagner, Co-Author of *Unleash Today*

When I worked as a policy advocate in Brussels, part of my job was to meet and greet a number of stakeholders on a daily basis. Some people would give me one, two, or three kisses on the cheek while others shook hands, depending on their cultural background. I had to learn to interpret different styles of greetings within seconds. Who were the people who stood out negatively? Those, mostly women, who shook my hand as if their hand

---

[*] *Unleash Today* expert and CEO at Inclusive Search in London, UK.

was limp and floppy. The handshake suggested that the meeting would be boring, which was not always the case.

Lesson learned
Pudding handshakes can easily be interpreted as insecurity and/or incompetence. Be prepared and anticipate which greeting is the most appropriate in the cultural setting you are in. In some countries, kisses on the cheek or bowing are more common.

11
Dress Code and Hair

> *Dress to impress—not just for them but yourself.*
>
> **Sarah Wagner**

Once you've made a winning first impression with a confident nonverbal communication style, you need to solidify it with the right outfit. A chic and comfortable outfit contributes to a good first impression. Studies show that a person's attire conveys positive qualities, such as good character, sociability, competence, and intelligence.[11] Just like your posture, the way you dress is also a visible sign to others about how you feel.

You should aim to dress in a way that empowers you. What holds true for everyone is that, if your clothes make you feel confident, you will impress others around you. Dress in as many colours as you want, wear heels or don't, but be yourself. Most importantly: own it.

By dressing to impress (yourself), you don't give in to the superficial judgement of others! Others should primarily remember you because you're good at what you do, prepared, and deliver great work. Yet, before someone can judge your competence, this person is likely to have assessed your outfit already and subconsciously developed a first impression.

Take the example of Facebook COO Sherly Sandberg, author of *Lean In* (2013). She is hardly ever seen in anything but an elegant outfit of bright colours and heels. Sandberg is clearly aware of the impact of clothing on her perceived competence.

So, how should you get ready for your first day at work? 'Better overdressed than underdressed' is our mantra. You can always turn your outfit down once you've identified what the general dress code in the office is. If you walk into a room full of dark suits wearing bright clothes, take advantage of your unique position!

Did you know that different clothing colours evoke certain human responses? For instance, blue conveys leadership while white makes people feel that you're very organised. Here is a colour guide[12] to help you to get ready for your next meeting or interview:

Colour	Meaning
Black	Power, authority, drama
White	Truth, simplicity, cleanliness
Grey	Sophistication, neutrality, practicality
Brown	Calmness, reliability, stability
Red	Energy, passion, action
Blue	Trust, confidence, calmness
Green	Balance, growth, self-reliance

Hello, Here I Am!

EXPERT MEMORY

Sarah Wagner, Co-Author of *Unleash Today*

When I started my new job, I decided to put on an elegant and timeless diamond green dress on my first day. Of course, I was totally overdressed, but I felt at ease and owned it. Every other person seemed to compliment me on my dress, and I knew I had made a lasting impression. When people spoke about the 'new colleague', they would often refer to 'the one in the green dress'.

Lesson learned
Make a positive, lasting impression with an elegant outfit on your first day at work.

You shouldn't only focus on your outfit, but also pay close attention to your hairstyle. Hair is a topic that's very important for some women and their self-esteem. Be aware of how the positive and negative perceptions of your hair (regarding length, texture, and colour) can tremendously impact you as a woman.

> **EXPERT MEMORY**
>
> **Olivia Nadine, Co-Founder of B•e Company, an organisation supporting artisan, minority-owned businesses in Beijing, China**
>
> Sometimes my hair can make a more significant impression than I do. When I was younger, I wore it in an afro, and it was often the first thing someone noticed about me. However, when getting ready for a job interview or an important work event, I usually put in the extra effort to make sure my hair isn't the star of the show.
>
> There is an idiom that says African American women have to be twice as good, smart, strong, and capable to get the same achievements and opportunities as our nonblack counterparts. The same goes for our first impressions: they have to be twice as good as well. Knowing the negative stereotypes stacked against African American women, every new connection is a chance to shift the perspective a bit.
>
> **Lesson learned**
> While some people can wear their natural hair down or in a simple ponytail and be considered professional,

Afro-hair doesn't always have the option, so we must be adaptive. Living abroad, away from my trusted hairstylist, meant that I had to become an expert in my hair. With my hair taken care of, there is nothing in my way from making a great first impression and being remembered for what I truly bring to the table.

12
Language and Tone

> *The way I sound makes me 'me'. It makes me memorable and now, I use my accent as an easy conversation starter.*
>
> **Maja Marszalek**[*]

When we talk to others, we assume that they understand what we're saying because we know what we're trying to express. But this isn't always the case. Your attitude, perception, emotions, context, and thoughts can create communication barriers. In order to ensure your message is perceived in the way you delivered it, you should put yourself in your receiver's shoes.

The way you speak conveys a lot about your level of confidence and has an impact on your image. We recommend playing with your verbal communication style. Different things work for different people. Here are some general tips that might be useful to you:

- **To sound trustworthy, vary the pitch, tone, and volume of your voice.** A speaker with a low pitched voice (male or female) is perceived almost

---

[*] *Unleash Today* expert and Director at ACA Compliance group in London, UK

> **EXPERT MEMORY**
>
> **Maja Marszalek, Director at ACA Compliance group in London, UK**
>
> A lot has changed since my first job in London. I used to speak to C-level executives on the phone daily. After the standard 'How are you's, the second question was always, 'Where is your accent from?' or the more direct, 'Where are you from?' I used to get frustrated with this so much that when the time came
>
> One day, my firm organised a presentation workshop where each of us had to stand in the middle of the meeting room and present. It's an awful exercise that makes everybody stare at and judge you. What was surprising, however, was the fact that every time I would stand there and speak, the room would go quiet. By having an accent, I was the one who they remembered, as I sounded different and it meant they needed to focus on what was being said.
>
> Since that workshop, I use my accent as my strength. The way I sound makes me 'me'. It makes me memorable and now, I use my accent as an easy conversation starter. I no longer take offence if somebody points it out. My accent is a great conversation starter to share my story with people.
>
> **Lesson learned**
>
> It takes so little to replace your so-called disadvantages and make them your biggest advantages. You never know what will make you unforgettable.

universally as being more authoritative. Females tend to raise their voices at the end of sentences, as if they're asking a question or seeking approval. Instead, let your voice start on one note, rise in pitch throughout the sentence, and then drop back down again. The goal isn't to sound manlier, but to bring some variety into your conversation and avoid sounding monotone.

- **Reduce fillers by speaking slowly and listening to your voice.** Pay attention to how fast you speak and try to speak at a slower, more relaxed pace. If you speak slowly, you're less likely to use fillers such as 'hm', 'like', and 'well'. Recording yourself and listening back to the tape or voice memo is a great way to become more confident with your voice.

- **Play with language.** Communication comes alive with examples and personal stories. People will listen more closely when you make your thoughts more understandable through concrete illustrations, comparisons, or examples.

- **Do not be afraid of silence!** This is probably one of the hardest lessons to learn, particularly for extroverts, but pauses can be powerful tools of emphasis and confidence. Use them to your advantage. Silence will grab others' attention.

Fig. 5
Silence is a powerful tool

> **EXPERT MEMORY**
>
> **Sarah Wagner and Kate Surala, Authors of *Unleash Today***
>
> We've discovered the power of silence. As extroverts, it's been extremely difficult to understand that not all words are meant to be expressed. Leaders know how to use silence as a tactic for speaking up for themselves and as an opportunity to lead.
>
> Imagine you only had a few moments to say what you need to say in a meeting. On average, in one minute, you should be able to convey your message and open the floor for questions. When you get questions, you can't answer every question, so simply respond to one or two. Your words will be more memorable than the ones of those who chime in at every possible chance.
>
> **Lesson learned**
> Use silence to your advantage. Silence can yield more power than words.

13
Mastering Your First Weeks

> *Knowledge is power.*
>
> **Francis Bacon**

In addition to making a good first impression, we also want to ensure you have a smooth start. Preparation is the key for everything. If you're prepared, you can hardly be taken by surprise. You have a minefield in front of you. We are here to share our practical tips to make sure that you don't step into one.

Observe and Learn

> *My secret weapon: watch before you act!*
>
> **Sarah Wagner**

Observe and learn about the office dynamics. See where you can fit best and how you can shine brightest. You'll slowly start to see various patterns. For instance, watch if people take a lunch break during a specific hour, observe who takes smoking breaks with whom, when important meetings take place, and who's involved. Identify who the real decision makers are, how they approach problems, and how decisions are communicated to the rest of the team.

Try to get invited to as many meetings as possible and ask your work colleagues out to lunch or for coffee. However, don't engage in any internal gossiping, as this could harm your reputation very quickly and significantly burden you in the long run. Remember, you can only make a first impression once.

> **EXPERT MEMORY**
>
> **Sarah Wagner, Co-Author of *Unleash Today***
>
> When I started my first job, a new boss was hired at the same time. Since she was also new, she needed support to learn as quickly as possible, and to get familiar with the key stakeholders and processes. I realised this was an opportunity for me to be proactive. I suggested rearranging the office, organising team workshops, and streamlining work processes. It meant more work for me, but I also got the attention of my boss that I would not have gotten otherwise. Several months later, I was offered a full-time position with a new title, salary, and much more responsibility.
>
> **Lesson learned**
>
> Observe what your line manager or executives need and how you can help them fulfil those needs. Don't just sit back and wait for these projects to land in your lap. Actively offer to help when it's appropriate.

Unleash Today

Ask the Right Questions

> *The more questions you ask, the more you will learn and the quicker you can grow.*
>
> **Maja Marszalek**

The more people you meet and, most importantly, the more questions you ask, the more you will learn. Prepare for your first day on the job by putting together questions you can ask your manager in advance, such as:

- What preparations could I make before my first day?
- What reading/course should I do so I can get up to speed?
- What are the deadlines/priorities for the next week, month, and quarter?
- How often would you like to meet and what is your preferred method for updating information?
- Who is the best person to contact about the project?

Try it! Have a conversation with your manager and ask about their role, the company, and your responsibilities. When you ask a question, listen to what they say rather than spending the time thinking what you're going to ask next. This might be difficult if you're an introvert or just a little shy, but you'll learn more than you think in this way. When you're talking, you're only repeating what you already know.

Also, showing an interest in your manager and their work will leave a good impression, as you're showing a dedication to getting things right and respecting their achievements.

Working Hours

> *It's so easy to give away too much of ourselves in areas that are not helpful—working long hours, striving for perfection, saying yes to everything, and pleasing others with our high standards.*

Liz Mearns[*]

A recent study found that more than one in five employees admit to putting in ten hours of unpaid work in a week.[13] That means that for an average 40 hour week, those employees are giving an extra 25 per cent for free.

When you start your new role, you might be wondering what the typical working hours are. How working hours are exercised and executed in practise may differ from what is delineated in your contract. Over time, you'll develop a feeling for when you are expected to stay longer and when it is fine to leave a bit earlier. You'll also learn whether office time is appreciated or if you could work remotely.

Since the COVID-19 pandemic forced many of us to remain at home, we have noticed that employers all over the world have become more flexible with working

---

[*] *Unleash Today* expert and Founder of The Head Coach in Cheshire, UK.

hours and rules for working remotely. That being said, even if your employer allows you to work from home, we encourage you to show up in the office once in a while, if circumstances allow and it is safe to go into work. Don't underestimate the importance of showing your face and having a little chit chat with colleagues. This means you'll be in other people's mind and could be considered for additional tasks when the time comes.

Urgent versus Important

> *I have two kinds of problems: the urgent and the important. The urgent are not important, and the important are never urgent.*
>
> **Dwight D. Eisenhower**

If you want to make the best first impression while working with your colleagues, you can clarify the urgency and importance of the task you are working on. Urgent isn't the same as important and you should learn the difference as early as possible in your career. Knowing the difference will help you to manage your time more effectively and prioritise in stressful situations.

We advise you to follow Eisenhower's principle (see the image opposite) that orders tasks on the urgent/important matrix, helping you to prioritise tasks by urgency and importance. In doing so, you're sorting out less important and urgent tasks that you should either delegate or drop. How important is the project? Does it need to be finished right now?

THE EISENHOWER DECISION MATRIX

	Urgent	Not Urgent
Important	**Do** — Do it Now.	**Decide** — Schedule a time to do it
Not Important	**Delegate** — WHO CAN DO IT FOR YOU?	**Delete** — ELIMINATE IT

You want to build trust between you and your supervisor. There will be days when you can afford to say, 'I have to leave at six pm because I have plans'. Get your priorities straight.

As a young, ambitious woman, we recommend that you only use the term 'urgent' when something is really urgent. We encourage you to discuss what 'urgent' means with you managers and colleagues to ensure you know what it means in your organisation.

> **EXPERT MEMORY**
>
> **Kate Surala, Co-Author of *Unleash Today***
>
> When it comes to working on projects: know your limits. Your sibling's wedding will (hopefully) only happen once, so clear communication is the solution. You might want to discuss the pros and cons of attending directly with your supervisor and ask for their advice. Do you finish the project on the way to the wedding or do you ask for an extension? You don't want to find out that the project wasn't important at all and you're supposed to be delivering it next week anyway.
>
> **Lesson learned**
> Evaluate the situation based on the urgent and important spectrum. Weigh the pros and cons. Don't compromise on one time events; discuss them with your supervisor.

13

Other Tips to Unleash in Your Workplace

> *Honour your skills, continue to learn, and provide value in your work and each day will bring new success.*
>
> **Sharon Torrence Jones**[*]

Here are a few practical hacks that will make your start smooth and help you to ensure others see the best in you from the beginning.

Never plan personal activities on the busiest day of the week

Everyone seems to be super excited after the weekend to get things done and will bombard you with emails on Mondays. The same goes for Thursdays, as people realise the weekend is very close and they need to meet deadlines before Friday night. You should prepare for these busy days, rather than cancelling external meetings or plans at the last minute.

Always budget some buffer time between meetings

It's almost certain that most of the meetings you attend

---

[*] *Unleash Today* expert, CTE teacher, and Founder and CEO of the Dottie Rose Foundation in Charlotte, US.

will overrun. You don't want to end up in a situation when you are late for your next meeting, then the following one, or even have to cancel. You should also allow time for travel. How many times have you been stuck on the train in between stations and not been able to message the person you're meeting that you'll be late? It's very embarrassing and you're presenting yourself badly and disrespecting the other person by wasting their time.

Always ask when you're expected to deliver a task or project

In the beginning, you may consider everything is absolutely urgent and needs to be done as soon as possible. Speed does not always guarantee quality. Your key takeaway here is to always ask the person who assigns the task to you what their expectations are and when the deadline is.

Learn to say 'no' early on

We're still learning this skill. It's very easy in theory but very difficult in practise. We remember the days when we would just say 'yes' to absolutely everything to please our colleagues or boss. That is not a sustainable way of working. You can't please your boss if you don't please yourself first.

How do you say 'no' in an acceptable way? If you're working on multiple projects at once that have close deadlines, you could ask your line manager if you could change one of the deadlines. Unless they tell you to reprioritise or accept the new deadline, you'll sound like someone who is in charge of their schedule.

> **EXPERT MEMORY**
>
> **Kate Surala, Co-Author of *Unleash Today***
>
> My mum used to say 'yes' to everyone at work and she would end up covering multiple colleagues at the same time, spending her weekends working. I'm sure she became sick and got cancer from all the stress and extreme workload. My mum taught me a very important lesson and, although it might sound very selfish at first, it will be beneficial to you: 'Think of yourself first and do you best to try to help others, but don't kill yourself.' It's much worse to disappoint someone by not delivering what you promised rather than saying 'no'.
>
> **Lesson learned**
>
> Try to evaluate your workload every morning before you get on with your first task. Always over-budget than under-budget. Learn how to say 'no' when necessary and to identify when 'necessary' applies.

Send future emails

Outlook and other email providers have a 'secret' function of delayed delivery. Imagine you're working on a project and you already know that a certain individual will not respond within the set deadline and you will have to chase them. We see chasing as time wasted and we hate wasting time. What can you do about it? Set these emails to be sent on the date of the deadline by using delayed delivery function. You can set up emails to be sent in a few minutes, hours, days, but also months! You can do this immediately when sending the initial email setting up the deadline. How can you then remember that you've chased your colleagues in two weeks' time? You simply CC or BCC yourself to ensure the email was sent. It's as simple as that!

Follow up by email after a personal meeting

Even when your conversation with a person is over, your job isn't finished yet. To ensure your first impressions stick, it's wise to write a personalised follow up message. The note should recap the conversation in a way that shows you have gained some insights, share an article you have mentioned, or do what you have promised. You want to show that your conversation had an impact while also bringing yourself to the table.

Schedule in 'me time' during the day

You might be feeling the increasing pressure for time and be tempted to give up on your free time. However, hobbies can make people substantially better at their jobs. It's no surprise that allowing yourself to spend at least fifteen minutes a day focussing on your feelings can reawaken your energy. Take a moment to go for a walk, have a cup of tea, or stay in silence. You could always ask your HR department if you could have a flexible cycle to work scheme or purchase a corporate pass to the local gym.

There are many more aspects that can contribute to making a good first impression, as you'll discover. Create your own recipe and write down your thoughts.

HELLO, HERE I AM!

ANSWER

14

Unleash Today Challenge: How to Make a Grand Entrance

Imagine tomorrow is your first day at work in your new role. How would you prepare yourself before embarking on this new professional journey? Try to think of everything you have learned in this chapter and envision additional ways of preparation.

ANSWER

Hello, Here I Am!

Expert Advice

Richard Pickard, CEO at Inclusive Search in London, UK

Start out with your goal in mind from day one. Where do you think this opportunity might take you in the next three to five years? What would success look like to you? I believe the smartest person in any room is usually the best prepared person. So, before you walk through the door, there is an opportunity for research. Let's begin with what expectations your new boss will have of you. Many hiring managers are happy to sit down with a new joiner for an informal coffee in the weeks before you arrive for your first day.

Spend some time online bringing yourself up to date on what has been moving and shaking in that company during the past few weeks. You can ask questions about their new market trends, new product launches, quarterly earnings results, and others. You can also search the company name on YouTube and LinkedIn, check out whether the leaders have spoken at recent conferences, given an overview of the company's growth story, and review the backgrounds of the team members, their educational, cultural, and employment backgrounds.

Think about how you will project your warmth, approachability, reliability, enthusiasm, authenticity, confidence, dignity, and focus. Speak clearly (not too loud, but not too quiet) and don't forget to smile!

It's the night before your first day and you've figured out your route to the office, you know the travel time, you've allowed 30 minutes extra time for unexpected delays, and you know the outfit you are going to wear. It's almost time to go get 'em! You're going to arrive nice and calm, always five minutes early.

As you travel, be aware that first days are always overwhelming, with lots of new information, too many names, and your perception that people are judging you. Don't panic, keep it simple. Deep breathing exercises really do help. Remind yourself that you were offered this job because you already came across as the most impressive match to the requirements of this role. Make sure that from the first moment people meet you they walk away feeling you are enthusiastic, positive, and willing to learn and smile. Look people in the eye, have a good posture, and a firm handshake.

There is absolutely nothing wrong with rehearsing in the mirror! You will feel a little strange at first—but familiarity creates confidence. Embrace the feeling of being out of your comfort zone (as this is when you will grow) and be brave!

Lesson learned

You only get one chance to make a first impression, so take time to prepare. Think about all the things you can control regarding how others will feel after interactions with you. Display a combination of confidence and focus, as well as warmth and authenticity. Smile, maintain strong eye contact, and listen carefully about what people are telling you. Use the person's name. Make an authentic personal connection.

Step Two: Strengthening Your Confidence Muscle

In our Step Two, we will be discussing how to:

- Become resilient and let go
- Overcome fear and self-doubt
- Boost your self-esteem and awareness
- Claim your seat at the table
- Fake it until you become it
- Practise to become confident

15

An Introduction to Confidence

> *Confidence never goes out of style.*
> **Sarah Wagner**

Imagine you're invited to a meeting, but when you get there you notice there aren't enough seats for everyone. Instead of taking one of the free chairs, you decide to stand at the back. Although you listen carefully to everything being said, you don't raise your hand to ask questions or voice your opinion. You might be worried that people might think you don't understand anything and fear that you would embarrass yourself in front of the others. Sounds familiar?

The phenomenon of capable people being plagued by self-doubt is often referred to as 'imposter syndrome'. While all people are susceptible to it, studies show that women are more likely to be affected by it.[14] Women tend to dwell on negative feelings and they worry about whether they are liked, attractive, or too dominant.

We may tell ourselves that we are incompetent and not worth the money we earn or the positions we hold,[15] but we're not the only ones. Even Sheryl Sandberg, COO* of Facebook, admits that there are still days when she feels like a fraud. She puts it well when noting that, in addition to institutional obstacles, women 'face a battle from within'.[16]

There is a plethora of articles online stipulating that a lack of confidence is holding women back. These articles usually provide so-called remedies to help women dismantle their imaginary hurdles. What we've found problematic about this self-confidence formula is the implication that women are patients. What's the treatment? Encourage women to be confident and strong, and they will become leaders in the workplace.[17]

Many women suffer from an 'acute lack of confidence',[18] but we don't choose to be less confident than men. Girls start out as confident leaders of their universes.[19] However, typically during puberty, they turn into more watchful and timid versions of themselves while the average boy becomes far more confident.[20]

Research suggests that the largest gender difference in self-reported confidence exists below the age of twenty-five. The level of confidence of women in their mid-twenties is at a startling 32 per cent in comparison to men's confidence of 49 per cent. However, men's confidence stagnates in their mid-thirties while women's reaches 40 per cent. It is only by the age of forty that the self-declared confidence gap usually disappears, and the confidence level of women and men is on par at 53 per cent and 55 per cent respectively. By the age of sixty, women eventually rate themselves as more confident than men.[21]

---

* Chief Operating Officer

We believe change is needed to ensure that women break the barriers society imposes on their self-confidence and unleash their full potential at an earlier stage in their life and in the workspace, in particular. All too often, they believe that hard work, good results, and competence are sufficient to excel and be recognised. However, studies show that confidence and self-assurance impact your success just as much as competence.[22]

In this Step, we will show you that all women can be confident when they let go of societal conditioning and self-doubt. Imagine confidence as a muscle in your body: you won't get a six pack unless you work out. As women, we have unlearned how to use our confidence muscle early in life. We are here to teach you to activate it again. The following parts in our book will provide you with tips on how your confidence muscle can be strengthened with the right exercises at any stage in your life.

16
Hard Work and Resilience

> *There is a future me that will be very happy I never gave up.*
>
> **Sarah Wagner**

Everyone can learn to be confident, but building your confidence is work in progress.[23] Confidence can be nourished through hard work, determination, and time.[24] While it won't happen overnight, you can take small steps every day to become more confident. You need to make the act of 'confidence building' a serious part of your life and consider it a goal that requires a development plan. Let's explore some tactics you might want to employ to boost your confidence.

Resilience and Letting Go

> *That which does not kill us, makes us stronger.*
>
> **Friedrich Nietzsche**

Developing confidence requires you to get out of your comfort zone and expose yourself to risks and failure. Failure is the stairway to success. If you want to succeed at gaining confidence, you have to learn to pick yourself up despite setbacks. Once you learn to embrace failure as an inherent part of your professional and personal life, you'll be able to move on more easily after a setback. You can't win without ever having lost!

While this might sound easy, we know that reality is very different. It's normal that your confidence level will fluctuate. One day you might feel like a queen, ready to conquer the world, and the next you would rather hide under your duvet. If you find yourself in the latter situation, we advise you follow this approach:

- **Acknowledge when you are having a bad day** and reach a low point. Recognising your emotional state allows you to accept your feelings. Be as compassionate with yourself as you are with others.

- **Create a mental break.** Once you have acknowledged that you're having a bad day, create distance between yourself and the problem. If it becomes too much, you must give yourself a break to regain your energy. Often, if you write down the facts and compare them with the image in your head, you will find that your mind is tricking you into thinking things are worse than they are.

- **Keep the bigger picture in mind** and put things into perspective. Ask yourself if the problem will still be important in a year. If the answer is 'no', then let it go. Reflect on your progress, write it down to internalise it, and picture how far you've already come. Don't let your mind trick you!

- **Stop ruminating.** Many of you will sit at home and think about work. You might think about what you did or didn't do, what you said, or your reaction to a comment. What a waste of time! You can't change what happened and overthinking will prevent you from moving on.

EXPERT MEMORY

Sarah Wagner and Kate Surala, Authors of *Unleash Today*

As we were writing this book, we experienced many highs and lows. The idea of helping other women become their best self-motivated us to spend our evenings, early mornings, and weekends writing this book. Not everyone seemed to believe in us and our idea, though. When we looked for publishers, we were told we did not have sufficient credibility in our twenties. When we approached a CEO to provide expert advice in our book, he replied that we hadn't achieved enough yet to write a book. For a moment or two, these comments made us think we couldn't do it. Was there some truth to the doubts they voiced?

But then we distanced ourselves from these emotions and thoughts. We consciously acknowledged the low point, accepted that not everyone would like our idea, reflected on what we could learn from these experiences, and moved on. We were more convinced than ever in our mission to help young ambitious women to maximise their potential. We did it and here is our book as evidence that this is possible.

Lesson learned
Everyone has an opinion; it's up to you to either accept it or reject it.

Here are some of the tools we have used to deal with a spiralling mind. They can help you prevent negative thoughts from taking over:

- **Notice when you're stuck in a rut.** Overthinking can turn into a bad habit and it's important to be aware of this from the beginning.

- **Challenge your negative thoughts!** Acknowledge that your thoughts might focus on the negatives and block out the positives, resulting in a skewed perception of reality. You can find more details about this topic in Step Five on love.

- **Focus on productive thoughts** that lead to positive actions, finding solutions, and/or ways to prevent the problem in the future.

- **Distract yourself.** Change your thoughts by changing your activities. Take up a sport or join a debate or project that will make you think about something else!

> **EXPERT MEMORY**
>
> **Paul Newton, former member of the Executive Team at Bupa in London, UK**
>
> One of the most difficult challenges we face in life is dealing with failure, especially when it's in the form of negative feedback. However, failure drives success. The worst thing we can do is to attribute our failure to the flaws and failings of others or to outside circumstances.
>
> When I was the head of a multi-award winning, global legal team at Bupa, I was held accountable for my team's results, even though there were many measures that looked like they were beyond my control. My results early on were so bad I was put into the 'remedial class'. However, the results weren't the problem—I was.
>
> My thinking was all wrong. I had to embrace feedback and hold myself accountable, even for feedback I had little control over, or I felt was unjustified. The intention wasn't to beat myself up, but simply to learn from what was going wrong and to turn it around.
>
> In the end, the biggest reward wasn't the fact that my team received both internal and external recognition and national and international industry awards. It was the way I was changed by the experience and that it made me a better leader (though still imperfect as my team would have been quick to point out!).
>
> **Lesson learned**
>
> Failure can be leveraged to produce success. Feedback is a gift to be embraced, even if it hurts. Accepting you are the source of the problem means you can be the source of the solution.

Resilience and Letting Go

> *Courage is not the absence of fear, but rather the assessment that something is more important than fear.*
>
> **Franklin D. Roosevelt**

We're often surprised to meet someone who believes confident people display a 'natural bravery', as if they had a magic button to take their fear away. However, courageous people aren't born like this. They learned to face their fear and act in spite of its existence. Once you name your fear, it loses its power. Try it now with the following exercise:

What makes you afraid? Write your thoughts down.

> **ANSWER**

Once you have identified your fears, you can train your confidence! Just like your body strength you can train your confidence muscle by overriding fear with action. Start taking action and leave your fear behind so you can achieve your dreams. We assist you in developing an action plan in Step Three on overcoming perfectionism.

> " *If it excites you, do it,*
> *If it scares you, do it,*
> *If you don't know how to yet, find a way*
> *and take the first step.* "
>
> **Franklin D. Roosevelt**[*]

---

[*] *Unleash Today* expert and a Mindset and Leadership Coach in London, UK.

A common rule in driving is to refrain from going through a traffic light when you're unsure if you'll make it before it turns red. However, the opposite applies at work. We advise when in doubt, do it anyway!

Whenever you feel like something is too big for you, just do it! It might seem frightening, but as soon as you're on the road you'll realise that it isn't so bad. Stop thinking about what others might say and let go of all the what-ifs.

Lastly, take comfort in the fact that everyone feels fear. It's how you mask it that develops you as a person. Read relevant books and speak to encouraging people who will help you find the words to talk the fear away.* Ready to jump off the cliff and pursue your dreams?

---

* You can find a list of our favourite books on our *Unleash Today* website (www.unleashtoday.com).

EXPERT MEMORY

Cheryl Miller Houser, Founder and CEO at Creative Breed in New York, US

Before I launched my own company, I was the Head of Production at a large TV production company. I had initially been happy in the job, but began to feel a yearning to move on. I stayed in that job for several years longer than I should have, becoming increasingly more miserable.

I stayed because of fear. I was afraid of walking away from a secure income, even though I had saved enough to give myself a long runway. I was afraid of who I would be if I left my job, since my sense of self was tied to a fancy title and an established company.

One day, the founder of the company did something so against my values that I felt compelled to resign. At first, I felt relief, and then terror. And then I embraced my new-found freedom to forge my own path forward and started my own production company. Now I push myself outside my comfort zone every day. Although I still sometimes feel fear when I face a major new challenge, I see how capable I am when I conquer it.

Lesson learned

The more we push ourselves outside our comfort zone and overcome our fears, the stronger and braver we become. It's truly like developing a muscle. As we conquer our fears and challenges, we build confidence, uncover strengths, and realise that we're capable of so much more than we ever could imagine.

Self-Esteem and Awareness

> *I've learned how self-esteem is my most valuable asset and nobody can take that away from me.*

Rebecca Perrin[*]

Being confident is, in part, not allowing other people's judgments to influence your self-esteem. Don't just try to be who you are, but fully own every aspect of what makes you who you are. Be proud of yourself. Self-esteem must come from within you instead of from outside sources, like others' recognition.

Fully owning yourself can be difficult, particularly if you're operating in a system that wasn't built for women. We've heard it all! Throughout our careers, people have told us that we should relax and respect hierarchies. Whenever we followed this advice, we managed to blend in for a while, but we realised we had the potential to achieve so much more by being ourselves.

Being strong-minded and direct are strengths that many people aspire to develop, and we shouldn't unlearn them to suit others. Many people who say that you're too much usually struggle to be confident, or are just jealous. It usually means they're intimidated by your power and authenticity! Rather than trying to improve someone's attitude, take it as a compliment when people criticise your level of confidence.

---

[*] *Unleash Today* expert, Communications Expert, Professional Writer, and Host of Women Talk Shop podcast in Toronto, Canada.

If people disregard you as they think you're a shy pushover, it would be worth working on your posture (see Step One for more details). Shy people tend to curl up into themselves and try to make themselves look as small as possible. Having a good posture with squared shoulders and an open chest makes you feel stronger. Feeling stronger physically will help you to feel stronger mentally as well, boosting your confidence.[25] There are exercises that can help improve your posture and, in doing so, you will also increase your confidence. It's worth checking out videos on online streaming channels (our *Unleash Today* YouTube channel provides various webinars on this topic).

Eventually, you'll rub someone up the wrong way. Accept this. You won't be liked by everyone. A conscious realisation of the path you're on will help you to build up the resilience you need to deal with the possible crash that you'll face along the way. You're part of a tapestry of women who are seeking to rewrite the rules by refusing to blend in. Be prepared to face obstacles and disagreements and build up the strength to swim against the stream.

Award-winning author Elaine Welteroth says, 'As a FOD,* sometimes just being yourself is the radical act. When you occupy space in a system that wasn't built for you, your authenticity is your activism.'[26] You have every right in the world to take up that space with your feelings, body and ideas. You do not need to shrink or hide any part of yourself. Don't let the world cage you!

---

* First, Only, Different. The term was coined by Shonda Rhimes to address the pressure of being an African American, female, showrunner and the burden of extra responsibility she experienced in her position.

EXPERT MEMORY

Anonymous

'Leave it. Jane can do it.'

I heard those words following a meeting where a confidential document had been distributed. I was meant to collect all the papers and shred them on the team's behalf. I froze, astonished at the order. I needed to inhale and exhale a few times.

A male colleague stepped in and offered to follow the order instead. I learned to rehearse a few sentences to be prepared for similar situations in the future. One example would be: 'Thank you for the idea, but I think everyone should shred their own document, so we all remember the importance of confidentiality.'

Lesson learned

Maintaining confidence is a life-long struggle. Remind yourself that confident women have always had to fight and will continue to do so, until we bring about change. It's best to prepare and develop routines to help you. (See Step Five on self love for further tips and Step Six on dealing with difficult situations).

17

Change Your Attitude: Raise Your Voice and Sit at the Table

> *The thing women have yet to learn is nobody gives you power. You just take it.*
>
> **Roseanne Barr**

Nobody, not even the kindest boss, will ever serve you a promotion or pay rise on a silver platter. They won't just acknowledge your hard work someday and reward you accordingly. At most, your hard work will get a 'thank you'.

Fig. 8
Find your seat at the table

Learn to ask for what you think you deserve, or you'll never get it! Imagine you were your employer and only had a limited budget and positions. Would you just hand out titles and higher salaries if you saw someone excel at their work? Don't just wait for your work to be recognised. Make sure you discuss your performance and combine those discussions with requests for bonuses and promotions. We share more tips on how to master your career progression in Step Seven on growth and development in the workplace.

> **Expert Memory**
>
> **Sarah Wagner, Co-Author of *Unleash Today***
>
> I was always often annoyed by how often many of my male colleagues fought for attention and recognition from our boss in meetings. Most women just watched and listened. While I'm sure my boss noticed the competition, she let it happen as she benefited from the fight for the best ideas. The truth is, a meeting with your boss is one of the few opportunities where you can demonstrate your competence and creativity. Be smart and take advantage of them!
>
> **Lesson learned**
>
> You can be yourself and authentic while playing the rules. Either throw your hat into the ring or miss out on the chance of success.

Unleash Today

Claiming Your Seat

> *If they don't give you a seat at the table, bring a folding chair.*
>
> **Shirly Chisholm***

We encourage you to become more conscious of your behaviour and to take charge by stepping forward and claiming a seat at the table. Make it a habit to raise your hand during discussions, to speak up first, and lead presentations whenever possible. Make an effort to stop hiding behind your colleagues and refrain from overthinking how people might feel about you. This is particularly relevant with the number of virtual meetings we have since COVID-19. Turn on your camera and raise your virtual hand rather than muting yourself and staying in the background. Imposter syndrome, adieu! Be the strong woman we know you are.

Remind yourself that, while you're occupied with self-doubt, your colleagues may have already raised the point that you intended to bring up. Make it a habit to always share your ideas and viewpoints. Even if you think your contribution might not be worth gold, it's still worth throwing it on the table.

We understand that it might be more difficult for introverted women to claim their seat. Here are some of our tips on helping introverts, or people who're just a bit shy, to find their seat:

- **Remind yourself of your self-worth.** You bring value to the discussions and others should be grateful

---

* First black woman elected as a Congresswoman in the US.

- **Only think about yourself** and not what others are thinking about you.

- **Focus on the discussion** rather than your response to what has been said. Enjoy listening, take notes, and make comments on the points that interest you and you have thoughts on.

- **Write down any relevant questions** before an event if you are worried about saying them in public, as it'll help you to articulate yourself in the moment.

- **Get a feel for the meeting or event style** and adjust your body language and tone accordingly. You can make comments once you feel comfortable.

  You can address points via email after an event if you're too shy to ask the question or comment in person.

- **It's ok to say you're nervous.** Many people feel like this and, by acknowledging it, you will feel more comfortable.

EXPERT MEMORY

Denise Kellner, Editorial Lead at *Unleash Today*

I often struggle with trying to find the right words at events. Over the years, I've witnessed that men are often the first to raise questions in Q&A sessions. They don't overthink but immediately ask, triggering discussion and taking part in the debate. Even Jo

Swinson, a former member of the UK parliament, has struggled to speak up and taken too long to think of how to perfectly phrase a question, only to find that no more questions were being taken.[27]

Lesson learned
Don't try to be perfect. Ask the questions that are on your mind. Don't wait until it's too late. Others don't wait, so why should you?

Fake it Till You Become It

> *I've not mastered my own uncertainty of being visible, but I know how to look confident to get my message across and keep practising.*
>
> **Katharina Krentz**[*]

You don't have to be entirely free of self-doubt or fully prepared from the start. By taking the leap into a daunting situation, you're freeing yourself of doubt. Be patient with yourself and practise. In the meantime, we recommend you fake it until you become it. If you want people to think that you are confident, act like the person you want to be, and true confidence will follow. Acting is a good way of overcoming your fear and stopping yourself from procrastinating. You can imagine using your 'confident face mask'—the way

---
[*] *Unleash Today* expert, Corporate HR Transformation Lead at Bosch, and Founder of Connecting Humans, living in Leonberg, Germany.

you see yourself when you're at a confidence high-point until you become naturally confident.

> **EXPERT MEMORY**
>
> **Maren Assmus, Personal stylist in Berlin, Germany**
>
> My business partner, Janine, and I had a meeting in the most prestigious department store in Germany, the kind of meeting where you get 15 minutes to impress. Our meeting was right after her pedicure appointment which left her a few minutes before our big meeting with the boss of the department store.
> But her nail varnish wasn't dry yet and if she had put on her shoes, they would've ruined her shiny polish. That's when I said, 'Let's fake it till we make it! We're stylists and whatever we wear is the trend.'
> So, Janine went to the meeting barefoot. I saw the manager's eyes rest on Janine's feet. All I said

was, 'That's how people wear it these days, didn't you know?' We all smiled, and it was the perfect icebreaker.

Lesson learned
Sometimes things don't work out like you planned. Then you have to make a decision within a split second before someone else makes it for you. Stand with whatever you decide, even if you're not sure it'll work out.

Using Humour and Improv to Gain More Confidence

> *Confidence shouldn't come from knowing what's going to happen; confidence should come from knowing that whatever happens, you'll be able to adapt.*

Andrew Tarvin[*]

One way of projecting confidence is to make a joke. People connect with strong emotions and confident people often enjoy a laugh with others. Humour in the workplace can be very empowering and could be used as a tool for responding to awkward situations, as we will further discuss in Step Six, focussing on how to handle difficult situations.

Humour
Humour is a universal human trait and is a very effective tool to be applied in various circumstances. Bringing humour to

---
[*] *Unleash Today* expert, Comedian, Improviser, Humourist, and Founder and CEO of Humor That Works in New York, US.

the workplace can bring about a number of benefits such as enhancing productivity, reducing stress, getting people to listen, and increasing likability or fostering rapport.[28]

Researchers have found that people perceive those who use humour as more confident and competent than those not willing to crack a joke.[29] Making jokes can also help you develop your confidence. By making others laugh, you gain their acknowledgment. Don't say that you're not funny. Humour is a skill everyone can learn. Here are a few simple, comedic techniques you can use:

- **Don't abandon your joke** before the punchline. When you crack a joke, follow it up with a statement or two, or you might not get a laugh.
- **Use observational comedy.** Pay attention to the absurdities of life and point them out as if you don't understand them.
- **Trust your instincts** to identify the appropriate time for making a joke and avoid making self-deprecating jokes revolving around your insecurities. Rather make situational jokes.

Improvisational Theatre

Improvisational theatre (improv) is a form of live theatre where characters, conversations, and a story are made up in the moment without previous preparation. Typically, you're confident when you're prepared for a situation, and improv is a great tool to prepare for unexpected circumstances. With improv, there is a constant risk of failure as you don't get to prepare for the audience's reactions. Not knowing what the outcome is will help you become more comfortable in difficult situations. Improv teaches you to be calm and react quickly in spite of stress and fear.

Start with easy improv exercises in front of your mirror or with family or friends. Once you're ready, you can implement your new skills at work. Here are a few exercises we do:

- **First-letter-last-letter game.** In this game, the first letter of the word you say has to start with the last letter of the previous word. For example, if I say 'chair', the next person could say 'ribbon'.
- **Thank you game.** With this game, you have to begin every sentence with 'thank you'.
- **Thumbs up game.** Look into the mirror and hold up your thumb on one hand and the index finger of the other. Then quickly swap them several times.

Reading and Mirroring Expressions

> *Read people like books from start to finish. If you skip pages, you might miss important insights.*
>
> **Kate Surala**

As many people fake confidence, you should learn to read them. There are traces which give away people's 'masked' confidence. For instance, start by watching other people's feet; they reveal a lot. People can control their hand and arm movements, but legs and feet are often unpractised.

Strengthening Your Confidence Muscle

They'll tap, wiggle, or wrap around one another, which may suggest that someone wants to leave a discussion, is nervous or not fully engaged.

You can also benefit from other people. To develop confidence, mirror your opposite's expressions and postures. Imagine you find yourself in a situation where you want to agree with someone else's statement or idea. If you want to show that you agree with a colleague's point and avoid excessive nodding—studies found that this can be also seen as a weakness—you can imitate their body language.

When you mirror other people with intent, it can have a positive side-effect and be an important part of building rapport with someone else. Doing so will make the other person feel understood and accepted. However, we acknowledge this technique can be especially difficult or awkward if you don't identify with the expressions to be mirrored.

Write down the facial expressions that you would like to actively avoid (frown, rolling eyes, etc.):

Answer:

> **EXPERT MEMORY**
>
> **Sarah Wagner and Kate Surala, Authors of *Unleash Today***
>
> Both of us are often asked how we manage to develop such a high level of confidence at a young age. Apparently, we come across as very confident in many situations. Sometimes, this makes us laugh, as we've been in various situations where we didn't feel confident at all. But here is a secret to keep in mind: most people out there aren't confident at all. They just pretend to be, and you should develop an eye to identify their level of confidence by observing them carefully. Knowing how confident a person is will help you to know how to approach and influence them and boost your own confidence at the same time.
>
> **Lesson learned**
> Next time you see a person who gives you the impression they are confident, look a little closer. Watch if they are nervous, speak fast, or tremble. Observe how they react to you and others.

Practise to Become Confident

> *I no longer approach presenting with fear and hatred. I seize every opportunity to present as a career defining moment.*
>
> **Mita Mallick**[*]

---

[*] *Unleash Today* expert and Head of Inclusion, Equity, and Impact at Carta, in New York, US.

STRENGTHENING YOUR CONFIDENCE MUSCLE

Being confident is a learned skill. Public speaking is a task that requires confidence whether you're presenting or speaking up in a meeting. Although you might dislike—or even hate—public speaking as it may make you nervous, it's a skill that you need to master to get far in your career. You might be afraid that things will go wrong but if you don't take risks, you won't open yourself up to more visibility and new opportunities.

You may practise for years and prepare to the maximum, but you might end up feeling very nervous regardless. Accept that a certain feeling of nervousness will accompany you for your entire life. It won't go away, no matter how experienced you grow and how much you practise you get. Rather, develop some techniques to keep your nervousness under control. You can also embrace it as a positive sentiment that helps you to focus and concentrate.

> **EXPERT ADVICE**
>
> **Mita Mallick, Head of Inclusion, Equity, and Impact at Carta in New York, US**
>
> For me, getting over my hatred of presenting was about practise and preparation. I practised talking points while driving, in the shower, while I cooked. I practised presenting with my husband, trusted colleagues at work. I raised my hand for opportunities to present. Sharing an innovation at a staff meeting. Volunteering to lead the team exercise. Offering to close the meeting. I practised, practised, and practised some more. Now, I don't approach presenting with fear and hatred. I seize every opportunity to present as a career defining moment. And now I actually enjoy presenting.

> **EXPERT MEMORY**
>
> **Sophie Gould, Head of Learning and Development at Flex Legal in London, UK**
>
> I used to be very nervous before presentations. What if I was asked a question I didn't know the answer to? Other presenters seemed so confident and never forgot their words. I found mentors who I had seen presenting and had a style I liked. It was a shock to hear how they still got nervous before presenting—they seemed so natural at it. Here are the tips they shared with me and some other tips I have picked up along the way:
>
> - If you are invited to present, think carefully about the audience and the topic. Is it relevant to your role or interests and can you add value? If not, politely say 'no'.

- Rehearse, rehearse, rehearse! I always write out what I am going to say in full, record myself saying it, and listen back (at this stage, I usually cut out about half of what I was going to say!). The most important thing to remember about presenting is that no one in the audience knows what you are going to say so if you miss a bit no one will know.
- When it comes to the presentation, my heart begins to pound so I always give myself a few seconds on stage to look at the audience and begin to engage them without yet speaking. Remember to introduce yourself, your topic, and what you will be covering.
- Don't be afraid of a few seconds of silence if you need to catch your breath. Wait for someone to ask a question or consider your answer to a question posed—it may feel like an eternity to you, but the audience will be unlikely to notice.
- If someone asks a question, you don't know the answer to, my top tip is to throw it back to the audience. Perhaps say, 'That's a really interesting question. Do any of you have any thoughts on that?'
- Finally, sum up at the end. Remind them of what you said you would cover, remind them how you covered it, and highlight any learning points for them to take away.

Lesson learned

Get used to the thought that you will always be nervous before a presentation. Learn to embrace this nervousness and turn it into positive energy.

Excelling at presenting is particularly relevant for entrepreneurs, who regularly have to pitch in front of potential investors. In these cases, there is really something at stake and the pressure is real. You have to convince others about your idea by telling an authentic story. Learning your script by heart doesn't automatically translate into success, as you might not be able to transmit your enthusiasm as well as you would otherwise. Rather than learning a script by heart word by word develop some techniques to keep your nervousness under control.

> **EXPERT MEMORY**
>
> **Galit Zuckerman, who raised 30 million dollars to found her biometric software company in Israel**
>
> I must have pitched my company hundreds of times. And so many times I've been self-critical of my presentation. However, I had a story to tell, and I knew it was a good one.
>
> I think that the most effective meetings that eventually translated into investments were those where I worried much less about speaking. Those were meetings where I was comfortable, just talking with another interesting person. Just realising that taught me my first lesson for introduction meetings with investors: RELAX.
>
> Before my meeting, I usually briefly review my pitch and presentation, which we've crafted with years of experience and with feedback from many experienced people around me. I usually have my favourite coffee and allow myself a sweet treat to give me a boost if

I need it. When you arrive at a meeting with positive energies, it will inevitably go much better.

I usually try to start a meeting by asking the investors to introduce themselves before I begin my pitch, so everyone feels more comfortable and you understand what kind of information they are looking for. To keep my audience engaged, I try not to give a presentation, but to tell a story (even if a slide deck is being displayed on the screen). At the end, I leave some time for questions and also a fruitful discussion.

Remember it's normal you will face many 'Nos' before getting to 'Yes'. Use each interaction to learn and improve for the next. Keep in mind that you are building a network, so that people who say no today may still be your potential investors in the next round or even at the end of your current round…

Lesson learned

Just relax. Believe in yourself and in your company so that you can engage comfortably with your investor audience. If you know that your company or idea is great, you'll be able to make it to the next step. Tell a story rather than reading out a script.

18
Unleash Today Challenge: Confidence

Imagine you've just started a new job at your dream company. The moment you arrive, you're told that an important meeting is about to start that you should join. The management team will be discussing the annual strategy on a topic you specialise in. You know that strategic planning is your strong suit, so you go ahead and enter a room full of men. Everyone is looking at you and then you're asked to deliver your perspective on a matter without having anything prepared. What would you do?

ANSWER

> **EXPERT ADVICE**
>
> **Gina Miller, Co-Founder at SCM Direct and the Lead Claimant in the Brexit case against the UK government**
>
> As this is your dream company, you have done your homework when it comes to this topic. You think back quickly to what they said at the interview about your positive attributes and how they are connected with their strategic goals. You can think of three big points, 'the power of three': people form immediate three-second impressions that can be hard to dislodge when meeting someone new. They usually tend to only remember or be able to disseminate three ideas. You also need to work out who the three most important people are at the meeting.
>
> You know you're nervous and the dreaded imposter syndrome will be doing its best to get into your

head, but you must overcome any negative feelings. Firstly, it's important to take a very deep breath and remain relaxed, not just with your body but your mind and face, too. Remind yourself that when you knock on the door to enter, it is not too light or too hard, one decisive knock and then open the door about halfway. Resist at all costs the first word out of your mouth being 'Sorry?' or something in a questioning tone.

Then there's the big question of where to sit. If the meeting has already started, there may not be a spare seat or there may be one against a back wall. If it's against a wall, you need to pick it up and ask very politely for the men to create a space for you at the table—you have to try to make it near the centre—not the front or back. You don't have the seniority to be at the top, but they think you have something to contribute so why sit at the back? After all, they asked you to join the meeting.

When you're nervous or caught off guard, remember that women's voices tend to go up an octave or two and we also tend to speak faster. So, the second rule: your words have to be deliberately lower and slower. Remember to breathe between points and don't look down. Posture is important, too. If you own your space and fill it with confidence, those are the unconscious messages and signs others will pick up.

It is an internal meeting so you need to show you can be collegiate. Even if you know the answer, make sure to ask the men for their views, too—you know they like to be the 'peacock', so allow them just enough space to do that. Listen carefully to their responses and comments, along with the inevitable mansplaining (physically and verbally), which can give you an edge when you respond to what they're saying.

Begin with a complement or two, then move the conversation onto your point or action. For extra brownie points, it's worth bringing in any analogy/reference to a sport, hobby/interest, part of the country/world they come from. Acknowledgement and a little flattery not only go a long way, but it will help them remember you both on an intellectual and emotional level. And you want to be remembered.

As the meeting is coming to a close, you must quickly work out how to stay at the table and remain connected with the team. Take the initiative to ask whether there is a task you can own and report back to them on?

Until you're out of sight, you will show no nerves, walk away with as much confidence and grace as you walked into the room with. We talk about bringing our whole self to work and to me that means bringing your EQ as well as your IQ. To influence progress and change, you need to be part of the strategic decision-making machinery that can result in the business being responsible and employing our social capital for the benefit of all our stakeholders.

Lesson learned

It's your passion so do not let anyone tell you where to be, that you don't deserve to be there or not to use your voice. This is your dream company, and you dream of making a reality of the good we can do.

Step Three:
I'm a Recovering Perfectionist

In our Step Three, we will be discussing how to:

- Change your attitude towards success
- Define and implement your goals
- Create a personal vision board
- Establish your excellence standards
- Find your accountability partner
- Recognise your emotional triggers and achieve a positive mindset

19

An Introduction to Perfectionism

> *Perfect does not exist. Accept it. Strive for excellence instead.*
>
> **Kate Surala**

It's late on Friday night and you're the last one left in the office. You can barely keep your eyes open while you go through the memo you've been working on for days. An image of your friends enjoying a night out pops into your mind while you're alone. But your inner voice pressures you to keep going. You need it to be perfect.

Finally, you hit send. You drag yourself home for a late night dinner and all you want to do is go to sleep. Your perfectionism got the best of you once again!

If you've ever felt the urge to ensure that everything you do is perfect, let us assure you that you're not alone. Many of us struggle with perfectionism. A study confirmed that perfectionism has risen among students of all ages and genders. Today, the average graduate is more likely to have perfectionist tendencies than a student in the 1990s or early 2000s.[30]

This increase has been correlated with a rise in depression and anxiety. Unrealistic expectations prevent people from seeing their work objectively and impair their ability to assess its worth. Perfectionism brings about feelings of failure, guilt, and self-esteem.[31]

The pursuit of perfectionism holds many women back in their personal and professional lives. We know that female perfectionism isn't biological, but a result of our socialisation.[32] Most girls are taught to play it safe and get the best grades. However, boys are often taught to explore and are encouraged to be adventurous. Somehow, being brave has become a more masculine trait, while females are encouraged to be perfect instead. As a result, women are aiming to be perfect before they can even be themselves.[33] How can we replace this never ending desire for perfectionism and accept that excellence is sufficient?

20

Choose Your 'Perfection' Wisely

> *Perfect is the enemy of good.*
>
> **Voltaire**

Perfectionism makes you see yourself as defective and flawed. It's like a destructive companion, constantly criticising you, leaving you drained and anxious. Perfectionism means seeking to get everything right in the eyes of others. As the image below shows, seeking perfection means aiming for the impossible. Instead, you should channel your energy towards an attainable goal: excellence.

By pursuing perfection at all times, you're holding yourself to unrealistically high standards. It's not worth pursuing perfectionism. Perfectionism is dangerous and, eventually, destructive to your own happiness. You might be able to uphold artificially high standards for a period of time, but remember that both your professional and personal life are a marathon, not a sprint.

Excellence means focussing your attention on the overall result rather than being bogged down by small mistakes. If you want the best in your life and career, pursue excellence.

The Perfectionism Scale

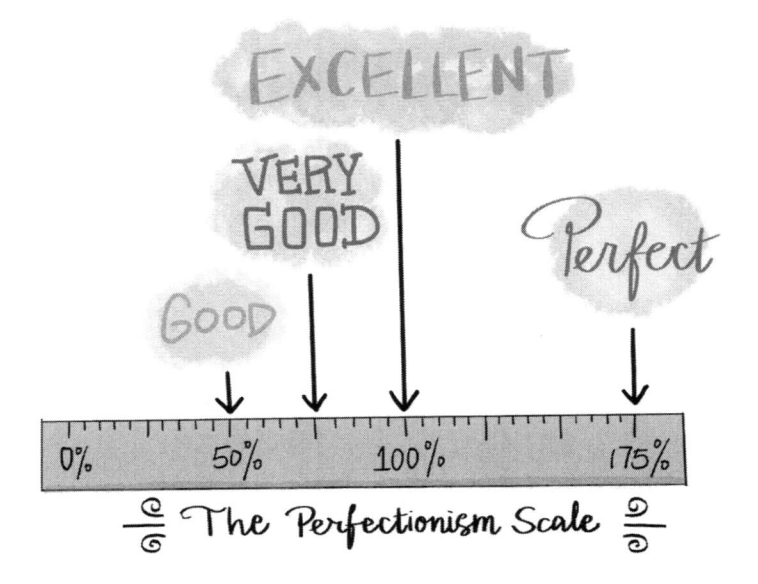

Change Your Attitude Towards Your Successes

> *When you aim for perfection, you discover it's a moving target.*

Geoffrey Fisher, Archbishop of Canterbury

The pursuit of perfection is a vicious cycle that will never stop until you stop it. You might get caught up in living in the future, judging your self-worth by the achievement of unattainable goals. Once you have accomplished one goal, you might not consider it a success a few days later and immediately start planning your next goal.

For perfectionists, performance is intertwined with a sense of self. This can be changed with a different mindset.[34] However, this switch isn't easy when you've lived as a perfectionist all your life. It's a continuous effort.

The secret is to embrace excellence as the new perfect. Keep in mind that the pleasure you get from achieving a goal often only lasts moments before moving on to a higher aim. You keep planning, achieving your goals, and falling back into misery, feeling that you have not done enough. The resulting disappointments can feel discouraging, can generate depression and lead to self-loathing.

Being overly goal-driven can be harmful and prevent you from living in the moment. Therefore, it's essential to find a balance between having goals to guide your life and rushing after a dream that prevents you from embracing the here and now. We discuss more tips on love habits in Step Five.

Defining Your Goals: Have a Clear Idea of What You Want to Achieve

> *Our goals can only be reached through a vehicle of a plan, in which we must fervently believe, and upon which we must vigorously act. There is no other route to success.*
>
> **Pablo Picasso**

Goals are a part of every aspect of your life, providing a sense of direction, motivation, and focus. In order to set a clear goal, you must have a target. But how can you create your formula for success and set the right goals? We recommend using the well established SMART method for goal setting,[35] which stands for:

- **Specific**: well defined, clear, and unambiguous
- **Measurable**: specific criteria can measure your progress towards your accomplishment
- **Achievable**: attainable
- **Realistic**: within reach and relevant to your purpose and values
- **Timely**: a clearly defined timeline, including a start and target date to increase urgency[36]

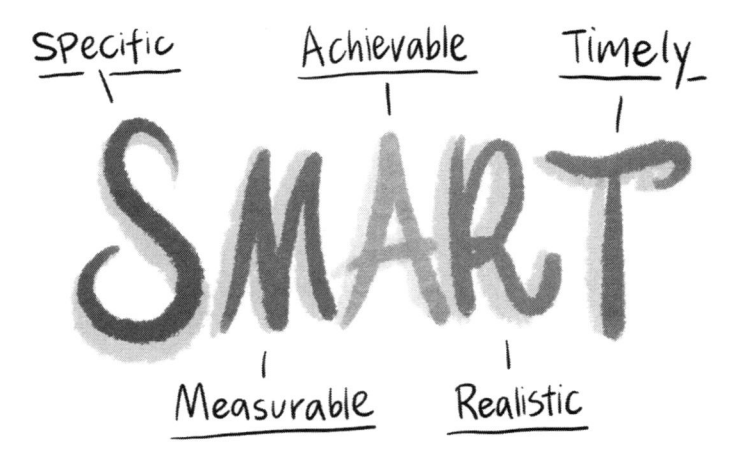

You should start with the right definition of your goal and a clear idea of where you want to go next. Never forget what your motivation is by reminding yourself of your purpose and values. Ensure that your professional goals align with these, as they will help you to decide where you want to go.

Academics who research goal setting suggest asking yourself the following five questions, which will help you to make your goals as concrete and realistic as possible:

- Who is involved with this goal?
- What do I want to accomplish?
- Where is this goal going to be achieved?
- When do I want to achieve this goal?
- Why do I want to achieve this goal?[37]

Using the SMART method and asking yourself these questions will help you to accomplish the right and concrete goals, aligning with your excellence standard, purpose, and values. By setting general and unrealistic goals, such as 'I want to be the best at X', many people will set themselves up for failure.

> **EXPERT MEMORY**
>
> **Kate Surala, Co-Author of *Unleash Today***
>
> One of my biggest dreams was to study at the University of Oxford. It seemed impossible but the goal kept me going. When I was studying my Bachelor's degree in Maastricht, I decided I would do anything to achieve my dream. I even printed out a picture of Radcliffe Camera, a famous library in Oxford, and taped it to my wall. It accompanied me during the best and worst moments at Maastricht. Once I even wanted to throw it

away, as I felt I would never get there. But, on 9 March 2016, I received an email from the course coordinator for the Master's degree in Law and Finance. I was offered a conditional offer. I couldn't believe it. I cried over the phone to my parents. You know you're nervous and the dreaded imposter syndrome will be doing its best to get into your head, but you must overcome any negative feelings.

However, the first time I arrived and saw Radcliffe Camera, I didn't feel happy for long. I felt a sense of fulfilment for a few days but after I'd settled, I started thinking, 'What's my next goal?' I'm really happy I achieved one of my biggest dreams, but I want to emphasise that it's not healthy to live from one goal to the next. The key is to craft your plans carefully and execute them one by one while enjoying the process.

Lesson learned
Don't only live in the future. Enjoy the present and embrace the now.

Take Kate's Oxford situation as an example. A general goal would be, 'I would like to study at the University of Oxford'. However, a more specific goal would be, 'I would like to study a Master's degree in Law and Finance at the University of Oxford during the academic year 2016/2017, and successfully graduate in order to start my career in London'.

It's important to remember that maintaining a healthy lifestyle and work-life balance is just as important as building your career. Aduke shares how she handled so many tasks without getting overwhelmed.

> **EXPERT MEMORY**
>
> **Aduke Onafowokan, Principal Consultant at Full-Service Diversity and Inclusivitii and Founder of The Sister Sister Global Network in London, UK**
>
> My life can be really hectic as a Mum of two, next to running Sister Sister Network and my management consultancy. I remember being particularly overwhelmed while I was working on a project for the Ministry of Defence, I had multiple conflicting priorities everywhere. I remember just having this sinking feeling I was failing at being a mum, wife, and everything else.
>
> Then it hit me that I was not processing what success and competency meant positively. This idea that you can do it all, have it all every time can be a trap.
>
> The first step is to understand that it's a process and that you are very much part of that process. Push yourself but don't put yourself down. Life is not meant to be perfect, but to be experienced. My advice is to remember that effort matters just as much as outcome—showing up, trying your best and being there is an achievement.
>
> It is also important to have a clear action plan. I use a weekly plan to coordinate all the moving parts of my life, from school meetings to client reviews, I can tell ahead of time which weeks are going to be crazy and mentally prepare for this. When I have to make a compromise, I know ahead of time what exactly I am compromising.

Finally, it's ok to ask for help, especially when you are overwhelmed. You do not have to do it all alone. There is an African proverb that I love: 'Alone you go faster, together you go further'.

Lesson learned
Effort really matters. Define success not just based on your outcomes, but also your effort and don't beat yourself too much when things don't pan out as planned. Have a comprehensive plan, and don't forget to ask for help.

Create a Personal Vision Board

> *Don't allow your value, your vision or your voice to be diluted by someone else's capacity to 'see'.*

Debbie Hayes[*]

Visualisation is one of the most powerful methods that can help you to define your goals. According to Rhona Byrne, 'When you are visualising, you are emitting a powerful frequency out into the Universe'.[38] Even Olympic athletes have been using vision boards for decades to improve performance.[39]

By creating an inspirational collage, your future goals will feel more tangible and easier to define. Depicting

---
[*] *Unleash Today* expert and Coach and Author in Sandbach, UK.

your goals in this way will stimulate your emotions, which is especially important as many people's minds respond better to visual stimulation rather than words.[40] By looking at your vision board daily, you'll become more motivated, making it easier to reach your goals.[41] In early 2020, we sat down and created a vision board that shows how we are writing this book, growing our team, and helping so many women like yourself to Unleash Today!

But how do you create an empowering vision board? Start by writing down your dreams and trying to visualise them. Try to find matching images, as the most fun thing to do is to create a collage and compose a vision board.[42]

Unleash Today

Celebrate Your Successes

> *Life is not a competition, focus inward, love yourself, and be who you truly are.*

Kate Surala

'Focus on yourself and don't compare yourself to others.' We've all heard this at least once, but it's easier said than done. It's a bad habit that we are all guilty of at times and it often leaves us thinking we can never measure up to other people's accomplishments. Such negative thoughts are dangerous, as they undermine your confidence. You can stop this vicious cycle by remembering our six tips:

1. You are unique
Learn to embrace your individuality and cherish the characteristics that make you unique. In times of self-doubt, it's common to think that you have no gifts or talents, but this isn't the case. Everyone is gifted in some way and it's up to you to find and exploit these gifts.

You have to change your perspective and think of how exceptional you are. Ask yourself these questions and jot your answers in a mind map to celebrate your unique personality traits!

- What have you achieved so far?
- What are your strengths?
- What are you most proud of?

2. Nobody is perfect

We compare ourselves to others daily and social media is a major culprit. It gives us the illusion that everyone—whether it's friends, family, or colleagues—has a perfect life. Studies continuously prove that social media has a damaging effect on mental health, especially for young women.[43]

Social media encourages us to present positive and attractive images that might be misleading to some and harmful to others. Psychological research[44] has shown that this representation can lead to anxiety and acute stress that could cause severe depression. Researchers believe that an increase in perfectionism is likely to be linked to social media.

Apart from taking the drastic measure of deleting your social media accounts, what can you do to stop comparing yourself to others? Here are a few of our tips to free yourself from this unhealthy grip:

- **Take a break** from social media by temporarily locking yourself out of your accounts.

- **Social media detoxes** for a set number of days and/or weeks means you can invest your time in other things while keeping in contact with friends and family.

- **Set aside a specific time of the day** for social media and implement a time limit to reduce the number of hours you're on social media.

- **Focus on a few social media networks** and follow the accounts that inspire you. Follow visionary personalities that motivate you to act and pursue your goals.

- **Unfollow people** who make you feel bad about yourself.

- **Reduce the pressure you put on yourself.** You don't have to see everyone's updates, post all the time, or follow everyone in your life.

- **Feel encouraged** to share imperfect moments in your life. By introducing a more human and realistic approach to social media, you might motivate others to do the same.

3. Everyone's life is different
The time you spend comparing yourself to others will make you feel miserable and life might seem like it is

filled with obstacles. Regardless of what advantages other people might have, it's a waste of time to compare your life to someone else's. You never know the background of a person's success and all the details of their story. Instead, focus on yourself and on what you want to accomplish and figure out how you are going to achieve your goals. To prevent destructive thoughts, think about how you can change your life to get where you want to be. What can you do to help to kickstart your progress?

- **Stop comparing yourself to other people** and determining their success based on their clothes, house, followers, or salary. Externalities are rarely an objective measure.
- **Don't compare your worst to their best.** Comparing your failures to other people's successes leads to disappointment. Before anyone can succeed, they have to fail first.
- **Remember that comparisons don't have an end.** Once you start going down that road, you'll never be satisfied.

4. Honour your inner power

Perfectionism comes in different forms. From self-orientated perfection (I have to be perfect) to socially prescribed perfectionism (others expect me to be perfect) and other-orientated perfectionism (I expect others to be perfect).

> **EXPERT MEMORY**
>
> **Max Masure Transgender User Experience Researcher and Inclusion Consultant in New York, US**
>
> Question the expectations others have towards you and those you have towards others, and your inner compass will reboot. Observe who you see as an authority figure. Is this person legitimately equipped to give you constructive feedback about your work? Do you trust this person with authority because you are used to people-pleasing? Surround yourself with people who ignite your inner power and make it grow. Speak your truth when you believe justice is at stake. We suffocate our inner power if we stay silent.
>
> Practise honouring time for yourself by answering to people who expect an instant response. 'I'll take a moment to think about it, and I'll get back to you.' Question the value in the toxic culture of rushing. If people need you to produce a lot quickly and meet unrealistic deadlines, challenge that perspective and find your own metrics of success.
>
> **Lesson learned**
> The answer lies within you. Honour your inner power and Unleash Today!

5. Keep a log of your successes

When you're comparing yourself to others, you'll struggle to appreciate your achievements. It's so easy to forget about all your previous accomplishments. Keeping a record of your achievements will give you the confidence you need to reach your goals. Buy yourself a nice journal to make the writing process an enjoyable activity or start completing an Excel sheet. Choose a method which feels most convenient to you and encourages you to regularly record your successes.

> **EXPERT MEMORY**
>
> **Kate Surala, Co-Author of *Unleash Today***
>
> I keep a log of all my successes in a specific folder so I can quickly retrieve them before my performance review. Try to keep a note of all your contributions to various projects, assignments, and additional tasks with your job description. This way you can demonstrate how you've gone above and beyond with your achievements next time you ask for a promotion.
>
> **Lesson learned**
> Keep a log of your personal victories at work so you can quickly retrieve them in moments when you need to remind yourself or others of your success.

6. Celebrate your successes

When you've finally achieved your goal, it's important to celebrate your success and reward yourself. This doesn't mean you need to spend a fortune on a party, but mostly to take a moment to honour your perseverance and zeal to cross the finish line. It's also a time to appreciate the process, your effort, and those who've supported you. How do you celebrate in a healthy way?

- **Celebrate with your loved ones.** Including others in your celebration is a wonderful way to build and strengthen your personal connections.

- **Be present in the moment.** Stop living in the future and ground yourself in the here and now. It's important to appreciate what you've already done and not rush off to your next goal.

- **Spoil yourself.** Celebrate in a way that nurtures your mind, body, and spirit by doing what you enjoy the most. This could be treating yourself to a massage, a shopping spree, or staying at home to watch a nice movie.

> *Sometimes, when I'm feeling a little low, I check my LinkedIn profile outlining my career trajectory and see how much I've already achieved and that makes me really proud.*

Denise Kellner[*]

When people celebrate their success stories, we often see them assigning their success to luck. Women in particular are likely to use phrases like 'I was lucky to receive this award' or 'I was lucky to be promoted to partner'. However, these milestones aren't achieved by luck, but by hard work. Next time you think you're lucky to be where you are, stop and think about it. Are you lucky or just very determined?

---

[*] *Unleash Today* Editorial Lead and Editor in London, UK.

EXPERT MEMORY

Kate Surala, Co-Author of *Unleash Today*

I bought a bracelet a few years ago. Every time I would celebrate a major event, I buy a new charm. My first charm was gifted to me by my very close friend, who celebrated our friendship with a heart. The second charm was a ring full of white flowers, acknowledging my first paycheck. My favourite one is from when I challenged myself to go on a seven day trip to the Caribbean alone after splitting up with my ex-boyfriend. It was the best holiday I have ever been on.

Lesson learned

Celebrate the special moments with a symbol that will remind you of their significance.

21

Implement the New Excellent

> *I'm a perfectionist. I'm pretty much insatiable. I feel there are so many things I can improve on.*
>
> **Serena Williams**

Once you have defined your goals and understand them, you should review your overall standard setting. How do you approach your life and how does this differ from your approach to your career? Are you bringing your whole self to work, or do you prefer leaving your personal life and emotional interests at home? All these questions play into what is often called 'personal branding', which is a way of establishing and promoting your unique skills, experiences, and personal characteristics that we will further discuss in Step Four.

Set Your Excellence Standard

> *My life has been nothing but a failure.*
>
> **Claude Monet**[45]

Life-long pursuit of perfection is unsustainable, which is why you need to set excellence as your target standard. You should develop the mindset that continual development is the norm and accept that failure is a part of your journey to success. Excellence is about doing the right thing, but excluding the unnecessary details. Excellence means focussing your attention on the overall result rather than being bogged down by concerns over small mistakes.

Sharing an idea or project while it's being developed can be extremely useful, especially if you want to receive feedback from others. Learn to become comfortable with moving quickly and potentially making mistakes along the way. Acting with a certain degree of discomfort and uncertainty is something we're not used to because educational institutions focus on preparing us for an employee position rather than entrepreneurship.

But what is the perfect standard? There isn't one! This is why we refer to excellence instead. We want you to establish your individual excellence stamp, as the standard varies from person to person.

> **EXPERT MEMORY**
>
> **Elizabeth van den Bergh, Founder of a public speaking consultancy in Brussels, Belgium**
>
> If perfectionism is holding yourself accountable to ridiculously high standards and the symptoms are procrastination and imposter syndrome, then yes, I've definitely had my share of it. Even if I would never admit it—until now.
>
> In becoming an entrepreneur, I've learnt that you can't be a perfectionist. By default, you're testing

products and services to fit the market. You have to keep moving forward and try out new ideas before they are matured. Perfectionism can prevent you from being innovative and effective.

In the past, for one of the first training sessions I conducted, I'd prepared and prepared for days. A far better approach is to ask your participants about what their specific challenges and expectations are with regard to the respective topic, so you can make it relevant and focus on concrete learning points. Ultimately, all participants want to know what's in it for them, what they will learn, and how this course will improve their life. I am fully applying this principle of testing and improving for my upcoming online course. It isn't going to be perfect, but is going to be excellent. And it won't just have a big impact on the participants' professional lives, but also their personal lives.

Lesson learned

Perfectionism holds you back and is the ultimate enemy of your creativity and productivity. Think of the participant journey and shifting from 'Look at how smart I am' to 'How can I serve you best?'[46]

Your Personal Excellence Stamp

What does it mean to give things your personal excellence stamp? Your excellence stamp stands for the excellent work that shows you have done everything in your power to finalise the required work, whilst staying within the realm of reason. When we say you should give a piece of work your excellence stamp, we mean that you would be willing to sign your name under a project or piece you have worked on and be held responsible.

Questions such as 'How do I want to be perceived?' and 'What would I like to achieve?' can help you during the process of establishing your personal excellence stamp. Remember your values and purposes and start using them at work. Then ask yourself what categorises the work you see as acceptable, good, excellent, and perfect.

Setting goal breakdowns to achieve your aim will help you to define your excellence stamp even better. It can be as simple as looking for six words that you believe best describe you. Form two sentences using three words in each and you've made yourself a personal slogan![47] Kate's example would be: 'Kate's work style is solution-driven, innovative, and energetic. She is a self-starter, full of passion for detail and has an analytical mind.'

Whenever you find yourself in a stressful situation and you feel under pressure to make a good impression and deliver great work, remind yourself of your stamp and slogan. Think about what you need to do, not more and not less, to be able to put your stamp on your work.

> **EXPERT MEMORY**
>
> **Sarah Wagner, Co-Author of *Unleash Today***
>
> It was midnight on a Sunday. Kate and I had been writing on this book for about twelve hours over Skype as Kate was sitting in London and I was in Beijing. After announcing I had to go to bed (I was seven hours ahead of her, after all), I remembered that this chapter was still missing my memories. I was exhausted, but I wanted the book to be excellent. Had it been a few

years ago, I would've stayed up to finish it until the morning. Instead, I shut down my computer. That is when I got the idea for this memory and, I have to admit, I did still write it down that evening. But then I went to bed.

Lesson learned
You should not work yourself to the ground to deliver a perfect result.

How to Work Hard and Stay Motivated

It's difficult for anyone to stay motivated and work hard all the time. We're all human and it's impossible to be productive every minute of the day. It's ok to experience delays and procrastinate occasionally.

EXPERT MEMORY

Kate Surala, Co-Author of *Unleash Today*

My to do lists are always too ambitious, and I add way too many items to them. When I go through my list to see what I've achieved, I usually end up being disappointed. Sometimes, I don't even start a very complex task because I feel I cannot give it 100 per cent, so I tend to procrastinate and delay, starting with the less urgent or smaller tasks.

Lesson learned
To gauge if a task is achievable, specify how much you like it, and how difficult it is. This will help you to set realistic and achievable to do lists. By 'achievable', we mean to specify the time the task will probably take and add an additional 20 per cent buffer time on top.

But how do you make sure you stay motivated and get your work done, having just determined your excellent standard? Here are a few of our personal tips:

- **Make hard look easy and break it down.** If a task looks too difficult, think about your task as a puzzle that you're trying to solve and break it down into smaller components that you can do one by one. Make it fun and prove to yourself that you're capable of solving the challenge.

- **Take a step back and take control.** When you're overwhelmed by personal and professional responsibilities, take a step back and take control of your tasks. Prioritise your work and start with the most unpleasant task. When it's done, you'll be relieved, and your motivation will increase.

- **Work for yourself, not others.** Focus on your self-worth, the experience you're getting from your job, and how big a learning curve you'll be experiencing.[48]

- **Surround yourself with motivated and inspiring people.** Discussing your progress with like-minded people will motivate you and others.

- **Remember your purpose.** What are you trying to achieve? Why are you working so hard in the first place? Think back to your reflection exercises at the end of Step One.

- **Get comfortable with discomfort.** Expand your comfort zone by choosing not to run away from discomfort. For example, if you're an introvert and are daunted about meeting new people at a networking event, stay a little longer and push yourself to strike up a conversation. If you practise this enough, you'll become less uncomfortable.

- **Rely on others and their knowledge.** When you lack confidence and are a perfectionist, there's a chance that you suffer from an inability to listen and take on feedback. However, others will be able to support you with a wide range of knowledge and experience.

> **EXPERT MEMORY**
>
> **Charlotte Roule, the CEO of Engie China and Vice President of the European Union Chamber of Commerce in Shanghai, China**
>
> Although I am not an engineer, I had the opportunity to develop a major industrial project.
>
> Should I have aimed for perfection, I would have needed to learn a massive amount of technical knowledge whilst not being able to give enough time to the project. Hence, I chose to get to really know the people involved instead, so that I could understand them, their strengths, and where they potentially needed help.
>
> The project was interesting, but also challenging. And yet, it proved to be successful. Seeing how willing people were to contribute made me grow more confident when asking for support. It also set a very good example of how much professional pride can reinforce the team, collectively. If you pursue perfectionism, you don't let others express their knowledge or talents. You also

deprive yourself of the possibility to be challenged. Accepting you cannot be perfect is a way to build a stronger and more confident foundation.

Lesson learned
Trust yourself and, most importantly, get to know and trust the people you're working with the best achievements are collective ones. That's how you'll lead best and avoid falling into the perfectionism trap.

Find Your Accountability Partner

> *Accountability is the glue that bonds commitment to results.*
>
> **Bob Proctor**

After you've defined your goals, it's time to set up a personal advisory board and find your accountability partner. While perfectionism is often linked with the desire to avoid criticism, it's essential for you to know how you are doing and what you could do better in order to grow and improve. With the right mindset, feedback will help you to identify opportunities for improvement and help build more skills.

Personal advisory board
Think of your goals as a project that an organisation is pursuing. Companies usually have a board that reviews important decisions. We recommend that you find a

personal advisory board to help steer your decisions and achieve your goals. By personal advisory board, we mean people you respect and would consider trusted advisers on your career. They could be family members, friends, professional contacts, coaches or mentors. In Step Four, we help you to engage with these professionals via networking, and in Step Seven we discuss the importance of having and finding the right coach and mentor.

Your personal advisory board should be composed of people of different ages, genders, and professional backgrounds. Also make sure that you don't have too many people advising you. While there is no perfect number, two to three is a reasonable amount in our board. Getting an abundance of contradicting feedback can become confusing. Your board should challenge and advise you on how to improve your skills, support you through your projects, and help you to (re)define your purpose.

When you've formed your board, you could ask the following questions:

- When I outline my strengths, do you see any inconsistencies?
- What's the best way to strengthen or develop these skills?
- What's the most efficient route to get what I need?
- What can I learn from your experiences?
- Should I embrace the next professional challenge; who could help me get there?

> **EXPERT MEMORY**
>
> **Kate Surala, Co-Author of *Unleash Today***
>
> My personal advisory board is composed of my family, Sarah, my mentor, and two very close professional contacts. When I need a second opinion, I call them and discuss my dilemma with them separately. The key is that they don't know each other, so they can't find out what the other is saying. By telling them ideas, such as my next career move, I'm able to listen to their feedback and realistic expectations. My personal advisory board helps me identify the show stoppers and other limitations of my plan even before these issues arise.
>
> **Lesson learned**
>
> Set up your personal advisory board and run key decisions and goals by them before you start pursuing them. Reflect on their suggestions and comments, then revise your decisions accordingly.

Accountability partner

An accountability partner is someone who'll help you to achieve your goal. Partnering with someone who'll support you through difficult situations will give you energy and help you to get back on track. However, your partner will also give you feedback on your ideas and behaviour.

How do you find your accountability partner? It's best to look for someone you admire as well as someone who is easy for you to reach. Ask yourself which one of your friends or people in your professional network shares your values. Are their strengths your weaknesses?

Don't be afraid to reach out and ask to meet for coffee when it suits them. Be upfront with your expectations and let them know what you would like to discuss, but allow them the opportunity to decline without making it awkward for them. Let them know whether it's about your career progress or a difficult situation at work and that you would like their advice on. The key is to find a person who has expertise in the area that you need and is happy to help.

Remember that there are many people out there who are willing to invest their time and energy in you, but you need to have the courage to ask for their support first. If they say 'no' or don't reply, it's better to have asked than if you hadn't tried in the first place. If you don't try, you're saying 'no' to yourself and to the opportunity of learning from someone else's experiences. Open yourself to the opinions of others, even if you make yourself vulnerable.

> **EXPERT MEMORY**
>
> **Sarah Wagner, Co-Author of *Unleash Today***
>
> I remember the day Kate called to inform me I could officially call her my partner in crime—our way of saying accountability partners. I was so excited, as I'd been waiting for years to refer to her like that. As Head of Compliance, she didn't want it to be termed as 'crime', but this is exactly what it feels like to me. She listens when I'm sad and asks me how I am, truly caring about the answer. I can give and ask for honest feedback. She tells me what I could improve and what I did well. I can tell her when she annoys me. She's like a mirror: always there and telling the truth, even if I don't feel like seeing it. And I am the same to her.

> **Lesson learned**
> Having an accountability partner is both a blessing and a curse, as they tell you everything you want and don't want to hear.

Recognise Your Triggers and Avoid a Burnout

> *Perfectionism goes out the window when you spend a month in bed. At that point, it's all about survival.*
>
> **Georgia Brooks**[*]

While goal setting has its advantages, it also has the potential to cause problems. If you push yourself towards your own goals with negative incentives, your stress and anxiety levels can increase.[49]

Pressure to be perfect can come from ourselves or others. Regardless of who causes the pressure, it can be very destructive and ultimately lead to a burnout. Herbert J. Freudenberger defines a burnout as 'a state of fatigue or frustration brought about by devotion to a cause, way of life, or relationship that failed to produce the expected reward.' Another definition is 'a state of physical, emotional, and mental exhaustion caused by long term involvement in emotional demanding situations'.[50]

---

[*] *Unleash Today* expert and Founder and Managing Director at Fempower Initiative in Brussels, Belgium.

EXPERT MEMORY

Liz Mearns, Founder of The Head Coach in Cheshire, UK

'You've lost your spark,' she said. 'What's happened to you? Your energy used to light up a room and now it doesn't.' I will never forget that conversation. It was one of those life-defining moments.

It got me thinking about my spark and what it was. I realised that sparkiness was a big part of me, my personal brand. I was always known for it but somewhere… somehow, my usual sparky enthusiasm and energy had fizzled out and, worse, it was apparent to other people. It could be due to tiredness, burnout, perfectionism, or anxiety. Either way, it's a red flag, a warning sign that something is wrong. Here are my three top tips to stay focussed and avoid letting your spark burn out.

- **Don't ignore tiredness.** So often we soldier on, trying to be all things to all people. However, lack of energy is a real sign we need to ease up. So, listen, acknowledge, and give yourself what you need.

- **Have just three things on your to do list every day.** It's overwhelming and stressful to work through a marathon list each day. By all means get it all out of your head and onto paper, but then pick three things which are both achievable and gratifying.

- **Become an expert at your thing and stop trying to be good at everything.** Stop letting life happen to you, get in the driver's seat, recognise your

> weaknesses and outsource or get help with them—ask! Then spend more of your precious time doing the things you are GOOD at or simply spend time with family, friends, or on your own.
>
> **Lesson learned**
> No one is coming to save you. You are in charge of yourself. If you are not taking care of your own energy, resourcefulness, creativity, happiness, emotional, and physical wellbeing, then who is?

Being ambitious is almost synonymous with a perpetual state of stress and even the most motivated go-getters need to hit the pause button every now and then. According to research conducted at Yale University, one in five 'highly engaged' US workers report feeling high levels of burnout.[51] A Gallup study found that nearly a quarter of employees often or always feel a burnout.[52]

Women, in particular millennials, don't often relax during working hours and tend to experience burnout early on in their careers, some already hit this stage before they're thirty![53] Men are more likely to take breaks throughout the day for personal activities, such as walking, going to the gym, or just relaxing.[54] Ladies, we encourage you to take that short break. It will be worth it!

Below is an illustration of the most common signs of burnout. These signs usually come without you noticing. You can go from bright-eyed and bushy-tailed to seriously burnt-out very quickly.

So, what can you do to avoid a burnout? Our team at *Unleash Today* has put together several tips for you:

- **Work with purpose.** Rediscovering your purpose can go a long way towards helping you avoid a burnout. Revisit Step One to remind yourself of your values and purpose you have set for yourself.

- **Get a lot of sleep.** Sleeping helps us to recover from mental and physical exertion. Research proves that sleep deprivation, such as sleeping for four to five hours a night, has negative effects on performance in cognitive tests. Most adults need between seven and nine hours of sleep per night to function at their best.

- **Learn to say 'no'.** Understand when it's time to reject an offer to take on extra work. Be firm and direct when saying 'no'. It's much better than saying yes, committing to something and having to justify incomplete work later on.

- **Schedule in some 'me time'.** Try to squeeze in a few moments in the middle of your day to relax and recharge. Taking regular breaks will help you focus in the long run and enjoy the process even more. Our tips are to unplug and, instead of reading emails or checking social media, go for a walk or simply stare out of the window and daydream. Journaling is also a great method to help you release your negative feelings and reduce stress. More tips on this in Step Five.

- **Eat and exercise regularly.** Diet and exercise are an important part of a healthy life, both in and outside of work. If you eat ready meals all the

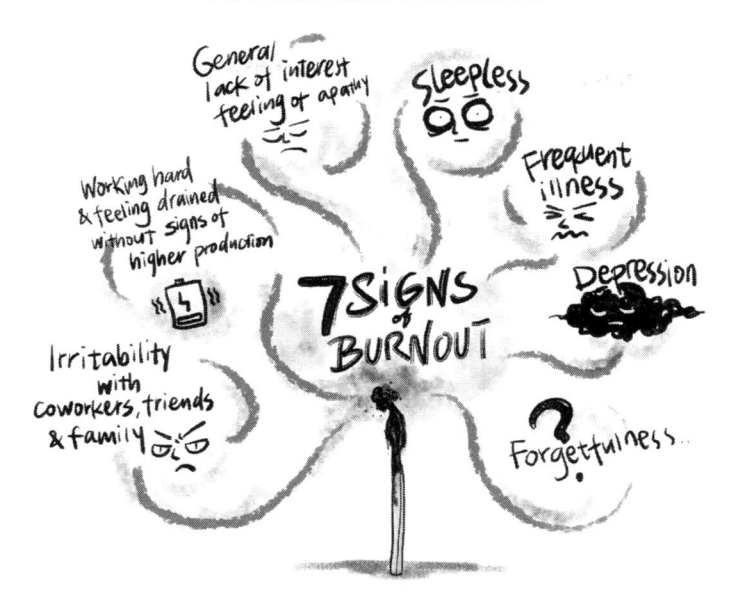

7 Signs of Burnout
- General lack of interest, feeling of apathy
- Sleepless
- Frequent illness
- Depression
- Forgetfulness
- Irritability with coworkers, friends & family
- Working hard & feeling drained without signs of higher production

time and don't move, you are at increased risk of developing health problems. Fit your workout into your schedule by getting up earlier or exercising during your lunch break. You might also feel more motivated by teaming up with your accountability partner or a friend.

- **Spread out your holiday evenly over the year.** Working long hours without a day off or taking holiday is not sustainable. Try to spread your holiday over the year evenly. We recommend that you unleash during a long weekend or proper holiday at least once every three months.

EXPERT MEMORY

Georgia Brooks, Founder and Managing Director at Fempower Initiative in Brussels, Belgium

By the time I started working, my perfectionism was both a driving and debilitating force. Deadlines? I was always early. Goals? If I didn't meet every single one—early!—then I felt like a failure. Everyone who knows me says I'm a perfectionist. Always have been, and most likely always will be.

On the plus side, my perfectionist tendencies meant a job in copywriting and editing came naturally. There is nothing more soothing to a perfectionist than correcting mistakes. It's little wonder that by the age of twenty-five I was made the then-youngest editor at a publishing house.

Things started to unravel a few years later when I set up my own organisation in another country. I pushed myself so hard, and everything had to be so right, that I was doing a thousand tasks at once. In March 2018, everything fell down on top of me. After coming down with the flu and bronchitis while travelling extensively for work, it worsened to such a degree I had to go to hospital.

Finally, back home, I was diagnosed with exhaustion and put on two months' sick leave. It was torture. And yet, it was illuminating. The world kept turning. My organisation kept running.

Post-sick leave, my work and personal life looks completely different. I don't travel as much, say 'no', and take better care of my health. While my perfectionist tendencies will never go away, I try not to let them dictate my life.

Lesson learned
Take care of yourself and don't let anything that might harm you drive your life. As the Egyptian proverb goes 'A beautiful thing is never perfect.'

How to Change Your Mindset and Enjoy the Process

> *Perfectionism is complicated to deal with. But reflecting on it is even more difficult.*

Wendy Degens[*]

If you're struggling with perfectionism, you might have honed the skills of spotting mistakes in even your best work. This habit is very difficult to stop, but it is possible. Look at yourself and name three positive things that you're experiencing right now.

Focussing on the things that work rather than things that don't will help you to soften the critical voice in your head. The next time you start thinking about what went wrong with your work, look for three other qualities that you do like. The more you practise this habit, the more naturally it will come.

As two former perfectionists, we were used to hearing a critical voice telling us that our work wasn't

---

[*] *Unleash Today* expert and Journalist at Maastricht University's independent weekly Obersevant, Maastricht, the Netherlands.

good enough and we hadn't tried hard enough. It also said we would never manage to write a book while working full-time. What helps to ignore this voice is to stop thinking about the end result by focussing on the journey.

You can enjoy the process more by getting involved with your accountability partner or even a group of friends. If you feel down or unmotivated, ask your friend to remind you of and appreciate the positive moments you have experienced.

EXPERT MEMORY

Marie Sina, Content Editor at *Unleash Today*

When I began writing my undergraduate dissertation, I kept telling myself that I chose the wrong topic and I wouldn't get an outstanding grade. I was so convinced that I was on the completely wrong path that I went to my supervisor at the very last minute and told him I wanted to change my topic. When he assured me that I was on the right track, I didn't believe him. Eventually, I no longer had the time to mull over my topic. Once I stopped second guessing myself, I had more time to focus on my work. Finally, I was convinced that I'd composed a decent piece of academic work. I ended up receiving eighty points (high distinction), as well as a commendation for academic excellence.

Lesson learned
It's normal to have self-doubt. What counts is to eventually ditch destructive thoughts and move one. They only slow you down.

I'M A RECOVERING PERFECTIONIST

Turn Your Mistakes into Valuable Lessons

> *It's not the setbacks but how we turn them into successes that defines us.*

Zaheer Ahmad[*]

Making mistakes is unavoidable. Not being able to achieve all your goals is a natural process of building your brand and legacy and should be seen as an opportunity to grow. The best things always come from trial and error rather than from instant perfection.

This is something that Walt Disney knew about. He would often reminisce about his first failed attempts at creating his animation brand, stating, 'I think it's important to have a good hard failure when you're young. I learned a lot out of that. Because it makes you kind of aware of what can happen to you.'[55]

One of the traits of perfectionism is to avoid situations with the potential to fail. However, it's natural to make mistakes. To overcome these tendencies, you must do the opposite, such as demonstrating increased efforts to look for challenges requiring skills and experiences you're not yet competent in. Remember that failure is part of everyone's development.

The good news is that you can take steps to learn from your mistakes. However, this doesn't happen automatically—it requires reflection. Turning our negative

---

[*] *Unleash Today* expert and Inclusion and Diversity Global Lead at GSK, in London, UK.

experiences and failures into valuable lessons was the key purpose of writing this book. We wanted to share our experiences with you so you can get ahead of your peers and apply our advice in your everyday life, which include:

- **Acknowledge your mistakes.**
- **Identify what went wrong.**
- **Make a plan** and focus on what you could do differently next time.
- If you have to **tell someone about your mistake**, be as factual and level headed as possible.
- **Move forward** stronger and more knowledgeable. Recognise that each mistake can be an opportunity to build mental resilience and improve.
- **Don't lose faith in yourself.** Stay positive and confident.

I'M A RECOVERING PERFECTIONIST

22
Unleash Today
Challenge: Perfectionism

Imagine that you've been working on a project for the past two months and the deadline is fast approaching. You have to submit a first draft to your manager the coming day. The project is still missing an executive summary, which isn't a requirement. Yet, you want the draft to be perfect and plan to put in the extra work. The evening before the submission date, your best friend is celebrating her birthday and you promised to drop by after work. You're faced with a decision: should you stay in the office, polish the draft and add the summary, or submit it as it is? What would you do?

ANSWER

EXPERT ADVICE

Lisa Magill, Co-Founder and CEO of Aleria in San Diego, US

Rather than aim for perfection, good leaders should strive to be approachable and open to solving problems in different ways. Looking back on various projects throughout my career, I can point to flaws and ways we could have improved. But I can just as easily point to a long list of unnecessary features we built, products we trashed, and other projects where I stressed over the wrong details. You want to find that balance, come to a point of completion where you feel good enough about your work, then move on… and go enjoy your best friend's birthday party.

Rather than spending the evening perfecting the document, put together notes of the ideas you have so that you can revisit them later. In an email or in notes attached to the draft document, present questions that touch on the additional changes you had in mind.

As an example, you could ask clarifying questions, such as: Would it be helpful to include an executive summary? Do you believe this section would be clearer if we provide an additional example?

It's important to remember the requirements for the project and to base decisions on expectations that have been set with your team. Given that this is a first draft, you know that you'll have the opportunity to further improve the project, taking into account the additional ideas that you have as well as any feedback you receive from your manager.

Lesson learned

Rather than aim for perfection, strive for excellence.

Step Four: Mastering the Art of Networking

In Step Four, you will learn how to:

- Embrace the value of a strong and trusted network
- Overcome networking aversion
- Learn the perks and perils of networking as a woman
- Build your own brand
- Start virtual networking and community building
- Conquer networking events step-by-step

23
An Introduction to Networking

> *If networking were a human, you would fall in love with it.*

Sarah Wagner

Imagine a client has invited you to a networking event. Despite feeling tired, you decide to attend because the event is a great opportunity to nurture your client relationship and form new connections. The idea of speaking to strangers makes you nervous. When you arrive, you see a number of groups, many of which are already engaged in conversation, making you feel anxious and tense. You have the impression that many of the people already know each other. You feel out of place and really want to go home. You notice your throat tightening, making it hard to get your words out. You don't have the courage to start talking to all these strangers, so you end up drinking your wine in the corner by yourself.

If you have ever stood alone at a networking event, write down how it made you feel:

Answer

From the outside, networking might seem superficial, boring, or intimidating. To appreciate the benefits of networking, you need to recognise its importance and long-term value. It's nothing less than a change of mindset: networking can open doors to new worlds and ways of thinking, and it can deepen your knowledge and ability to innovate.[56] Networking can expand your job opportunities and ultimately improve your quality of work.[57] It's also an empowering tool as it gives you access to people and enhances your status and authority. In a nutshell, networking is one of the most important activities you'll be involved in throughout your career. Whether you are a career starter or experienced professional, networking is worth any time you put into it. Most importantly, it's a skill that can and should be learned. It is far more than just sipping champagne at a reception and should be strategically planned and executed accordingly.

Yet, it's a skill we are neither taught in school nor university. Worse, for the majority of people networking feels like a burden that is to be avoided at all costs. Many feel uncomfortable while attempting to network. To some, it may seem like an unethical and unilateral transaction: asking for something without giving anything in return. However, meaningful networking is actually a two-way street where both parties benefit and provide at the same time.

If you approach networking with the right mindset—excitement and curiosity—many possibilities can unfold and you can learn to enjoy it. It really isn't as intimidating as you think. You just need to practise, like you would with any other skill.

We share with you our personal tips to turn from the passive bystander to a rising networking star. In the first part, we focus on how you can overcome your networking aversion by showcasing why you cannot go without it. We will provide you with a hands-on step-by-step guide on how to build your personal brand and establish a lasting network.

24

Falling in Love with Networking

> *Your network is your net worth.*
> **Richard Branson**

Networking isn't usually at the top of everyone's to do list as it can be time consuming and often awkward. When you have appointments for work and family commitments, the last thing you feel like prioritising is a networking event with strangers. We are here to tell you that you should!

The Value of a Strong and Trusted Network

Networking is worth your time because connecting to other circles and businesses pays off.[58] Having a strong network of trusted allies gives you better access to knowledgeable people who can help further your career. Networking has a myriad of other benefits too. It enhances your social skills, self-esteem, self-confidence, and keeps you up-to-date with key trends and industry news.

EXPERT MEMORY

Denise McQuaid, CEO and Board Advisor who embraced her first C level leadership role at age twenty-nine from Dublin, Ireland

No woman is an island: Networking is a valuable strategy at each and every stage of your career development. Networking allows your island to become populated with long term relationships and it is important that you place it at the core of your career. Networking is not just about handing out and collecting business cards. It is about connecting; establishing and building relationships that are mutually beneficial for you and others.

If you nurture this army of network contacts early in your career it will allow you to find role models—those that have gone before you and paved the way—upon whom to base your behaviour. You cannot be what you cannot see. Role models provide a vision for who we aspire to be. You must embark on finding them consciously and strategically and do not limit yourself to one! Try to apply a growth and global mindset to both networking and identifying role models.

Lesson learned

Networking is a skill that you should practise and use to build a support army that gives you advice in difficult situations. Connecting with people in your company, various departments and divisions is equally crucial as connecting with people in different fields and outside of the workplace.

However you perceive networking, it's a necessary skill if you are serious about progressing in your professional life. Your network is at the heart of a successful career and is just as important as a good education. For instance, the strong network that elite universities provide their graduates helps propel them further in their chosen profession.

Considering how important networking is to further your own career, it's rather strange that the art of networking still isn't part of the modern curricula at universities.[59] As networking is not yet a commonly taught skill, we tend to underestimate its importance. We urge you to create your own opportunities instead of relying on the limited resources provided by your university or workplace. It's especially important during a job search, whether you're straight out of university or switching careers.

During your studies you should already start reaching out to professionals in your chosen industry. You can do this by asking your family and friends to connect you to their colleagues or contacts. Alternatively, LinkedIn and our website provide a vast pool of contacts to get you started. You'll be surprised by how many people respond positively to personalised contact requests on LinkedIn or by email, if you show gratitude for their time and support.[60] We would be delighted if you'd reach out to us on LinkedIn! Send us your favourite part of the book or let us know if there is a step you would like to receive further advice on.

In your contact request, you should clarify why you are reaching out, for instance, that you would like to inquire about a certain company or industry or the professional background of that specific person.

> **Kate Surala, Co-Author of *Unleash Today***
>
> EXPERT MEMORY
>
> I am genuinely interested in meeting new people as it expands my horizons. For instance, if I see someone interesting on LinkedIn, I am not shy to reach out and send a personalised request. An example would be, 'Hi Bijan, I am reaching out to you as we have something very important in common: passion for empowering women to reach their full potential. I have seen your recent post celebrating the top talent in AI. I really appreciate you bringing this up and please continue doing so! All the best, Kate' Bijan and I connected,

scheduled a virtual coffee, and found out more about each other and our interests. Bijan was so inspired by our Unleash Today project and agreed to join our team as a Data Analytics Expert.

Lesson learned
I always ask myself the following question when my imposter syndrome creeps in and wants to prevent me from sending out a connection request, 'What is the worst that can happen?' My response is, 'They will ignore it, but that's their loss.' Go, lady, send out the message!

As you network with people in your own company or industry, you will uncover new opportunities to connect with mentors and advisors who can help increase your visibility. These interactions provide you with new ideas, access to industry influencers, and a support network. Doors will open easier and faster, which will allow you to move forward and upward quicker.

Networking is also helpful if you plan to switch jobs or change industries.

EXPERT **M**EMORY

Liselotte Grönlund, Digital Marketing Team Lead at *Unleash Today*

I was unsure what to do after my Bachelor's degree: whether to go back to my home country to access the legal bar or further specialise in my preferred area by doing a Master's degree. I was lost. I reached out to several experts I randomly contacted on LinkedIn and also got connections from Kate and Sarah. Soon, I had several insightful conversations about different career paths. Having spoken to people who shared their honest experience with me, I managed to make a decision I felt confident about.

Lesson learned
You can network at any time. Always show your appreciation if someone replies to your requests for advice. However, not every piece of advice from your network is equally relevant and effective. It can be contradictory.

EXPERT MEMORY

Tijen Onaran, CEO and Founder of Global Digital Women in Berlin, Germany

'Mom, I quit my job today!' On the other end of the phone line was my mother, who probably went into shock. I knew that my professional life had to take a new direction. As it soon turned out, my network was to play an essential role in it.

The bad news first: networks are not an inexhaustible source of new jobs and business opportunities that arise like a miracle. Nevertheless, I consider networking to be absolutely essential when it comes to starting a new career. My first business idea was a direct result of a conversation with a mentor. She advised me to do exactly what I could do best: advising people on PR issues. My network became my first contact point to find clients.

If you are well networked, you have better access to people and especially to topics. A good network is based on trust. Whoever trusts you, is also open to working with you. That helps a lot in your job, because there are always situations where you need to cooperate.

Last but not least, a network has to be more than a directory of people you have met or heard of. A thousand contacts on Twitter or LinkedIn are not yet a network. Networking contains the word 'work' for a reason. You have to work for it and only this work pays off in the end. Networking involves becoming visible as a person, having and original topic to talk about, developing and representing an attitude, exchanging and meeting with others, helping others, empowering them and organising together.

Lesson learned
I am firmly convinced that you always achieve more together than alone. This is exactly what a strong network guarantees.

Change Your Mindset: Overcoming Your Networking Aversion

Most people have a 'promotion' or 'prevention' mindset. Those belonging to the former group see the potential for growth and the accomplishments that networking can bring. Those in the latter group consider networking as something they're obliged to participate in for professional reasons.[61] Prevention-focussed people see networking as a 'necessary evil', so they do it less often and with less conviction, which almost certainly prevents advancement in their jobs.

Take a moment to think about which category you fall into. Write down an example to show how you came to this conclusion.

Answer:

Fortunately, if you have a prevention mindset, you can change your mentality.[62] Try *not* to think of networking as an immediate transaction, but rather focus on getting to know who you're speaking to and identify common interests. Building long-term relationships will determine what you could offer the other person in the future. If you just selfishly think about what you can gain from the other person, you won't get very far.

Mutual learning

There are two ways you can approach a work-related event. You can pretend you like small talk, or you can actually embrace opportunities by engaging and being open to the unforeseeable. Rather than thinking about what a person

> **EXPERT MEMORY**
>
> **Divya Sharma, Executive Director at the Climate Group, with twenty years of experience working as consultant in India and other jurisdictions**
>
> There are two types of networks: business and personal. I feel a moral obligation to help others if I'm in the position to do so.
>
> Part of being a consultant means one needs to approach networking from a more strategic and business-minded perspective. Yet, by building those networks, I still keep a sense of empathy, a genuineness of intent. For me, a business interaction cannot be devoid of a personal, more humane touch, looking at a person as a whole and thereby creating a level of trust. In my experience, this is also very fulfilling and gives you a sense of satisfaction That's why my networks are very long-lasting.
>
> **Lesson learned**
> Networking is a mutual, humane, and long-term investment.

could offer you the moment you meet them, think of what you can learn from them. Ask about their career and position, even hobbies and interests. You will come across as more likeable if you show an active interest in the other person.

Keep in mind that most people are focussed on themselves in conversations. Therefore, you should make sure you ask questions about them and acknowledge their responses. But what questions do you ask? We all have had moments in which we struggle to come up with a compelling question. This is why we like to use the FORD model.[63] This stands for **Family**, **Occupation**, **Relax**, and **Deep**. Armed with the FORD tool you will be able to control a conversation and create a rapport by asking questions like:

- Where are you from?
- What company do you work for?
- What's the greatest challenge in your business?
- What's your plan for the next few years?
- You sound very busy. What do you do to relax?
- What inspires you in your job?
- How do you establish trust with your clients and stakeholders?
- Is there something you have recently tried in your current role that you would recommend?
- What is the best bakery in town?

At the same time, be careful to strike the right balance between asking questions and giving insights about who you are. Otherwise, the other person might leave the conversation not knowing anything about you or even perceive you as being too interrogating. Only asking questions also means that you have no opportunity to impress others with your own skills and experiences.

> **Expert Memory**
>
> **Sarah Wagner, Co-Author of *Unleash Today***
>
> I used to be anxious ahead of networking events as I was unsure what to say. Since I wasn't sure what to talk about, I focussed on actively listening and asking questions that demonstrated my genuine curiosity. I ended up taking in a lot of information while creating a bond with another person. At the end of the evening I often heard, 'Oh, now I did not hear anything about your work, actually. Let's catch up another time.'
>
> **Lesson learned**
> General curiosity is compelling because people want to talk about themselves. Learn to ask compelling questions indicating genuine interest. Focus on coming across as authentic rather than feigning interest. You can train asking meaningful questions.

Common interest

Meaningful connections aren't created through casual interactions. Once you've asked several questions and identified if your goals align, you can determine whether it's worth taking the conversations further.

To be even more strategic, you can also identify shared interests ahead of an event by doing some research, which we will discuss in the second part of this Step.

> **EXPERT MEMORY**
>
> **Kate Surala, Co-Author of *Unleash Today***
>
> Before a conference or an evening lecture, I like to look up the speakers and organisers. It helps me to determine two things: firstly, whether I am truly interested in the topic and it's worth my time; and secondly, to learn more about the speaker's background so I can both demonstrate my research and show I'm passionate about their work. People are usually astonished that you have looked them up and invested time in understanding their career path and interests. How would you feel if someone approached you at an event having done their research about you? I bet you would be especially pleased to answer their questions and remember them long after the event.
>
> **Lesson learned**
> Look up the speakers and organisers before an event that you will attend to lead a more informative discussion and create a better bond with your new contact.

Share your strength

As you get to know a contact, you can identify how you can help them achieve their goals. Go beyond the obvious. Perhaps you have another contact who is selling a product to make their business more efficient, or a professor who specialises in their industry.

A study conducted by Cornell University demonstrated that juniors often feel powerless and less likely to join networking activities, even though they might be the ones to benefit the most.[64] We're often intimidated by the situation and automatically assume that no one will be interested in speaking to us. However, even if you're a junior professional, you can still be a valuable contact to someone you meet at a networking event. The Cornell study also shows that senior professionals actually feel more comfortable networking with juniors.

> **EXPERT MEMORY**
>
> **Sarah Wagner, Co-Author of *Unleash Today***
>
> I remember all too well how often I entered a networking room as a junior professional and started sweating because I created an image in my head of how a conversation would go. I'd approach someone who would realise I was junior and would end the conversation. Once I changed my attitude by worrying less about my limited experience and network, I was able to display more confidence.
>
> **Lesson learned**
>
> As a junior professional, you need to be bold. Never put yourself down with the thought that you don't have anything to offer. Be curious, put yourself out there, and just go for it!

Regardless of your position, you always have a wide range of resources at your disposal. Whether it's your connections, technical support, or knowledge of the industry, you might be able to give them new insights. For instance, if you've read a compelling news article or a report about a topic the other person is interested in, mention it to them or email them a link later on. This is an easy way to be helpful despite not having a big network at your disposal.

Let's practise. Imagine you are at a networking event and trying to establish a connection with someone. Write down three things you have to offer. What skills or strengths do you provide that others might not have?

> **ANSWER**

> **EXPERT MEMORY**
>
> **Rachel Morarjee, Director at the Economist Corporate Network in London, UK**
>
> To network effectively, look beyond yourself. You often see memes talking about how introverts hate meaningless conversations, as if extroverts love going to parties surrounded by strangers and making small talk. I'll let you in on a secret: almost no one on the planet enjoys making meaningless small talk with people they

don't know. Normal reactions range from feeling mildly uncomfortable and out of place, to one friend who said that if he was sent to hell, he would spend his entire afterlife having to make small talk at diplomatic cocktail parties.

For the last few years, I worked as a network director for the Economist Group, and a large part of my job was to go to events and talk to people. So, as someone who did this for a living, the best tip I can offer is that it really helps to have something to say that will lead to common ground with the people around you.

If you are quite new to the world of work, you are probably wondering how you might go about doing this. If you are a woman, the harsh reality is that for much of your professional life you will walk a tightrope between being perceived as too assertive and being criticised for being too much of a wallflower. There is a simple solution to this problem, which is to be asking questions, making connections or reaching out to other people on behalf of others.

The aftermath of COVID-19 is a nerve-wracking time to be entering the job market and many of you reading this you will be anxious about how you will accrue professional experience and build the skills you need to take you to the next stage of your career. The good news, however, is that there has been no better time in recent memory to be an activist. From environmental protection and women's issues to LGBTQIA+ rights and children's education there has never been a more urgent need to get involved with a cause, nor better access to the technology to help you do so.

'What does this have to do with networking?' you may be wondering. If you start volunteering you will have a reason to approach influential people on behalf of others you are helping, a legitimate excuse to ask for their advice, and you don't need to worry about being seen as pushy because you will be reaching out in service of something greater than yourself.

Working in service to something greater removes much of the ego from networking and reaching out to others. In doing so, it gets rid of the worst cause of nerves, such as 'Why should anyone talk to me?'

Lesson learned

Get a piece of paper and form two columns. Write the causes that inspire and energise you on one side and the skills that you have on the other. Then start researching organisations that need your help. Once you get involved in something bigger than yourself, you will find yourself meeting like-minded people.

25

The Art of Networking: You Can Learn It!

> *Plan, practise, rehearse—there is nothing like coincidence.*
>
> **Sarah Wagner**

Some people look like they have a natural talent for speaking to strangers. They're always confident and know what to say. Just like everyone else, people who look confident also get nervous before approaching a stranger. However, you can be successful when networking if you diligently plan each step. We still get nervous before networking events at times, but our trick is that, when we show up to an event, we're prepared!

Building and managing a network is a skill that can be learned. You're not born a good or bad networker. Everyone can learn to network, but it's hard work and involves a lot of practise.

Networking Events: A Guide

We want you to make the most of the networking events and, having attended hundreds of them, we know what you're going through. Below are some of our tips on how to prepare for and follow up after an event, and everything that goes in between.

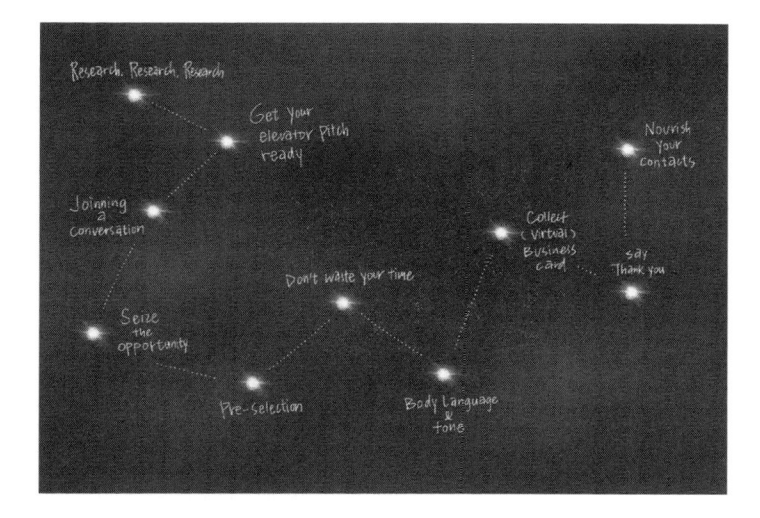

Research, research, research

Before embarking on your networking journey, you need to know what your goal is. Are you new to the city and trying to make as many new contacts as possible? Then go for the quantity of contacts. Are you already established and want a big professional circle? Then focus on the quality of contacts. Other reasons for attending a networking event include:

- Meeting new and/or specific people or potential clients
- Getting inspiration and input
- Getting out of your comfort zone

- Gathering intelligence
- Job hunting
- Presenting and selling your work
- Enjoying a casual evening over free drinks

Never just go to an event for the sake of it. Be as respectful with your own time as you are with that of others by taking the time to look up the organiser and speakers in advance. Once you've done your research, you can assess what kind of professionals you're likely to meet. With this background information, assess whether attending the event will bring you closer to your goal. If the answer is 'yes', make the time to go. If not, don't go.

Research the people speaking at these events and identify things that you could mention to them. Knowing the person and trying to understand their personality will help you determine their needs and set you up for a positive first impression.

If possible, contact individuals ahead of the event to tell them that you're excited to meet them. Tell them that you're looking forward to talking about topics relevant to the panel discussion. When you introduce yourself to the person at the event, remind them that you had contacted them previously.

Get your elevator pitch ready

If you plan on approaching a speaker at an event, you should prioritise networking with them. High-level speakers don't usually stay long after an event, so you should intercept them immediately after the panel or while they're leaving.

To stand out, have a catch phrase ready to help you join in or start a conversation, such as:

- 'I heard you speak about [topic]. Can I chime in?'
- 'I'm sorry, I've just arrived and don't know many people. Could I join you?'
- 'Do you know what the next session is about and which room it's in?'
- 'Are you also here to see [speaker's/company's name]?'
- 'This cake is delicious. It's the main reason I come to these events.' [Wait for laughter.]
- 'I heard you discussing [topic] and I love [topic]. Would it be ok if I join you?'

Have an introduction ready and practise it before an event so it sounds authentic and sells your strengths while getting to the point. Also prepare some keywords, dates, and names that you can drop into the conversation to show that you're not just anybody. In professional conversations, name dropping shows others that you have a valuable network.

An example of an introduction is:

Hello, I'm Jaki Smith, the Editor and Production Lead for *Unleash Today*. We are a passionate movement looking to empower young and ambitious women to maximise their potential in the workplace. I'm looking to get into the publishing industry and am excited to be sharing Kate and Sarah's book and my contributions with you. What brought you here?

Also prepare an elevator pitch that goes beyond your introduction. Your elevator pitch should be adjusted, depending on the person's seniority, age, and gender, and should demonstrate you're worth speaking to. Essentially, it's a sales pitch aimed at creating exclusivity around you and what you have to offer. An example would be:

Hi there, I'm Jaki. I'm a recent graduate from UCL where I earned a Master's degree in Publishing and gained valuable insight into the industry. I'm looking to enter the world of publishing and am currently the Editor and Production Lead for *Unleash Today*, a passionate movement aiming to empower young, ambitious women to maximise their career potential. I hope to find a position that will test my skills and give me the opportunity to contribute my ideas, like I do at *Unleash Today*.

Joining a conversation

It can be daunting to enter a discussion, particularly if it's on a topic you're not familiar with. Here are a few things you can do:

- **Get used to feeling uncomfortable.** Embrace feeling like you're stepping outside your comfort zone.

- **Look out for people standing alone**, looking at their phones. They're missing out on great conversations—make sure that you don't! Hide your phone in your bag so you don't get tempted to look at it.

- **Remember that we're all in the same boat.** Many people attending the event will be just as intimidated and unsure of what to say as you are.

- **Why are you here?** You decide to go to an event for a reason and you'll regret going home without meeting new people. You have nothing to lose by approaching a stranger.

> **EXPERT MEMORY**
>
> **Denise Kellner, Editorial Lead at *Unleash Today***
>
> At legal networking events, the partners are snatched up immediately. What I tend to do is put away my notepad a little earlier than anyone else, before the discussion finishes. Then, when the event is over, I can dash out and be the first to engage with the speaker.
>
> **Lesson learned**
> Never be a passive participant at an event. There is so much for you to benefit from if you think ahead.

Seize the opportunity

Not every step of a networking event can be planned. You never know who'll show up or who you'll bump into on the way out. Be prepared to react in the moment. Don't think twice, seize the opportunity.

> **EXPERT MEMORY**
>
> **Sarah Wagner, Co-Author of *Unleash Today***
>
> On International Women's Day, I used to attended a big event organised by Brussels' biggest EU newspaper. People who attend need a special invitation, which is why I knew it was a great opportunity to network. On my way out, I met a woman in the lift. In this moment, I realised that inspiring women are actually recognisable.

> The ride was only a few seconds long, but I dared to make the pictch and today she is a good friend and trusted advisor to me and Kate.
>
> **Lesson learned**
> Follow your gut and act quickly when you grasp an opportunity. You might not get a second chance.

Pre-selection

When you enter a room, invest time to screen your surroundings and get a feel for the atmosphere. Look carefully at the people around you. A person's clothing, body language, and attitude can often tell you if they are interesting to you. Don't waste time on people who aren't of interest.

If you're joining a dinner or sitting down for a debate, don't just sit anywhere. Look at the people already sitting down and think about who you'd like to speak to.

Don't waste your time

If you feel like you've ended up talking to the wrong person, have the courage to leave the conversation politely. However, don't judge the person or conversation too quickly, show genuine interest in anyone you meet before coming to a conclusion.

Instead of thinking up an excuse, simply thank the person for the conversation and excuse yourself. If you feel uncomfortable, you can add something like 'I'm going to say "hello" to a friend', or 'I'm just going to pop to the restroom/get another drink'.

Use the moment someone leaves their seat to engage in a new conversation with someone else. It will help create a new dynamic in the room and people will soon copy you. It's all about being polite but determined.

Body language and tone

Using the right body language is just as important as saying the right words. Be conscious that you make a strong first impression* before you get a chance to open your mouth. To make the right impression, you should wear something that will increase your visibility, such as an elegant dress or bold colours. It can make introductions easier, especially if someone compliments your clothes.

Look into everyone's eyes when joining a group and shake their hands. Your hands are important and you should be using them while explaining something. Articulate things clearly and be engaging. Make people want to notice you. The key is to actively listen and show genuine interest in the other person. In order to show you're a great listener, pay attention to the other person's:

- Posture, eyes, and smile
- Energy and attitude
- Positive responses

Paying attention to these things can help you to establish trust. Moreover, you can make use of the following techniques while talking to someone:

- **Mirroring** is a technique that gets the other person to talk without you having to say much. Asking a question by repeating the last three words they said

---

* For more information on how to make a great first impression, please see Step One.

implies that you're listening to them. For instance, your new connection says, 'I have recently joined a big asset management firm in Frankfurt as an ESG* analyst supporting their research team.' You can respond, 'I have heard a lot about ESG lately and I would be keen to enter this industry. I recently completed my thesis which concluded that the majority of ESG funds outperform the wider market over ten years. Could you share a few insights from your role?'

- **Labelling** emotions gives the impression that you're aware of the other person. This can trigger contemplation and make them feel heard. When you see someone talking very passionately about their new work project, you could say, 'You seem very passionate about this project, what is the most valuable lesson that you have learned so far?'

- **Repeating their name** helps you to remember their name, which people like. Make a special effort to remember someone's name by using it as often as possible. 'That's such valuable advice, Louise,' will land much better than just 'That's such valuable advice.'

Collect (virtual) business cards

Some people keep an online diary while others prefer a traditional journal to keep track of their contacts. We would recommend using different methods, including:

---

* Environmental, social, and corporate governance

- **Online networks**, such as LinkedIn. This network allows you to scan an individual's QR code in the app and makes it easier to find them online.

- **A book or folder** to collect physical business cards.

- **A digital document** (such as Microsoft Word or Excel) or list-making app (like Trello) to write down contact details.

- **Informal communication channels**, such as WhatsApp or, in China, WeChat.

Keep in mind that new technologies are changing the way we network. Be aware that there are differences depending on which sector you're in, but the best way of knowing how to contact someone is to ask them how to reach them in the future. While diplomats tend to prefer being contacted by the phone, people in other industries commonly use social media.

Say thank you

Make sure you email people the day after getting to know them to thank them for their time and advice. Ideally, this should happen within twenty-four hours and never more than forty-eight hours after the meeting. Ensure to make the message personal by mentioning aspects of your conversation to show you listened. Remember to keep it short, as short messages are more powerful.

Building a lasting relationship can be difficult, our advice is simple: do what you say. If you agreed to meet, suggest a concrete date and demonstrate that you're serious about the commitment.

If you contact people online and they take the time for a call or coffee to share their experience and advice with you, show your appreciation. For instance, a sample message could look like the following:

Dear Miranda,

I just wanted to take a moment to thank you for taking the time to speak to me and for connecting me with your friend James. He has already gotten back to me with some proposals as to how my application would be most successful and even offered to meet over coffee to provide further help.

I truly appreciate your support and hope to stay in contact in the future. Please do not hesitate to contact me in case I can be of help with anything!

Best wishes,
Sarah

Nourish your contacts

It's not sufficient to just send a message after the first meeting. You should follow-up regularly by asking how the contact is, to make sure they don't forget about you. This is especially important if your goal is to get to know the person better.

Instead of sending an email or message over social media, you can be more discrete. Start following and connecting with the person on Twitter and LinkedIn. If you're active on social media, the professional will see your posts in their newsfeed and you can actively choose to display content that will draw attention to your work.

> **EXPERT MEMORY**
>
> **Kate Surala, Co-Author of *Unleash Today***
>
> I met a fascinating female role model at the Inspiring Women in Business Conference in London. She gave a great talk and her tips deeply resonated with me. I wanted to learn more about her achievements, so followed up with an email. She was very busy travelling in the US, as I later learned, and I didn't get a response. But since she inspired me so much, I followed up a month later. I didn't get a response immediately, but eventually she suggested that we meet up.
>
> **Lesson learned**
>
> Follow up, follow up, follow up! If you're truly interested in a person, send personal messages. Ensure that you space them out so that you don't bombard them with messages. If you don't get a response after a month, simply move on so that you don't come across as annoying.

26

How to Get Comfortable with Promoting and Selling Yourself

> *Know what you want, who you are, and what you have to offer.*

Sarah Wagner

Many women may excel at selling projects, events, or other services. However, when it comes to promoting themselves, some tend to start stuttering, turn red, or turn silent. It's so important that you get comfortable with selling yourself. Self-promotion is a muscle we as women need to learn to flex more often, for ourselves and for other women. Have the courage to go after what you want and support other women doing the same.

Building Your Brand

Start by developing your personal brand: build a value-based professional reputation and shape your image before others get the chance to do so. Your personal brand means being vocal about who you are and what you have to offer. Be transparent about your contributions, performance, and values, as well as the strengths and power skills you have at your disposal. Always remember that you have the power to control your brand.

> **EXPERT MEMORY**
>
> **Sarah Wagner, Co-Author of *Unleash Today***
>
> During my first few working years, I needed an outlet for my emotions. I started capturing my feelings by writing them down rather than keeping them bottled up. It felt like therapy. At some point, I decided that if I wanted to bring about change in this world, I had to share my opinion with a wider audience. So, I started publishing my articles on LinkedIn. Within a short amount of time, my followership grew tremendously; people from all over the world commented and got in touch with me. I realised I was not alone. People in my work environment began to demonstrate interest as well. Soon I was known as the 'feminist' in the office. I was invited to speak at events and consulted on questions surrounding inclusion and diversity. I was developing my brand.
>
> **Lesson learned**
> Use online platforms like LinkedIn to develop a brand. Actively share your opinion articles and leave comments below other people's contributions to demonstrate what you stand for. Engage with people online to grow your followership and expand your network of supporters.

To promote yourself and become visible, you can make use of various tools. First off, your inner attitude is a key requisite to successfully managing your brand. When you network, be yourself and be proud of who you are—that's your unique tool. Sit down and reflect on all elements you want to be known for, tie them in with your life experiences and opinions and dare to stand and speak up. In this context, learn to become a good storyteller. Telling a coherent story is one very meaningful tool to establish your brand and improve your memorability. By creating a consistent story about what you do best, what makes you unique and special, and what you stand for, you make it very easy for people to remember you. You want to make sure you captivate the interest and attention of listeners by sharing your why and what you really care about.

Be Your Own Saleswoman

Every time you enter the networking arena, you should have the goal to sell yourself. To encourage people to spend time listening to you, you must believe in what you're selling: yourself. Don't think of this as negative, as everything in life is sales.

Nobody will learn about your great work and experience unless you tell them about it. If you share these details, they might be able to provide valuable feedback or contacts. Imagine you have an invisible USP* pinned to your chest. Only you can see it, so you need to describe it to everyone else. Be a saleswoman for yourself and your company and/or cause.

Selling your brand is about creating a profile both online and off to show the world the positive impact you have on your company culture and/or community. Here

---

* Unique selling point

are some concrete tips on how to build your brand and sell your skills:

- **Participate in networking events** (career fairs, diversity groups, chamber of commerce events, receptions, promotions, policy debates, gallery openings, etc.) and look for opportunities to share your viewpoints.
- **Elevate your profile** by polishing your CV and using the right keywords for every application.
- **Build strong online profiles** on career portals, such as LinkedIn.
- **Offer a solution to a problem** rather than a final product. Present yourself and what you have to offer with passion and personalise everything that you mention.

- **Be present, visible, and leave traces.** Find ways to make sure people remember you by adding them on LinkedIn, following up, wearing bright clothes, or engaging candidly in conversations.
- **Be persistent and assertive.** If you go to a (virtual) event to speak to a specific person, don't let them intimidate you.
- **Find your own networking style.** Be your authentic self rather than copying someone else.
- **Let go of being everyone's darling.** Not everyone will like or agree with you. Those who believe in you will support and accompany you in good and bad times.

You may be the hardest worker in your firm and deliver the best results, but more often than not your hard work won't get recognised if people are not aware of your existence and performance. If you want to maximise your career success, you need to create opportunities. Creating opportunities begins with creating your own brand.

Practical Branding Tools: Virtual Networking and Community Building

> *'Build it and they will come' only works in the movies. Social media is a 'build it, nurture it, engage them, and they may come and stay'.*

Seth Godin

Social media is an essential tool in elevating your profile. If you want to get your voice out there, you'll have to spend time on social media. You may perceive social media as something fun to do in your free time, but it's more than that. It can be really hard work on the one hand, and an essential career boost on the other. But how do you use social media effectively?

> **EXPERT MEMORY**
>
> **Irène Kilubi, Founder of brandPreneurs and brandFluencers in Munich, Germany**
>
> Networking has moved online. You can use the internet to reach out to your professional and social community. LinkedIn, Twitter, and Facebook are some of the best platforms you can use to network with people who identify with you. Freelancers and entrepreneurs can also use the same platforms to create communities. However, there are several things you should consider before you build meaningful virtual connections:
>
> - **Optimise your online presence** by creating an authentic bio to improve people's perception of you and engage in meaningful discussions.
> - **Build your social proof** by requesting testimonials from employers and also recommendations from clients.
> - **Manage your time wisely** and focus on activities necessary for personal growth.

> **Lesson learned**
> Although it might seem easy, virtual community building can be challenging. It's a process that requires a lot of patience, since it might take time before you get a meaningful audience.

To build your social profile and optimise your online presence, don't underestimate the value of LinkedIn. It should become your best friend and here are a few things you should pay attention to:

- **Have a complete LinkedIn profile** with a headline that summarises you in a few words and includes a call for action.

- **Give a detailed overview** of your professional experience and education. Tell a story about yourself, your interests and how the various points on your profile link together.

- **Show your network what you know** and what you find interesting. Publishing articles and writing posts showcases your interests, insights and personality to potential employers and draws attention to how well rounded and engaged you are.

- **Regularly share content** to ensure that your posts appear at the top of the newsfeed for your LinkedIn network.

- **Ask current or former colleagues to give you a reference** or assess your skills.

27
Unleash Today Challenge: Networking

Imagine you've decided that you must overcome your networking aversion and expand your network. You are terribly shy and you don't know where to start, have no particular skill set, and are in a relatively junior position. What first steps can you take to becoming a successful networker?

Answer:

EXPERT ADVICE

Katharina Krenz, Corporate HR Transformation lead at Bosch and Founder of Connecting Humans in Leonberg, Germany

Networking opens doors to new opportunities, knowledge and inspiring people. You need to be part of an active network to stay informed, connected, and visible.

I am naturally more the shy, introverted type of person. I thought I'm not special, not talented, or particularly bright enough, so what do I have to offer to other people? How could a connection with me be valuable for someone else? And how should I get in touch with other people, personally offline and online?

Content-based exchange was easy, I trusted my knowledge and experience enough to feel safe. But approaching other people openly, even specifically addressing foreign experts, was very difficult and cost me a lot of effort and energy every single time. I was satisfied, when other people approached me and invited me to join their network. But I left it up to chance to make new connections, and I wasn't being strategic in my approach.

During the beginning of 2015, I had a personal 'aha!' moment: networking is an art, and it is not only a talent. It can also be learned by anyone who is open and curious about other people.

I've learned to build relationships on a very personal level and to make it useful and fun for everybody involved. If you know who you are, what drives you and what you have to offer, it is easy to connect to others in an authentic way. This isn't fake or manipulative, but genuinely based on attention, appreciation and recognition and your curiosity for other people.

And the best thing is that you can practise networking online as well as offline, on social media, at events, even in meetings and workshop situations. It is a practical learning-by-doing journey, enabling you to find out what suits you in approaching other people and how to overcome your fears and uncertainties.

I recommend the following steps to help you to network:

- **Be aware of your USP** and create your own personal brand. What topics do you want to be known for? What should people remember when they hear your name?
- **Find your channels.** Where do you want to be visible? There's no need to be active on all social media platforms. Try things out and adapt them according to your experiences.

- **Create your virtual identity.** It's necessary to have a virtual identity, so fill in a social media platform to show who you are, what interests you, and what you stand for.
- **Connect to others** by following participants of an event of inspiring people. Start liking and commenting on their posts.
- **Build your networks.** There are many different types of networks that add value to you and your career. Original and continuous contributions are important for building networks. Often, we remember who helps us, which adds value and builds trust.
- **Stay true to yourself** and be honest with yourself. When you know who you are, you'll know what your USP is and will be authentic. Others will recognise when you pretend and you'll lose credibility.

Step Five: Project 'Love'

In this section, you will learn how to:

- Nurture your self-love and share it with your colleagues
- Develop a self-love routine to overcome negativity
- Value meditation, gratitude, affirmations, and mindfulness
- Balance your diet, exercise, and sleeping habits
- Be in charge of your emotions in the workplace
- Reject thankless tasks in the office.

28

An Introduction to Project Love

> *Love you,*
> *Open heartedly, and feel the*
> *Valour through self-acceptance,*
> *Everyday, all day.*

Kate Surala

Your alarm clock goes off, you get up tired and you know all the caffeine in the world won't wake you up: it's going to be one of those days.

The thought of getting out of bed and working on your numerous deadlines makes you feel like hiding, safe and sound, under your duvet. Negative and stressful thoughts rush through your head. You criticise yourself, telling yourself that you didn't go to sleep early enough, or that you don't have what it takes to succeed. You feel overwhelmed, dejected, and hopeless.

Before 2020, the word 'lockdown' seemed alien. We never imagined we would be holed up inside our homes, unable to meet family and friends. However hard the pandemic has been, it has taught us to appreciate the things that we take for granted. Whether that's a sit-down meal at your favourite restaurant or the warm embrace of your loved one. It also helped us all to turn our attention inwards and focus on how we feel about ourselves. This drastic change in our day-to-day lives proved to be an opportunity to reflect on our circumstances and tune out the opinions of others.

With or without COVID-19, you should learn how to turn negativity into a superpower and find love within—it is an essential step in unleashing your true potential. Rather than being drowned in negativity, you should learn to flip it into positive energy and motivation to act and get things done by developing a self-love routine and personal love habits.

It is proven that women are more likely to struggle with a lack of self-love, which can greatly influence your mental health and self-esteem.[65] By not believing in your own abilities, we might not treat ourselves with sufficient respect and fall into a patterned mindset of self-doubt.[66]

Particularly in the age of social media, you may fall into the trap of constantly comparing yourself to other seemingly successful women. This also applies to the workplace, where you might be surrounded by other women with seemingly more success and influence. This will have a serious effect on your self-love and self-esteem, the impact of which should not be underestimated. How do they do it, you wonder? What do they do differently?

Self-love means to invest time in your own happiness and your physical and mental wellbeing. In this Step, we will provide you with the tools to unleash your self-love and share it with others. That means to set your own boundaries for yourself and extend it to the environment you operate in. We discuss tips on how to start a new routine and learn the value of gratitude.

29

Turning Negativity into Your Superpower

> *We need to go inward instead of outward, and learn to trust our own inner guide, preserving our identity and finding the answers from within.*

Jane Fulton Alt

Imagine you have just received a rejection email after applying for your dream job. Several thoughts probably cross your mind. You might go through every detail of the interview in your head, scrutinising every single thing you said and regretting the things you failed to mention. You might even think you'll never find a job!

Negativity bias is our tendency to register negative stimuli more readily and to dwell on negative events, instead of focussing on the positives. Fortunately, optimism can be learned! Instead of obsessing over the negatives, try to focus on the positives. For example, think about how you managed to get to the last round in the hiring process. The hiring manager(s) might have given you some valuable feedback that you can implement during your next interview that might lead to an even more exciting job. Later on, you might find out that the reason you weren't hired was because of a hiring freeze and had little to do with your performance.

Particularly in stressful situations, but also in general, our mind gets flooded with negative thoughts that prevent us from putting ourselves out there and taking risks.[67] These negative thoughts can cause stress and can even lead to severe mental and physical illnesses. So, how can you get out of this vicious cycle?

Prevent the spiral of negativity in your head by nurturing your body, mind and soul on a regular basis. You cannot prevent negative thoughts but develop a strong immune system to block them before they impact your behaviour and actions.

There are lots of ways to do this. Seek out your path to relaxation through trial and error. What we have found most effective is identifying our personal love habits, routines that strengthen our love from within, and implementing these into our daily routines. Write down your activities in a journal regularly to develop a routine. Further in this Step we provide more concrete tips on how to successfully create a habit.

What are some mindfulness exercises that you would like to incorporate into your daily routine? Write down your thoughts in the box below. Here are a few examples to get you started:

- **Body scan meditation.** Lie on your back with your arms and legs extended, palms facing up. Focus your attention slowly on each part of your body. Take note of the sensations, emotions, or thoughts that you associate with every part of your body.

- **Pay attention.** Take the time to experience your environment with all senses, engage in mindful seeing, listening, touching, tasting, and smelling. For example, when eating lunch, enjoy the smell, taste, and sight of your food.

- **Focus on your breathing.** Sit down and take a deep breath—exhale and inhale slowly—with your eyes closed. Focus on your breath as it moves in and out of your body.

ANSWER

Overcoming Your Negativity: Starting a Journal

> *Worries and tension are like birds.*
> *We cannot stop them from flying near us,*
> *but we can certainly stop them from*
> *making a nest in our mind.*

Rishika Jain

One particularly helpful tool to overcome your negativity bias is to keep a journal. When you write down your emotions and thoughts, you'll be able to discover how you can challenge those that are holding you back. You can use the ABC method[68] to help process negative events:

- **A**ctivating events are situations that trigger a chain of thoughts and emotions inside you, which can be internal or external.
- **B**elief includes your thoughts and feelings about the event and can be so subtle that you don't notice them or are very intrusive.
- **C**onsequences are the results of your actions or feelings during the A and B stages.

An example would be: I heard my colleague speaking loudly on the phone (A). → I need silence to work (B). → I felt annoyed, as I think the colleague was speaking loudly on purpose in order to get on my nerves after we had had an unpleasant conversation earlier that day (C). →Therefore, I slammed the door and went downstairs.

Once you have written down the event following this structure, identify the links between circumstances, thoughts, and emotions. The final step is to challenge and falsify these thoughts. What evidence do I have to support my belief? Is it logical that the consequence will follow? What concrete proof do I have of the truth of this belief? In this example, has the colleague really started speaking louder than usual just because of the previous disagreement?

Big or small, it's all about describing the event and your feelings in detail, using facts and non-judgemental language. Once you've written it down in this structure, identify the links between the circumstance and your emotions. The final step is to challenge these thoughts. Has the colleague really started speaking louder than usual just because of the previous disagreement? Ask yourself questions, such as 'Was the "consequence" (your reaction) the logical approach to this situation?'

Think back to the past few days. Can you apply the ABC method to an event that triggered negative emotions? Write down the process in the box below.

ANSWER

Alice Fiorica, Psychologist, CBT Therapist and Mindfulness Teacher in London, UK

Stress is the result of our perception. It's what comes out of the rapport between your perceived demands and resources. The good news is that the key word is always 'perceived', so just changing our perception reduces stress.

But how do you change your perception? Firstly, identify all your demands and write them down. Then, differentiate between which ones are real problems (ones that you need to attend to or there'll be bad consequences) and those that are what if... statements. All the what if... statements are problems that aren't happening now and may never materialise. Now, ask yourself: can I do anything about it? If the answer is no, then you need to let that worry go.

Some techniques of lowering your stress levels are:

- **Mindfulness** is a skill at the core of letting go. If a thought isn't helpful, choose to let it go and to focus your mental energy on a more helpful thought.
- **Accepting** uncertainty, as life is uncertain. Embrace the fact that sometimes outcomes are out of our control and do what is right for you now.

Lesson learned

Reading about how to reduce your stress will not reduce your stress levels. Only changing your behaviour by practising these techniques will lessen your stress.

> *Don't be a prisoner of your past and future thoughts and start living right now!*

Kate Surala

It's natural to catch yourself thinking about your plans for tomorrow or remembering details of an uncomfortable conversation from yesterday. The key to unleashing your full potential is to live in the here and now.[69] We've come up with a few daily steps to make every day count:

- **Be genuine and make small gestures of kindness** to the people around you.

- **Make time for personal connections** with people you might take for granted, regardless of who they are, even if you're in a rush. This can also be done virtually.

- **Establish which aspects of your daily life are outside of your control.** For instance, if you lose your job you can't control the fact that you were fired or laid off. What you can control is how you react to it. You can decide whether you take steps to find a new job as well as whether you take care of yourself through a nutritional diet and sufficient sleep.

30

Start Unleashing Your Inner Goddess

> *Find the love you seek, by first finding the love within yourself. Learn to rest in that place within you that is your true home.*
>
> **Sri Sri Ravi Shankar**

Now that you have recognised your negativity, it's time to find ways to overcome it by turning your negative thoughts into self-love. We will demonstrate to you how meditation, gratitude, and affirmations are beneficial for identifying your own love habits and implementing them into your day-to-day schedule.

Meditation Time!

Neuroscientists from the University of Harvard have found that individuals who regularly practise meditation report lower levels of stress, anxiety, depression, and chronic pain. Regular meditation also improves the quality of your sleep[70] and immune system.[71]

Just like exercise, you get better at meditation with time so, don't expect an immediate change! It can take about forty days to change a habit and ninety days to confirm it. Then, it takes 120 to integrate the new habit into who you are, and 1,000 days to master it.

When you learn how to make meditation work for you, you'll notice that your focus and tranquillity will influence your daily life. You'll feel less stressed in difficult situations and less likely to be overwhelmed by negative emotions.

If you've never tried meditation before, we recommend starting with a guided session, letting a professional talk you through the routine. This can be done either in person, or via audio or video.

> **EXPERT MEMORY**
>
> **Kate Surala, Co-Author of *Unleash Today***
>
> I first listened to a guided meditation session in February 2017 at the age of twenty-four after a friend introduced me to it. I was feeling very stressed and overwhelmed during my exam period, so she proposed to try meditation to calm down during my lunch break, breaking up my study sessions. The yogi always ended the session with a ten minute meditation with a short gratitude exercise. I remember the first time, lying down, closing my eyes after an intense workout and trying to calm down my thoughts that were only focussed on the future. 'Will I manage to hand in the assignment due tonight?' 'I have nothing left for dinner. I need to go to the supermarket and buy some food.' I could not keep my mind still. It took me weeks before I started seeing results. However, after a persistent effort, I suddenly realised that I felt less tense during my meditation classes and during the

day. The days that I started with a ten minute meditation session became more joyful.

Lesson Learned
Practise meditation to improve your mood, sleep, and immunity system. However, be patient to see the full results.

Gratitude

Being grateful will allow you to unleash and enjoy all the moments in life: helping you cultivate awareness and take nothing for granted. You can practise this by saying what you're grateful for out loud, or even write it down. Over time, your perspective will change and you'll see life as a gift, even with its ups and downs. But how do you start practising gratitude in everyday life?

Gratitude is something very individual. There is no perfect recipe or timing for practising gratitude. You should find your own personal routine. Do you want to write every morning before getting up to work or rather every now and then when you feel down? We encourage you to find your individual routine, building on whatever format and frequency works for you.

Gratitude countdown
Practising gratitude is useful for daily life, but it's particularly helpful in those moments when you feel lost. When something is getting you down, you can start by listing five to ten things that you are grateful for in that

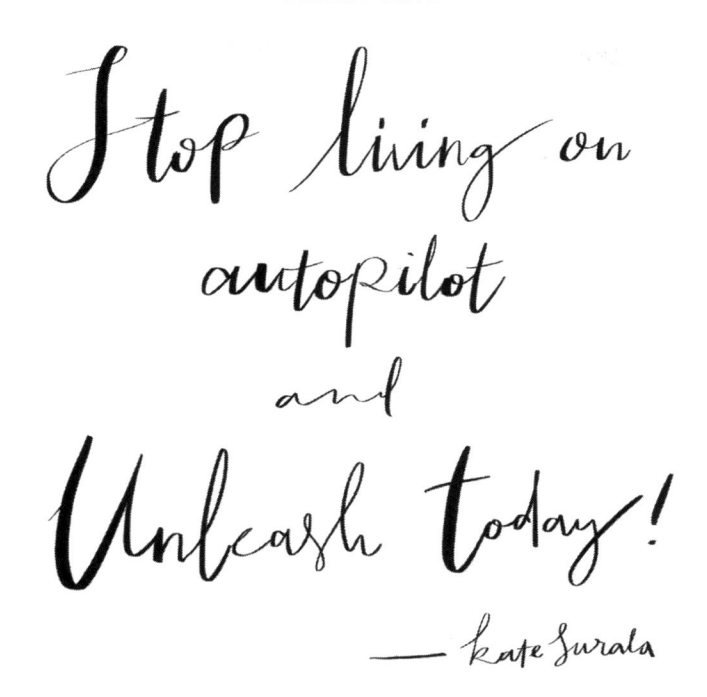

> *Stop living on autopilot and Unleash today!*
> — Kate Surala

moment. Trying it out should make you feel thankful, but a voice in your head may say, 'I can't think of anything else!'

When doing a gratitude countdown, we tend to start off by naming material items in our lives, but the more we list, the more likely we are to name things that actually matter to us. You should try to be as specific as possible when writing your list. The more details you give, the greater the feeling of gratitude. After writing your first two points, ask yourself 'why'. We like to end some days with a gratitude countdown to fully experience and appreciate all the little moments from the day. Try sharing this beautiful exercise with someone else, such as your friend, partner, or family member. You'll be amazed how effective it can be![72]

> **EXPERT ADVICE**
>
> **Debbie Hayes, Experienced Coach in Sandbach, UK**
>
> Practicing EFT, aka tapping can work wonders to help remove subconscious sabotaging thoughts and help you align with your true north. My breakthrough was to create a mantra I could tap in to remind me of my value. Below is my example of an **A-Z of Enoughness**:
>
> I am amazing enough. I am brave enough. I am courageous enough. I am decisive enough. I am energised enough. I am fierce enough. I am grateful enough. I am heroic enough. I am intuitive enough. I am joyous enough. I am knowledgeable enough. I am lovable enough. I am magnificent enough. I am noble enough. I am optimistic enough. I am powerful enough. I am quintessential enough. I am robust enough. I am strong enough. I am thoughtful enough. I am understanding enough. I am vivacious enough. I am wise enough. I am extraordinary enough. I am youthful enough. I am zealous enough.

Similar to Debbie, we encourage you to apply your gratitude exercise as a tool to use when you find yourself in a tough situation. Embrace this challenge and start with us now. While we were writing this chapter, trying to meet our tight deadline created a lot of stress. Here's what we wrote for our gratitude exercise. We were grateful for:

The technology we use every day which enables us to write down our thoughts and ideas and turn them into this incredible book. Our creativity and optimism throughout our lives.

PROJECT 'LOVE'

Our loving families and friends who support us every day.

Being the true 'us' without limitations.

Having such an amazing team helping us to write this book. To them, we cannot be grateful enough.

Now it's your turn: what are you grateful for? Try out the gratitude countdown.

> **ANSWER**
>
>
>
>
>
>

You might find it quite difficult at first. When you're not feeling your best, you will likely struggle to find anything to be grateful for at all. However, we promise you, by the end of the countdown your mood will be brightened, and you will be able to view your struggles in a larger context.[73]

Set your affirmations

Affirmations are motivational messages. These could be small statements that you say to yourself throughout the day to make yourself feel better. Using affirmations daily will help you to subconsciously replace negative thoughts with positive ones.

> **EXPERT MEMORY**
>
> **Sarah Wagner, Co-Author of *Unleash Today***
>
> Whenever I had an exam or important task due in school or university, my mother would leave me little messages on my bed or table which said things like, 'I am so proud of you, you got this. Stay calm, you know you have everything you need to master this.' It motivated me tremendously and reminded me that yes, I actually was prepared and capable of doing this.
>
> **Lesson learned**
> Write your own messages of affirmation by leaving post-it notes around your apartment that make you feel good, such as 'You got this!' or 'You look amazing!'

You can also use affirmations to help boost your motivation. Repeating these affirmations will help you to reprogramme your subconscious by focussing on this desire to achieve your goal.

Kate has included some of her favourite affirmations to give you some ideas of what yours could look like. Once you've read through them, write yours down in the box below.

20 January 2020: 'I am confident, yet humble. I empower others, including myself.' *Unleash Today* was taking off then and this is when we realised that we would like to ask others for help with this ambitious project. Now we have a dedicated team of 29 people.

12 March 2020: 'I choose to be free and myself at all times.' It was the start of the first lockdown of the year in the UK as a result of COVID-19 and this affirmation helped her to see the world more positively.

Write down your personal affirmation for today. It's important for you to use present tense and avoid any negative wordings. For instance, if you said, 'I will start working on my new project and no one will disturb me during its completion,' could it be transformed into a more effective affirmation? Such as, 'I am successfully completing XYZ, the process is quick and easy, and I am enjoying the results of this project.' Excited to create your own affirmation for today?

ANSWER

Other Ways to Stay Motivated

Our book is packed with our favourite inspiring quotes that we like to write down on sticky notes and display around our apartment. Kate likes sticking these quotes in her bathroom and looks at them when she brushes her teeth. Sarah likes to stick her motivational quotes to her fridge and front door so that she sees them every time she prepares a meal and leaves the house. We also share various motivational messages on our Instagram and LinkedIn channel as well as newsletter, so make sure to follow us!*

To start your day right, you could also buy a pack of motivational cards with affirmations to help you start manifesting limitless abundance today.

Our other favourite way to unleash is drinking tea, and colouring a book with positive affirmations for confidence and relaxation. Find your own way to unleash your inner child and keep yourself motivated and in good spirits.

---

* Subscribe to our newsletter via this link: https://www.unleashtoday.com/copy-of-get-in-touch

31
Develop Your Love Habits

Early on in this Step, we advised you to develop your self-love routines. However, establishing or changing your love habits is not all that easy. Developing routines that strengthen our love from within takes time. Nowadays, driven by the internet and social media, we always crave instant gratification. The natural instinct is that we want to see results as soon as possible. It's like a soldier rushing into battle too soon without having carefully thought through their strategy. As mentioned earlier in this Step, it can take about forty days to change a habit, ninety days to confirm it, 120 to integrate the new habit into who you are, and 1,000 days to master it.[74] Take one step at a time; miracles don't happen overnight.

Here are our *Unleash Today* tips to establish a new routine that you'll stick to:

- Define your routine and only commit to one change at a time.

- Break each large goal into smaller goals.
- Establish a plan and book your 'goal time' in your diary. For example, if you want to do twenty minutes of yoga every day, schedule an appointment for yourself every morning and add it to your daily to do list.
- Be prepared. When deciding on a new routine, make sure you have all the necessary equipment available. It will make it easier for you to say 'no' to your excuses and thoughts of delaying it.
- Share your new routine with your accountability partner (see tips on how to find one in Step Three).
- Reward yourself with something fun once you have completed your routine on a consistent basis.

Think of these love habits as a 'shopping list' where you can pick and choose items depending on your mood or a specific situation. In the following, we have outlined some habits that have worked particularly well for us:

1. Identify what boosts and drains your energy

Your energy level directly impacts your mood. When you're too exhausted and frustrated with everything around you, it's time to pause and think about how to get your energy back. Your energy levels are also deeply influenced by your personality. We recommend you invest some time getting to know your personality, as each person has different methods to recharge their battery. It's all about finding the right balance. As the following illustration shows, there are, for instance, key differences between the ways in which introverts and extroverts regain their energy.

Extroverts tend to show a preference for socialising with others, whereas introverts prefer to spend their time on their own, for instance reading a book.[75]

There are various free personality tests available online to get a better picture of who you are and which love habits suit you best.[76]

Now it's your turn. Mark the things that give you energy in green and things that drain your energy in red:[77]

- Being alone
- Being with people
- Spending time with friends
- Spending time with family
- Spending time with your partner
- Pursuing a passion like painting
- Doing sports
- Tidying up
- Reading
- Going out for a drink
- Going out to dance
- Listening to music
- Watching a movie
- Playing a party game
- Travelling
- Doing nothing
- Going shopping/doing groceries
- Working with your colleagues
- Studying for exams
- Having challenges
- Having unfinished work/ your to do list

2. Food that gives you energy

Some of us tend to snack and eat junk food when we are stressed. Find out whether you are prone to emotional eating and try to identify your triggers. Do you eat certain types of food when you are stressed or sad?

> **ANSWER**

You can learn to fight your cravings by remembering how you felt after making your way through a huge bowl of ice cream. The best way of getting energy is to eat well and take care of your body. Try to change your eating habits by filling your kitchen with fresh fruit and vegetables (bananas, sweet potatoes, apples, eggs, spinach, and if you have a sweet tooth, dark chocolate is your best friend!)

> **EXPERT MEMORY**
>
> **Denise Kellner, Editorial Lead *Unleash Today***
>
> I love food and I love cooking. Always have and always will. Cooking has, without a doubt, always helped me to slow down, become more present, and enjoy the fruits (often quite literally) of my labour. Making a simple meal that isn't only delicious, but which also has nutritional value, will fill your belly and mind with joy

Lesson learned

See the joy in cooking and start simple. You'll learn a lot and will become hungry (yes, pun very much intended) for more!

It's important to listen to your body and know when it's hungry. Don't feel obliged to follow rigid rules telling you when you should eat. Listen to yourself to find the right time for you. The same applies to portion sizes and the number of meals you eat a day. Some people prefer eating five, smaller meals while others prefer larger portions two or three times a day.

EXPERT MEMORY

Sarah Wagner, Co-Author of *Unleash Today*

I confess I've been an emotional eater most of my life. During my studies, when I sat for hours studying for exams and writing papers, I would eat a pack of sweets just to survive the night. The same goes for moments of anger, frustration, or nervousness. I'd always end up indulging my sweet tooth. Today, I know that getting much needed sleep is a more effective solution. Now, when I feel tense or angry, I go for a run or take a nap instead of opening a box of chocolates.

Lesson learned

Whenever you consider engaging in emotional eating, pause for a moment and listen to your body. Is food or sugar really what you need right now? Or is your body instead asking for rest or exercise?

3. Maintain a healthy sleep routine

Sleep is a vital component of everyone's life that leads to better health.[78] Yet, we often neglect it as something we can just catch up on later. We have put together a list of helpful tips to make sure you get that good night's sleep:

- Don't consume caffeine late in the day. Caffeine can stay elevated in your blood for six to eight hours. Replace it with a decaf coffee or herbal tea.

- Reduce blue light exposure in the evening. Switch off your electronic devices at least one hour before your bedtime. This will also help you to clear your head.[79]

- Establish a sleeping routine. Try to get up and go to bed at the same time to support your body's circadian rhythm.

- Relax and clear your head before your bedtime. Try listening to relaxing music, taking a hot bath, reading a book, meditation, or deep breathing.

> **EXPERT MEMORY**
>
> **Sarah Wagner, Co-Author of *Unleash Today***
>
> During the busiest days of writing *Unleash Today*, I was so tired that I hit my head very hard on my wardrobe. This forced me to stay at home for several days. Rather than saving time by pushing myself during night shifts, I lost a lot of time by being so tired that I injured myself.
>
> **Lesson learned**
> If you are a workaholic, force yourself to take regular breaks and never compromise on your sleep. Do not see

rest as unnecessary or wasteful, see it as an investment in yourself, your productivity, and health.

4. Exercise

Doing sports or engaging in any other physical activity improves your endurance and fitness. It also increases your self-esteem when achieving your objectives and thereby strengthens your confidence. If you're not a gym junkie, a simple walk can do miracles. If you're busy and don't have a chance to escape work, we recommend finding a private place (one of Sarah's and Kate's favourite spots is the bathroom) and turn on your favourite song for a little dance. It will boost your energy for the next meeting and you'll feel refreshed![80]

> **EXPERT MEMORY**
>
> **Sarah Wagner, Co-Author of *Unleash Today***
>
> We all know that taking a break, whether that's by going for a walk or doing a little stretching, is helpful to recharge our batteries. Yet, when I am stressed by an approaching deadline, I have difficulties prioritising exercise in my mind. An hour in the gym seems like a loss of time if you have an important deadline to meet. However, in those moments imagine how you'll feel afterwards: refreshed, awakened, and ready to conquer that deadline!
>
> **Lesson learned**
> Exercise should be a priority even when time is tight. Some time to break a sweat and focus on yourself can give you the energy you need to perform your best.

5. Take regular holidays

Booking a few days off gives you a great chance to escape from your daily routine, discover new places, and switch off your phone. Starting as young professionals, we thought that holidays would hold back our career progression because we would miss important meetings and might even be perceived as slackers. But this is a lie!

Treat yourself to a nice relaxing holiday. Consider signing up for a solo trip with a travel agency or go on an all-inclusive laid back holiday. If you can't afford to go away for one or two weeks, take a Friday and/or Monday off and enjoy a long weekend away.

> **EXPERT MEMORY**
>
> **Sarah Wagner, Co-Author of *Unleash Today***
>
> Arriving in China, a new country on a different continent, trying to integrate into a new team while taking care of various tasks in a foreign language was tough and truly exhausting. One day I decided I needed a day of rest. In the first six months of my contract, I had the right to two days off per month. Before I could even ask for a holiday, my boss told me that she did not appreciate any of us taking a holiday during the probation period. I took sick leave instead, after being mentally exhausted.
>
> **Lesson learned**
> Know your limits and what is best for you. Be aware of the toll work can take on your body and consequences you might face.

6. Spoil yourself

Being kind to yourself and doing something that you enjoy—going out to dinner, visiting the hairdresser, or buying a new book—is good for you and your long-term mental health and well-being. You don't even have to spend money to spoil yourself. You could even simply write a letter to yourself with everything that you are grateful for.

EXPERT MEMORY

Avril Chester, CEO and Founder of Cancer Central in Eastbourne, UK

It's incredibly easy to slip into that 'just one more hour' or 'I'll just finish this', which always ends up much longer than originally planned.

I learned this technique later in my career thanks to Adele King's incredible talk 'Life Lessons from Cancer'. When work is overwhelming, what small luxury can you schedule into your diary? Once a week,

I spoil myself and have a cup of tea in bed. It doesn't sound like much, but it's the best thing ever.

Begone alarm clock! This is me time.

I might call my parents, text friends, or simply start into space. I'm here, feeling rebellious in my jim-jams, sipping my tea with glee. I start the day controlling it rather than it controlling me.

Lesson learned
Be kind to yourself. Carve out your time. Let go of your arbitrary expectations.

7. Maintain healthy relationships

Being happy and finding your love within also means surrounding yourself with the right people and maintaining healthy relationships. These relationships could include your interactions with friends, colleagues, family, and loved ones.

EXPERT MEMORY

Júlia Aldenucci, Photographer from Brazil

My husband was always the kind of guy with a lot of female friends. In the beginning, some women would tell me to 'watch out!' But I always thought the opposite. If this guy can have a conversation with women without romantic interest, he probably admires them and values their ideas. That was key to our relationship! Also, we were always very honest about our feelings and intentions, so when we decided to be together, I knew we were ready to commit.

Today we have a daughter and we share every single task. He can do and, more importantly, he likes and wants to do every one of them. When I became pregnant, he took part in every decision, attended every doctor appointment, and was there at every ultrasound.

How does this help me to succeed in my career? Well, when I say, 'I really need to focus on this now.' I can really do it. He doesn't interrupt me every single minute to ask where our daughter's doll is or what she is trying to say. He can put her to sleep, he can play with her, he can understand why she's crying, or cook something for her. He feels comfortable with taking decisions, and good ones! He understands that my work is something important, not only for me but for us. He plays his part so that I'm not overwhelmed at the end of the day.

Lesson learned

Find the right person. Find the person who admires and supports you.

32
Self Love at Work

> *I like super women. Be smart, be brave, be demanding, be cheeky (yes, that too!), and be weak at times. To show this is also a sign of strength. Be ambitious, be curious, be passionate, be uncomfortable.*
>
> **Natascha Zelko**[*]

Loving yourself means that you're true to your authentic self and extend your love to others, including your co-workers. For you to be happy and satisfied at work you should bring your whole self rather than putting up a facade. We spend so many hours in our lifetime at work that it should be a priority of ours to find a workplace that fits with our personal values, convictions, and interests. There are different ways to extend your self love to your surroundings, including saying 'no' to certain tasks, taking a break to eat, and going for a walk when you feel like it.

Being Vulnerable Is a Strength

We're always told to be 'professional' at work and to leave our personal lives at the door of the office. But who

---

[*] *Unleash Today* expert and Co-Founder and Chief Editor at F10 FemaleOneZero in Berlin, Germany.

benefits from you being a robot? You shouldn't have to hide your feelings and put too much effort into behaving how others expect you to behave. In her book *Radical Candor* (2019), Kim Scott explains that when people try to 'keep it professional', they fail to care personally.[81] As a consequence, nobody feels comfortable being who they really are. Some companies have found that people who embrace authenticity at work are considerably happier and less stressed.[82]

While everyone has different comfort levels with workplace socialising, we believe that getting to know your colleagues beyond the 'How was your weekend?' chit-chat is valuable. Making the effort to understand and get to know your colleagues rather than making assumptions will help you to build relationships regardless of seniority level or background. Empathy can go a long way and can lead to better collaboration between you and your colleagues.

So, show the real you rather than pretending to be someone else. We're at our most confident when we're our true selves and demonstrate our vulnerability. You don't have to discuss your personal relationships, but what about your hobbies, favourite food, or the music you like?

To Cry or Not to Cry?

When it comes to crying, there's a fine line between being candid and professional. Tears can be powerful elicitors of concern, but also suspicion. While the sight of tears can cause people to pay attention, they could also portray you as weak or inept.

Studies prove that women are more prone to cry for both negative and positive reasons.[83] Research also shows that the crying of women can be interpreted as a sign of emotional instability.[84]

There are moments when you just can't and shouldn't hold back your tears. Yet, always be aware of the negative perception you're likely to face as a consequence. Try to find a safe place to cry and identify the colleagues that you can show this emotion to as a way of preventing a negative impact on your career.

> **EXPERT MEMORY**
>
> **Kate Surala, Co-Author of *Unleash Today***
>
> I never thought that I would say these words, but crying is good. When I'm going through tough times, I carry concealer in my handbag, just in case I need to correct it after crying in the office bathroom. If a situation gets too much or someone is rude to me, I say, 'I need to excuse myself. I'll be back in a few minutes.' Never allow your enemy to see your weakness.
>
> **Lesson learned**
> Find your safe place, whether it's at home with a loved one or alone, and just let it out.

How to Set Boundaries

Have you ever been in a situation at work that left you thinking 'I should never have agreed to this'? No worries, we've all been there! We encourage you to listen to your gut and learn how to say 'no'. Learn to resist your need to accept thankless tasks. Remember to love yourself and listen to your body and well being.

EXPERT MEMORY

Kate Surala, Co-Author of *Unleash Today*

It has happened to all of us. You have a very productive meeting, you agree to send XYZ to your colleague, and you never find time to do it! One day, I got very angry with myself after going through my endless to do lists after various meetings. I decided to set a new routine, scheduling in a fifteen minute 'follow up time' after every meeting. I would consciously book in a fifteen minute slot after every meeting to take care of immediate tasks like sending out invites for the next meeting, responding to a few questions which were raised, or letting the attendees know that it was nice to meet them.

Lesson learned
Try out a fifteen minute follow up time after each meeting.

Project 'Love'

Research by the American Economic Review shows that women are more likely to volunteer for tasks that aren't going to help their careers.[85] However, this isn't because women are inherently more altruistic. Interestingly, the survey shows that when participants were placed in same-sex groups, the volunteering rate was the same. Research has also found that women are assigned to do tasks that aren't in their job description more often. When a manager, regardless of their gender, decides to pick someone for a thankless task, they 44 per cent more likely to ask a woman to volunteer. The reason for picking a female is because they know 'she is going to say yes'.[86]

We've spoken to many women in senior roles and this scenario keeps happening, even to women at the top.[87] Even in 2021, predominantly women are asked to make coffee in meetings and shred paper during their full-time job that doesn't involve any of these tasks. Be prepared to act appropriately when this happens to you. We want to see you unleash by breaking out of the volunteer role women are squeezed into while in the office. Actively remind yourself to say 'No!'

> **EXPERT MEMORY**
>
> **Kate Surala, Co-Author of *Unleash Today***
>
> I was asked to prepare a coffee at my first client meeting in Luxembourg. I was the only woman in the room. The other seven men were comfortably sitting in the leather chairs and waiting for me to get up, miss the introduction round, and complete the task I was most qualified for in their eyes. My male colleagues remained silent. To break the silence, I eventually got up and went

to search for a coffee machine in offices I had never visited before. Today, I know I made a mistake at that very moment. I would discourage you from following this approach. There are several options on how you can respond in such a situation. For instance, you could just bring the coffee (not a good solution, in my view), you could pretend you overheard what they said and carry on (not a good solution either), you could stand up and scream 'how dare you' and leave (absolutely not to be recommended), or you could respond smartly. This is how I would respond in this situation today: 'Oh, that's a great idea, let's ask the receptionist to bring us all some coffee. I would like a black with no sugar please.'

Lesson learned

Make a joke out of an awkward situation and offer a solution. Ask for an assistant's help.

33

Unleash Today Challenge: Project Love

Imagine that you've been asked to prepare coffee at your first client meeting. You have just joined the firm as a junior and you are the only woman in the room. You are daunted as you are surrounded by men only and you don't know what to do. You came to this company to learn about marketing, not about coffee. What would you do? Take a few minutes to think about your response before reading Johan's advice below.

ANSWER

> EXPERT ADVICE

Johan Ysewyn, Partner at Covington & Burling LLP in Brussels, Belgium

Most importantly, you can't say 'No', because you could be perceived as 'unhelpful'. Depending on the context and the relationship you have with the people in the room, you could turn the situation by making it more light hearted. You could say, 'Maybe we should all go to the coffee machine and serve ourselves' or 'Sure, could someone help me to bring in the coffee?'

Another option is to serve the coffee and say nothing until you raise it diplomatically with your boss afterwards. You could say something like, 'My job is to help you. Serving coffee isn't good for my reputation. I hope you understand that if you already put me on the "backburner" with this client, I can't help you as effectively. I'm afraid that the client will have lost all confidence and trust in me from the beginning. I can't do my job properly if you don't give me the level of confidence and trust.'

Step Six: Dealing with Difficult Situations

In this section, you will learn how to:

- Grow from challenging colleagues
- Respond to sexism in the workplace
- Develop a positive relationship with your boss
- Stay calm and keep your emotions under control

34

An Introduction to Difficult Situations

> *Sometimes I forget how strong a woman I am until I'm put in a situation where I have no choice but to show my strength.*
>
> **Sarah Wagner**

Do you remember when you were at university and you worked on group projects? We do, and we haven't forgotten about the frustration we experienced, particularly towards passive team members that relied solely on the hard work of others. There were those who didn't want to cooperate and those who struggled to keep up. We'd ask our professors why we couldn't just do the project on our own, but the response was 'in real life, you can't choose your colleagues either'. Back then, we laughed. Now we know they were right.

If you are reading this book, chances are you're a driven and hard-working woman with grand goals. This could mean that some colleagues might dislike you because they're jealous of your zeal. In fact, as a powerful woman, particularly as you move up to the higher ranks, you're likely to have more envious colleagues than supporters. All the more, it is important for you to learn to deal with your various co-workers. If you want to become a good leader, you will need to get along with all types of people. We will share our secrets on how to navigate difficult situations while bringing out the best in yourself and others.

Work environments and people are different and, while you will never get along well with everyone, you need to learn to collaborate. The only option is to accept this and learn how to handle situations with difficult people, including those you would rather want to avoid. You can't change someone's personality, but you can try to find a healthy and productive way of dealing with it.

How you interact with others determines the level of success you'll achieve in your personal and professional life. It's extremely difficult to hide dislike. However, if you want to become successful, you must learn to channel your emotions and befriend your enemies. Foes can teach you as much, or even more, than friends. It is equally crucial to get along with your boss, whether you agree with them or not. Learning to effectively 'manage' your boss by developing a mutually rewarding working relationship is essential to the success of your career and your wellbeing at the company.

Sometimes, emotions run high, particularly if sexist remarks are at play. As women continue to deal with sexism in the workplace to this day, it is important to address ways to proactively handle it. In the final section, we will therefore provide you with tips to identify your emotional trigger points and stay in control when your emotions run high.

35

Don't Run Just Yet, Lady!

> *Where there is no struggle,*
> *there is no strength.*
>
> **Oprah Winfrey**

You have no idea how often we called each other during our junior careers, swearing we would quit our jobs because we were fed up with certain colleagues. While many of our experiences were painful and kept us awake at night, they all made us stronger and taught us how to do things differently. All too often, we saw other colleagues leave their jobs after just a few months because they didn't feel at ease with their work environment.

Millennials in particular are a job-hopping generation by nature.[88] They move on quickly if they identify a lack of career advancement, spot development opportunities or determine a mismatch of values or expectation for compensation.[89] We're convinced that escape is usually a quick fix rather than an effective solution. Quitting your job won't necessarily enhance your work satisfaction in the long run. Endurance is important for your professional growth as you learn to face your problems in the work environment.

Here are some tips and tricks on how to prevent conflicts when interacting with your colleagues:

- **Don't gossip.** When you're angry, it can be difficult to hide your emotions and it's tempting to share your negative feelings towards a co-worker. However, it's imperative that you remain friendly and respectful. You also need to watch your body language. Subtle signs like rolling your eyes can be interpreted negatively.

- **Don't complain.** It won't help the relationship with your colleagues. It certainly won't make you a stronger candidate for a promotion or help your team to be more productive.

> **EXPERT MEMORY**
>
> **Sarah Wagner, Co-Author of *Unleash Today***
>
> Whenever I was annoyed with a colleague, I would roll my eyes, very clearly showing my dissatisfaction. I couldn't help it. If a colleague was being patronising or repeating what someone else had already said, I wanted everyone to realise that this colleague was hijacking the meeting. Obviously, it was totally useless, because I was the one making a fool out of myself. Rather than actively contributing, I was complaining about my colleague.
>
> **Lesson learned**
>
> Don't show your discontentment in front of other people. If you need to complain about someone, do it in private outside of the office. If the colleague causes actual problems at work, speak to your (HR) Manager and ask them for advice to improve the work relationship. They might be able to rearrange projects, so you don't have to regularly interact with this colleague.

- **Assess whether it's worth being honest in all situations.** Sometimes, too much honesty can cause tension, especially if the other person can't take the truth. Other times, it just doesn't make a difference whether you communicate your feelings or not.

- **Find an ally and support network to back you.** Carefully consider what you share with your colleagues and/or line manager. Often people will be your friend, but don't want to put themselves in the line of fire for you. Others might only see you as a colleague and may not have the time to support you. Look out for real allies who'll offer advice, information, and protection. Alliances like this don't appear overnight but must be built up over time.

> **EXPERT MEMORY**
>
> **Denise Kellner, Editorial Lead *Unleash Today***
>
> I remember a time when several colleagues and I had a similar problem with our supervisor. We had voiced our concerns amongst ourselves and agreed to reach out to her to discuss the problems we were facing. When it came to the discussion, I was the only one addressing the issues and the rest of the team stayed quiet, making me look like the 'bad guy'.
>
> **Lesson learned**
> If you and your colleagues face similar problems with a supervisor or a boss, remember that you should discuss these individually and not rely on the backing of others.

Think about who at your firm is a potential ally you can reach out to:

ANSWER

- **Kill with kindness.** Acting as sweet as pie doesn't come easily when you are boiling inside. But, by acting kindly, you'll come across as professional and that's what counts. Make sure to use simple pleasantries like 'hello' and 'bye' with your colleagues and refrain from responding to pettiness and bad behaviour. Show that you are able to deliver results in spite of personal discrepancies. The key thing to remember is Michelle Obama's catchphrase: 'When they go low, we go high!' If you're kind, people won't be able to say anything bad against you. All of your colleagues will just say, 'Her? No, she's always so kind to everyone.'

- **Don't focus on being liked.** Be aware that you won't be liked by everyone, so try not to take it personally if someone doesn't. Be polite to everyone regardless and vent at home if you need to.

- **Re-adjust your focus.** Don't waste your energy on disliking someone when you could use your time more efficiently. Focus on yourself, family, friends, job, and other things that make you happy. Try to find something positive about the person you dislike. What are some of their positive attributes and skills? What could you learn from them?

Think about the colleague who you dislike and try to identify three aspects that you could learn from them.

> **ANSWER**

- **Document any bad behaviour.** If you are involved in a serious conflict, keep a detailed record of when, where, and what was said verbatim in case you need to raise your concerns formally. If worse comes to worst, you can recall what happened and provide evidence to the Head of HR or even your legal representative, in the case of the last resort. If you know the colleague doesn't mind lying, avoid face-to-face conversations and communicate via email. Communicating by writing is very helpful as every interaction is recorded. If offensive language is used in a face-to-face conversation or over the phone, you can write up an email to pinpoint which remarks you thought were out of line, while putting exactly what was said in quotation marks.

- **Dare to have that difficult talk.** Most people try to avoid challenging conversations. However, progress can often only be achieved if we address the issue with the people involved. Therefore, we challenge you to identify an underlying conflict in your professional life that can be resolved with a candid conversation.

Once you have embraced the idea and are ready to face a difficult talk, we encourage you to prepare a script of what you want to say. Here are a few tips to approach that conversation:

- **Plan ahead.** Work out when and where to have the conversation and allow sufficient time to prepare. Think about what you want to say and schedule the conversation for a time that is convenient for both of you.

- **Have a personal encounter.** Try to have the conversation in person rather than over the phone or email. You may also have coffee and tea to create an amicable atmosphere.

- **Show empathy and change perspective.** Listen carefully to the other person's concerns. Try to put yourself in the other person's shoes. This might help you to have a more objective understanding of the problem. Summarise their points occasionally to make sure you understand what they are saying.

- **Be clear and persevere.** When it's your turn to speak, have your first sentence prepared. Be as specific about the issue as possible, and clear about what is expected and the outcome you want to see.

- **Agree to disagree** and determine objectives. Establishing where you disagree can be a positive way forward. Finish with clearly agreed objectives, including a timeframe and schedule the next conversation.

36

Speak Up, Don't Endure!

> *Never accept unacceptable behaviour or you will make it acceptable.*
>
> **Anonymous**

Our daily lives are full of casual sexism, whether it's a supposedly harmless joke at the expense of women, or a male colleague receiving unjust preferential treatment. Sexism is so deeply ingrained in our language and professional culture that it often goes unnoticed. Phrases such as 'don't be so bossy', 'you're getting emotional', and 'nice work, sweetheart' are still frequently uttered in the workplace without anyone speaking up and demanding change.

Unfortunately, women continue to find themselves in situations where they have to deal with inappropriate behaviour. It's likely that, as a young woman starting your career in particular, you'll find yourself in a situation where you're not being taken seriously, ignored, or interrupted by your male colleagues. You might also deal with mansplaining.[90] Situations like this can make you feel uncomfortable and alienated and they shouldn't be taken lightly. A recent study shows that subtle sexism in the

Dealing with Difficult Situations

workplace may affect women more than overt harassment.⁹¹ As a young professional, you might not feel that you have the authority to challenge casual sexism. But this doesn't mean you should just accept it.

> **EXPERT MEMORY**
>
> **Marwa Kassem, Master Trainer and Learning Consultant in Cairo, Egypt**
>
> During one of my training workshops with a reputable multinational organisation in Egypt, I was engaging with the three day programme and thought it was successful. After it ended, I sat down to read the feedback on the evaluation forms. One of them stopped me in my tracks. The entire page was empty, except for one sentence at the bottom of the page. Just then, my phone rang and, with trembling hands, I answered my manager.

'How was it?' she asked excitedly.

I broke down crying. Between sobs, I told her what was written that 'The trainer should be a man or a veiled woman.'

She laughed! Then she said, 'Who cares? The guy obviously had a message to send. What did the others write?' When I told her I had very encouraging comments, she answered, 'Well, that proves my point.'

Lesson learned
Who you are is not up to anyone else to decide but you! You are worthy, you are mighty, and you are enough.

Unfortunately, there is no one-size-fits-all solution for dealing with sexism. You must take into consideration a variety of factors, such as who the person is and the level of inappropriateness, before responding. Sometimes it does make more sense to let something go, but we do encourage you to stand up for yourself if you feel strongly about an issue. The most important thing is that you remember your values, set your boundaries, and know whom to listen to and when you should listen only to yourself.

Expert Memory

Anonymous, working in a financial services firm in London, UK

In 1995, I started my second job as a trainee accountant with a media company in Knightsbridge. It was a small company of about thirty employees and the Christmas parties were something everyone looked forward to.

They were held outside London with no expense

spared. My second Christmas party with the company had a theme of Victoriana and individual costumes were hired for all the staff. Following the meal, the CEO suggested we play a game before starting the dancing. He suggested the game should be a competition to find the most 'buxom wench' (the woman with the largest breasts).

I was amazed that no one objected. Instead, everyone followed the CEO's instructions and the women lined up along the wall. I deliberately stood at the far end of the line, already feeling uncomfortable. He then summoned two men from marketing to be judges. He asked them to use their hands to cup each woman's breast so that they could feel whose were the largest. As they moved along the line closer to me, I became more and more amazed that no one was challenging them. The women giggled and the onlooking men cheered. When they reached me, I pushed the hand away and said, 'Don't come anywhere near me.' I walked away from the line, approached my male boss who was looking on, and said, 'I can't believe this.'

The rest of the evening was marred by feelings of anger and disbelief. Back in the office, my boss asked me if I had enjoyed the party and I expressed my continued disbelief. I vowed never to attend a Christmas party with that firm again and moved to a new job in May.

Lesson learned

Leaders set the standard for the whole company and few people challenge them. Don't be afraid to be the one who challenges, even if it means standing alone.

If you decide to speak up, think about the way you want to communicate the issue. You should determine who you will speak to and what communication tool you will employ. More often than not, the person who offended you isn't insensitive but simply unaware of their bias.

Sometimes it can be helpful to make a joke about it rather than publicly condemning the person, as the following example demonstrates:

> **EXPERT MEMORY**
>
> **Sonja Stuchtey, Chair of the Supervisory Board at Alliance4Europe in Munich, Germany**
>
> The day we had to present the results of our analysis, we entered the old-fashioned office of a paternalistic and highly hierarchical institution. I was twenty-four years old, smart, self-assured, and the bedrock for one particularly delicate consulting project within this huge corporation. The CEO, one of those very accomplished old men, pulled his chair back a bit and listened rather inattentively until I revealed some provoking insights on head counts and expenses. 'That is not true!' he said in a firm voice. 'The data is from your own accounting—verified during site visits. All well documented and substantiated facts,' I replied confidently.
>
> 'This cannot be true. Are you the CEO of this company or am I?' He grabbed his phone. Then his face fell as the person on the other side of the line confirmed my data.
>
> The partner of my firm grinned. He looked at the old chairman and remarked casually, 'Among men, this would mean a schnapps now!'

> **Lesson learned**
> Believe in your capabilities and trust yourself in any situation.

While you can use humour to defuse a situation, there are other solutions you can pursue as well. Do you want to address the issue right away or remain anonymous and approach HR? In the following, we present three options to deal with sexist remarks and other inappropriate behaviour.

1. The indirect route

Sometimes you might feel like you are the only one seeing or experiencing inappropriate behaviour. In such situations, speak to your allies about your experiences and ask how they feel about what transpired. The concept of an ally goes much further than simply sharing experiences. Real allies will speak up and help you to build power in numbers. If you decide to publicly call people out for their behaviour, it's vital to have someone confirm your perception or experience.

Are they experiencing the same? They will help you put things into perspective, particularly if they've been working at the company or in the industry for longer. They might provide context that this is a deep-rooted issue within your company culture. While speaking to your allies will not directly solve your problems, their back-up may give you confidence to take the next step, i.e. speak up or approach the HR or line manager.

It's easy to feel helpless and isolated. When you're one woman facing a fraternity-style workplace.

2. The direct route

Speak up and point out the issue without condemning. Firstly, don't accept double standards—question them. Questioning people's behaviour forces them to reconsider their actions. For instance, if your boss calls all your male colleagues by their first name but addresses you by your last name, ask why everyone except for you is on a first name basis.

We also encourage you to speak up for other women. Be an ally for them just as you would want them to support you. Inappropriate behaviour affects the entire team's dynamic and morale.

EXPERT MEMORY

Sarah Wagner, Co-Author of *Unleash Today*

I remember working with my female colleagues at our all-female island in the office. Suddenly, one of our male colleagues came over, asking, 'Girls, please join our meeting.'

I addressed the fact that I didn't want to be addressed as 'girl', given that I wouldn't call him 'boy'. He was perplexed and didn't understand what my problem was. Later, we had a long discussion about the subtle sexism of our language. Bringing up the issue made him reflect and be more aware of his usage of words.

Lesson learned

Dare to speak up, but be careful about your method of communication. Being funny or subtle is sometimes more fruitful than condemnation.

3. The double route

Speak to your line manager or HR. Regardless of the option you choose, you can always consult HR as well, if your company has an HR department. Annual or performance reviews would be a good moment to bring these points up. As always when raising a problem, it's useful to also provide a possible solution. For instance, you could propose to implement awareness training for staff or mentoring programmes for your colleagues.

37

Smart Ladies Manage Their Bosses

> *If you are forced out of your job by a fearful boss who feels threatened by you, don't feel bad. Keep your flame growing, whether other people like it or not.*

Liz Ryan

No two bosses are the same and, frankly, there are both those who are incredibly talented and those that are woefully incompetent. There are bosses who seek to grow and learn and are open for feedback. Whereas others might not care, are overwhelmed with the situation, or simply enjoy having power over others.

Unfortunately, being a good boss and managing people is a skill we don't usually learn in school or university. Then, we're thrown into working life and are suddenly supposed to know how to deal with colleagues and superiors. More often than not, you're learning on the job.

We spend most of our waking hours at work, so if the relationship with our boss is a difficult one, those hours will be gruelling. Learning to work with and 'manage' your boss is essential to the success of your career and your wellbeing at the company. You don't have to be manipulative, there are smart ways to develop a mutually beneficial working relationship with the person above you in your organisation.

We are here to teach you some smart habits and skills to understand and effectively manage your boss.

A general solution is to spend time getting to know your boss. This way, you can adjust your actions and behaviour around them more effectively. Speak to colleagues and listen to informal conversations to find out how they're perceived by others. In case your boss doesn't fall under the competent and likable category, we have come up with the following types of difficult bosses that you are likely to come across in your work life. We will share our tips on how to keep working with them and grow your professional relationship.

1. The overwhelmed type
Some people just aren't yet equipped to assume responsibilities of a manager, let alone of a leader. They may get angry quickly, are rude and dismissive, or just

don't appreciate your hard work. They might have many skills, but leading a team just isn't one of them.

There are various reasons why an overwhelmed person could end up in a managing position. They may have assumed the position because nobody else was available or interested at the time, or they inherited the role because they've been at the company the longest. Never automatically assume that your boss is competent by virtue of their position.

If you feel as though your boss is incapable of holding their position, be smart about not showing your anger towards them. Avoid challenging your boss or revealing their incompetence in any way, as this might backfire. Always remember that, while they might be incompetent, they have the power to damage your career, particularly if no one else is assessing your performance.

EXPERT MEMORY

Kate Surala, Co-Author of *Unleash Today*

One of my former bosses was completely 'hands off' and used to say 'sink or swim' to new joiners. The only things that I was given on my first day were a table and a chair. I had to figure everything out on my own, from introductions to the team to understanding the complex structure of the organisation. Rather than being frustrated, I accepted that I needed to develop my own career and get an understanding of my responsibilities myself. I reached out for external help, found a mentor and coach, and established a wide network of connections in my industry to help resolve any issues I was facing.

> **Lesson learned**
> Build and nurture your external network in the same industry and learn from a role model who is willing to mentor or coach you. If you're not managed, see this as an opportunity to learn from someone else of your own preference!

2. The jealous type

It can happen rather quickly. One day you're enjoying your job, your boss supports you, and gives you opportunities to shine. Then, suddenly, you seem to be doing everything wrong. Your boss complains constantly and you're no longer able to please them, no matter how hard you try. How did you go from the dream team to their least favourite person?

The answer could be that your boss realised how talented you really are. Now you might be a threat to their position. While your boss might have ten to twenty years more experience, it's what they don't have that bothers them. For example, you might have become popular among the company executives or clients, or you display too much knowledge in a key area.

Only truly confident and self-assured bosses can be comfortable with employees who have the potential to surpass them. In fact, they seek to be surrounded by people who are better than them in certain areas to assemble the best team possible and achieve great results together.

At an early stage, identify how confident your boss is so that you don't overstep any boundaries. Once you step on their toes, it's difficult to rekindle the relationship.

Spend time observing their insecurities and try to identify the source. For instance, your boss might dislike confrontation and criticism because they're afraid of being unpopular with the staff. In this case, try to write emails or choose to discuss difficult topics over casual encounters. Try to avoid showing that you know their weak points and give them extra credit when you know they're doing something well.

> **EXPERT MEMORY**
>
> **Anonymous leading professional in the tech industry**
>
> When I changed jobs, I wanted to show how capable and connected I was. Networking and establishing big stakeholder circles had always been one of my strengths, so I reached out to various professionals before assuming the position. By the time I arrived, I already had a whole range of people I wanted to meet over lunch and learn from their work. When I received my performance review, I was asked to respect hierarchies and refrain from contacting stakeholders without my boss' approval.
>
> **Lesson learned**
> Watch before you act. While certain behaviours are appreciated by confident bosses, you need to be very careful not to step on the foot of an insecure boss. Also consider cultural differences, particularly when it comes to hierarchy.

3. The royal type

Some just think they are better than everyone else. They believe they can treat people any way they want and create a toxic environment. They make fun of colleagues, exhibit no emotional intelligence, and talk about others behind their back. You can't learn anything from a royal boss except how *not* to manage a team. A lousy boss can be a great teacher as you learn what *not to do* when you become one.

Our tip is to change your mindset when hurt or frustrated. Every time your boss treats you badly, write down your feelings and how you would have behaved differently in the situation. See it as an exercise on your way into the management team.

> **EXPERT MEMORY**
>
> **Marie Sina, Content Editor at *Unleash Today***
>
> When I was working as an intern, I was collaborating with my boss on a report for a client. By the time the deadline rolled around, my boss had not completed his part. When the client complained in an email about the incomplete work, my boss replied that the intern had not completed it on time. I was furious but unsure how to react. I was just an intern and did not want to fall out with my boss. At the same time, I was not going to let him blame me for his own error. After deliberating how best to approach him, I mustered up the confidence to address him in person. I told him politely but decisively that I thought it was unjust of him to blame me and asked him to straighten out the situation. He immediately saw reason, apologised, and clarified what had happened in an email to the client.

> **Lesson learned**
> Even when you are the underdog, you should not let your boss disrespect you by being untruthful. Stand up for yourself in a deliberate and well thought out manner.

Moreover, you could find yourself working with a 'Queen Bee', a female boss who perceives other women as a threat and tries to hinder another woman's advancement. We see this particularly with the baby boomer generation, who had to face a tougher glass ceiling and direct discrimination. Unfortunately, some develop the 'If I went through it, why should it be easier for her?' attitude.

With royal types, in the long run, it is about acting or leaving—a decision only you can take for yourself. Are there reasons justifying why it's worth staying on (e.g. potential change of management, particularly good compensation, etc.)? Always listen to your heart and take care of your mental health. If the situation gets out of hand, seek help from your HR department, or, if you don't have one, you could reach out to organisations that provide free advice, such as ACAS and Citizens Advice in the UK.

EXPERT MEMORY

Natasha Necarti, Business Development Director at Crafty Art in London, UK

Before I joined the family business, I worked for a corporate firm that tendered for projects and I enjoyed the first couple of years working there. However, there were some signals along the way that showed that things weren't quite right.

I remember a particular situation where the entire team had a deadline but, while everyone else (including the managers) could go home, I was expected to stay in the office and work on my own. There were times when I was expected to come into the office alone on weekends too. I was even asked to pick up my line manager from the station or drop her off. My colleagues told me to say 'No', but I was made to feel that I had no choice.

I stayed in the hope that things would get better. The bullying got so bad it made me ill. I would suffer from frequent migraines and started having panic attacks.

The final straw came when I returned from my grandad's funeral. I had called my line manager to ask for a day of leave and explained my grief. But she told me that I was faking it, that I was a liar, and if I valued my job I would be in work.

After that, I left my job. I had a great salary and we had bills to pay, but I had to question what was important. I had to regain my confidence. Looking back on it, my fear was that I wasn't good enough for anything else. I feared I wouldn't be able to find another job.

Lesson learned

After this, I promised myself that I would never treat any of my staff in this way. Everyone deserves respect and common decency, and that's the goal that I have set myself to remember.

4. The perfectionist micromanager

Having a perfectionist boss micromanaging you can be difficult as you may feel you'll never fulfil their expectations. They might expect you to arrive early and leave late, cancel dates, and forget hobbies, because that's what they do.

What is important to keep in mind is that perfectionists often don't mean to impose cruel working hours or tasks. Rather, their micromanaging style is a reflection of the pressure they put on themselves.

With these types of bosses, try to subtly show them that the expectations they have for themselves shouldn't be the same for the rest of their team. Instead of protesting by not fulfilling tasks, put things into perspective and let them know that you have too much on your plate. You shouldn't have to justify not wanting to work an unsustainable amount of overtime. Sometimes, a perfectionist is so focussed on doing the job perfectly that they forget that people have other things to do.

> **EXPERT MEMORY**
>
> **Anonymous young female professional working in public policy**
>
> My boss always stayed until 9pm. Whenever I left—around normal working hours, but still later than contracted—I got a strange look. My boss expected me to stay longer. While I was keen to uphold a healthy work-life balance, I felt like I shouldn't have to justify why I wanted to leave on time. For colleagues with kids, this was never questioned. But, strangely, as a single woman I somehow felt an expectation to spend my evenings in the office. Although I often arrived one

to two hours before my boss, I felt I couldn't satisfy her. I got bad job performance reviews and decided to raise the issue that I preferred to work early and leave on time. The situation improved.

Lesson learned

It's difficult to impress a perfectionist. Know your limits, stick to your standards, and communicate them clearly. Discussing expectations and lifestyles can help to create mutual understanding.

5. The sneaky type

A sneaky boss can be sly and cutthroat in how they approach clients and employees. They may lack integrity and be unethical, without shying away from lying and intimidating others to get their way. Their actions may have a long-lasting impact on your self-esteem and confidence, so it's essential you set your limits and not let them wear you down.

One way is to speak with your boss in private when a situation becomes too dire. Talk about your own feelings rather than making the conversation about what your boss is doing wrong. Be smart by using phrases such as 'I feel as though' or 'The way I see it is'.

> **EXPERT MEMORY**
>
> **Rebecca Perrin, Strategic Communications Expert and Professional Writer as well as Host of Women Talk Shop Podcast in Toronto, Canada**
>
> My career was smooth sailing until the company I worked for swelled by debt and the CEO sold it to a risk-loving buyer in New York City in 2013, and the layoffs started.
>
> I hatched a plan to design a new job position that would bridge the gap between lifestyle content and integrated marketing with the hope to keep my job. I booked an appointment to pitch it to the VP of my department.
>
> My VP's response was encouraging and he asked me to do a little more research, create a job posting, for formality's sake, and come up with a salary that I thought made good sense for the role. HR set up a series of three interviews that I soared through and then waited for my official offer to come through.
>
> The offer never came to me. Instead, it went to a guy from outside the organisation whom I'd never met but had previously worked with my VP at a sports channel. I was gutted. I felt humiliated. And worse, I thought I had done something wrong. Had I not interviewed well? Was I not skilled enough? Did they think I was too young? Too much of a woman?
>
> Unfortunately, I was laid off—the same day I shook hands with the new guy who got 'my' job. My self-esteem plummeted and the outcome was detrimental to my career development for a long while. When I moved into a new role at a magazine, I was fearful of asking

for help, scared to ask questions for clarification, and anxious to aim higher than my perceived limits. I thought that these things would make me seem vulnerable or imperfect and put me at risk for being found out as someone who wasn't really that smart after all. I burned out and got laid off from that job too.

My next move was to seek the help of a therapist and work on my self-esteem. It was the smartest move I've ever made. I still battle with imposter syndrome and fear of failure, but therapy helped me develop a much stronger sense of self, and now I think I'm resourceful and just as capable as everyone else.

Lesson learned

It's unfortunate that I suffered through this circumstance so early on in my career and if the same thing were to happen today, I would likely defend myself more intentionally and push back against such blatant nepotism and, likely, systemic gender bias in the workplace. The silver lining is that I've learned how self-esteem is my most valuable asset and nobody can take that away from me.

38

Keeping Your Emotions Under Control

> *Leaving your emotions freely flowing at your workplace is like driving a car with no seatbelt on. It can go wrong very quickly.*
>
> **Kate Surala**

Every strong emotion has, at its root, an impulse to action. Learning to manage these impulses is the basis of emotional intelligence. Knowing how to calm down in the workplace when emotions run high is particularly important as the ability to think and speak clearly dissolves during an emotional peak.

Everyone has triggers, such as specific topics, that create physical or emotional discomfort. Identifying and understanding your triggers will help you to take adequate action to protect your mental health. You will feel in control of your emotions more easily and quickly in moments of distress.

How do you know what your emotional triggers are? Think of a stressful situation you encountered this past week and try to work backwards. What was the first thing that made you feel uncomfortable? What was the worst? Write your thoughts in the box opposite.

Dealing with Difficult Situations

> **ANSWER**

Being able to identify your triggers to prepare a targeted reaction is an effective strategy to take control of your emotions. In the following, we and our guest experts share more tips to be in charge of your emotion. We encourage you to try out different methods until you have found what works best for you.

Too often, we get stuck in emotional patterns, which disempower us from doing what we are really capable of. You have the power to decide what meaning you give to events and experiences in your life. In every difficult situation that triggers an emotional response you and only you have the power to decide what to make out of the situation.

> **EXPERT ADVICE**
>
> **Drew Povey, Leadership Coach and Mentor in London, UK**
>
> If you're feeling stressed, just take a minute and use the three Ps. I really like it because it makes a big difference very quickly. It's about pausing, taking perspective, and resetting priorities.

- **Pause.** We're often working on autopilot. Just press pause for a minute, but it doesn't mean stop. When you take a moment, you become aware.

- **Perspective.** When you're doing that, though, the next part is to get a really good perspective of what's going on. Zoom out and have a look at the bigger picture.

- **Priorities.** Reset your priorities. What's the most important thing now?

Here are a few more tips for a quick fix next time you find yourself in a nerve-racking situation and an important meeting is around the corner:

- **Step back and put things into perspective.** Sometimes it can help to just step out for a moment and get some fresh air. Listen to a podcast or favourite song—or even our *Unleash Today* playlist—and you'll be in a better mood when you return to the office.

- **Detoxify.** In moments of anger, negative thoughts are flooding your brain. Challenge these thoughts and realise that you don't have to believe them.

- **Write down your thoughts.** Writing down your experiences can help you to calm down by reflecting on a situation. It also fulfils the need to share your experiences.

- **Distance yourself from the emotions you feel in a certain moment.** Remember you're not your emotions and they'll eventually pass. Make a conscious effort to let them pass and act later if necessary.

- **Get some sleep.** Get a good night's sleep to find your voice again and wake up ready to use it! We're particularly negative when we're tired and can act irrationally.

- **Look at motivational quotes.** Follow Instagram accounts that feature daily quotes for motivation and encouragement. Sometimes a photo or quote is more impactful than talking something through for hours. Try our *Unleash Today* Instagram account.

- **Listen to empowering music.** This is a very individual thing. We've put together an *Unleash Today* Spotify playlist that could help you to regain your energy every morning, but you could always make your own.

Another strategy to calm down is the five 'why' techniques. We recommend using this technique when you come back from work and you have more time to analyse what's gone wrong during the day. At work, we often do not have the space, intimacy or time to properly digest an experience.

Our 'whys' technique

- **Identify the problem** by taking a piece of paper and writing down what bothers you at the moment. For example, 'I'm frustrated with my boss.'

- **Ask your first 'why'.** Ask yourself why you feel the way you do and provide a response. An example would be 'Why do I feel frustrated with my boss?' and your answer could be that they were being unfair.

- **Keep going with the 'whys'.** You'll keep coming up with various reasons why you feel frustrated or anxious about a particular situation.

- **The next step is acceptance.** Accept the facts, look at it from a different perspective, and also repeat some of the reasons why you're feeling the way you do. By repeating these, you'll feel your emotions peak at some point and then deteriorate.

Give it a go! Identity your problem and use the why technique to get to the bottom of your underlying negative thoughts and accept it.

Answer

39

Unleash Today Challenge: Dealing with Difficult Situations and People

Imagine that you're stuck in your current role at a company that has a toxic environment. Your new boss is a micromanager, the atmosphere has changed since their arrival, and people are not happy working for them. You have a mortgage to pay and you feel you cannot leave your current workplace. What do you do if you aren't working for them and don't want to take the risk and resign?

Answer:

EXPERT ADVICE

Michelle Simard, Senior Corporate Commercial Lawyer specialising in Privacy and Cybersecurity in Toronto, Canada

It has happened to me a lot. You're going to have haters and you're going to have people who would love you. They might say you are 'too emotional' or 'too loud', labelling is important, because the unknown is scary.

At the end of the day, it's about your values. Two of my key representatives are my honesty and genuineness and the people that do like me see that I am honourable and I'm credible. What I've realised is I'm never going to win against people who just don't like me.

I have been threatening for bosses, I usually outshine them. But I'm well aware of it. Instead of fighting your enemies, try to relate to them. It's not that easy sometimes.

Sometimes you have to talk to them in a language that they're more receptive to. You have make them feel comfortable and win people over this, despite how you look and who you are as a person.

My other tip is to surround yourself with people who love you. Spend time with friends and surround yourself with upbeat, energetic, and grateful people. When you start thinking about all the shit in your life, try saying to yourself: 'This is just one phase of my life, and I'm going to get out of it. I'm just going to put my time in, because I have to and I'm going to create a plan right now that I'm going to get out of this box, this black hole that I'm in.'

Lesson learned

Try to speak their language, resonate with them, and surround yourself with people that love you. Don't forget to remind yourself that you got this!

Step Seven: Opportunities Don't Just Appear, You Create Them

In this last Step, you will learn how to:

- Get into the driving seat of your career
- Overcome setbacks and have the courage to grasp opportunities
- Find a mentor, coach, and sponsor
- Ask for training at your firm
- Improve your skills with free learning courses, webinars, and workshops

40
An Introduction to Creating Opportunities

> *The best part about life is the realisation that you will never stop learning.*
>
> **Kate Surala**

Imagine yourself in a few years' time. You have been in your job for some time now and you're no longer as excited to wake up and start your working day. Instead, you ask yourself if there is something wrong with you or with the firm that you work for. You feel like you have been stuck in your position for a while and your manager does not seem to care about your career progression.

You're sitting at home, scrolling through LinkedIn to discover one of your school friends became CEO of a start-up, another founded her own company, and your university acquaintance fulfilled his lifelong dream of becoming a pilot. You suddenly realise that you might have wasted years pursuing dreams that weren't yours. You feel regretful, angry, and sad. You chose the path of least resistance and did not push yourself outside your comfort zone.

It's not too late to transform these negative feelings into powerful catalysts for change. This final Step is all about how to keep growing in your workplace, learn new skills in your current job, and take the leap if you want to switch careers. Step Seven will help you to embrace continuous learning by yourself and with the support from others.

41
Learn How to Step Outside of Your Comfort Zone

> *Most people don't aim too high and miss. They aim too low and hit.*
>
> **Les Brown**

Embracing continuous learning in your career is the key to success and job satisfaction. You might have entered the workplace thinking that your time as a student is over, but that's far from reality. If you want to keep growing as a professional, you should embrace continuous learning and get used to stepping outside of your comfort zone. As outlined in the illustration below, you need to leave your comfort zone and pass through your fear and learning zone to reach your growth zone.

You can't run before you learn how to walk: getting into your growth zone doesn't happen overnight. The hardest part is to be persistent and start with entering the fear zone. People are afraid of starting new things because it's unlikely that they'll be good at them straight away. Likewise, thinking about planning or switching your career might scare you, as you would have to start all over again.

It's important to take risks, as every risk you take comes with more experience. Don't let your risk aversion

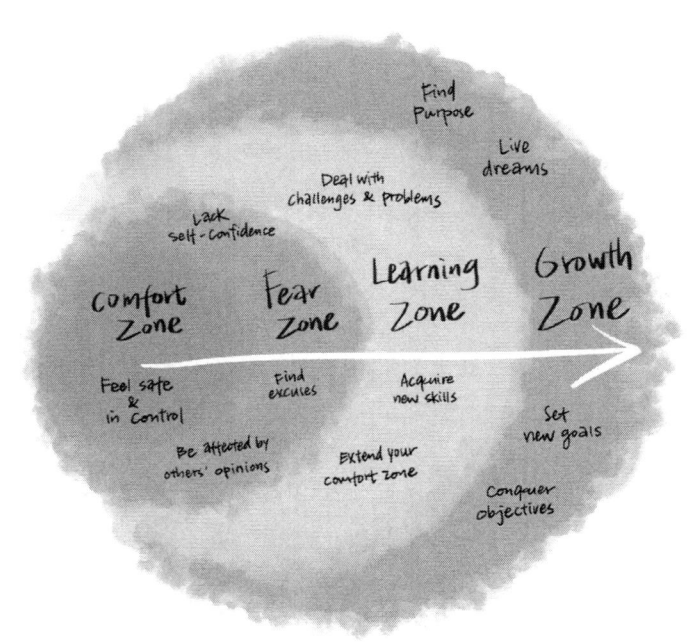

Figure: Four concentric zones diagram

- **Comfort Zone**: Feel safe & in control; Be affected by others' opinions
- **Fear Zone**: Lack self-confidence; Find excuses
- **Learning Zone**: Deal with challenges & problems; Acquire new skills; Extend your comfort zone
- **Growth Zone**: Find purpose; Live dreams; Set new goals; Conquer objectives

dictate your career moves. However, it's important to remember that it's easier to bounce back early in your career if things don't go as planned. If you're fresh out of university and start off in a career that's not right for you, you will not have lost much time and can find another position quickly. When you're already older, have a mortgage, and potentially a family on the way, taking risks can cause a lot of pressure. So, if you are unhappy with your career, act earlier than later to make the most of your 'freedom' as a young professional.

Your career starts to decay the moment you decide you don't need to improve anymore and remain in your comfort zone. Try to regularly assess yourself from a new angle. As soon as you realise you're too comfortable, seek to reinvent yourself. Try something new, such as learning a new skill, even if it might not seem like it's related to your career. Apple Co-Founder Steve Jobs, for example, pursued a calligraphy course in university and applied that knowledge later on to develop the typography for the Macintosh, the first personal computer that supported multiple fonts.

Be in the Driver's Seat of Your Career

> *The first part of being influential is influencing yourself.*
>
> **Chris Helder**

Nobody will take care of your career but you. You might think that your manager will come in and draft the ideal career plan for you, dictate your career objectives, and tell you exactly what you need to do to achieve them. While there may be a few very caring bosses and line managers, who will take the time to discuss your professional career plans, you should never rely on that to happen. Don't sit down and wait; take control of your own career path.

It all starts with dreams and ambition. The evidence is in your hands. Whatever your goal is in life, it should be your own pursuit, rather than someone else's dream. Would your parents like you to become a doctor or a lawyer? Is this your parents' wish or your own? Take your faith in your own hands. You are in the driving seat of your career, not your parents or anyone else.

EXPERT MEMORY

Helen Mountfield QC, Barrister at Matrix Chambers in London and Principle of Mansfield College in Oxford, UK

Looking back on my career, there are a few things I would do differently. I would try to acquire more self-confidence earlier in my career rather than letting misogyny put me down and to cause me to internalise self-doubt. I would feel more entitled to live my own life rather than doing things that I felt were expected of me. I would also have tried to do less and give myself permission to go slower in the middle of my career.

Time is a definite resource. For instance, I have three children and after each maternity leave, I came back to full-time work, partly for financial reasons and partly to prove that I was serious about work, while also trying to work very hard at being a good parent. I felt I had to prove something to everyone—my children, my partner, and my job. I also felt pressure towards other women, too. For quite a long time, I felt a responsibility to become a full-time judge. I am a part-time judge and I enjoy that, but I wasn't sure that was what I wanted to do as my whole job. We obviously need more women as full-time judges, but I felt quite liberated once I realised that didn't mean that I had to do it, and that the truly feminist thing to do was to lead the life I want to lead.

Lesson learned

Give yourself the permission to follow your heart and intuition rather than following the path that others believe you should take. Only you know what is best for you.

Opportunities Don't Just Appear, You Create Them

Speak about your plans and share them with others. Through voicing them you create a community of accountability partners, because they'll ask you how you're progressing in your pursuit. Make sure you surround yourself with people who support you in achieving your career plan rather than belittling it.

In order to establish a goal that will push you outside of your comfort zone, we encourage you to develop a career plan. You can start by drawing up a mind map, a pros and cons list, or anything else that will help you map out your path. They are good indicators for you to help you put your thoughts down on paper. Ultimately, though, you should follow your heart and do what feels right. In the end, it's about passion, drive, and the willingness to fulfil a dream, which will put you on the route of lasting satisfaction in the workplace and in life.

Make sure your plan is unique to you, don't simply copy someone else's career plan. However, you can consider other people's professional development as an inspiration and a starting point for yourself. If you're still lost and don't know what your career plan is, you can look to your role models for inspiration, for example.

Below you will find an example of what this could look like:

Career Plan	0–3 Years Experience	3-5 Years Experience	5-8 Years Experience
Role	Junior Legal Officer	Senior Legal Officer	Manager
Responsibility	Learn the basics of the job and network with other colleagues	Expertise in contract law, advise on property matters and financial crime	Lead a team
Skills	Legal writing, negotiations, and presentation skills	Become an expert in my field by shadowing some experts in the industry	Delegation, learn to handle difficult situations, and be a leader rather than a manager
Qualifications	Legal Practice Course	Financial crime certification	Management course and Scrum project management course

You may now say 'But I don't know where I want to be in five years. I've just started'. We're not saying you have to have every detail ironed out, but you could aim to have a broad outline based on your values and purpose you identified in the Introduction. Another benefit of starting your career plan is that it will also help you define what you don't want, which is equally important as listing all your goals!

> **EXPERT MEMORY**
>
> **Marie Sina, Content Editor at *Unleash Today***
>
> While studying in London, I spent a lot of time establishing my career plan. I had always been fairly certain I wanted to be a journalist. However, before committing to this path, I explored a variety of options to make an informed decision on my future. First, I established what other careers were also appealing to me: working for the EU, working in political consulting, and working in public affairs. Then, I invested a lot of time into exploring each of these: I interned at the European Parliament, attended an open day at a political consultancy, went to a variety of careers fairs, and spoke to multiple women working in public affairs. In the end, I was still convinced that journalism was the right choice for me. Upon graduating, I accepted a spot in a journalism training programme with an international broadcaster in Germany.
>
> **Lesson learned**
> Building your own career plan takes time and dedication. I can assure you it is absolutely worth it. It will enable you to make more informed choices that have a lasting positive impact on your life.

As you might not come up with your career plan overnight, we encourage you to invest time to define it. Think about having a dream company or organisation that has everything you need. Close your eyes and imagine walking through the door, meeting your dream colleagues, attending a meeting about your dream topic, and doing your dream task. How would your ideal day at your dream company look like? Try to be as specific as possible and write down your thoughts:

ANSWER

Be Flexible and Patient with Your Career Plan

Life is unpredictable and you should approach it with flexibility and an openness to change. Reconsider your career goals when necessary, discuss them, ask others whether they can give you an introduction to people working in your desired industry, and help you get closer to your goal.

While we encourage you to develop a career plan, miracles don't happen overnight. Achieving your career goals is a long-term process and can't be rushed. If you're a very ambitious and driven woman, you're likely to be impatient and want to see results immediately. We often hear that millennials in general are impatient, and there might be some truth to it. Learn to accept that, for impactful life developments to unfold, you need time. So, get comfortable with not having everything under control at all times! You need to learn how to be flexible and work with plan B, C, or D. Equally, learning new skills will pay off in the long run, if you are patient enough.

> **EXPERT MEMORY**
>
> **Sarah Wagner, Co-Author of *Unleash Today***
>
> I liked living and working in Brussels. Yet, after three years, I decided to leave. Why? I was afraid I would end up doing the same type of job my entire life and eventually stop learning and growing. Whenever I asked colleagues why they stayed, they could not say why they were doing what they were doing. Often, they referred convenience or named their partner or kids as reasons. So, I quit my job and moved to the other side of the world. Was it frightening? Hell, yes! Do I regret it? Not a bit. I knew exactly why I was doing what I was doing.
>
> **Lesson learned:**
>
> If you want to continue growing, you need to regularly change. Don't stick with the 'easy' option. Change does not necessarily mean you quit your job and leave your hometown. Change can happen in various ways.

Our top four tips to becoming more patient while pursuing your career plan

1. Your career and life as a whole are **a marathon, not a sprint**. Don't force anything.

2. Career success is related to so many things: relationships with colleagues and stakeholders, culture at the firm, knowledge of your sector, and performance. **Ask yourself if you're conscious of all of them. And work on those aspects you are lacking.**

3. If you plan everything to the smallest detail, there's no time for the beauty of surprise and for the unforeseen to unfold. Rather than running from goal to goal, appreciate the moment.

4. Stressing and worrying over things only deprives our energy and makes us sick. Most things we worry about aren't even worth our attention.

EXPERT MEMORY

Alexis Rose, Chief Operating Officer at Becoming X in London, UK

When I was a junior manager, I worked on a huge deal for about a year in a bid management role that was a real stretch for me. The day we got the call to tell us we hadn't won, I cried. One of the senior leaders took me to one side and told me, 'You will learn more from the experience of losing than you would have learned if we had won.' But, because we'd lost, I ended up taking a completely different path that resulted in an exciting secondment, which directed my career in a way I hadn't envisaged.

Lesson learned

Think of your career as a cross country orienteering expedition, not a sprint. Don't be afraid of unexpected setbacks or to take risks. You never know where it might lead!

42

Keep Learning and Never Stay Still

> *Once you stop learning, you start dying.*
> **Albert Einstein**

There are so many ways you can gain knowledge and push yourself outside your comfort zone. Don't wait for your employer to provide you with learning opportunities, instead take your growth into your own hands. In the following section you will learn how to explore training at your existing company or request a training that you would like to receive. We will also teach you to be courageous and take initiative, exploring webinars, scheduling virtual coffees, and learning from your mistakes.

How to Benefit from Training

Extra training will help you improve your performance, address your potential weaknesses, and broaden your own professional horizons. Think about what you can gain from taking on extra training: you can increase your confidence in your own abilities, receive additional qualifications, and stand out from the crowd in a job interview. If you are unhappy in your current role, you can take on extra training in order to tailor your CV to your desired career path.

Some organisations, mostly bigger corporations, have a tailored training programme beyond possible compulsory training. Such training programmes might target different skill sets, for instance how to operate various systems at your workplace, manage a team, or master emotional intelligence. Usually, smaller companies do not have these programmes in place. This means you will have to actively approach your manager and ask for the specific training that you would like to receive. In this case, we encourage you to be proactive and suggest training that would mean you to become better at your tasks. Find out what you want and where you want to go, then discuss it with your line manager or HR department. Your destiny is in your hands!

> **EXPERT MEMORY**
>
> **Elinor Stutz, Founder of Smooth Sale in Washington DC, US**
>
> My new sales career terrified me. As the lone pioneer saleswoman, training wasn't permitted because management believed I would fail. My solution was to have prospective clients teach me how they prefer to buy. Next, I took a three month-long public speaking class. The first night, I timidly announced my name; the last night, I became the Grand Prize Winner!
>
> As for sales, I became the star. For eleven years, I was repeatedly in need of a new job.

> **Lesson learned**
> Learn every day. QLC—question, listen, clarify—every situation. Speak up with a smile. Use negativity as your motivational force. Live life your way.

Tips on how to ask for training

When asking for training, be clever about how you phrase it. Don't simply state what training you want, but clarify how the company would benefit from paying for a particular course. What skills would you learn that could help the company to advance? Make it about the company's progress rather than your personal development. Put yourself into their shoes. Why should they invest in you?

- **Have a clear understanding of the training** you would like to attend and how it would benefit your firm. Know the price and how much time you'll need to complete it to start thinking about arranging a cover for yourself if necessary. Be specific and have a very concrete proposal at hand when asking for training.

- **Schedule a separate meeting with your HR** or line manager to discuss this proposal or include it on the agenda at your weekly meeting. Tell them in advance about the subject matter of the meeting so they are prepared and can respond to your request.

- **Offer to create a presentation for the team** or send a summary from the workshop or conference to people that might benefit from it. Try to turn your knowledge into valuable knowledge for your firm.

- **Don't forget how important networking is** and keep a log of your contacts from the event.

> **EXPERT MEMORY**
>
> **Kate Surala, Co-Author of *Unleash Today***
>
> After two years at my previous firm, I was made a partner. I was excited, but daunted. It was a big step up in my career and I wanted to make sure that I was prepared for the additional responsibility. I started looking for coaches to help me develop my leadership skills and started compiling information about potential coaches, including the costs, to create a proposal. Although my proposal mainly focussed on the benefits for the firm, it was rejected due to budgetary constraints. I was disappointed, but I didn't stop there. I found an online course on leadership skills for women that I worked on in the evenings. I invested my savings into this course as I knew it was an absolute must for my career progression.
>
> **Lesson learned**
> Even if your proposal for a training course or conference gets rejected, find an alternative that will help you develop these skills.

Just Do It and Offer to Help!

If you want to learn something new, volunteering can open the door to new experiences and responsibilities, as well. If a task presents itself, be courageous and ask if you can help out. But don't just volunteer for anything. You should choose tasks which will propel you forward on your career path. For example, organising a virtual social event might help you progress your career. You will meet new work colleagues and establish a rapport with them.

> **Expert Memory**
>
> **Gemma Greaves, Co-Founder of Nurture and Founder of Cabal in Twickenham, UK**
>
> While I was at university, I did a student placement at the Foreign & Commonwealth Office, where we made documentaries. Although I was employed as an office administrator, I found that the more I showed interest, curiosity, and was helpful, the more opportunities outside my original role arose. I made myself really useful (indispensable) to the producers and in turn learnt all about the documentaries we were making.
>
> I noticed we were spending a significant amount of money on copyright clearance and realised there might be an opportunity to do it a different way. When I spoke to the producer in charge, she was excited and supportive, but when I took the idea to the more junior associate producer she laughed in my face. After picking myself up off the floor, I decided to have the courage of my convictions, seize the opportunity, and give it a go. Within a few days I had made a sizable commercial impact and was fortunate enough to take the lead role in the project and others.
>
> **Lesson learned**
> If you believe in something, don't take 'No' for an answer—there is always another way. Going outside

> your comfort zone is where the true learning begins and where you can have a bigger impact. Having the courage of your convictions can lead to personal and professional success.

There are many more opportunities to ensure continuous career development:

- **Read about leadership trends** and best practices.
- **Shadow someone from another team**, department, or even a partner company.
- **Have lunch with recent retirees** and enquire about their experience and ask their counsel on current issues.
- **Have a lunch or coffee with a different person at your company** every day rather than always meeting with the same colleague.
- **Teach others what you've learned.** By sharing your knowledge, you reinforce your lessons and strengthen your reputation.
- **Learn what matters** to your colleagues and what their goals are so you can identify mutual interests and possibly work together.
- **Read about your industry and related industries.** Find out what happened in the past and what's happening today.

Other Learning Opportunities Out There

This world provides so many opportunities for growth. We can easily become overwhelmed trying to identify the right offer for us. If you take the time to identify what possibilities are around you, you're likely to come across evening classes, language schools, or life-long university learning schemes.

There are also many online courses and webinars available. Due to the COVID-19 pandemic, most of the materials are now widely available at your fingertips. These courses are for everyone, but they are particularly useful for those who don't get any other support and might not have the financial resources set aside for career growth. Online courses are also great for busy people who need flexibility.

If you don't have time to take an entire course, try looking for (free) pre-recorded webinars online. Via our *Unleash Today* website, you can find a full library of great webinars and very useful tips on our YouTube channel.

Below, we have gathered our top tips on how to find the ideal webinar for you:

- **Start with Google and create a list of top choices.**
- **Define the skill you would like to learn.** It could be anything from leadership skills to how to handle your emotions at your workplace.
- **Read up on the speaker(s)**, the organisation, and their previous events to evaluate whether to join or not.

- **Sign up for their newsletter**, follow the provider on social media, and connect with them via LinkedIn. You can do the same with *Unleash Today*.

To start with, here is an overview of the top online courses, and some of them are free:

Free	Some free courses	Paid
Alison	Coursera	LinkedIn Learning
Codeacademy	FutureLearn	Masterclass
edx	Udacity	Skillshare
Forage		Udemy
Khan Academy		

How to Turn a Bad Experience into Lessons Learned

> *Bad experiences teach us much more than the good ones.*
>
> **Kate Surala**

Anytime you go through a difficult experience, rather than feeling sorry for yourself, try to focus on the lessons you've learned and how you can build your resilience and advance your career. Bad experiences teach us much more than praise or positive feedback. Rather than perceiving them as wasted time, there is always some gain to be discovered. Some of life's greatest lessons come packaged in hard experiences. We encourage you to embrace unfortunate events and learn from them!

> **EXPERT MEMORY**
>
> **Karina Robinson, Headhunter and Senior Advisor in London, UK**
>
> I've been made redundant so many times it's an effort to remember them all. Yet each experience taught me a huge amount. I have generally tried to leave on good terms, but I haven't always managed. If I were to live my life again, I would still take on those jobs.
>
> When you have the luxury of choice, by all means focus on whether the employer delivers what their mission statement implies. When you turn down a job, help other candidates and the organisation by saying why. If, for instance, there are not enough women in senior roles, so you doubt they are committed to women, mention it. Losing a candidate who joins a competitor will focus their mind.
>
> **Lesson learned**
> Making change happen depends on having a seat at the table. If you get kicked off the table, dust yourself off and move on the next job.

The more times you fail, the quicker you can learn from your mistakes and progress in your career. Don't give up if you are applying for your next promotion or thinking about changing careers. It's all about trial and error.

OPPORTUNITIES DON'T JUST APPEAR, YOU CREATE THEM

> **Vivienne Artz OBE, Chief Privacy Officer at London Stock Exchange in London, UK**
>
> EXPERT MEMORY
>
> No matter how successful and capable you are, you won't always achieve your ambitions the first time round. So, when you have a set back, it's essential to learn what you can from the experience and use it to 'rise from the ashes'.
>
> It was a female colleague who had applied for a promotion and, of the two candidates, she was clearly the more accomplished and deserving. Instead of letting this experience hold her back, it had helped her prioritise her goals and focus on her ambitions. We stayed in touch and her career went from strength to strength, eclipsing anything she may have achieved at the firm she left. She had never let her earlier 'defeat' sour her own attitude or set her back.
>
> I remembered her example when I applied for one of my first leadership roles and was turned down. Just a few months later it became vacant again and I was then asked to reapply. Having shown professionalism (despite my disappointment) meant I was very much in the ring when the next opportunity arose, and it was a game changer for me, both in my career and personal development.
>
> **Lesson learned**
> Just as we should be gracious in victory, so we should be gracious in defeat—both are essential in achieving your ambitions.

Is Your Current Job a Stepping Stone?

You might have accepted your current job just to survive, not because it is the right job for you. If you can't find the optimal job or you landed something that you don't enjoy as much as you thought, see this opportunity as a stepping stone that helps you move closer to your ideal job.

A stepping stone in your career can be temporary, freelance, contract, or part-time work. This position can provide you the financial support you need and possibly create free time in your week, so that you can focus on looking for the ideal job you are passionate about.

> **EXPERT MEMORY**
>
> **Blandine Crutzen, French Language Translator at *Unleash Today***
>
> I'd been looking for a job for ten months when a recruiter contacted me on LinkedIn. I knew from the job title that it was not my dream job, but I decided to give it a go. I read the job description and called the recruiter to get more information. Eventually, I was offered the job. I accepted it, ready to get the most out of this experience. I started in January 2021 and I have already met inspiring people and developed new skills. By asking for feedback on my job interview and the personality test I took, I also learned a lot about myself and what I should keep in mind while looking for new opportunities. This job gives me the stability I need to keep looking for my dream job. I'm on my way there, and every step counts.

> I try to always keep a positive attitude, convinced there is something to learn in every situation.
>
> **Lesson learned**
> Keeping an open mind and a positive attitude will allow you to learn from every experience. As Mel Robbins phrased it so nicely, remember that 'Your dream doesn't have an expiration date. So, take a deep breath and try again!'

How to grow from a stepping stone job into your dream job:

- If you are looking to switch industries, a temporary position gives you the opportunity to 'try it' before you commit to your next major career role.

- Build your CV by volunteering outside of your job—get involved in projects that will equip you with the skills that you need for your dream job.

- If your current employment contract allows it, start working as a freelancer during the evening to gain more experience in your desired industry.

- Don't rule out temporary roles. After making the best first impression and following our tips in Step One, you're well set to get an offer to stay and transition into a full-time employment.

Kate Surala, Co-Author of *Unleash Today*

EXPERT MEMORY

When I was changing jobs, I found a very senior temporary role at a company that was on my radar. I knew the position was demanding around ten years of experience and I only had four. I wanted to gain experience working for the company, so I applied nevertheless. I realised that there is less competition for temporary roles if you are available immediately, as the company is usually looking for someone to join as soon as possible. I got to a third round and was told that they are about to advertise a permanent role that would fit my profile even better. In the end, I wasn't selected for the role. However, I was referred internally for another role at a different department. I applied for the other role and received an offer!

Lesson learned

Never close a door that has just opened in front of you. Open the door and see if there is another one that leads to your ideal job.

43
Unleash Your Growth with Others

> *Asking for help doesn't cost anything but courage. You are not alone.*
>
> **Sarah Wagner**

If you're not growing in your workplace, you're stagnating in your career. However, rather than becoming frustrated and quitting your job as a consequence, think about how to continue your journey with the help of others. You are not alone, look for the right people to help you with your endeavour.

Find Your Role Model(s)

> *Being a role model is the most powerful form of educating.*
>
> **John Wooden**

Role models act as a guide to help you understand who you would like to become in the future, or whose skills and achievements you would like to pursue. As success is a subjective term, try to look for role models who have done something impressive or act admirably in your eyes. It could be anyone from your mum, best friends, a TV presenter, an Olympic gold medallist, or a stay-at-home dad.

Who is or could be seen as your role model and what skill of theirs would you like to embrace?

ANSWER

Kate Surala, Co-Author of *Unleash Today*

EXPERT MEMORY

One of my role models (yes, you can have many!) is Gina Miller—one of our experts that you met in our challenge in Step Two, a business owner and activist who initiated the court case against the British government over its authority to implement Brexit without approval from Parliament. Her key characteristics that resonate with me are courage, persistence, resilience, and being outspoken. Asking 'What would Gina do?' at a low point gives me the energy to keep going.

> **Lesson learned**
> Identify the key characteristics of your role model and remind yourself of these traits when you're moving from your comfort zone to your growth zone. Keep going—you got it!

Mentors, Sponsors, and Coaches

Understanding what the difference is between a mentor, sponsor, and coach is crucial for your career development. Why? Your mentor, sponsor, or coach could help you grow in your current company or completely switch careers. We will help you look for a pivotal person who can provide you with insight on the missing element in your career plan.

Mentor

A mentor is someone who talks with you about your career goals, plans, and aspirations. Your mentor can suggest people you should talk to, opportunities that shouldn't be missed, and obstacles that you should be aware of. Mentors can be any professionals and don't necessarily have to work in the same company, have the same academic background, or career as you. They give you general career advice and help you develop transferable skills.

Mentoring is usually a long-term commitment and someone who you could call regularly to discuss your career progress. You can find your mentor on LinkedIn by typing in 'mentor' or 'pro bono advice'. If you're after a more established mentoring programme, reach out to an association in your industry and ask whether you could join. For instance, if you are working in the finance industry, search for 'finance associations in Berlin' or 'young finance professionals.'

Some might be paid, but others might already be included in your membership. You could also just approach a professional you look up to and inquire whether they would be available to mentor you. Remember, that you are not restricted by borders. You can get your mentor from a completely different country and industry. They will be able to provide you with a completely different take on your career progression. You can find more details on how to find and work with your mentor in our webinars on YouTube—search for our channel *Unleash Today*.

Sponsor

This is someone who talks about you when you're not in a meeting or event. Sponsors* usually proactively search for opportunities to promote you and it's crucial to find someone who can advocate for your success and help you to climb the career ladder.[92] Usually these are colleagues who are positioned higher up in your organisation and have a good relationship with your line manager. Your role model can easily turn into your sponsor or mentor. Reach out to various contacts at your firm, see how they support the success of others and approach them for your first coffee.

Coach

A coach is someone who trains you as you're trying to achieve something specific. You might want to hire a

---

* The concept of a sponsor is currently more known and used in Anglo-Saxon countries.

coach to help you master your leadership style, establish your executive presence, or simply find your passion and purpose. They can also just be someone who listens and helps you to structure your thoughts and ideas. Some organisations sponsor coaching sessions while others have in-house coaches. Or you could decide to pay for your own coach. If this is the case, you can find an overview of established coaches on our website.

How to Progress Your Career by Asking for Feedback

People will give you a lot of solicited and some unsolicited feedback. Learn to embrace both and perceive them as something positive. Be aware that the opinion of another person isn't the eternal truth. It's just a point of view, so never take anything personally.

Unfortunately, we are still surrounded by jealous managers who may want to hurt you and make you feel bad (think back to Step Five). While it might not seem apparent and difficult to implement, the best response in our view is to simply thank them and move on. As a general rule, only take advice from people you would ask for advice in the first place.

Asking for feedback is the quickest and cheapest (it's free!) way to grow. Who doesn't ask, doesn't get. If you're enquiring for concrete feedback about your career plans and prospects, single out specific people whose opinions you truly value, like your accountability partner. It is also a good idea to ask for regular feedback from your manager and colleagues. Asking for feedback indicates to your employer that you are serious about improving and learning as a professional and that you are able to deal with constructive feedback in a professional way.

> **EXPERT MEMORY**
>
> **Sarah Wagner, Co-Author of *Unleash Today***
>
> I remember receiving very puzzling feedback about my outfit. I was shocked for a moment but, after careful consideration, decided not to take any of this feedback on board and stick to the advice outlined in Step One.
>
> **Lesson learned**
> Take feedback seriously, but eventually decide what aspects of it you take on board and use to grow.

44

Unleash Today Challenge: Learning and Growing

As a young woman, you've been in your job for some time and you're not as excited about your job as you were in your first few months. You haven't been provided with any training or coaching, and your manager isn't very interested in your career progression. You feel helpless because you're not being listened to. What should you do?

ANSWER

EXPERT ADVICE

Jennifer Brown, Founder and CEO of Jennifer Brown Consulting in New York, US

Right now, many millennial women quit. They get tired of pay inequalities and lack of advancement opportunities. They feel isolated, because they don't have an outlet where they can have frank conversations about bias or the fact that the system isn't changing as fast as it needs to.

That's why it's important that millennial women are clear on what they need in order to thrive and hold their organisations accountable. This could mean flexible work schedules, more learning and development opportunities, different work responsibilities, or something else.

When you enter a system, you want to have a positive impact on that system, and leadership urgently needs that feedback and honest assessment of why people don't bring their full selves to work. Companies should be more worried than they are about losing people. They should care if you feel disengaged, or don't feel welcomed, valued, respected, and heard.

No matter what size your organisation, joining a resource network within your organisation where you can have honest conversations about your individual experiences is an excellent way to ensure you feel less alone and less isolated. That community can also become a mechanism for career development from a networking perspective, as well as a forum for other employees to learn about differences in a safe environment. If there is not a pre-existing network for certain kinds of identities in your workplace, you could look into creating one. This way, you can lead change from the lower levels of your organisation. You don't need positional power to do this. You can do it informally while building the community that you need and strengthening your voice through the collective.

Lesson learned

Learn, grow, and acquire new skills and progress with your career.

Your Unleash Today Journey

We are so proud of you. Look at what you have learned on our *Unleash Today* journey.

Step One: Hello, Here I Am!

- You only get one chance to make a first impression. Take time to prepare.
- Smile, maintain strong eye contact, and listen closely like you actually care about what people are telling you. Power pose when needed.
- Pudding handshakes can easily be interpreted as insecurity and/or incompetence.
- A calm and controlled voice will bring you more listeners and authority.
- Actively offer help when appropriate to ease your line manager's workload.

Step Two: Strengthening Your Confidence Muscle

- Failure can be leveraged to produce success.
- The more we push ourselves outside our comfort zone and overcome our fears, the braver we become.
- Claim the seat at the table. Fake it Till You Become It.
- Practise, practise, practise. Being confident is a learned skill.

Step Three: I'm a Recovering Perfectionist

- Seeking perfection means aiming for the impossible. Instead, you should channel your energy towards an attainable goal: excellence.
- We recommend using the SMART method for goal setting: smart, measurable, achievable, realistic, and timely.
- Enjoy the present and embrace the now.
- Set up a sixty or ninety day plan, and don't forget to ask for help. Celebrate your success and don't compare yourself to others.
- Find your accountability partner and advisory board. Turn your mistakes into valuable lessons.

Step Four: Mastering the Art of Networking

- Networking is a skill that you should practise and use to build a support army that gives you advice in difficult situations.

- Try out the FORD model, which stands for Family, Occupation, Relax, and Deep, when meeting someone new.

- Get your elevator pitch, including your unique selling point, ready. Build your brand and get comfortable with self-promotion.

Step Five: Project 'Love'

- Only changing your behaviour by practising meditation, accepting uncertainty, and other techniques can change your negativity bias.

- Develop your love habits. Maintain a healthy sleep routine, exercise, take regular holidays, spoil yourself, and surround yourself with the right people who support you.

- Set boundaries at your workplace and learn how to say 'No' when needed.

Step Six: Dealing with Difficult Situations

- Don't gossip and complain at work. Keep this to yourself or share it only with people that you really trust. If the colleague causes actual problems at work, speak to your (HR) Manager and ask them for advice to improve the work relationship.

- Speak up, don't endure if you experience casual sexism or receive inappropriate comments, even if it means standing alone.

- Keep your emotions under control, offload only when you are in a safe place.

Step Seven: Opportunities Don't Just Appear, You Create Them

- Embracing continuous learning in your career is the key to success and ongoing satisfaction.
- If you want to continue growing, you need to change regularly. We advise that you don't stick with the 'easy' option. Step outside your comfort zone and start learning and growing.
- Don't be afraid of unexpected setbacks or to take risks. You never know where it might lead!
- Ask for training, just do it, and explore other learning opportunities out there.
- Find your role models, mentors, sponsors, and coaches.
- Take feedback seriously, but eventually decide what aspects of it you take on board and use to grow.

Unleash Today

You are ready. Now go and unleash today!

Here is to all women:
May we empower them,
May we encourage them,
May we love them,
May we praise them,
May we untame them,
May we unleash them.

Notes

How to Unleash Today...

1   Study of over 3,000 men and 4,000 women, by Zenger, J. and Folkman, J. (2019) 'Research: Women Score Higher Than Men in Most Leadership Skills', *Harvard Business Review* (https://hbr.org/2019/06/research-women-score-higher-than-men-in-most-leadership-skills).

For more information, read Dabiero, U. (2019) 'Women reach peak career confidence around age 40, research shows', *Business Insider* (https://www.businessinsider.com/the-surprising-moment-that-women-reach-peak-career-confidence-2019-7?r=DE&IR=T)

Step One: Hello, Here I Am!

2   For more information on this subject we recommend Zebrowitz, L.A. and Montepare, J.A. (2008) 'Social Psychological Face Perception: Why Appearance Matters', *Soc Personal Psychol Compass* (https://www.ncbi.nlm.nih.gov/pmc/articles/PMC2811283/) DOI: 10.1111/j.1751-9004.2008.00109.x

More information can be found in Cehic, E. (2015) 'First impressions: What your clothing says about you', *Smarter Business* (https://www.smarterbusiness.telstra.com.au/growth/business-strategy/first-impressions-what-your-clothing-says-about-you)

3   Cuddy, A. (2012) 'Your body language may shape who you are', *TED* (https://www.ted.com/talks/amy_cuddy_your_body_language_may_shape_who_you_are/transcript#t-133561) and a study that links the way people walk and their mood: Mediacentre (2014) 'Research shows the way we walk affects our mood', *Queen's University* (https://www.queensu.ca/gazette/media/research-shows-way-we-walk-affects-our-mood)

Another article written by Kilburn M. (2017) 'How your body language can improve your mood', *Avogel* (https://www.avogel.co.uk/health/stress-anxiety-low-mood/how-your-body-language-can-improve-your-mood/#:~:text=Body%20language%20can%20not%20only,we%20are%20faced%20with%20stress)

4   Cuddy, A. (2012) 'Your body language may shape who you are', *TED*

(https://www.ted.com/talks/amy_cuddy_your_body_language_may_shape_who_you_are/up-next?language=en)

5   Carney, D.A et al (2010) 'Power Posing: Brief Nonverbal Displays Affect Neuroendocrine Levels and Risk Tolerance', *Psychological Science*, 21: 10. DOI: 10.1177/0956797610383437. PMID 20855902 (https://www0.gsb.columbia.edu/mygsb/faculty/research/pubfiles/4679/power.poses_.PS_.2010.pdf)

6   Cuddy, A. (2018) P*resence: Bringing Your Boldest Self to Your Biggest Challenges*, Little, Brown, p. 40

7   Jimbere, J. (2018) 'Tips for Positive Body Language that Conveys Competence', *Radical Joy For Women* (https://www.radicaljoyseekingwomen.com/blog/tips-for-positive-body-language-that-conveys-competence)

8   Frith C, (2009), 'Role of facial expressions in social interactions', *Royal Society Publishing* (https://royalsocietypublishing.org/doi/abs/10.1098/rstb.2009.0142)

9   byte (no date) 'Women's Experiences with Being Told to Smile, *byte* (https://www.byteme.com/pages/womens-experiences)

10   Kinsey Goman, C. (2008) *The Nonverbal Advantage: Secrets and Science of Body Language at Work*, San Francisco, Berrett-Koehler Publishers, Inc., p.184

11   Damhorst ML. (1990) 'In Search of a Common Thread: Classification of Information Communicated Through Dress', *Clothing and Textiles Research Journal*, (8)2:1-12. DOI:10.1177/0887302X9000800201(https://journals.sagepub.com/doi/pdf/10.1177/0887302X9000800201#articleCitationDownloadContainer)

12   Doyle, A. (2019) 'The Best Colors to Wear to a Job Interview', *the balance careers* (https://www.thebalancecareers.com/what-colors-to-wear-to-a-job-interview-2061165)

13   Hannah, F. (2018) 'British people work an average of 469 unpaid hours a year', *The Independent* (https://www.independent.co.uk/money/spend-save/uk-people-unpaid-work-hours-year-british-workers-a8266676.html)

Step Two: Strengthening Your Confidence Muscle

14   Sandberg, S. (2015) *Lean In: Women, Work, and the Will to Lead*, WH Allen, p. 29

15   Studies prove that women are less self-assured than men. A study by Cornell University suggests that women generally underestimate their abilities and performance while men overestimate both. However, their performance doesn't differ in quality or quantity. Kay, K. and Shipman, C. (2014) 'The Confidence Gap', *The Atlantic*, (https://www.theatlantic.com/magazine/archive/2014/05/the-confidence-gap/359815/)

16   Sandberg, S. (2015) *Lean In: Women, Work, and the Will to Lead*,

Notes

WH Allen, p. 28

17   Currently, only 4.9 per cent of Fortune 500 CEOs and 2 per cent of S&P 500 CEOs are women. See the *Catalyst*'s website (https://www.catalyst.org/research/women-in-sp-500-companies/) for more information.

18   Kay, K. and Shipman, C. (2014), 'The Confidence Gap', *The Atlantic*, p. 3

19   Ibid

20   A survey of 1,200 girls aged eight to eighteen found that puberty kills a girl's confidence, with it peaking at age nine. A 1991 study conducted by the American Association of University discovered that girls 'lost their self-esteem on the way to adolescence. Other studies have proven that girls have a range of interested and strong opinions that tend to disappear when they enter the 'dating age'. Girls tend to lose their voices as they confront patriarchal demands to become subservient and silent to be more attractive to males, which can cause problems with self-esteem. For more information, see Shipman, C., Kay, K., and Riley, J.'s article on puberty (https://www.theatlantic.com/family/archive/2018/09/puberty-girls-confidence/563804/)

21   Folkman J., Zenger J., (2019) 'Research: Women Score Higher Than Men in Most Leadership Skills', *Harvard Business Review* (https://hbr.org/2019/06/research-women-score-higher-than-men-in-most-leadership-skills)

22   Kay, K. and Shipman, C. (2014), 'The Confidence Gap', *The Atlantic* (https://www.theatlantic.com/magazine/archive/2014/05/the-confidence-gap/359815/)

23   A person's confidence level is influenced by a host of genetic factors that don't seem to have anything to do with his or her sex. However, male and female brains do display differences in structure and chemistry, differences that may encourage unique patterns of thinking and behaviour, and that could affect confidence. See Kay, K. and Shipman, C. (2014) 'The Confidence Code', *The Atlantic* (https://www.theatlantic.com/magazine/archive/2014/05/the-confidence-gap/359815/)

24   Science doesn't have a clear answer to this yet. A person's confidence level is influenced by a host of genetic factors that don't seem to have anything to do with his or her sex. However, male and female brains do display differences in structure and chemistry, differences that may encourage unique patterns of thinking and behaviour, and that could affect confidence. See Kay, K. and Shipman, C. (2014) 'The Confidence Code', *The Atlantic* (https://www.theatlantic.com/magazine/archive/2014/05/the-confidence-gap/359815/)

25   Robbins, T. (no date) 'How to Be Confident', *Tony Robbins* (https://www.tonyrobbins.com/building-confidence/how-to-be-confident/)

26   Welteroth, E. (2019), *More Than Enough*, Ebury Press, p. 200

27   Swinson, J. (2018) *Equal Power: Gender Equality and How to Achieve It*, Atlantic Books, pp. 15–18

28   Tarvin, A. (2014) '30 Benefits of Humor at Work', *Humor That Works* (https://www.humorthatworks.com/benefits/30-benefits-of-humor-at-work/)

29   Zipkin, N. (2017) 'Why Telling Jokes at Work Makes You Appear More Confident', *Entrepreneur* (https://www.entrepreneur.com/article/287679)

Step Three: I'm a Recovering Perfectionist

30   Thomas Curran and Andrew Hill's recent meta-analysis of rates of perfectionism from 1989 to 2016. The first study to compare perfectionism across generations, Curran and Hill found significant increases among more recent graduates in the US, UK, and Canada. Curran, T. and Hill, A. (2017) 'Perfectionism Is Increasing Over Time', *American Psychological Association*, 145: 4 (https://www.apa.org/pubs/journals/releases/bul-bul0000138.pdf)

31   Hamachek, D.E. (1978) 'Psychodynamics of normal and neurotic perfectionism', *Psychology*, 15, pp. 27–33

32   Thomas Curran et. all (2020) 'A test of social learning and parent socialization perspectives on the development of perfectionism', *Research Gate*, 160 (https://www.researchgate.net/publication/339433945_A_test_of_social_learning_and_parent_socialization_perspectives_on_the_development_of_perfectionism)

33   Saujani, R. (2016) 'Teach girls bravery, not perfection', *TED* (https://www.ted.com/talks/reshma_saujani_teach_girls_bravery_not_perfection/up-next?language=en)

34   Ben-Shahar, T. (2009) *The Pursuit of Perfect: How to Stop Chasing Perfection and Start Living a Richer*, Happier Life, USA: McGraw Hill

35   MindTools (no date) 'SMART Goals: How to Make Your Goals Achievable', *Mind Tools* (https://www.mindtools.com/pages/article/smart-goals.htm)

36   Wade, D.T. (2009) 'Goal setting in rehabilitation: an overview of what, why and how', *Clinical Rehabilitation*, 23, pp. 293–294 (https://journals.sagepub.com/doi/pdf/10.1177/0269215509103551)

37   MindTools (no date) 'Golden Rules of Goal Setting', *Mind Tools* (https://www.mindtools.com/pages/article/newHTE_90.htm)

38   Byrne, R. (2006) *The Secret*, UK: Simon & Schuster

39   Rider, E. (2015) 'The Reason Vision Boards Work and How to Make One', *HuffPost* (https://www.huffpost.com/entry/the-scientific-reason-why_b_6392274?guce_referrer=aHR0cHM6Ly93d3cuZ29vZ2xlLmNvbS8&guce_referrer_sig=AQAAABqg-yoCI5thJzaCmsam-TtJjJ-LndJBmoj-Q1azkI8Pqewg0ySqjhDSqUsHhvlleCt5jb4XJ6N0TG9QCBHciKvKoceM8-AVxP6AgXGUlQ2xPa3SagDU8irFw3oumtPtvMW8KThbEVNF7WsxROsD5vIHqLRXPkMLbXY_M7AL7fDn&guccounter=2)

40   Robertsons, C. (2014) 'How to Influence Your Subconscious Mind to Achieve Your Goals', *Will Powered* (http://www.willpowered.co/learn/how-to-influence-the-subconscious-mind)

41   Gunter, P. (no date) 'Vision Board - A Powerful Tool To Manifest Your Dream Life', *The Law of Attraction* (https://www.thelawofattraction.com/vision-board/)

42   For further practical tips on how to create the right board for you and stay focussed, we encourage you to read Christine Kane's article on 'How

NOTES

to Make a Vision Board'. Kane, C. (no date) 'How to Make a Vision Board', *Christine Kane* (https://christinekane.com/how-to-make-a-vision-board/)

43 The Young Health Movement recently found that nine in ten young women say that they are unhappy with the way they look. Edmonds, R. (no date) 'Anxiety, loneliness and Fear of Missing Out: The impact of social media on young people's mental health', *Centre for Mental Health* (https://www.centreformentalhealth.org.uk/blogs/anxiety-loneliness-and-fear-missing-out-impact-social-media-young-peoples-mental-health)

44 Dhir, A. et al. (2018) 'Online social media fatigue and psychological wellbeing—A study of compulsive use, fear of missing out, fatigue, anxiety and depression', *International Journal of Information Management*, 40, p. 1 (https://www.sciencedirect.com/science/article/abs/pii/S0268401217310629)

45 This famous artist was a perfectionist who often destroyed his own paintings in a temper, including 15 paintings that were meant to open an exhibition. Fernandez, C. (2016) 'Monet slashed 250 lily paintings: Artist destroyed hundreds of works shortly before his death because he thought they weren't good enough', *Daily Mail* (https://www.dailymail.co.uk/news/article-3752099/Monet-slashed-250-lily-paintings-Artist-destroyed-hundreds-works-shortly-death-thought-weren-t-good-enough.html)

46 Brower, T. (2020) 'Perfection Versus Excellence: 4 Ways to Ensure Perfectionism Doesn't Prevent Progress', *Forbes*, (https://www.forbes.com/sites/tracybrower/2020/02/02/perfection-versus-excellence-4-ways-to-ensure-perfection-doesnt-prevent-progress/#1c8d0c0d53ef)

47 Barron J. (2019), *The Visual MBA, A Quick Guide to Everything You'll Learn in Two Years of Business School*, Great Britain, Penguin Business

48 Rohn, J. (2015) '9 Jim Rohn Quotes That Will Inspire You To Work Harder on Yourself', *Pick the Brain* (https://www.pickthebrain.com/blog/9-jim-rohn-quotes-will-inspire-work-harder/)

49 Locke E.A., (1996), 'Motivation through Goal Setting', *Applied and Preventive Psychology*, Volume 5, Issue 2, pp. 117–124 (https://doi.org/10.1016/S0962-1849(96)80005-9)

50 Kraft U. (2006) 'Burned Out: Your job is extremely fulfilling. It is also extremely demanding-And you feel overwhelmed. You are not alone', *Scientific American Mind*, pp. 29–33

51 Horton, A.P. (2019) 'How do you know if you're about to burn out?', *Fast Company* (https://www.fastcompany.com/90311958/hhow-to-identify-and-overcome-burnout)

52 Wigert, B. and Agrawal, S. (2018) 'Employee Burnout, Part 1: The 5 Main Causes', *Gallup* (https://www.gallup.com/workplace/237059/employee-burnout-part-main-causes.aspx)

53 Faw, L. (2011) 'Why Millennial Women Are Burning Out At Work By 30', *Forbes* (https://www.forbes.com/sites/larissafaw/2011/11/11/why-millennial-women-are-burning-out-at-work-by-30/#2e588502664d)

54 Captivate Network, (2011), 'Captivate Office Pulse Survey Reveals Men are Happier than Women in their Work-Life Balance', *Office Pulse* (https://officepulse.captivate.com/work-life-balance)

55   Barrett K., Greene R., (2001), *The personal story of Walt Disney*, Disney Editions

Step Four: Mastering the Art of Networking

56   For more information, please read Casciaro, T. et al (2016) 'Learn to Love Networking', *Harvard Business Review* (https://hbr.org/2016/05/learn-to-love-networking?utm_campaign=hbr&utm_medium=social&utm_source=linkedin)

57   Kagan, J. (2020) 'Networking', *Investopedia* (https://www.investopedia.com/terms/n/networking.asp)

58   Dang, D. (no date) 'Top 9 Benefits Of Networking in Business', *Entrepreneur Facts* (https://entrepreneurshipfacts.com/top-9-benefits-of-networking-in-business/)

59   The positive effect of networking on job and business opportunities, status, and power has been proven by various studies. Camedda D., Mirman-Flores A., Ryan-Mangan A., (2017), 'Young researchers need help with academic networking', *University World News* (https://www.universityworldnews.com/post.php?story=20170906091434215)

60   If you are interested in more tips, you can find our webinar on networking on *Unleash Today*'s YouTube channel (https://www.youtube.com/watch?v=yZNLxGGvg1g)

61   Casciaro, T. et al. (2016) 'Learn to Love Networking', *Harvard Business Review* (https://hbr.org/2016/05/learn-to-love-networking?utm_campaign=hbr&utm_medium=social&utm_source=linkedin)

62   Dweck, C. (2012) *Mindset: How You Can Fulfil Your Potential*, Robinson.

63   Developed by leadership and communication speaker Chris Helder. For more information, read Helder, C. (2013) *The Ultimate Book of Influence*, Wiley

64   Casciaro, T. (2016) 'Learn to Love Networking', *Harvard Business Review* (https://hbr.org/2016/05/learn-to-love-networking?utm_campaign=hbr&utm_medium=social&utm_source=linkedin)

65   'However, there was a notable disparity between men and women's confidence levels, with more women than men experiencing a lack of confidence in the workplace (79% of women vs 62% of men).' O'Brien S. (2019), '79% of women regularly lack confidence at work', *PALIFE* (https://palife.co.uk/news/79-of-women-regularly-lack-confidence-at-work/)

66   Gold A. (2016), 'Why self-esteem is important for mental health, National alliance on mental illness', *NAMI* (https://www.nami.org/Blogs/NAMI-Blog/July-2016/Why-Self-Esteem-Is-Important-for-Mental-Health#:~:text=Someone%20with%20low%20self%2Desteem,potentially%20

NOTES

dangerous%20way%20to%20live)

67 The amount of cortisol, which is a chemical that relates to one's hormones and stress levels in your brain, tends to flow more freely and spurs negative thoughts. When imminent danger arises, your brain releases this chemical as a way to warn you. As a consequence, you are more likely to experience negative rather than positive thoughts.

68 This method was developed by CBT and Ragnarson. Riggenbach, J. (2012) *The CBT Toolbox: A Workbook for Clients and Clinicians*, PESI

69 Tolle, E. (1999) *The Power of Now - A guide to spiritual Enlightenment*, New Worlds Library, p. 41

70 Crain, E. (no date) 'How Meditation Can Help You Sleep Better', *Men's Journal* (https://www.mensjournal.com/health-fitness/how-meditation-can-help-you-sleep-better-20150225/).

71 Corliss, J. (2014) 'Mindfulness meditation may ease anxiety, mental stress', *Harvard Health Publishing* (https://www.health.harvard.edu/blog/mindfulness-meditation-may-ease-anxiety-mental-stress-201401086967)

72 Tamara Levitt confirms that this will allow you to recall a 'distinct memory or setting an actual scene in our mind's eye, which naturally evokes an authentic feeling of gratefulness.' Levitt T., (no date), 'Gratitude, Calm Masterclass Toolkit', *NHS Wales*, p.15 (https://phw.nhs.wales/topics/latest-information-on-novel-coronavirus-covid-19/staff-information-page/staff-wellbeing-docs-folder/gratitude-toolkit/)

73 You can read more about the gratitude countdown on this website: Levitt, T. (2012) 'The Gratitude Countdown', *Calm* (https://blog.calm.com/blog/the-gratitude-countdown)

74 For more information on mastering habits, we recommend that you read Rubin, G. (2013) *Happier at Home*, Two Roads, or Clear, J. (2018) *Atomic Habits*, Random House Business

75 Check out this Ted Talk that addresses this topic in more detail: Cain, S. (2012) 'The power of introverts', *TED* (https://www.ted.com/talks/susan_cain_the_power_of_introverts)

76 For example: https://www.16personalities.com

77 Ein guter Verlag (2021) *Ein Guter Plan*

78 We recommend that you read some more useful tips on how to maintain your healthy sleep routine in E, A. (2016) *The Sleep Revolution: Transforming Your Life, One Night at a Time*, Virgin Digital

79 This is due to its effect on your circadian rhythm, tricking your brain into thinking it's still daytime. This reduces hormones like melatonin, which help you relax and get deep sleep. Figueiro, M.G.; Wood B.; Plitnick B.; and Rea M.S. (2011) 'The impact of light from computer monitors on melatonin levels in college students', *Neuroendocrinology Letters*, 32: 2 (https://www.nel.edu/userfiles/articlesnew/NEL320211A03.pdf)

80 Our Unleash Today Editor Jaki Smith recommends the FitOn App that has specialised workday workouts that take between five and fifteen minutes. The advantage of FitOn is that it's also 100 per cent free (unless you want to have access to a diet plan).

81 Scott, K. (2019), *Radical Candor*, St. Martin's Press, p. 12

82 Levy G. S., (2019) 'Can You Really Be Yourself at Work?', *The Oprah Magazine* (https://www.oprahmag.com/life/work-money/a27457513/can-you-really-be-yourself-at-work/)

83 Mathell, P.; Vingerhoets, J.; and van Heck, G. (2001) 'Personality, Gender and Crying', *European Journal of Personality*, 15, pp.19–28. The most consistent finding from this research is that women cry more often than men.

84 Ibid

85 Babcock, L. et al. (2017) 'Gender Differences in Accepting and Receiving Requests for Tasks with Low Promotability', *American Economic Review*, 107: 3, pp. 714–747. DOI: 10.1257/aer.20141734 (https://pubs.aeaweb.org/doi/pdfplus/10.1257/aer.20141734)

86 Torres M., (2019), 'How Women Should Say No To Thankless Office Tasks', *Huffpost* (https://www.huffpost.com/entry/women-serve-coffee-at-work-how-to-say-no_l_5d35c9bfe4b004b6adb352a5)

87 Surala, K. (2019) '"I was assumed to be the 'tea-girl' or note-taker when I was the only women in the room"', *University of Oxford*, (https://www.law.ox.ac.uk/news/2019-11-15-i-was-assumed-be-tea-girl-or-note-taker-when-i-was-only-woman-room)

88 Adkins, A. (no date) 'Millennials: The Job-Hopping Generation', *Gallup* (https://www.gallup.com/workplace/231587/millennials-job-hopping-generation.aspx)

89 A recent study found that 49% of millennials would quit their job within two years. Friedman, Z. (2019) '49% Of Millennials Would Quit Their Job Within 2 Years', *Forbes* (https://www.forbes.com/sites/zackfriedman/2019/05/22/millennials-disillusioned-future/?sh=2a2b2f54353e#453beb58353e)

90 According to the Cambridge dictionary mansplaining is 'the act of explaining something to someone in a way that suggests that they are stupid; used especially when a man explains something to a woman that she already understands' (https://dictionary.cambridge.org/fr/dictionnaire/anglais/mansplaining)

91 Sojo VE, Wood RE, Genat AE.(2016) 'Harmful Workplace Experiences and Women's Occupational Well-Being: A Meta-Analysis', *Psychology of Women Quarterly*, 40: 1, pp. 10–40 (https://journals.sagepub.com/doi/10.1177/0361684315599346)

92 Harris, C. (2019) 'How to find the person who can help you get ahead at work', *TED* (https://www.youtube.com/watch?v=gpE_W50OTUc&feature=youtu.be)

Acknowledgements

We would like to extend our gratitude to the many people that have supported us on the *Unleash Today* journey. We would like to thank our families, close friends, and anyone who has believed in our vision and told us to 'keep going' when we wanted to give up. Writing this book allowed us to turn pain and frustration into healings for others. It taught us to make sense of our personal experiences and to realise how strongly we feel about fighting for the change we aspire to see in society. By being vulnerable and telling our stories we are able to help other women to overcome similar obstacles and guide them on their way to become resilient, confident and empowered in their careers. We cannot wait to see all the women out there unleash their potential!

This book owes its existence to many wonderful women and men out there—listed and not listed! Putting together our lessons learned and experiences would have been impossible without the support of our *Unleash Today* team and the generous sharing of experiences and advice of our many experts in our networks, in particular. You can see the profiles of our guest contributors and our team members on our website www.unleashtoday.com. Thank you as well to all the women and men who participated in our webinars, workshops, and blog posts and were brave enough to share their personal stories with us.

To help us self-publish this book and reach women globally, we would like to thank our amazing *Unleash Today* team. We could not have done this without you, thank you!

Alexandra Hilberer - Project Leader

Anna Ivanova - Events Lead

Anna Marino - Social Media Strategist

Bijan Ranjbar - Data Analytics Expert

Blandine Crutzen - French Translator

Carolina Cicati - Events Host

Claire Pattison - Event and Promotion Strategist

Clare Oxenbury-Palmer - Copy Editor

Denise Kellner - Editorial Lead

Emilia Placek - PR Specialist

Farhin Binte Siddique - PR Specialist

Henry Castelein - Visual Artist

Laila Souza Hansen - PR Specialist

Liselotte Grönlund - Digital Marketing Team Lead

Acknowledgements

Lucía Burillo - Social Media Strategist

Jaki Smith - Editor and Production Lead

Maxima Lucia Sutter - Strategy and Innovation Expert

Marie Sina - Content Editor

Melanie Rose - Operations Lead

Reneta Georgieva - Social Media Strategist

Sam Hotham - Copy Editor

Selina Zehnder - Launch Strategist

Sharon (Zhe) Shi - Illustrator

Shivani Nair - Content Creation Expert

Théo Aldenucci - Creative Lead

Uyen Phan - Events Leader

Yajing Hu - PR Specialist China

Printed in Great Britain
by Amazon